Following a hectic career across continents and countries, Lynda is now happily retired in the West Midlands. She has two gorgeous grandchildren, two manic Labradors and four recalcitrant cats. Oh, and an academic husband.

She is kept very busy by all of the above. But come the spring and summer, gardening is also necessary!

When not otherwise occupied, Lynda enjoys travelling and exploring the world.

To Angela – a source of bright ideas always.

Lynda Thrift

THE SAGA OF THE SWORD

AUSTIN MACAULEY PUBLISHERS™

LONDON * CAMBRIDGE * NEW YORK * SHARJAH

A CIP catalogue record for this title is available from the British Library.

ISBN 9781398491915 (Paperback)
ISBN 9781398491922 (ePub e-book)

www.austinmacauley.com

First Published 2022
Austin Macauley Publishers Ltd®
1 Canada Square
Canary Wharf
London
E14 5AA

I would like to thank my long-suffering family and friends for their support and patience as I bounced from one idea to another. Their comments and thoughts have been more than invaluable in bringing this story together.

I would also like to thank Melissa Byrne for her artistic design and imagery. Her illustrations have captured the story's fire and adventure.

Prologue

It was the end of a hot steamy summer's day.

James had been kept busy entertaining his mother and Great Aunt as they celebrated his Great Aunt's eightieth birthday. Now, he stood by his open bedroom window. Trying to cool down and thinking over everything that has passed.

He was still bemused by his Great Aunt's choice of celebration, particularly as it was quite an important milestone to reach in anyone's life. But from what he knew of his relative, her life had been anything but ordinary.

Great Aunt Pauline had achieved much during her eighty years. She was now a world-renowned expert in Viking history. But her story began back in the 1970s, when she decided to investigate possible trade routes between Europe and the Middle East during the Dark Ages.

While she had been doing fieldwork in Iraq, she had been caught up in the confusion and fear that accompanied the political turmoil of the time. Indeed, she and her fellow researchers had been missing for several weeks at the height of the unrest.

Through a series of daring adventures, she and her colleagues had made it safely back, but at great personal risk. James had seen the newspaper cuttings from the time, telling of how they had escaped the clutches of the regime, arriving back in the UK to a fanfare of attention. She could have become a female Indiana Jones on the back of it all.

But that wasn't her style. Instead, she climbed her way steadily to the top of the academic ladder, marrying her physicist husband on the way.

Celebrating this milestone birthday was in keeping with her quietly eccentric personality, but James was sure it wouldn't have been what he would have chosen.

First there was a dry presentation of a prestigious award—not to her but to a dear friend—that she wanted to watch.

Then there was a delicate afternoon tea at the Randolph Hotel.

And that was when things became really strange. For she had invited her academic chum to join them and he turned out to be someone that James knew really well.

Exceptionally well in fact. Yet he hadn't realised that his Great Aunt also knew him.

No, mused James as he went to lie on the bed and wait for a cool breeze to filter through the now-open window, it had all been very odd.

Especially what had just happened.

He thought he saw that friend standing outside down on the street, dressed as a Viking. At least he thought it was his friend. It was quite difficult to be sure in the dark, especially as he seemed to be painted in some sort of circus makeup. James couldn't be completely sure, but was his face blue?

Then, James thought back to when he was seven years old.

His adventures had begun when he went to stay with another of his relatives when he went to visit them in the north of England.

With a shiver, James started to recall the very first dream that he had experienced up there.

He couldn't be totally certain, but the chap in the street didn't merely resemble his long-lost friend, he also looked remarkably like someone he saw in in that dream, all those years ago.

As he lay thinking, the memories came flooding back.

It had all started when he was seven, and school was breaking up for the summer holidays…

Part One
The Child

Chapter 1.1
Start of the Summer Holidays

James had been waiting for this day to come for ages. He thought that it would never arrive.

But now, as the teacher told the class to pack up their things for the last time before they broke up, he realised that it had.

After half past three—in a whole ten minutes' time—he would rush out of his classroom and say goodbye to his schoolfriends.

And this time, he wouldn't be saying "See you tomorrow…"

No, this time it would be "See you in six weeks' time!"

The bell rang.

This was it.

The Summer Holidays were finally here.

There would be no more school until September, and that was just ages away.

James picked up his packed bag, full of all the work he had done this term. He threw the straps around his shoulders and joined the queue of children waiting by the outside door.

James peered out hopefully.

His mother had promised to pick him up from school and go to the sweet shop as a special treat to mark the end of the school year.

It wasn't straightforward to see what was happening. His best friends had already taken up their positions in front of him, and so his view to the outside world was pretty much blocked. But he tried to see out anyway. He might catch a glimpse of familiar skirt or blouse.

Then, on the stoke of half past three precisely, the teaching assistant threw open the door and started to call out the names of the children.

In reply, the person who was collecting the child would step forward. They had to tell the teaching assistant a safe word before their child could leave with them.

Eventually, it was James' turn.

His name was called as he stood next the teaching assistant. He was very nervous now. He couldn't see his mother anywhere. James hoped she hadn't forgotten.

James knew that his Mum worked very hard, and quite often, work things took a bit longer than they were supposed to. But there was a visit to the sweet shop at risk here.

Then, just in the nick of time, just before he was bundled back into the classroom to wait with the "late collections", he saw his mother rushing around the corner and towards the classroom.

"There she is, Miss," he shouted as his mother got closer.

"I know, young man," came the crisp reply, "But I can't let you go to her until I have the safe word!"

James understood why the teaching assistant needed to make sure that the person that he would run to was his mother. Nevertheless, he still wanted to rush out.

But he didn't. He was a good boy. Also, the teaching assistant had a very firm grip on his backpack!

"Gosh," gasped his mother as she came within hearing, "I didn't think I was going to be on time, but the safe word is…"

It matched the word which the teaching assistant had on her list. She let go of James and he ran straight to his mother and gave her a huge hug.

"Come on," he said from between the folds of her skirt, "We're going to the sweet shop now!"

His mother smiled her agreement. At the same time, she was thinking that he was so grown up. James probably wouldn't want to greet her like this from school again when September came.

After all, he was a big boy now.

She ruffled James hair and took his backpack.

"Come on then," she said, "Let's find those sweets…"

And with that, they started to walk back home, via the promised sweet shop.

Later that evening, James was getting ready for bed.

The cat looked on sleepily from the foot of his bed, where it had curled up, ready for a lovely long snooze.

James had finished his shower and brushed his teeth.

Now he was arranging his toys in order of priority in case he woke up in the middle of the night. He might be a whole seven years old, but he didn't want to feel scared and his toys helped him feel safe. It was essential that he knew exactly where each one was before he went to sleep in case it was still dark when he woke up.

His mother looked on.

James hopped into bed, and his mother sat down on the chair next to it. The cat grumbled and shifted off the bed. It clearly wasn't big enough for the toys, James, and him. The cat would have to find somewhere less crowded to spend the rest of the night.

Now it was story time.

James snuggled down under the duvet, eyes closed, ready for this evening's offering.

But things were a little different tonight. His mother hadn't opened the book from which she usually read.

James waited.

"I know we usually have a story before I switch off the light. Tonight is going to be a little bit different because I have a surprise for you!" said Mum.

James sat up. He suddenly wasn't very sleepy. What was his mother talking about?

His mother continued.

"Do you remember how we stayed with Great Aunty Marian last year?"

James didn't. Last year was a long time ago. He sometimes had difficulty remembering what he had for breakfast!

"Tomorrow, we are going to stay with your Great Aunty Marian. Just like last year. But that was last year, and you have grown up so much. I thought that you might like to stay there without me. Just like I used to when I was your age!"

Now that his mother had mentioned it, he did have some memories of Great Aunty Marian. He remembered that she lived in a house with a backyard rather than a garden. And that the house backed onto a narrow-cobbled road.

James thought about this idea and then said carefully, "It might be a big adventure for me..."

His mother looked pleased. James had clearly said the right thing.

15

Then he remembered more and was suddenly a little bit scared.

He recalled that he had tried to make friends with the local children, but that they wouldn't play with him.

They said that he talked funny and that he was posh. He didn't think that he did or was. But the local children wouldn't listen and ran away.

"But what if I don't like it?" he asked, "Can I come home?"

"Of course, you can. I will call Great Aunty Marian every evening. I will ask her how you are, and then I will ask you. If you really want to come home, you can. But I know your Great Aunty Marian would really like you to stay. She doesn't get to see you very often!"

James thought about this. It had been a whole year since he had been to see his Great Aunt. And a year is an awfully long time. Especially when you are old, he supposed.

His mother chattered on nervously.

"I know it's a big thing for you to stay somewhere without me. We haven't had an adventure like this before. I won't just leave you with Great Aunty Marian until I know you are settled in. So, I will stay for a night or two to make sure that everything is alright. Then I will have to come home. After all, you might be big enough to look after yourself without me for a few days, but Tom can't manage by himself."

His mother looked round towards the cat who was now making a bed for himself on the pile of discarded school uniform which James had left on the bedroom floor.

James grabbed his favourite plastic dinosaur and asked, "Can I take Timmy Rex with me?"

"Yes," replied his mother, "We are going there by car, so we can pack as many toys as you want!"

Brave words. James liked a challenge…

James started to plan which of his toys he should pack, and which he should leave behind.

As he did so, his eyelids grew heavy, and before he got to adding his Action Man to his list, he was fast asleep.

Chapter 1.2
Settling In

It had been a long journey to Great Aunty Marian's house. His mother had had to drive along busy motorways and down several quite narrow roads before she shouted:

"Look—see those tall chimneys? They used to be part of the cotton mills where your Great Aunty Marian worked when she was young!"

James looked up from his iPad. He could just make out two thin long brick towers, which he presumed were the mill chimneys that his mother was talking about.

His mother was still talking.

"The mills closed down long ago, and all the looms that used to weave the cloth are gone. The looms could only be used to weave cloth so once the mills closed, I think they were broken down for scrap metal."

"What's scrap?" asked James, who wasn't really that interested and hadn't, truth to tell, been listening either. He had just reached a critical level in the game he was playing on his iPad. That was far more important.

"It's metal that can be reused. It's sold on before being melted down to make other things."

"Oh," said James and went back to his computer game.

Not too many minutes later, James looked up again. The car was pulling into a parking spot outside a neat, terraced house.

"Come on," said his mother as she opened car door next to where he was sitting, "We're here!"

Great Aunty Marian had obviously been listening for the car to arrive.

Before James had a chance to take off his seat belt, the door to the neat, terraced house opened and a tallish comfortable-looking lady with bright spectacles stood on the doorstep.

His mother ran straight towards her and gave her a hug.

His mother beckoned to James, who hopped down onto the pavement.

"Come and say hello!"

James hoped that Great Aunty Marian didn't expect him to hug her as well. Mum might remember her from last year, but his memories were still quite hazy.

The three of them went into Great Aunty Marian's home. They walked along a narrow corridor which opened into a cosy little sitting room.

The room was dominated by a huge wooden fireplace, which had horse brasses hanging all around it.

"What are those?" he asked.

"They used to put these on the horses that pulled the carts."

"But horses don't pull carts?" said James, who couldn't understand this at all.

"You ride horses." he stated with certainty.

Great Aunty Marian looked at her great nephew and smiled.

"In the olden days, when I was a little girl, there were no cars or lorries. If you wanted to have anything delivered—like coal or beer—it had to be loaded onto a cart. The cart was pulled by a huge horse.

When the town had a fair, the horses would be dressed up with these brasses. They looked ever so imposing."

Then Great Aunty Marian reached over to the mantlepiece, and picked up a trio of bells, all fastened together.

"This thing here," she said, shaking the bells so they tinkled merrily, "was worn on the horse's head. It would have huge ostrich feathers on top and would have looked magnificent!"

James wanted to play with those bells so much, but Great Aunty Marian put them back before he had a chance to ask if he could.

Great Aunty Marian continued, "All these horse brasses were worn by your Great, Great, Grandfather's horse when he was on show. He was a beautiful black Shire horse—almost as black as the coal he used to deliver during the week."

Great Aunty Marian looked wistful. She was remembering things from her childhood, which was a long time ago.

Then, she pulled herself together and said, "Come on, let's sit down at the table!"

James looked to his mother, and that was when he noticed that the table behind them was laid out with all manner of lovely things to eat.

There were sausages (his favourite) and tomato sauce, and crisps too. For his mother there was a lemon drizzle cake (homemade, of course) and a bottle of fizzy pop was next to the teapot and cups.

"I thought you might be hungry after all that driving, and so I have made afternoon tea."

"This is lovely, Aunty."

His mother was clearly very pleased with this. So was James. Now he thought about it, he was quite peckish.

When they had eaten their fill, Great Aunty Marian showed his mother and James to their bedroom. It was quite small, but there was room for a pair of single beds.

"I hope you don't mind sharing with your Mum while she stays here with you. You can have the room all to yourself when she goes." said Great Aunty Marian.

James was secretly delighted.

Although he was a big boy now, he had to admit that it was a comforting thought that Mummy would be snuggled up close next to him as he got used to this new place.

The next job was to unpack the car and make sure that James knew exactly where each of his toys could live while he stayed here.

Chapter 1.3
Playing Out

James's mother had gone home yesterday.

It had been a lonely night, all by himself in that room. But Timmy Rex and Action Man had been there to help him cope.

Now, James had just finished lunch (or dinner as Great Aunty Marian called it. She called dinner tea too. It was very confusing.)

What to do next?

Great Aunty Marian had put up the ironing board and brought out a huge washing basket full of newly dry clothes.

"I am going to get on with some ironing," she stated, "You should go and play outside. It's a lovely day."

James thought that he might play with his iPad instead. But when he dug it from his pile of things in his bedroom, he realised that it wouldn't work. It had run out of charge.

Reluctantly, he returned to the sitting room.

As he opened the door, Great Aunty Marian looked up from steaming a frilly blouse.

"You could go to the park," she suggested, "If you follow the path at the bottom of the road, you will see signs to it.

It's really a rather pretty and wild park, although it has all the things you like there too—like swings and slides! You'll love it up there!"

James wasn't convinced but he thought he might as well give it a try. It would be more fun than watching the steam rise as Great Aunty Marian did her ironing.

He ran upstairs, put on his trainers, and put his waterproof coat in his backpack (just in case it decided to rain).

He then returned to the sitting room where Great Aunty Marian was now working on a particularly troublesome pleated skirt.

"I have decided to go to the park!" he announced.

"Good," came the reply, "But remember—you must be back in time for tea!"

With that, Great Aunty Marian returned to the job in hand and James set off.

James felt very grown up. At home, his mother would not have allowed him to go out without an adult. But Great Aunty Marian seemed to think that it was okay. Things were clearly different up north!

It was a bit of a trek to get to the park.

James had to first walk all the way through town, taking extra care not to step off the pavement. He wasn't too keen on being squished by a passing car.

James remembered all the advice his mother had given him when they walked home from school, or the shops, or wherever. He remembered to look both ways when he had to cross the road. That he should use at a zebra crossing if there was one. And most importantly, he remembered to listen all the time as well.

James wove his way down several cobbled streets, past the corner shop and over by the library. All the while, he followed the signs. Each one had an arrow pointing in the direction of the park. Underneath in large letters, was the instruction "This way to the Waterfalls".

Just after he had passed the library, the signs led to a narrow and very stony footpath which twisted and turned around drystone walls. It was impossible to see too far ahead.

James was starting to think that he would never reach the promised swings and slide, when suddenly, the path opened into an enormous area of grass. It wasn't a field because there were no cows or sheep there. Neither was there any evidence of them, such as tufts of wool or cow poo.

But it wasn't a playing field either.

James thought that this was very peculiar. However, right at the far end of the field, he could just make out the promised play equipment.

He was clearly in the right place.

As he started to run towards the swings, he heard the sound of rushing water close by.

He stopped to listen. It was very close.

James thought that he would see if he could find the water. After all, he had the whole afternoon to play on the swings. Even he thought he might become a little bored after a little while as he had no one to play with.

The stream was hidden from immediate sight by a small gathering of trees.

James poked his head through the branches and found the stream. Only it wasn't just a stream.

He realised that he was at the head of a waterfall down which the stream was vanishing.

As the water disappeared, it splashed up a fine spray in which he could see rainbows. It was very pretty and totally unexpected.

So that must be why the park was called the Waterfalls. Although there was only one waterfall, so technically at least, James felt the park should really be called Waterfall.

James stood and watched the water splashing downwards.

He was miles away. So far away that he jumped when he heard a voice on the other side of the stream shouting a cheery hello.

When James looked across the water, he realised that the hello had come from a young boy who looked to be about his age.

Perhaps he would want to play. James really hoped so. It would be nice to have friend here.

The young boy shouted again.

"Hello! Who are you?" he asked.

"I'm James, and I don't live here. I am staying with my Great Aunty Marian. Who are you?"

The boy called back.

"I'm Gordon and I do live here. Do you want to play with me?"

Did James ever!

"How do I cross the stream?" he asked.

Gordon told him that there was an old grass-covered bridge further upstream. James would know it when he saw it. There was an old slimy concrete paddling pool built into the stream right next to it. You really couldn't miss it!

"We'll meet you there!" shouted Gordon as James ran off. He was so keen to reach the bridge that it was only when he stopped for breath that James realised that Gordon had said "We".

Was there someone else to play with too?

It wasn't hard at all to spot the bridge. And there, on the opposite side, stood Gordon who now had a lovely rough border collie dog at his side.

"Hello again, James!" said Gordon, "Meet my dog. She is called Gem. Because she is a real jewel!"

James was delighted. He had found a friend. It was lovely to meet someone who didn't think he was a snob or talked funny.

It seemed that he and Gordon had a lot in common. They both loved dinosaurs and Action Man toys for example.

However, James was surprised when Gordon told him that he was one of eight children in his family. As well as having five sisters, he had two brothers.

James privately thought that having so many brothers and sisters wouldn't be much fun. He wasn't used to having other children around him other than at school. At home, there was just him and his mother.

Gordon told James about his family.

Most importantly Gordon was the baby of the family. The older members had left school as soon as they could and were already working.

This shocked James.

"But what about going to university?" he asked.

"There's no chance of that happening round here!" came the reply.

"Me Mum needs the extra money to help feed us all!"

With that, Gordon ran off towards the bridge, shouting "I'll race you to the swings!"

The boys spent the afternoon playing.

James had so much fun. The boys built dams in the stream, getting their feet soaked in the process. Several times James slipped and almost fell in!

Then they climbed to the top of the witch's hat roundabout. It was ever so high and the roundabout swung high and low as they climbed. James felt that he was being very naughty. If his mother had been there, he knew she would never allowed him to do any of this. She would have been so scared that he would fall off, and so stopped him before he had a chance to even get started!

Gem sat down quietly nearby and watched it all.

All too soon, though, it was time to go home.

"Me Mum said I had to be back in time for tea!" said Gordon.

"So did Great Aunty Marian!"

They both checked their watches.

James was surprised that Gordon was wearing an old-fashioned mechanical watch that you had to wind up.

Gordon noticed and told him that it had been a present from his Dad.

James supposed that it was an old watch that his father didn't want any more.

Both watches agreed on the time though. It was time to go home.

"Which way do you go?" asked James.

He was hoping that he would have a little more time with his new friend if they had to go in the same direction. But Gordon lived over the hill in the opposite direction completely.

"Never mind," said Gordon, "I think I can play out again tomorrow. Will you be able to as well?"

The boys agreed that they would meet up by the grass covered bridge straight after dinner the following day.

But now, the boys needed to rush home so that they would be back in time for tea.

James arrived home as Great Aunty Marian was laying the table.

"Did you have fun?" she asked.

"Oh yes," replied James, "And I have made a friend and we're going to meet up tomorrow after dinner!"

"That's grand!" said Great Aunty Marian, "Shall I pack you a picnic?"

James was so pleased. A new friend and a picnic to look forward to.

He would also take Timmy Rex to show Gordon.

Later that night, as he went to bed, he told Action Man all about his new friend.

Maybe staying with Great Aunty Marian would turn out to be fun after all.

Chapter 1.4
Another Exciting Day

James woke early the following day. He was so excited.

He was going to meet his new friend Gordon by the grass-covered bridge at the Waterfalls after dinner. His Great Aunty Marian was going to pack him a picnic too.

He could hardly wait.

The morning just seemed to drag by.

Great Aunty Marian had some shopping to do in town, and he had to go with her.

James realised that Great Aunty Marian did things very differently to his mother. For a start, Great Aunty Marian walked to the shops. He didn't think that she even had a car!

Fortunately, it wasn't a long walk.

James saw that Great Aunty Marian only bought enough food for the next couple of meals. He was used to his mother ordering a big shop online and a delivery van turning up with a week's worth of goodies.

They called at the bread shop first.

"There is nothing like a slice of fresh baked bread and butter," said Great Aunty Marian as they emerged out of the bakery. "And have you ever tried bilberry tarts? They are delicious. The berries grow up on the moors among all the heather. You have to be careful because they grow next to similar-looking berries which are poisonous. But the bakers here have a secret supply which they put into these lovely little pies. I've bought a couple for us. You can try one at dinner time!"

The next shop was the butchers, where Great Aunty Marian bought some sausages for James, and some tripe for herself.

"What's tripe?" asked James.

It turned out that tripe was the lining of a cow's stomach. Great Aunty Marion was going to boil it in milk with some onions and pepper.

James wished he hadn't asked. He thought that tripe sounded disgusting.

Thank goodness he was going to have the sausages. At least he hoped they were for him.

The final stop was at the newsagents where Great Aunty Marian picked up a copy of the daily newspaper.

How quaint!

James's mother got all her news from the internet!

But, if Great Aunty Marian didn't have a car, come to think of it, perhaps she didn't have a computer?

James hadn't thought to ask Great Aunty Marian for her password to the internet before now. Now, he wasn't at all sure that she even had the internet.

James felt for his mobile phone which he always kept in the zipped pocket in his trousers. His mother had told him that it was for emergency use only—like if he needed a lift home from a friend's home. But it also had a mobile hotspot which was linked to his iPad. Without that, he wouldn't have been able to play his computer games in the car as they drove up.

Or, as he realised with a sudden shock, play them here when his iPad was fully charged!

Thank goodness for the mobile hotspot!

James made a mental note to remember to charge up both his iPad and his phone otherwise he wouldn't be able to use either of them!

As they sat down with a welcome drink after all that shopping and walking, Great Aunty Marian's telephone rang. It was an old-fashioned thing which lived on the wall next to the kitchen door.

It was his mother calling to find out how everything was working out.

Great Aunty Marian passed the receiver to James. He hadn't really noticed before, but it was different to the phones at home. For a start off, it was attached to the phone by a curly wire. Neither did it seem to be able to take photographs. And you couldn't send texts on it. But you could talk to people on it and make calls.

It was lovely to hear his mother's voice. But she sounded to be so far away. Never mind though. She had called like she had promised that she would.

James chatted to his mother for some time. He wanted to tell her what he had been doing. Well, most of what he had been doing. He didn't tell her everything because he didn't want to be told off. Or even worse, for his mother to tell him stay to at home with his Great Aunt the following day!

So he didn't say anything about how he had walked to the Waterfalls by himself. Neither did he mention that he had climbed all the way to the top of the witch's hat roundabout twice! But he did talk an awful lot about his new friend Gordon and his dog Gem.

His mother was so pleased. She had been worried that James might have been homesick and want to come back. But he seemed to have settled right in.

A small part of his mother was a bit sad too because she missed her boy. But him being away meant that she could get a lot of work out of the way so that when he did come home, she would be able to spend more time with him.

After dinner—which wasn't the dreaded tripe—that treat was apparently for the next day and only for Great Aunty Marion—Great Aunty Marian packed James a picnic.

Then as she opened the door and he ran out, she shouted to James's receding head, "Remember—be back in time for tea!"

James shouted a "bye" which was lost as he ran onto the path.

Before you knew it, he was on the grass-covered bridge waiting for Gordon and Gem.

He didn't have to wait very long. The unlikely couple appeared at just about the same time.

They touched base in the middle of the bridge.

Gem ran to James and jumped up at him.

"Hi there," said James, "I was worried you might not be able to get away!"

"I nearly didn't!" came the reply.

Apparently, Gordon's mother had wanted Gordon to help her with the washing up. But Gordon had explained that he had arranged to meet his new friend—"who wasn't from these parts"—straight after dinner. If he had to stay and help wash up, he would be late. It would have been rude to be late.

Gordon's mother had understood and assigned him another task for him instead. After all, with eight children in the family, they all had to pull their weight!

If he wanted to avoid the plates from dinner time, he would have to wash up at teatime instead. She made it clear that this would be a bigger job because all his brothers and sisters would be home for their tea so there would be more dirty plates.

James was impressed and pleased that his new friend thought that he was worth taking on extra work so that he could see James.

But the boys realised that they could have been in a bit of pickle if for some reason they couldn't make their meeting. They needed a way to get messages to each other if anything happened in the future. And, because they were boys, it had to be secret.

Gordon said that he knew of an old tree, just beyond the dry-stone wall which encircled the park. The boys quickly scrambled over the wall.

The tree was exactly where Gordon had said it was, and it looked exactly how he said it did.

Most importantly, there were several deep holes in the trunk where messages could be safely left without getting wet if it rained. If either of them was late or the other couldn't wait, the one who couldn't wait could leave a message in the hidey hole.

Perfect!

Now all the boys had to do was to make sure that it was safe. They needed to test the system.

They sat underneath the old tree canopy to think about this. James unpacked his picnic. It wasn't that long since dinnertime, but they were two growing lads, and they were hungry again.

As the tucked into the foil-wrapped cold sausages leftover from James's dinner, they pondered how to make sure that their messages would stay hidden from everyone but themselves.

Then, James had an idea.

"Why don't we use the foil from our sausages to wrap our messages in? They will be safe in there."

Gordon agreed but then had another thought.

"But the foil is greasy and will spoil the paper message."

Both boys thought for a little while longer.

Then James dug out the half empty bottle of orange squash.

Why don't we drink this up and then use it to put our messages in?

Perfect!

They finished off the orange squash and left the empty bottle in the tree hole, ready for use if needed.

The boys would check things out the following day to make sure things hadn't been moved.

Now it was time to get on with the more serious business of playing.

As the time for tea drew closer, Gordon suddenly remembered something.

He might not be able to play out tomorrow. His mother wanted to take him to the local shoe shop to get some new shoes for school.

It seemed that Gordon's school holidays started earlier than James's did. But they were the same length of time which meant that he had to go back to school before James did. Although that would be after James had gone home, Gordon still needed things like shoes to be ready to wear when the new term started.

James looked up in horror.

He would be lonely that afternoon without Gordon and Gem to play with.

He had enjoyed his morning of walking around the little old town and helping Great Aunty Marian. However, he didn't think that a daily trip to the bakers and the butchers was be the highlight of his day. Meeting his friend was far more important.

Then Gordon had an idea.

"I will come here tomorrow straight after dinner. Then I will take you to meet my mother. She said that she wanted to see you. And then, if you wanted to, you could come with us to the shoe shop."

James wasn't sure. Food shopping wasn't that interesting, and shoe shopping sounded much worse.

But then Gordon told James about something that sounded odd but exciting.

Gordon told James that you could see your foot bones at the shoe shop.

Because Gordon had grown since his last pair of shoes, he would need to have his feet measured so that his shoes would be the right size for his feet. At the shop where Gordon would get his new shoes, they didn't just use tape measures. They had a new-fangled machine that would show you the bones in your feet. Gordon didn't know what it was called, but it used X-rays and made your feet glow bright green.

James thought this all sounded very exciting. The place where he got his shoes certainly had no such thing.

He was intrigued. He wanted to see this machine. To be honest, James did wonder whether Gordon was telling the truth, or whether he was making it all up so that James would go with him.

No matter—he really did want to see this strange machine. James decided that he would join Gordon tomorrow.

But now, the time had flown by again and it was time to head home. Otherwise, he wouldn't be back in time for tea!

Chapter 1.5
The Shoe Shop

James's week with Great Aunty Marian was passing quickly. Indeed, he had hardly watched television or played with his computer games at all.

It was now Tuesday. James had been here since Saturday. It didn't feel like it. That was because of his new friend. Playing with Gordon made time go very quickly.

After breakfast, Great Aunty Marian told James to put on his coat as it was time to go shopping again.

She had thought that after yesterday's traipsing around, James might not want to come with her. But much to her surprise and delight, James was ready to leave the house before she was!

Today, the duo had to visit the local grocery shop at the end of town. It was a little further than they had walked on the previous day, but James didn't mind at all.

He was on a mission.

He wanted to check out the shoe shop to see if this magical machine was there before he met up with Gordon.

As they walked along, James asked Great Aunty Marian where the shop was.

It seemed that they would pass it on the way to the grocery shop.

"Good," thought James, "I will get a chance to check things out before I meet up with Gordon!"

Great Aunty Marian walked on purposely towards the grocery shop. James was afraid that she would forget to tell him when they were getting close to the shoe shop.

But no. Rather the opposite in fact.

"There is still a little way to go," began Great Aunty Marian, "but the old shoe shop is just over there."

She pointed vaguely ahead.

And then she started to tell James all about the shoe shop.

It had been in the town for as long as she could remember. Amazingly, through all that time, she said, it had been owned and run by the same family. Not the same people of course. The person who ran the shop now was the grandson of the man who had run the place when she was a young girl, and she got all her school shoes from there. As had all her brothers and sisters too. She had even got her first dance shoes from there.

They had been shiny black leather and very posh. She had been ever so proud of them.

James saw that his Great Aunt was becoming quite sad as she remembered those years.

"It was at one of those dances that I met your Great Uncle Leslie," she said, "He were so handsome..."

Then she suddenly stopped and pointed again. This time she pointed directly at a small old-fashioned looking shop.

Unfortunately, it was across the road and so James couldn't look inside as he had planned.

The outside of the shop looked like it needed a good coat of paint. From where James stood, he could see that the shop window was full of shoes of different types. Real shoes. Not trainers or stuff like that. And they all seemed to be brown.

Oh well. James would just have to wait until the afternoon to find out more about the magic machine.

Great Aunty Marian was still talking. Apparently, the person who ran the shop didn't have any children, and she wasn't sure if it would keep going when he retired. It would be a loss to the town, but most families now preferred to visit the big retail outlets to buy their footwear. These shops had a wider selection of shoes to choose from and they were usually much cheaper.

The afternoon eventually arrived, and James ran off towards the Waterfalls again.

"Be back in time for tea!" shouted Great Aunty Marian as he disappeared round the corner.

James was now very familiar with the way to the Waterfalls. He knew where it was safe to cross the road, and where not to for example. His knowledge also meant that he reached the grass-covered bridge in double quick time.

Given that he had left the house earlier than he needed to, that meant that he was very early. As he had a little time to spare, he decided to check in the tree hidey hole.

He put his arm deep into the hole and pulled out the orange plastic squash bottle. He could tell that no one had moved it so that was good.

As he waited, James decided to leave a message in the bottle for Gordon. He would write out his name and address on a scrap of paper which was at the bottom of his backpack and put it in the bottle. He always carried a notepad and pen with him everywhere. But he had never needed to use it before.

James decided to write out his address in capital letters. His mother had told him that his joined-up writing was very good, but nevertheless, James wanted to be sure that Gordon would be able to read his message if he found it.

Just as he was putting the bottle with its message back into the hidey hole, he heard Gordon and Gem arriving at the bridge.

James hurried back over the dry-stone wall and rushed up to the bridge.

"Phew!" announced Gordon.

"For one horrible moment, I thought you hadn't come. Then I would have to go home and tell me Mum that you hadn't turned up. She has made a cake especially for you!"

The boys didn't have time to play. They rushed back to Gordon's house, over the hill.

When they arrived, James was a little surprised. Clearly over at this end of town, it was quite posh. The road was all cobbled rather than tarmacked and there were no cars parked around. How super trendy was that?

Gordon opened the door to a small but tidy middle-of-the-terrace house, and ushered James inside.

Then he shouted at the top of his voice, "Mum—James is here!"

Gordon's mother came rushing towards them. She was busy drying her hands on a tea towel. James thought that she had probably just finished washing up or something.

She held out a damp hand and said, "Hello James-not-from-these-parts! Our Gordon hasn't stopped talking about you since he met you the other day. It's right grand to see you for meself!"

She then turned around and walked back in the direction she had come from. The boys followed her into a small sitting room which was not unlike that of

Great Aunty Marian. There were some differences. For example, James couldn't spot any radiators. Perhaps they had underfloor heating?

But just like at Great Aunty Marian's the room was dominated by a large highly polished but clearly much used table. It had eight chairs squashed around it.

Gordon noticed James looking at the table.

He said, "This is where we have all our meals."

James was slightly puzzled.

"But I thought you said you had two brothers and five sisters? There are only eight places?"

"Me Mum never gets a chance to sit down when we eat because there is always something else to do. Me dad doesn't get home till much later. So, it all works out!"

It made sense. Sort of.

James didn't have time to ponder this information because Gordon's mother appeared from the kitchen, balancing plates in one hand and the most scrumptious-looking cake in the other.

"That's the cake I was telling you about!" whispered Gordon.

Gem settled down in front of the fireplace, even though there wasn't a fire burning. It was summer after all!

James and Gordon sat at the table, and Gordon's mother cut them both a huge slice of cake.

It was as good as it looked. The boys quickly finished off their portions and didn't leave a single crumb.

"That was delicious!" said James.

"I'm right glad you enjoyed it, Young Man. I reckon I had to do a good job given I didn't know what you would expect!"

"Right you two," said Gordon's mother as she cleared the plates away. "Let's go shoe shopping!"

Gem stayed behind. Gordon's mother told James that Gem didn't like shopping because he would have to spend most of the time tied up outside the shops.

James agreed that didn't sound to be much fun.

Again, like Great Aunty Marian, they walked to the shops. It wasn't quite the same way as Gordon lived on the other side of town. But the shop looked the same. It still had that brown-painted, slightly neglected air to it.

Gordon's Mum pushed open the door and a bell tinkled.

An old man came to the counter.

"Hello, Mrs Holden," he said. "It must be nearly time for this young man to be getting ready to go back to school!"

He then turned to James.

"And who have we here?" he asked.

"This is my friend James. He's not from these parts. I told him about your magic X-ray machine, and he wanted to see it!" explained Gordon, "He's never seen one before!"

"Well I never," replied the old man, "Let's find you some shoes in the next size up from last year and then we can show James the magic machine!"

With that, the old man disappeared into the back of the shop.

James looked at his friend and asked, "But you haven't told him what you want?"

Gordon explained that there wasn't a choice. He would have exactly the same style of shoe this year as he had had last year. The only difference would be that it would be the next size up and not squash his feet. The shoes that he was wearing now had started to hurt so he knew he had grown.

James didn't quite understand. When he and his mother went shoe shopping, there was always a choice.

Still, as he was very aware, he wasn't from these parts. He knew that they did things differently here.

The old man returned from the back of the shop carrying a brown shoe box which he opened.

"Here we are, Young Man," he said as he passed the shoes to Gordon.

Gordon put them on and tied the laces.

Another strange thing.

None of James's shoes had laces. He wondered if Gordon had to have laces as part of his school uniform.

"How do they feel?" asked the old man.

"Much better than my old shoes." came the reply.

"Right then, let's check them out using the pedoscope!"

And then, to clarify, the old man turned to James and said, "That's the magic machine to you!"

Gordon and his mother followed the old man into the back of the shop. James thought that he ought to go too.

He followed the others as they went behind the counter into what appeared to be a storeroom.

The walls were lined with shelves stacked from top to bottom with boxes. James supposed they were all stuffed full of shoes in all shapes and sizes. If Gordon's brogues were anything to go by, James thought that they would all be brown.

But then his attention was drawn elsewhere. Straight ahead in fact. To a large wooden box on a plinth.

There was a hole at its base, and three portholes on the top.

James realised that this was the magic X-ray machine.

Gordon had told the truth.

The shopkeeper turned to Gordon and said "Right, Young Man. You know what to do. Up you go and put your feet and shoes into the hole."

Gordon leapt onto the plinth and stood very close to the box. His feet disappeared into the hole at the base.

The shopkeeper then turned away and flicked a switch. There was a humming sound, and shafts of green light appeared from the cracks in the box.

The shopkeeper looked down one of the portholes on the top. Mrs Holden looked down another. Gordon peered down the porthole directly in front of him.

"Come and see," he said as he beckoned to James. "Come and see my bones!"

James did as he was told. He went over to the plinth and took over viewing from the shopkeeper.

It was exactly as Gordon had said. James could see every bone in Gordon's feet. They were encased by the outline of his brand-new shoes. All against a vivid green background.

James was staggered. He had only ever seen Hallowe'en skeletons before. They were made of plastic and James was sure that they were not anatomically correct. Here were real bones in a real person's feet. He could even see Gordon wiggle his toes!

As James kept looking, the shopkeeper talked to Mrs Holden. They agreed that the shoes were an excellent fit and that she would buy them.

James suddenly felt brave.

"Could I have a go on your magic X-ray machine, Sir?"

The shopkeeper turned to him and asked if he was thinking of buying any shoes. James had to admit that he wasn't.

"Then, Young Man, I am afraid that I can't let you try out my pedoscope. It's the only one that I have. I won't be able to get another one if it breaks. I must keep it for paying customers only. I'm sorry."

James was very sad. He had fallen in love with that eerie green light and so wanted to see his bones silhouetted against it.

But it wasn't to be. Perhaps he could come back tomorrow with Great Aunty Marian and then he could have a go.

Now there was a thought.

Gordon jumped down from the machine. He said, "I told you it was good!"

James agreed.

Gordon put his old shoes back on and turned to his mother.

"Have we finished now?" he asked.

She said that they had, and that if they were quick, the boys would be able to play for half an hour at the Waterfalls before teatime.

The boys took the hint and ran off immediately, leaving Mrs Holden and the new shoes behind.

They had just enough time to have several goes on the swings (including jumping off—something else that James was not supposed to do!) before they had to return to their respective homes.

Before they did though, they again agreed to meet on the grass-covered bridge for another afternoon of fun on the morrow.

Now they had to go their separate ways if they were going to be back in time for tea.

Chapter 1.6
Pirates on the High Seas

Wednesday already!

James couldn't believe how quickly the time was flying by. He was having such fun with his new friend Gordon.

Straight after dinner, he grabbed his backpack and told Great Aunty Marian where he was heading. He thought that she had probably guessed already, but he needed to be sure she knew where he was.

Gordon and James met on the grass-covered bridge, just as they had on previous days. They sat at the centre of the bridge where they watched the stream pour into the concrete paddling pool below.

"What shall we do now?" asked James.

"Don't know!" replied Gordon, "Let's go and play on the roundabout while we make up our minds!"

That seemed to be a good idea and off the boys ran.

As they started to scramble their way to the top of the witch's hat roundabout, James had an idea.

"Let's pretend that we are pirates, searching for plunder!"

"What's plunder?" asked Gordon as he reached the top.

"It's stolen treasure. Jewels, gold, coins!" replied James.

He then told Gordon about a book he was reading at bedtime. It told of how pirates would sail across the foreign seas. They would rob ships of any treasure they were carrying. If the ship's crew wouldn't join them, the pirates would either kill them, or put them in a small rowing boat and leave them to die.

Pirates lived a life full of excitement and adventure.

Sometimes, when they found treasure that they really liked, they would take it to an island and bury it.

"Let's pretend we are pirates, trying to board a ship full of treasure!" shouted James.

"But don't we need Swords and stuff like that?" asked Gordon.

James paused from his climbing. Then he started to go back down to the ground.

"Where are you going?" Gordon shouted from the top of the roundabout.

"I'm going to find some Swords!" came the reply.

Before you knew it, James was back on the roundabout. This time, though, he was carrying two long straight sticks.

"I thought we could pretend they are Swords!"

Gordon thought this was a splendid idea and the two boys spent the next hour or so, climbing around the top of the roundabout. Every so often they would playfight with the sticks, shouting things like "Ahoy, me hearties!" and "Take that!"

Amazingly, neither of them hurt the other, and neither of them slipped or fell off. Given their enthusiasm for the game, this was a surprise!

Suddenly Gordon paused.

"Hush!" he demanded.

James stopped shouting.

Both boys listened.

Gordon had heard something.

It shouted like the roar of a tractor engine and it was getting louder.

"What's that?" wondered Gordon. "It sounds like a tractor, but as far as I know, all the tractors round here are busy with haymaking!"

The boys scrambled down from the roundabout and waited.

The noise came closer and grew louder.

James wanted to know what haymaking was. Remember—he wasn't from these parts.

As the boys waited to see what was going to happen, Gordon explained about haymaking.

Apparently not all fields were used to keep animals in. Neither were they used to grow things like wheat. No, instead, they grew grass. And at this time of year, the farmers would come along with their tractors and toppers and cut the grass. They would leave it to dry in the open air until it went yellow.

When the grass was dry and had turned yellow, it was hay. The hay was used during the winter when there wasn't anything else for the sheep or cows to eat.

When the hay was ready, all the young boys and teenagers from the town would come and help. The tractor would now have a bailer attached and the loose hay would be tied up with string into large cube-like parcels called bales.

The boys would stack the parcels into neat piles across the field, which James now learnt was called a meadow. Although that sounded like a simple job, it was jolly hard work as the hay bales were very heavy. Gordon had done this job for the first time last year and it fair wore him out!

Then Gordon told James that this year's grass had been cut earlier in the week. Because the weather had been so dry since, the hay was almost ready, and baling would start very soon. Indeed, he might not be able to play out on Friday or Saturday because he had to go and help with haymaking.

James was devastated. That meant that he only had today and tomorrow with his friend before he had to go home.

He had a thought.

"Can I come and help?"

But Gordon said no. It would be too dangerous for someone who wasn't from these parts to try and hay-make.

Oh dear.

"Let's enjoy now time!" said Gordon, and being an optimist, he also added, "Maybe they won't need me till Saturday!"

James reluctantly agreed. He had been having such fun. He didn't want it to end.

They heard the tractor shudder to halt.

As they ran to look over the dry-stone wall to see what was happening, Gordon shouted, "And there is always next year!"

They reached the wall and peered over. To their surprise, at some point since the previous day, a large wooden shed had sprung up. There was a very battered and dirty Land Rover parked beside it.

Standing next to the tractor, and in deep conversation with its driver, were two men. Each sported a very straggly bread and wore extremely muddy jeans.

The tractor was attached to a trailer on which a small digger was precariously balanced.

What on earth was going on?

Gordon and James watched as the men unloaded the digger.

Then the tractor and trailer drove off.

The two men who were left behind started to mark out areas of the grass under the tree and just beyond it.

When they were happy with their areas, one of the men with a straggly beard jumped on the digger and started to drive it to the first of the spots.

It was at this point that the two boys were spotted by the other man.

"Hello there!" he shouted.

He seemed friendly.

But Gordon and James had been warned about strangers, so they stayed where they were, on the park side of the dry-stone wall. They could run away if they needed to!

But they did want to know what was going on.

James wanted to run away, but Gordon held onto his tee shirt.

Gordon bravely waved back to the man, and shouted, "What are you doing?"

The man started to walk towards them.

"This is a mystery. A real adventure! We can get away if we need to. Let's find out what we can!" whispered Gordon.

By this time, the man with a straggly beard had reached his side of the wall.

"Hello, you two!" he repeated, and then asked them who they were.

Gordon returned the question. He wanted to know who the men with straggly beards and filthy jeans were. And while he was about it, where had that hut come from, and what was that digger doing?

Chapter 1.7
A Lesson in Archaeology

The man explained that he was something called a university professor. He studied a subject called Archaeology.

Neither James nor Gordon had heard of Archaeology.

The man could see that the boys were at a bit of a loss. They wanted to know more.

So, he went to explain.

The man driving the digger was also a professor at the same university.

They wanted to learn about the olden days.

Apparently, not all history was written down in books. Neither did it always tell the truth. And it most certainly didn't tell you a lot about everyday life in the olden days.

To find out what had really happened, you had to dig into the ground and try and find things—he called them "artefacts"—that would help you understand.

The man's friend who was now driving the digger, had discovered that there might be a village under the grass. He had discovered this from some old documents that he had found in a library.

However, other than a couple of lines in the documents, nothing else was mentioned.

The two professors had previously visited the site—which the boys realised was the field in which the professor was now standing—a few weeks ago.

The field appeared to be the one mentioned in the old document.

So, the two professors had decided to do some what the professor called "field work".

They were going to check out the field.

At the same time, it was a good opportunity to try out something that the professor had been working on back at the university. If it worked, it would make the professors' job a whole lot easier.

They were now going to try out a new machine.

The professor paused briefly to catch his breath.

"We wondered if we could use X-rays to show us where things might be buried."

Gordon interrupted.

"Like the machine in the shoe shop that shows up the bones in your feet?"

James thought that professor might be a bit cross at being interrupted. But no. He seemed rather pleased that the boys were paying such close attention.

He continued.

"Our machine works in a similar way. We discovered fairly quickly that X-rays don't work very well underground. So now we are trying out a type of radar instead.

Our experiments back in the laboratory show that radar can penetrate (that means go through) the ground and help us see things in the ground. In the lab, it works so much better than X-rays.

We are trying it out here now to see if it works in a real situation. If it works then all these areas that we have marked out should have things in them."

The professor pointed towards the ring-fenced areas.

He told the boys that they were going to become what he called trenches.

Gordon butted in again.

"They had trenches in World War One. Will they be like them?"

The professor replied, "They will be similar in that they will be rectangular holes in the ground. But that's where it will end. We want to dig things out, not live and fight in them like they did in the War!"

The boys watched as the digger moved from trench to trench.

The digger was removing what the professor called the "topsoil".

By taking it off, the job of digging down by hand and using trowels to where the things were would be quicker and easier. That task would be done by students. They would come to excavate deeper during the following week.

All the tools for the excavation had been brought by the Land Rover and were now in the shed ready for use when needed.

Gordon and James looked at each other.

"What's a student?" asked Gordon.

The professor looked at him and said, "It's someone who has gone to university to study after he has finished school. This dig is part of the course work."

Gordon didn't feel that he could ask any more. It was clear from the professor's way of talking that the professor thought the boys should know.

James timidly asked his question.

"What does "excavate" mean?"

The professor told them it was a posh word which meant to dig down carefully.

In Archaeology, you had to dig very carefully otherwise you might destroy what you were looking for. A lot of things that they were searching for had been in the ground for many hundreds of years and were very fragile.

"We want to finish taking the top layer off today so that the farmer can have his digger back. But the students won't be here until next week. We hope it won't rain between then and now otherwise it will be very hard work excavating! We don't use spades. We use trowels!"

When asked by Gordon if that would take a long time, the professor agreed. He also told them that by being careful, it might be possible to learn as much from what the artefact was buried in and where it had been found as you might from the artefact itself.

He made Archaeology sound very exciting.

The boys were enthralled. X-rays, radar, and the possibility of treasure!

The professor said that it was important that the site stayed as it was now.

It would be ready for the students to begin straightaway when they came.

It was all about "context"!

The boys didn't have time to ask the professor what he meant by that as James remembered the time. He looked at his watch and saw it was getting late.

He tapped Gordon's arm, and told him, "We need to head home or we won't be back in time for tea!"

With that, the boys said their farewell, and ran back towards the grass-covered bridge.

The professor shouted after them. "Please don't play on the site!"

But his words were lost to the boys as they ran back.

"See you tomorrow?" shouted Gordon.

"You bet!" shouted James as they went their opposite ways home.

Chapter 1.8
Buried Treasure

Gordon and James rendezvoused at their usual spot on the grass-covered bridge after dinner the following day.

Today, James had brought Timmy Rex. He had remembered what Gordon had told him about haymaking. And how Gordon might have to go and help on Friday.

Now that it was Thursday, James had realised that this might be the last time he would see Gordon before he went home on Saturday.

He wanted to make sure that they would meet up again next year if they could.

He had brought Timmy to help make sure that happened.

The boys sat on the bridge and dangled their feet over the edge. Gem lay down next to them.

"I do have to go and help with the haymaking tomorrow," Gordon glumly said, "It means I can't play out tomorrow—or for the rest of the school holidays. We have to get all the hay into the barns before it rains."

"I go home the day after tomorrow, too," added an equally sad James.

Then, he reached round to his backpack.

"Shall we meet here next year?" he asked Gordon as he fiddled with the backpack's clasps.

Gordon agreed readily.

James took Timmy Rex from his backpack.

"Will you look after Timmy while I am away?" he asked, "You can give him back when we meet up again?"

Gordon readily agreed. He thought Timmy was a splendid model of a dinosaur, and he was so happy that James was willing to trust him to look after it for a whole year!

With that settled, they decided to make the most of what time they had.

Gordon told Gem to look after Timmy while they got on with the serious business of playing.

"What shall we do today?" asked James.

Gordon had an idea.

Yesterday, before they had met the professors, they had been playing pirates. It had been a rattling good game too, with lots of action on the high seas. Well, the witch's hat roundabout anyway.

James went to fetch the sticks that they had been playing with.

"Do you remember telling me about pirates and buried treasure?" asked Gordon, as James came rushing back, "Why don't we play that today?"

James looked in the direction Gordon was facing.

He saw the field with its marked out trenches over the dry-stone wall.

"Excellent idea!" he agreed.

The boys quickly hopped over the dry-stone wall.

Gem stayed where she was. She had been told to guard Timmy Rex and that was what she was going to do. She knew that Gordon would be back at some point to relieve her of her duties. Until then, though, she would not allow anyone or anything near the precious plastic toy.

Once over the wall, the boys looked at all the trenches. The digger had done a very good job of taking off all the grass.

"Where shall we start looking?" asked James.

Gordon looked around and decided.

"Let's start with this one!"

The boys quickly got on with their play fighting. It was great fun in the trenches as they felt like they were really looking for treasure.

It was all becoming very intense.

James shouted, as he wielded his stick, "You shall not find the jewels!"

He charged towards Gordon, who tried to step back.

Only he didn't. Instead, he stumbled backwards and fell flat onto his back.

James snapped out his role as Captain Cutlass, and back to being best friend.

"Are you alright?" he asked as he peered over.

"I think so," gasped Gordon, "I didn't fall, though. I tripped."

"Perhaps it was a tree root?" wondered James.

Gordon scrambled to his feet, then knelt back down and started to pull the soil away.

"There's something here," he shouted, as he dug deeper.

"It might be buried treasure for real!" exclaimed James as he watched.

Gordon dug and dug. Then he asked James to help him dig some more.

Eventually, they realised that they had uncovered something that was most definitely not a tree root.

It was long and thin, and seemed to be wrapped in cloth. Or possibly leather. That bit wasn't too obvious as the material was quite rotted.

The boys tore the material away and exposed a magnificent Sword.

Wow! It was amazing. It looked like it was almost brand new.

"This can't have been buried in the ground for hundreds of years?" asked James. "Surely it would be rusty?"

"Maybe the cloth it was wrapped in protected it?" replied Gordon.

James wasn't convinced, but there didn't seem to be any other possible explanation. No one had been here since yesterday.

As they gazed at what they had found, both James and Gordon had the same horrible realisation at the same time.

They knew that they weren't supposed to be playing on the field now that it was all dug up and ready for the Archaeology professors' return.

How were they going to be able to explain away finding the Sword without getting into heaps of trouble?

They couldn't put it back in the ground. They had already made enough of a mess digging it out.

Indeed, James was getting quite concerned about that.

Gordon reassured him. He thought that the disturbed soil looked like a fox or badger had been digging—so they could probably get away with that.

But they couldn't show the Sword to the professors or the professors would know that they had been playing on the site when they shouldn't.

And they couldn't take it home as they would be told off for playing in a dangerous place.

What a dilemma.

Then James had an idea.

"Why don't we hide it somewhere safe. We can "find" it another time— perhaps next year—when all this has gone away?"

What a good idea. Gordon agreed whole-heartedly.

The next challenge was to find that safe place.

The boys looked around. The temporary shed where the professors' tools were stored wouldn't be any good. Neither would be hiding the Sword under the bridge where it could get washed away if the stream flooded.

Gordon and James had the same idea at exactly the same time.

Of course! It was obvious when you thought about it.

The hidey hole in the tree!

It was deep enough. It was sheltered enough. And, most importantly, it was secret enough!

Perfect!

James scrambled out of the shallow trench first, and Gordon passed the Sword to him. Then he got out.

They walked over to the tree, looking round all the while to make sure they weren't being watched.

James had a sudden thought as they got to the tree.

"Do you think the hole will be deep enough?"

"It will have to be!" came the reply.

Nevertheless, the boys cleared the hole as best they could of all the leaves and twigs that had fallen down there over time.

As they did so, James wondered about time. He felt like he had known Gordon for ever, but when he thought about it, they had only met four days ago.

Very strange.

Gordon carefully wrapped the Sword back up in the rotting material.

Now for the moment of truth. Would the Sword fit in the hole, and most importantly, would it be properly hidden?

James held his breath as Gordon gently lowered the Sword into the hole. It slipped in silently, until Gordon had to let go of it. It landed at the bottom with a muffled clang.

It fit. It was completely out of sight. No one would know it was there if they weren't looking for it.

James wondered if the Sword was now on top of his orange squash bottle. One thing that he knew now was that Gordon would not be able to find his hidden message now. Not until they retrieved the Sword.

Whenever that might be.

The boys returned to the bridge where Gem was still guarding Timmy Rex. She wagged her tail as they approached.

Gordon looked at his watch.

"You're not going to believe this," he said, "But it's nearly time to go! Hiding that Sword has used up our precious play time!"

Gordon and James felt very sad.

This was it.

They now had to go their separate ways for a whole year. And they had to leave now if they were to avoid getting into trouble because they weren't back in time for tea.

Chapter 1.9
Fast Forward

It had been a good year.

It had been a busy year.

James had moved up a class and was now in year 4. He was excelling in football and reading.

But all the while, he was counting the days until the summer holidays. Not for him, the excitement of Christmas and snow—although he thoroughly enjoyed them when they arrived.

Not for him the joy of Easter Egg hunts—although he relished the chocolate prizes.

No, James wanted to be reunited with his friend Gordon. He wanted to play pirates again on the witch's hat roundabout.

And most importantly, he wanted to sort out the situation with the Sword.

He knew he had to be patient and wait for the summer holidays. But it wasn't easy.

It was one thing to know something, but another to do it!

Time did that funny thing again.

It seemed to take forever for weeks to pass. But when he looked back to what he had done during that time, it only seemed like yesterday when they were driving home from Great Aunty Marian's.

He remembered that when he first went back to school his mother would walk with him. But now, as the school holidays drew ever closer, he was old enough to walk the short distance all by himself.

James decided that time was a strange old thing.

Slowly but surely the clock ticked onwards.

Then, one day, as James was finishing a particularly engrossing chapter in his favourite Harry Potter story, his mother announced, "I can't believe how quickly time has passed!"

His mother continued.

"It's nearly time for us to visit Great Aunty Marian again!"

James stopped reading immediately, put down his book and started to listen intently.

This was the news he had been waiting to hear for so long. Nearly time to reconnect with Gordon!

It seemed that his mother had more to tell.

Apparently, things were going to be a little bit different this year because she was going to stay for a few more days. His mother promised not to stop James from playing out or going to the Waterfalls though.

This year, there was going to be a big family party.

This was the first time that James had heard of any such event.

His mother explained.

Her mother, James's grandma, was one of eight children. Amazingly, they were all still alive, although they were now very old.

His mother said that when the eldest of the uncles and aunts had reached their 70th birthday, the rest of the family had held a huge party to celebrate. Since then, it had become a family tradition to have a party when one of the Great Uncles or Aunts had their 70th birthday.

Great Aunty Marian had her 70th birthday party when James was tiny. He couldn't remember he had been so little. A baby, in fact!

This year it was the turn of the youngest of the brothers and sisters to turn 70. This would be the last 70th birthday party of this generation. Great Aunty Marian—who seemed to be the organiser in chief—decided that it would be extra special.

James would meet all his great uncles and aunts. Because he was now a big boy, he would remember them too.

It would also be lovely for his mother to see all her uncles and aunts. She didn't get to see them very often now that they lived down south.

His mother planned to stay so that she could help Great Aunty Marian organise the party and clear up afterwards.

James didn't care about any of this. All that mattered to him was that they were going back and going back soon. He would see Gordon again.

James was beside himself with joy.

He marked up the fridge calendar so he could count down the days to the end of school and more importantly, the day when they would be going back to Great Aunty Marian's.

Now that he knew when all this was going to happen, time did that strange thing again. Each day passed more slowly than ever. However, before James knew it, it was time to pack!

This time, his mother had arranged for the next-door neighbour to look after Tom cat while they were away. So much better than using those automatic feeder things like they used last year. It meant that his mother could stay for longer rather than have to rush back to feed the cat.

Finally, James and his mother were in the car and on their way.

James became more and more excited the closer they got to Great Aunty Marian's.

By the time they reached her front door, his mother had become quite cross and fed up with James asking "are we nearly there yet" every five minutes.

As happened last year, Great Aunty Marian greeted them at the front door.

As before, and after unpacking, they all sat down to enjoy a drink and a chat.

It was too late to play out, so James had to curb his enthusiasm and listen to his mother and Great Aunty Marian discussing what had happened since their last visit.

James sat in front of the fireplace, playing with his computer. He was wearing his headphones but could still hear what was being said if he listened carefully.

At first, it seemed that the adults were talking about his Great Uncle. Great Aunty Marian was saying how well he had done. Her baby brother was the first in the family to go to university—and that was a major achievement back then, you know. He'd worked really hard though, passed all his exams, and never looked back.

He'd married well too—to a clever lady who did something at the university which sounded very high-falutin. They had travelled the world and even lived in foreign parts.

He'd had a very different life to what he would have had here, where he grew up. Not that he had forgotten his roots. No, baby brother came back whenever he could.

And now he was 70. It seemed impossible.

James' mother wanted to know about the party.

Great Aunty Marian said that it was all arranged. It was going to be held at the visitors' centre.

James looked up from his game.

He heard that bit.

"What's the visitors' centre?" he asked, "I haven't heard of that before."

Great Aunty Marian looked at James, and then she remembered how he had played at the Waterfalls last year.

"I'm afraid that you are going to see a lot of changes when you go to the Waterfalls!"

James felt an icy chill cross his heart. Would this mean that he might not find Gordon?

"The Waterfall is still there," said Great Aunty Marian, "But the park with the swings and roundabout have disappeared."

What?

James demanded to know more, despite his mother asking him to mind his manners.

This was important.

He even took off his headphones so that he could hear everything.

Apparently, shortly after James had gone home last year, there had been big excitement in the town.

Some archaeologists had come to explore the field next to the playground.

Another icy chill ran though James's veins. He hoped they hadn't found the Sword.

It seemed that they were following up an earlier dig. Although the earlier dig had promised much, nothing had been found.

But this time, using better equipment (Great Aunty Marian couldn't remember what it was called) these scientists had dug up a hoard of treasure. There were helmets, daggers, brooches—even coins and a couple of rotten leather pouches. It had been so important that the local tv had been round and put it on the telly. Great Aunty Marian was surprised that the news hadn't got to James.

Great Aunty Marian continued.

The treasure and where it was found (James remembered that was called "context!") was so important that the field was still being dug today.

But it all cost a lot of money.

So, the local Council and the university had applied for money to help. Great Aunty Marian mentioned something called the National Lottery.

It turned out that this National Lottery would give them half the money needed to continue exploring the field. But the Council and the university had to find the other half.

The Council decided that the best way to make money was to let people come and watch the site being dug. Alongside it, it built the visitors' centre which had a small museum attached.

This was why there had been such big changes and the playground had gone. The visitors' centre was where the witches' hat roundabout and swings had been.

When people came to see the dig, they could go to the visitors' centre look at some of things that had been found. Not the big things, of course, they had to be sent to the British Museum. But there were smaller items like bone combs, cloak pins and stuff like that were on display.

You could buy tickets there to let you into the field so you could watch the archaeologists digging.

The centre also had a small café which served an excellent cup of tea and slice of seed cake.

There was more bad news.

The grass-covered bridge over which James and Gordon had dangled their feet was gone too. In its place was a posh wooden construction with a barrier and kiosk at the far side. A man sat in the kiosk and collected tickets from the people who had bought them at the visitor's centre. Then he would let them through so that they could watch the dig.

The big field that James walked through to reach the playground was now a huge car park so that the visitors could leave their cars safely while they wandered around the place.

So many changes.

But Great Aunty Marian thought that it wasn't all bad. After all, the Waterfalls playground was old and very run down.

Apparently, the Council had built another playground over other side of town. It had everything. Not just swings and roundabouts, but see-saws, tunnels to run through, and monkey bars to climb on too. And, as Great Aunty Marian muttered to James's mother, rubber surfaces under the whole lot so that if a child fell off anything, they wouldn't injure themselves too much!

"Yes," concluded Great Aunty Marian, "There have been big changes because of that dig. As well as changing the Waterfalls, it has meant that the town has had lots of visitors and made many more jobs for the locals."

"But what about the Waterfalls?" asked James, "I liked it just as it was."

"You can go and see tomorrow." said his mother, "Then we can try out the new park. If this friend Gordon is as good a friend as you think, I am sure he will find you regardless of which park you go to."

Chapter 1.10
Disaster

James and his mother went to bed. Unlike last year though, his mother slept in Great Aunty Marian's box room. It was small, but just about big enough for a single bed. James slept where he had slept last year. It was what he was used to, and after all this worrying news, his mother didn't want to make him any more upset than he was.

And he was too big to share a room with his mother now. After all, he was eight.

He didn't sleep well at all. He tossed and turned. So many thoughts kept popping into his head.

Underlying them all was the fear of what he would find—or not—when he went to the Waterfalls. Surely it couldn't be as changed as Great Aunty Marian had said.

The following day, straight after dinner, he set off towards the Waterfalls.

Just like last year, he was told to be back in time for tea.

As he walked along the route that he had taken last year, he could see that things had changed. For example, there was a brand-new traffic light-controlled road crossing where he used to just look both ways. He also noticed that the streets all seemed to be busier. Many more people and cars.

As he drew closer to the turning to the Waterfalls, his feelings of dread increased.

Instead of the tiny narrow snicket leading to the large field, there was now a tarmacked road. It was wide enough for two cars to drive past each other. There was even a narrow pavement. Then there were the signposts. They were all brightly painted and unlike last year, when they indicated the way to the Waterfall, now they announced "this way to the Viking dig".

This was not looking good.

Then as he walked on, and just as Great Aunty Marian had said, the grassy field had gone. In its place was a car park with lots and lots of vehicles parked in it. And yet more signs. This time they were demanding that you should "Pay and display".

James could still hear the water rushing at the far edge of the carpark.

He went over to see.

At least the waterfall seemed untouched. But there was now a park bench next to it where people could sit and admire the view.

This was definitely not good.

James walked on.

He saw the visitors' centre, just as Great Aunty Marian had described it, precisely where the witches' hat roundabout had been.

James ran to the bridge.

"Please let Great Aunty Marian be wrong!" he thought, all the while knowing that she wasn't.

Just as she had said, there was a brand-new wooden bridge, and there was a kiosk right on it. With a barrier. And a man sitting in the kiosk.

From where he stood, James could just make out what was beyond the barrier.

The dry-stone wall had disappeared.

The field behind where it had been was now all bare earth and holes.

But the old tree was still there.

Perhaps Gordon had left a message for him in there?

How was he going to reach it to find out?

Even if he could get past the barrier, there were too many people either digging or watching the digging to get close.

There wasn't a lot James could do, other than turn round and walk back to Great Aunty Marian's.

James felt like crying, even though he was a big boy.

He now doubted that he would ever see his friend again.

He got back in plenty of time for tea.

His mother rushed to him as he walked into the front room. He was so despondent.

"James, James," she said in a very worried voice, "Was it as bad as Great Aunty Marian said?"

"It was worse!" replied James.

He was about to throw his backpack on one of the chairs when he realised that there was someone else in the room. Well, two people, who he hadn't met before, were there.

Not that he was bothered. He was far too upset to care.

"James," said his mother, "remember your manners!"

James looked up.

His mother and Great Aunty Marian were sat at the table. So was a man and a lady.

"Say hello to your Great Uncle!" ordered his mother.

James mumbled a quick "hi!"

He supposed he must have sounded very sulky because his Great Uncle was staring at him in a very strange way.

Great Aunty Marian thought so too.

She told James that here was her little baby brother. The one who was 70 years old, and whose party they were having tomorrow.

The lady sitting next to him was his wife, Great Aunty Pauline.

James thought he had better try to show some interest. He remembered that Great Aunty Marian had said that he worked at a university.

"Are you a professor?" he asked his Great Uncle.

"Indeed, I am," came the reply, "And so is Pauline."

James started to feel just a tiny bit interested.

"What do you study?"

"I'm a physicist," replied his Great Uncle, "I look at things and try to understand why they work in the way they do. It needs lots and lots of complicated mathematics and stuff."

Oh. James's interest fell. That sounded to be way too clever for him.

Then Great Aunty Pauline joined in.

"I'm an Archaeologist." She told him. "I study the Vikings. And I am afraid that its partly my fault that your playground has moved."

This was the last thing that James wanted to hear, Nevertheless, he had no choice.

Great Aunty Pauline continued her tale. To be fair, it hadn't been her fault directly. It was her team's.

Apparently, the field had been dug before and nothing had been found. (At this point James had to hide a wry smile as he remembered how he and Gordon had tripped over the Sword).

But, she continued, the ground radar that was used then was what she called state-of-the-art, and prone to mistakes.

So, the first dig had looked in all the wrong places.

However, since then, more accurate and better equipment had come along. And her team had the latest version. The team used it to scan the site and discovered where the first dig had got things wrong. Not badly wrong. Just wrong enough to stop them finding anything of interest. Had they looked a few inches to the left, they would have been bang on target.

The bottom line seemed to be that the people who were digging there had now found lots of stuff. It was all in excellent condition and was helping the university to understand how the Vikings lived all those years ago. There wasn't another site like it in England. Or even Europe. It meant that the park had to go so that the dig could continue. After all, it was now of national importance!

It was jolly good luck that her husband's birthday was tomorrow as it meant that she could not only come to the party but inspect progress at the site!

By this time, the teapot was empty. It was time for Great Aunty Marian's brother and his wife to leave.

They were staying in a local hotel and they had a meal booked for that evening.

They didn't want to be late.

Great Aunty Marian's brother gave James another strange look and then said goodbye to everyone.

They wanted to be back in time for tea, thought James.

Chapter 1.11
Party Planning

It was the day of the party.

His mother and Great Aunty Marian were in a great state of excitement and in a frenzy of organisation.

James wished he could run away to the Waterfalls and play with Gordon. But he couldn't. Not now.

Everything had changed, and he had no idea how he could get in touch with Gordon or if he would ever see him again.

James did offer to help with all the party preparations. His mother thought about this briefly, then sat him up to the table and gave him a pen and some cardboard squares. Then she produced a list.

"I want you to write the names of everyone on this list onto these squares," she said, "You will have to use your best handwriting. And only one name in each square! We will use them to mark up where everyone is going to sit for the meal."

James looked down the list. There were a lot of names on it. This was going to be a huge party.

Great Aunty Marian noticed that James was counting the names.

"There are a lot of names, aren't there," she observed, "That's because all the Great Uncles and Aunts had children, and they are all coming."

"Except your Grandma," added his mother, "She can't come because she's on holiday in Scotland."

James thought his Grandma should have perhaps made an effort, but then he knew his grandma was what his mother politely called eccentric. She didn't do things like other people.

He could tell that his mother wasn't happy about the situation. But, as he couldn't do anything about it, he decided to say nothing.

The list was long, so James needed to make a start.

As James copied each name carefully from the list, his mother was buttering slices of bread.

Great Aunty Marian put the finishing touches to several lemon drizzle cakes that she had made at some silly o'clock before he had got up.

Apparently, most of the other relatives were contributing to the feast as well. Aunty Marian referred to the event as a "Jacob's Join".

She explained to James that the term meant that everyone would bring something to the party (only she referred to it as a "do"!). She hoped that it would be just like the parties that they used to have when they were younger, and that it would bring back happy memories of those times for her brother.

The only big difference was that the do was being held at the visitors' centre because there wasn't a place big enough anywhere else that they could afford to hire.

James's mother explained that the café would deal with the drinks side of things, which would make it a bit easier for everyone.

James's mother continued making sandwiches.

She layered slices of ham between buttered slices of bread, and then packed them in foil. Then she prepared egg and cress. After that, cheese, and tomato.

James could see that it was going to be a fine feast.

Eventually every slice of bread was made into a sandwich of one sort or another, and the cakes were all fully iced. Great Aunty Marian carried one lot of goodies to his mother's car, and his mother followed with all the rest.

There was only just enough room for James to squeeze into the back, but he managed to fit in. He clutched the completed cardboard squares next to his chest and tried not to breathe too deeply. He hoped that he wouldn't sneeze before the car was emptied!

Although James was still very upset about what had happened to the Waterfalls, he had to admit to himself that the improved road to the visitors' centre was so much better than what had been there before. He hated to think what could have happened to the sandwiches and cakes if it had been as he remembered it! The cakes would have only been fit for trifle if the old road had still been there.

James could see that the visitors' centre was very busy and full of paying customers.

His mother could see that he was confused.

"We're going to put all this lot into the back kitchen where there is a cold room. It is like a huge fridge and it will keep everything fresh for the party later."

Thank goodness. James had been worried that the customers might be tempted to taste the goodies.

James handed the completed cardboard squares to his mother. She could see that he had done an excellent job. All the names were written in James's best handwriting.

"I think there will be quite a few people bringing things for the cold room!" said Great Aunty Marian, "We will come back after the café has closed for the day to set things up!"

With that, they all got back into the car and returned home.

The party was due to start at 7pm prompt.

As the café closed at 4pm, that allowed plenty of time for getting ready.

James went to have a shower as his mother prepared yet more food. This time it was battalions of scones which she was going to put on the tables with pots of strawberry jam and clotted cream. She told James that they always went down well with the family!

Eventually, his mother, Great Aunty Marion and James were all dressed in their best clothes and the car finally packed with the last load of delectable goodies for the evening.

As they drove up to the Waterfalls, Great Aunty Marian told his mother that there was going to be dancing. One of the other relations was going to bring his karaoke machine.

James smiled to himself. Little did Great Aunty Marian realise that it wouldn't just be dancing. There would be singing along to the music at the same time. He looked forward to seeing Great Aunty Marian doing that!

When they reached the café, James could see that the family had pulled together.

The café was transformed! Long tables were laid out around three sides of the room, with the fourth wall having a table packed with all manner of different sorts of food.

There was much that James recognised—like the sandwiches and lemon drizzle cakes. But there was some that he most certainly didn't. He stared at small brown pastry triangles. They smelt lovely, but James didn't have a clue what they were.

One of his relatives came up behind him as he looked at them and told him.

"They're samosas. I think they are Indian. These ones here are filled with savoury minced lamb, and those over there…" she pointed, "…are filled with potatoes, carrots and peas."

James wanted to try both.

He grabbed a plate and helped himself to one of each. Even though they smelt delicious, he didn't want to take any more just yet. After all, there was a risk that he might not like them.

As he did so, everyone fell silent. At first James thought he had done something wrong. But no, the guest of honour, his Great Uncle, and his wife had arrived.

They slowly walked to the end of the room as everyone watched them. Then, they checked the place cards and went to their places.

Everyone cheered.

Now it was time to eat.

James took his samosas back to his place next to his mother and Great Aunty Marian, and tucked in.

They were delicious. They were not too hot, but gloriously spicy and he wanted more.

He went back to the long table of food and started to eye up the options again.

Should he go for the sausage rolls or the crisps? Or perhaps both? And would he be able to fit another samosa in if he did?

As he pondered his next move, he realised that his Great Uncle was standing next to him.

He was looking at James with that strange expression again.

"Hello James," he said, "I was hoping our paths would cross again!"

James looked up and asked, "Why are you looking at me like that? I haven't done anything wrong, have I? Everyone else is eating…"

"No, you haven't! In fact, I would say that you have done everything right. You are standing in front of all this party food, so I would say that you are most certainly in the right place for tea!"

Chapter 1.12
A Mystery

James's Great Uncle helped himself to a huge plate of goodies.

Then he said to James, "How would you like to explore this place after we've finished eating? I am sure I can sneak away for a little while and we might be able to climb over that barrier now that everything has closed for the evening!"

James looked at his Great Uncle with awe. Was his relative a mind-reader?

That was exactly what he had been wishing he could do.

He needed to check out the tree to see if the Sword was still there, and perhaps more importantly, if Gordon had left any messages for him as to where they should meet up now.

James and his Great Uncle agreed to meet by the front door to the café. It was right next to the toilets so if they were missed, his mother would think that he had gone to the loo!

This was almost as exciting as playing out with Gordon!

James almost wished that the plate of food that he was carrying wasn't quite so enticing. But he was a boy, and a hungry one at that.

So, he went back to his place and finished off the delectable morsels as quickly as good manners would allow. Then he asked his mother if he may leave the table. He didn't say that he wanted to go to the loo, but from the way he was acting, that's what she thought he wanted to do!

As he left the big room, he turned to his Great Uncle and winked.

His Great Uncle winked back and stood up.

They rendezvoused by the toilets. It was getting quite chilly so they both had found their coats. His Great Uncle was now carrying a satchel as well.

They sneaked outside and walked quickly to the bridge. All the while, James kept looking around to make sure they weren't followed.

Honestly, it really did feel like he was with Gordon again, and that they were re-enacting what they did when they had hidden the Sword.

They reached the bridge. The barrier stood strong and firm in front of them.

"Don't worry," said his Great Uncle, "I will lift you over and then I will climb over. My legs are longer than yours!"

The tree stood in front of them. It was just as tall and impressive has it had been last year.

James ran round it, searching for his hidey hole.

He didn't have to search too hard.

There it was.

All the while his Great Uncle watched.

"Anyone would think you were looking for something!" he observed.

"I am," replied James, "I came up here last year—before all this horrid building and digging had started—with the best friend that I ever had. We played here every day for as long as I stayed. Apart from one day when we had to go and buy Gordon some new school shoes!"

"Sit down for a minute." Said his Great Uncle.

James did as he was asked and sat next to his Great Uncle. His Great Uncle took something out of his satchel. It looked like an old photograph. It was in faded colour with a sort of brown tinge.

"This is a photograph of me with my brothers and sisters. It was taken when I was about your age. Have a look."

James was a polite young man, so he did as he was asked.

He took the photo from his Great Uncle and looked at it. As he did so, his Great Uncle pointed to the grainy images.

"There is your Great Aunty Marian when she was a young girl," he was saying, when James burst out, "There's a boy on here that looks just like my friend Gordon! How can that be?"

His Great Uncle looked at him.

"You know, even though we met yesterday, and your mother introduced us, she didn't mention my name, did she?"

James nodded in agreement. Now his Great Uncle came to mention it, what did he know about this person he was sitting next to? All he knew was that he was his Great Uncle, and he was 70 years old.

"It is Gordon!" said his Great Uncle.

"Are you my Gordon's father?" asked James.

After all, James had been named after his father, so it was possible.

"No," replied his Great Uncle.

Then he reached into his satchel again.

This time he pulled out something that was wrapped up in pages from an old newspaper.

He handed it to James.

"I was given this a long time ago," he said, "I kept it by my bed till the winter, then I thought I should wrap it up and put it away to keep it safe."

James started to unwrap the yellowing newsprint. As he did so he could still read parts of the headlines.

"Kennedy shot in Dallas"

"Tragedy on the campaign trail"

And the date—22 November 1963.

Things were becoming very peculiar. James wasn't sure he liked this game anymore.

But curiosity drove him on. He wanted to know what this parcel contained.

He ripped the last layer off.

"TIMMY!"

It was Timmy Rex.

His favourite dinosaur.

The one he had given to Gordon on their last day together before he had had to go home, and Gordon had to go haymaking.

James looked at his plastic dinosaur in amazement.

Yes, it was definitely Timmy. It wasn't an imposter. James could see his teeth marks on Timmy's tail where he used to chew on the toy in the night.

James looked at his Great Uncle.

"I don't understand?"

His Great Uncle replied, "Neither do I, and I'm supposed to be a physicist who can explain these sorts of things. But, if I am right, and I am really your friend from last summer, we need to look in the hidey hole to see if our Sword is still there!"

That clinched it.

No one else knew about the Sword. Only James and Gordon.

This old man, whose 70th birthday his family was celebrating, was none other than his friend from last year.

How did he get so old?

James jumped up. Gordon would have done so as well, but he was feeling his age, so it was more of a dignified rise.

They walked round to the hidey hole. Neither needed to tell the other where to look.

They found the hole at same time.

James put his hand in. He reached deep down. His hand flailed around in thin air. He couldn't feel anything in there.

He took his arm out and turned to his Great Uncle.

"It's not there!" he said in a stunned voice, "I can't find it!"

"Let me have a go," said Gordon, "I'm now over six feet tall and my arms are a bit longer than yours!"

James watched and held his breath.

Was the Sword still there?

His Great Uncle leaned further into the hole. His arm had completely disappeared.

Suddenly, Great Uncle Gordon yelled loudly, "I've got it! I've only gone and got it!"

He stepped back, and slowly removed his arm from the hidey hole.

He stepped further back. As he did so, he pulled out a long thin shape of something. A rather nasty damp musty smell emerged at the same time.

James and his Great Uncle grinned at each other. It was just like old times.

Almost.

"It was right where we left it!" said Great Uncle Gordon.

James was speechless with delight.

They sat down on the grass under the tree. Great Uncle Gordon had the Sword across his knees.

James recovered the power of speech.

"What do we do now?" he asked.

"I have an idea!" came the reply, "We go back to the party and take the Sword with us. We will tell everyone where we found it—in the tree. They can't tell us off for playing where we did. All that is long ago. So, we won't get into trouble!"

"And," added Great Uncle Gordon, "We won't have been missed."

James finished the sentence.

"And we will be back in time for tea!"

Chapter 1.13
Back to the Party

Great Uncle and James were wrong. They had been missed.

As they walked back into the party room, Great Aunty Marian and his mother confronted them.

"Just where have you two been?" asked his mother in a worried voice.

James hid behind his Great Uncle.

"I'm so sorry. We were longer than we thought we would be," he apologetically said.

"We have found something which we think might be very important. But we need to show it to an expert to be sure!"

Then he looked over to Pauline, his wife, and Professor of Viking Archaeology.

"Pauline," Great Uncle Gordon shouted, "Have you a moment? Can you come over here? I think we have something that might interest you!"

Pauline put down her sausage roll and did as she was bid.

"What are you on about?" she asked.

In reply, Great Uncle Gordon handed her the smelly rotten pouch and Sword.

Pauline gasped in amazement.

"Where on earth did you get this from?"

And then, "If I'm not mistaken, this is a valuable ancient Viking Sword!"

She wanted to know exactly where they had found the object, and then she took out her mobile phone.

"I'm calling my team at the university. They need to get this back to the laboratory so we can verify exactly what you have found. From what you've told me, you found it in a tree? I will lay odds on that wasn't where the Sword was originally. I wonder how it got into the tree?"

Great Uncle Gordon and James looked at each other but didn't say a word.

What a marvellous and exciting end to a birthday party!

But there was still a whole heap of work to be done to make sure that Great Aunty Pauline's thoughts about the Sword were correct.

One of Pauline's team arrived remarkably quickly after her call. James wondered if he had been staying close by and had been working on the dig earlier in the day.

No matter, he was now going to take the Sword back to the university where it could be examined properly.

Great Aunty Pauline explained that because the Sword was so old, they couldn't just unwrap it. It had to be carefully taken apart. The material that it was wrapped in might be able to tell them as much about the Sword's history as the Sword itself.

James piped up. "You mean context?"

Great Aunty Pauline was impressed.

"Indeed, I do, Young Man."

It was clear that James was fascinated by the Sword, and the Vikings who probably made it.

Great Aunty Pauline took him to one side and said, "Would you like to come and visit the university laboratory with me while you are here? I can show you all the marvellous things that can be done scientifically to help us understand more about the Sword."

James looked at his mother. This was better than playing out with Gordon— or even Great Uncle Gordon as he now was. A visit to a real scientific laboratory!

"Can we? Please say yes!" he begged.

His mother pretended to think about it for a little while. Not too long though. Just long enough for James to think that she might say no.

Then she nodded and agreed.

Privately, his mother thought that a visit to the university might be good for James. She thought it might inspire him and give him something to work towards when he did his schoolwork. Parents are like that, you know.

That was agreed.

His mother and Great Aunty Pauline would sort out a day and time for James and his mother to visit the university.

But before that, there was a party to enjoy. James's best friend Gordon's birthday party to be precise!

The lights went out.

In walked Great Aunty Marian.

She was carrying an enormous cake. It had seven candles, and they were all lit.

"I couldn't manage seventy candles," she said as she advanced, "They would have been too hot. So, each of these little blighters represents ten years!"

Great Aunty Marian started to sing. Then everyone else joined in except Great Uncle Gordon.

He looked vaguely embarrassed but extremely pleased.

After two rounds of "Happy birthday" and "He's a jolly good fellow", Great Aunty Marian put the cake down on the table in front of him. She instructed him to blow the candles out and make a wish.

Great Uncle Gordon winked at James, then he closed his eyes and blew out all the candles in one breath.

James knew what Great Uncle Gordon had wished for.

It was the same as what he would have wished for it if had been his birthday.

He wanted to solve the mystery of the Sword!

James could hardly wait for his visit to the university.

It could be far more exciting than anything that had happened so far.

And he might find out more about the Sword too!

Chapter 1.14
Dreamtime

It was a very tired but excited little boy who went to bed late after the party.

After the birthday cake, there had been party games ("Just like we used to play when we were young!" according to Great Aunty Marian).

They had worn him out.

Now James was tucked up in bed with Timmy Rex by his side.

It had been a very peculiar day all round.

Despite wanting to think about it all, James fell quickly asleep.

And he started to dream.

Not about his usual exploring the jungles and finding dinosaur bones dreams though.

This was a very different dream. It was so vivid. So colourful. He could even smell things.

It was like he was watching from afar and looking down on a village from the olden days.

There were no cars, or tidy rows of houses.

In this village, the houses all seemed to be covered in hay. Smoke curled gently through holes in the roofs.

The houses were clustered around a central space, and a large bonfire was burning in the middle of it.

In his dream, there were people—men, women, and children—all dressed in heavy woollen cloth and looking like they hadn't had a good wash for weeks. They clustered around the bonfire.

Suddenly, some of the people moved away from each other, and made way for a large thickset man so he could stand by the fire.

He was dressed strangely. He had woollen trousers with thin rope wrapped around them. To keep them on, James supposed. The man wore a heavy thick cloak round his shoulders.

But James was really impressed with the helmet that the man was wearing, and the Sword which he was carrying.

It looked shiny and new. It had lots of what seemed to be scribbles on its side. The hilt appeared to have a bright yellow, almost glass-like, stone set in it.

James thought it looked remarkably like a new version of what he and his friend had found.

The man approached the bonfire and raised the Sword.

"Behold, the Sword of Eir!" he shouted.

The crowd bowed their heads in his direction.

The man stomped over to a small three-legged stool and sat down.

He took off his helmet. James could now see that his face was covered in bright blue swirls, very similar to those on the Sword.

The man balanced the Sword in front of him.

Then he began to speak. The man had the sleepy voice of a practiced storyteller.

But his face told a different story. It had the look of a battle-weary soldier.

His tale was very strange.

He had come to the village to present them with the Sword of Eir. For safekeeping.

The Sword was precious.

It had slain many enemies of the Vikings. Their blood had given the Sword magical power. But that power must be used with care. Because it could be dangerous. He, the Keeper of the Sword, was becoming old. Soon, he would not be able to look after the Sword. But it needed to be kept safely away from those who might try to abuse its power.

He was gifting the Sword to the village, and it would be their solemn duty to protect it from this day forth! Until the Sword found its new Keeper.

The people around him gasped.

The Sword was truly magnificent. It came with such responsibility.

They wanted to know more about its power, or things could go wrong.

One of the villagers spoke up. Could he be a village elder? Someone tasked with keeping the village safe and prosperous?

James's dream continued.

The village elder asked two questions of the storyteller.

First, he wanted to know what magical gift the Sword held, and then, how they might keep the Sword safe? They would not shirk their duty but needed to know these things to be able to carry it out.

The storyteller shuffled slightly to get more comfortable. Three-legged stools were not exactly designed for long tales.

"The mighty Sword of Eir has great magical powers!" he began.

The crowd drew closer.

"It has the power to rip the curtain that separates the past from the present. But only for the Him whom the Sword choses!"

The people were getting excited now. Could one of them be the chosen one who might be able to travel back and forth in time and space?

It was almost as if the storyteller had read their minds.

"The Sword will choose. The Sword will know. We humble mortals will not.

Its power stretches beyond its physical being. When it chooses, that person need only be nearby for its power to work.

But many evil people want this Sword for themselves. You must hide it safely until it decides it wants to be found! Many will search, but it must not be found by them. Only by the person whom the Sword chooses."

Gosh—this was a cracking dream. James hoped he would remember it when he woke up!

Down below in the village, the scene was changing.

James could see that it was daytime again. The storyteller and the three-legged stool were nowhere to be seen.

The village elder was there though, as were some of the men from the previous evening.

Other than them, the village was completely deserted.

It was clear that the elder was giving instructions.

One of the men ran into a house and returned with the Sword and a sheep skin.

As the village elder reverently wrapped the Sword in the furry pelt, the men were digging a deep hole.

The village elder came to look at the hole and nodded.

"That is just right. It is too deep for anyone to find the Sword unless we tell them where it is."

He jumped in the hole with the Sword and lay it down.

Carefully.

With reverence and fear.

One of the men had to help the village elder climb out of the hole afterwards.

When the village elder was back above ground, the men filled in the hole.

They covered it with stones and leaves.

By the time they finished, there was nothing to show that there had been a hole there.

The village elder was clearly pleased with their efforts.

He produced a large pouch from under his cloak.

"Let us drink to the mighty power of Eir" he said as he passed the pouch from man to man.

The men drank readily. It had been thirsty work.

By the time it was the village elder's turn to drink, the pouch was empty.

He didn't look too upset though.

As the men started to walk away from their work, one by one, they started to fall down.

They grabbed their throats.

And fell silent.

The village elder had poisoned them all, so that they could never tell of the Sword's resting place.

James woke up with a shudder.

That wasn't what he had thought would happen. Where had that dream come from?

He grabbed Timmy Rex and began to chew his toy's tail. Just like he did last year when he was worried.

There was no way that he was going to forget that!

James knew that he must tell Great Uncle Gordon and Great Aunty Pauline about the dream. He didn't understand why he felt this need, only that it could be important.

Chapter 1.15
Corridors of Learning

It was a long wait until first grey shafts of light crept under the curtains.

Poor Timmy Rex's tail had several more notches from James's chews. He hadn't been able to get back to sleep after that vivid but very disturbing dream.

But at least he had a name for the Sword now.

The Mighty Sword of Eir.

It sounded very impressive. He could hardly wait to tell Great Uncle Gordon.

James eyes felt itchy and sore from lack of sleep.

As he stumbled to the table for breakfast, his mother looked at him with concern.

"Are you alright, young man?" she asked, "I can ring up your Great Uncle and cancel our visit to the university if you are coming down with something."

Great Aunty Marion rushed over with a thermometer and took James's temperature.

It was normal.

"He hasn't got a fever!" she announced.

His mother and Great Aunt conferred. They decided that perhaps James had become over-excited the previous day at the party.

As result they thought he might have had a couple of bad dreams which meant he didn't sleep very well.

James allowed himself the smallest of smiles. Little did they know. But he wasn't going to tell them of his dream. Otherwise, they might not let him visit the university.

Anyway, after a bowl of cereal and a couple of slices of toast and home-made marmalade, he was feeling much happier!

Now it was time to get ready to visit the university.

Apparently, his mother had arranged to meet Great Uncle Gordon and Great Aunty Pauline at the campus, which James came to realise was what grown-ups called the place where the university buildings were.

They would all meet after dinner. That would allow his relatives time to get back home, unpack their car, feed their cat, and go to the university.

Meanwhile, his mother and James were going to treat Great Aunty Marian to a posh meal in a restaurant in the university town at dinnertime. Without a hint of tripe! Or, James thought, any washing up!

The family would rendezvous at three o'clock prompt.

James was so excited that he could barely eat his sausages and chips. His mother and Great Aunty Marian seemed to be taking for ever to finish their meals. And then they were thinking about pudding.

Time was doing that strange thing again. It was passing far too slowly!

Eventually, his mother and Great Aunty Marian finished their post-pudding cups of coffee. His mother asked for the bill.

At last. It was time to head over to the campus.

Now James was worried that his Great Uncle and Aunt might not turn up. They might have been delayed. Their cat might have run away. Anything could have happened to stop them coming.

James's mother parked the car in the Department of Physics car park, just as she had been instructed by Great Uncle Gordon. The building looked big and functional. Like it was built to have laboratories and clever people inside.

James's mother's timing could not have been better. As she switched off the engine, Great Uncle Gordon came rushing down the steps.

"You found us!" he said.

James thought that was a far more practical way of greeting than just a simple hello.

Great Uncle Gordon helped Great Aunty Marion out of the car and asked if anyone would like a cup of tea before their tour.

Both his mother and Great Aunty Marian said no. But Great Aunty Marian decided that it might be wise if she paid a visit to the loo before they set off! She had always been told to make sure you went before you set off anywhere because you never knew where the next facility would be!

His mother thought that would be a good idea for James too. James rolled his eyes but knew that he would have to go into the Gents otherwise he would never hear the last of it!

The tour began with a visit to the basement.

Great Uncle Gordon told James that this is where all the really sensitive equipment was. Sometimes, physicists had to measure the tiniest amounts of stuff (thankfully, he didn't go into detail). They could be so small that even the slightest vibration from, say, a passing car, or a beam of sunlight could affect the measurement.

James was amazed.

The machines looked to be huge and built so solidly of metal. How could they possibly be used to measure such small things?

There was a gentle clatter in the background.

"That noise is made by vacuum pumps!" explained Great Uncle Gordon, "Many of our experiments have to carried out with as little air as possible. These pumps get rid of it!"

James was fascinated. He had never seen such impressive machines before.

His mother shivered.

"It's a little chilly in here," she said.

Great Uncle Gordon explained some more.

Because the machines had to make such delicate measurements, they had to be kept at the same temperature all the time. Otherwise, the measurements would be affected.

Great Aunty Marian sniffed.

All this fuss to try to measure something that you couldn't even see. It didn't make sense.

Great Uncle Gordon begged to differ.

He reminded his sister that everything was made up of smaller things. If you didn't understand about the smallest of these, how could you really and truly understand the world?

Good point!

Great Uncle Gordon took them back upstairs and quickly showed them round the offices and lecture theatres. He explained that students would sit in the tiered rows and listen to their professors telling them stuff.

Then they would be told to go and find out more from the computers in the library.

At this point, Great Aunty Marian was heard to give another sniff. She didn't hold with these modern new-fangled computer things at all. Give her a good old-fashioned typewriter any day. You knew where you were with one of those!

Now it was time to head over to the Department of Archaeology. James would be able to see what was happening with the Sword.

James couldn't help himself.

He turned to Great Uncle Gordon and said, "Don't you mean the Mighty Sword of Eir?"

Gordon looked surprised.

"How did you know that?" he asked, "Your Great Aunt has only just started work on it. I know it's what her team have started to call it. How on earth did you find out?"

James smiled.

His dream had meant something.

Even if it had ended horribly.

"Can I tell you later?" he asked.

They were stopped from talking more by Great Aunty Pauline shouting across the road.

"Hello—come on over. This is really exciting!"

Everyone rushed to join her. They scurried down the narrow lino-lined corridor to what appeared to be a room full of tables and shelves.

Three cameras had been positioned around one of the tables, and two technicians were paying great attention to the Sword. They were gently scraping away some of the rotted leather from around the big yellow stone in the Sword's hilt.

Every word and action was being recorded so that nothing was missed.

The Sword was still in its leather pouch, but half of the blade was now exposed.

"We're about to remove the rest of the leather," she announced.

"Is it the remains of a sheepskin?" asked James.

"How on earth did you know that?" asked Great Aunty Pauline, "We have only just reached that conclusion ourselves!"

James and his mother watched as the technicians returned to scraping the hilt.

One of them began to gently scrape away more of the rotted leather.

"We're going to send this sample away for radiocarbon dating," explained the technician, "It's what the Sword was buried in. Because it's sheepskin and not metal we should be able to date it fairly precisely!"

Great Aunty Pauline explained that both the leather and Sword were probably about the same age. If they could find out how old the leather was, they would know how old the Sword was.

Great Aunty Pauline had more exciting news.

She thought that there was mention of the Sword in the ancient English Viking chronicles.

Great Aunty Marian's legs were getting tired with all the walking.

Great Aunty Pauline was thirsty with all the talking.

They decided it was time for a cup of tea and retired to the tearoom, where they could talk some more.

Yes, it was definitely time for tea!

Chapter 1.16
Codex Eiricus

As the group sat in the Department of Archaeology tearoom, Great Aunty Pauline told them more about what was happening.

First of all, she reminded them all about how the dig had got to where it was today. She particularly emphasised how the first dig hadn't found anything because those Archaeologists dug in the wrong place.

Then she told how their dig had been covered over and put back to how it was before and left there. That way, if another dig took place, any finds would be in context.

James didn't need to have that explained—he knew what context meant. He remembered how he had been told about it last year!

Two years ago, Great Aunty Pauline had decided to look up the old records of that dig. She thought it might be worth another look, especially as more accurate machines to look under the soil were now available.

It took her a while to raise the money for the dig. It wasn't cheap to fund ten or so archaeologists digging for several weeks, you know.

Even if they had to do the digging as part of their studies and weren't paid, they still needed somewhere to sleep and feeding. That all cost money.

Quite a lot.

Fortunately, though, the university had eventually managed to sort that out. By last year, they were ready at last, and the dig had started.

From the very beginning, it had yielded so much information.

The rest, she told them, they knew.

She talked about the treasure that they had found—the coins, the brooches, the cloak pins and even two almost complete shields.

But her work wasn't just about the dig.

Great Aunty Pauline said that she had been back to look through the library to see if there was any more information on the site.

After all, if the first professors had found mention of the village, perhaps, if she looked more thoroughly, there might be more?

There was.

She had been very lucky. It wasn't very often that you could match written evidence with artefacts.

It took her a while to find the information as it was hidden away in a much younger manuscript (she referred to it as "more recent"—which meant the same thing).

Even recent documents were very fragile and rare. They had to be kept in a special room. Great Aunty Pauline called it an archive. She said that it had minimum light as light would destroy the documents, and air conditioning so that everything was kept at the same temperature all the time.

"So historical documents live like the machines in the Physics department!" added Great Uncle Gordon.

Great Aunty Pauline nodded towards her husband and then continued.

It had been quite a challenge to track the evidence down. But she had.

She handed copies of the document to James.

"This is the Codex Eiricus!" she announced.

James took the paper but was puzzled.

Looking directly at James, Great Aunty Pauline went on to explain about the name "Codex Eiricus". It wasn't one that you would expect to see every day, was it?

Apparently the "Codex Eiricus" had been named by very learned gentlemen scholars at the University of Oxford when they first studied the manuscript. They were so clever that they gave it a name in Latin. Which, she said, was a dead language, and certainly most Viking folk wouldn't have spoken it.

Interestingly, the town where Great Aunty Marian lived was named after the Sword.

James had not known that.

The first part of its name—Eir—was the name of the Sword.

And "by" was the Viking word for town.

The scholars realised that the Codex related to Eirby, which was so close to here, they gave it to this university when it opened.

Great Aunty Marian gave another of her sniffs. She was not very impressed. Why give something such a fancy name. It made it sound better than it should as far as she was concerned.

Great Aunty Pauline continued regardless of Great Aunty Marian's scepticism.

The scholars didn't realise just how important these fragments were back then.

James looked at the sheet of paper. It looked like a jigsaw puzzle with most of the pieces missing.

He looked at his Great Aunty Pauline and waited for an explanation. He knew there had to be one.

Great Aunty Marian sniffed again. But that did not deter Great Aunty Pauline.

"The original document was written on vellum because the Vikings didn't know how to make paper. Vellum is made from sheepskin, you know. Because the vellum is so old and wasn't kept well, a lot of it has rotted away."

"Like the Sword's sheepskin!" added James.

James looked again at the sheet of paper in his hands. He could see that the yellowing fragments had what appeared to be scribbles all over them.

Great Aunty Pauline noticed.

"That's how the Vikings wrote. They didn't have our alphabet. Those scribbles are called runes. With time and patience, they can be translated.

I know that the Codex is all in bits, but I have managed to have a go at working out some of it.

It seems these pieces of vellum tell parts of the legend—or Saga—of Eir.

The Vikings were known as great storytellers."

James nodded.

So, Great Aunty Pauline went on, "Many of their tales have been translated from manuscripts like this. Most of those manuscripts are kept in places like Iceland or Sweden or Denmark though. They are called sagas and have characters like Erik the Red as their hero. This is the first story that relates directly to things round here!"

This all sounded very interesting, and if James was honest, far more exciting than the physics that he had been shown.

"Are you all sitting comfortably? Then I will tell you the Saga of Eir!"

Great Aunty Marian took a large sip of her tea which was now lukewarm.

His mother shifted slightly on her plastic chair.

James and Great Uncle Gordon waited for Great Aunty Pauline to begin.

They loved a good story and this one sounded like it was going to be fabulous!

However, as the tale unfolded, James slowly realised that it was almost—but not quite—the same as his dream.

This was very, very strange.

Great Aunty Pauline told them about the Storyteller. She said he had a blue face.

James chipped in.

"No, he had blue swirls all over his face. They looked very scary!"

Great Aunty Pauline looked at James with surprise.

"That's right. Exactly right. The Vikings either coloured themselves with woad or tattooed themselves with bright blue ink. But the story doesn't say that. It only mentions his blue face."

Great Aunty Pauline looked thoughtful.

"What else can you tell us about this Storyteller?" she asked.

James told them about how the Storyteller seemed tired.

That he had a huge responsibility that was becoming too much to bear.

How he had come to the village and sat by the bonfire.

James told them all about the helmet which the storyteller was wearing before he revealed his blue face.

That it was silver and had a bit that covered his nose.

Great Aunty Pauline was really impressed.

"Did you read all this somewhere?" she asked.

James went quiet.

He didn't really want to tell everyone here, especially his mother, about his dream.

They might think he was silly.

So, he mumbled, "I suppose."

Then he shut up.

Great Uncle Gordon realised James wasn't happy about continuing.

He looked at his watch.

"Goodness me," he announced, "Its half past five already!"

Then he said, "It's too late for you all to travel back on an empty tummy. Why don't you all come to our house. There's a fish and chip shop close by, and I will treat you all to a fish supper."

Great Aunty Marian thought this was a grand idea. Two meals cooked for her in one day.

Brilliant.

His mother wanted to see what a professor's house looked like, so she approved of the idea too.

And so, they all went round to Great Uncle Gordon's for tea!

Chapter 1.17
Fish, Chips and a Serving of a Dream

Before everyone left the university, Great Aunty Marian had been the first to place her order. She didn't mind what sort of fish Gordon and Pauline bought, but could they make sure that they got lots of mushy peas.

They were her favourite.

James shyly asked if they could see if there was a battered sausage on the menu. He hoped his mother wouldn't remember that he had already had sausages once that day.

They were his favourite.

Gordon and Pauline shared their postcode with their guests. Then, they set off in the direction of the fish and chip shop. They calculated that even with the detour, they would still be back home before their guests.

After all, James and his mother weren't from these parts. They didn't know the way so would have to travel slowly and listen carefully to the sat nav. Great Aunty Marian was well known in the family for not having a good sense of direction either.

Just as Gordon and Pauline had gambled, they were back home just before their guests.

Great Aunty Pauline was laying the table as the door opened.

"You didn't forget my mushy peas?" asked Great Aunty Marian as she came in.

"No, we did not. And we remembered to ask for batter scraps too!"

James wanted to know what batter scraps were. He'd never heard of them.

Great Aunty Marian explained that they were a great Northern treat when she was growing up.

The fish was dipped in mix of flour and milk and then put into hot oil to cook.

Sometimes though, not all the mixture stuck to the fish. The bits that dropped off cooked to a crisp alongside the fish. When the scraps were drained and put with the chips, they made the chips even more crunchy.

Great Aunty Marian thought that they, along with mushy peas, were a real treat at any time of day!

James, his mother and Great Aunty Marian were told to wash their hands and then sit down. Everything was ready for tea.

It was absolutely delicious.

Who would have thought that walking around a dry and dusty university could pep up an appetite?

It didn't take long for the fish and chips—and mushy peas—to be demolished.

Great Aunty Marian was right about the batter scraps too.

Great Aunty Pauline stood up and started to clear the plates away.

She looked at James and asked if he would help her with the washing up.

He was a polite young man and so readily agreed.

Once they were in the kitchen and the dishwasher fully loaded, Great Aunty Pauline turned to James.

"I could tell that you didn't want to say too much when we were at the university. But I think you know more than you were letting on back there.

I would really like to know what you were thinking of saying. I promise to listen and not laugh.

Just to prove it, I can tell you that your Great Uncle has shared with me his stories of when he was growing up. He particularly mentioned playing with a young boy who sounded to be remarkably like you. And, he told me about Timmy Rex."

James was encouraged by this.

So, he told Great Aunty Pauline all about his strange dream.

Great Aunty Pauline kept her promise. She proved to be an excellent listener and didn't interrupt once as he talked.

When he had finished, Great Aunty Pauline sighed deeply. Then she said to James, "This is truly remarkable. First of all, your dream matches what the Codex tells of how the Sword came to be where you found it. In the ground that is. Not in the tree trunk!

We found graves of several men close to where there had been a big bonfire.

There was a lot of ash and bones. We were able to date the bones using radiocarbon dating. So, we knew how old they were. But we didn't know why they were there.

It was clear from how the bones were buried that all the men they belonged to had died at the same time.

What we couldn't understand was why they had all died there together at the same time.

I looked at the Codex to see if there were any clues there. But the Codex is in too many pieces and large parts of the tale were missing.

Your dream gives us a very plausible way to fill in the gaps."

James was amazed. How had he managed to have such an important dream?

Great Aunty Pauline hadn't finished.

She told James that there were many things about Viking history and beliefs that had been lost.

It made understanding how they lived quite tricky.

She had found out some of the Sword of Eir legend though.

The Codex confirmed James's dream, that the Sword was supposed to have the power to rip the curtain that separates the past from the present.

But only for the person whom the Sword chose.

What the Codex hadn't told them was who that person might be. Or how they became that person.

Given what had happened to Gordon and James, and now this strange dream, Great Aunty Pauline had reached a conclusion.

It wasn't one that she could write about. There was no scientific proof to back it up. If she did publish it, she would be laughed at.

Scientists and academics don't like mystical mysteries. They like solid facts.

However, her theory was the only explanation that fitted what had happened.

She shared her thoughts with James as they stood by the dishwater.

Great Aunty Pauline thought that the Sword had chosen its next Keeper.

That next Keeper was James.

She didn't know why, but all the things that had happened to him pointed that way.

Great Aunty Pauline explained why she thought this.

First of all, James and Gordon had met and played out together last year when James was seven and Gordon was eight.

Yet Gordon was an eight-year-old child back in the 1960s. Not last year.

Everything that she knew and understood told her that it was impossible for these two boys to meet, play out and have fun together like they did last summer.

But it had happened. Timmy Rex proved that.

The only explanation was that James had somehow passed back in time so that he could meet up with the eight-year-old Gordon.

Another example—Great Aunty Pauline knew for a fact that the X-ray machines that James had watched Gordon use when he got his new shoes no longer existed. The government had decided many years ago that they were dangerous as the X-rays were so strong and too many of them made you sick.

They were all removed from shops in the 1970s. Long before James was born.

"So that's why I had never seen one before!" exclaimed James.

Great Aunty Pauline agreed. Then she continued.

"I know for a fact that there have been two excavations at the Waterfalls. But you thought that there had only been one."

James nodded in agreement.

Then, there was the fact that the boys had found the Sword as they had played together, when Gordon was eight and James was seven.

Again, Great Aunty Pauline didn't understand how that could have happened.

When the boys were playing in the trenches, only about a foot's depth of soil had been taken out.

But when the second excavation took place, it had found evidence that the Sword had been buried in a hole that was far deeper.

But the Sword was missing.

Of course, it was. It was in the tree trunk!

It was a mystery that something that was buried so deep should have suddenly been so close to the topsoil so that Gordon and James could pull it out.

But it had been.

Which is why Gordon had fallen over it.

Then the boys had retrieved the Sword and placed it in the tree trunk for safe keeping.

When James's holiday was coming to an end, James had given Timmy Rex to Gordon to look after until they met again.

Gordon had done so, even wrapping Timmy in newspaper to keep him safe.

James remembered the headlines. They were from 1963.

The next thing you knew was that somehow, time had reverted to now. Gordon and James had met up again. Only now, Gordon was so much older than James. Sixty-two years older to be precise.

Somehow, James had been taken back through time. He must have because he and Gordon had put the Sword in the trunk at the same time.

And, now, sixty-two years later, between the two of them, James, and Gordon, had retrieved the Sword yesterday from its hiding place, where they had left it.

There was no logical explanation.

Now the Sword was undergoing tests in the university laboratory.

All the tests so far showed that it was genuine. It had been made by the Vikings and was very old.

Great Aunty Pauline still needed to work out what the runes on its side meant.

She would be able to translate them, but it would take her a very long time.

That was something that she was really looking forward to. It would be an excellent research project for her retirement!

But so far, none of the physical evidence of the dig could explain James's experiences.

The only explanation was that the Codex story about the Sword was true.

That the Sword could blur time.

And the Sword had chosen its next Keeper. That Keeper was James!

The evidence supported this theory.

James was the one who had passed back in time.

He was the one who had the strange dream last night.

James decided that this was starting to feel a bit scary.

"I don't want to be the Sword's keeper!" he said.

"I'm not sure you have a choice!" came the reply.

However, if Great Aunty Pauline's theory was right, it shouldn't be too scary.

She reminded James that while he was at home and counting the days until he came back here, nothing strange or peculiar had happened to him.

It was only when he came to stay with Great Aunty Marian that time seemed to shift, and he had strange dreams.

So Great Aunty Pauline thought that James's life would only be affected by the Sword when he was close to it. Not necessarily right next to it. But, say, no more than a mile away from it.

For example, he may have some more strange dreams that night because the Sword was close by at the university.

But the dreams and visions should stop once he got back home.

"But does that mean I can't come and see you ever again if the Sword is here?" asked James.

Great Aunty Pauline smiled.

"I think you are going home tomorrow. You shouldn't be affected by the Sword once you are there.

And as soon as we have finished the tests here—and that is likely to be in the next day or so—the Sword will be sent to the British Museum in London.

You can come to see Great Aunty Marian as often as you want once the Sword has been taken there.

I suspect that when you grow up, you will want to visit London. But you will be older and will be able to deal with things then."

James realised that this was as good as it was likely to get.

And to be fair, in some ways it might make life a little bit different and maybe even exciting for him in the future.

Great Aunty Pauline put away the tea towel.

"Let's go back and join your mother. She will be wondering what has happened to us!"

Chapter 1.18
More Dreams

It had been another long day for James. He was very tired by the time he got back to Great Aunty Marian's.

But he didn't really want to go to bed. He felt a little afraid if he was honest. He wasn't keen on vivid dreams at all. Especially ones where people died.

He made sure that Timmy Rex was by his side and that the night light was on before he closed his eyes.

James didn't expect to sleep a wink, but much to his surprise, he fell asleep almost at once.

And was transported immediately into another world.

At the centre was the Mighty Sword of Eir. It looked like it was brand new. The steel blade was shiny except for the black runes etched along its length.

The yellow jewel in the silver hilt glowed warmly.

James realised that the stone was probably amber. His mother had told him all about amber when they had been talking about dinosaurs.

She had explained that it was tree sap from the time of the dinosaurs which had been turned into stone over time. It felt warm to the touch rather than cold like diamonds.

James's mother had also said that some people in the olden days thought that amber could make them better if they got sick.

That it could heal them.

The Sword seemed to be giving out halo of pale yellow, almost like sunlight.

Most importantly for James, though, was that none of this felt in the least bit scary or threatening to him.

As he looked at this vision in his dream, the Sword seemed to talk to him.

Not like it had a voice, though. More that James felt its thoughts inside his head.

He didn't feel frightened and didn't want to wake up.

He wanted to listen to the Sword.

He slept on peacefully.

The Sword told James that he was now its Keeper.

Its existence and his were now bound together until the Sword needed to move on.

James was its first Keeper since the Storyteller.

Many had tried to become the Sword's Keeper. They had all failed because the Sword did not want them. They wanted the Sword to give them power over others. That was not the Sword's way.

The Sword then told James about its beginning.

It had been made many hundreds of years ago, in very different times.

They were violent and vicious times when no one was safe.

The Sword had been forged with love by a man who wanted to protect his family. He had traded a prize cow for the amber jewel because he wanted the Sword to use its strength to heal rather than fight.

He had hoped that merely having such a weapon would be enough to keep his family safe and well.

But it was not to be.

The village was attacked, and the Sword had to be used to kill and hurt the enemy.

To keep his family safe.

Somehow, the blood of the dead had strengthened the Sword's power.

Then, one night, as the man and his family slept, the Sword was stolen.

The man who stole it used it in hate and anger. The hate and anger had strengthened the Sword's power even more. But the man did not know this.

He was not the Sword's Keeper. Merely someone who had the Sword.

He could not use the power of the Sword.

When he died, the Sword was buried with him, where it stayed for many years.

But it didn't stay buried.

The Sword found the Storyteller, who was a kind man.

A mystical man.

He understood that there are many things about the universe which cannot be explained.

He understood that it was his destiny to be with the Sword.

The Sword's power gave the Storyteller inspiration for his tales and sagas.

By looking back in time, the Storyteller could speak of events that happened long ago, so that those who listened might learn from past mistakes.

But it was a heavy burden to carry because people would listen but not learn.

The Storyteller was very old when he came to the village where he told his last story.

The one that James had seen in his earlier dream.

It was then that the Storyteller decided that he must part with this most precious gift.

He was now too old to carry on. He needed to rest.

But with no successor in sight, he decided that the Sword should be buried until it decided the time was right.

Until it found its new Keeper.

James turned over in his sleep. Timmy Rex fell on the floor but didn't wake him.

James's vision shifted.

He knew he was looking into the future.

He saw a crowd of teenage boys, all dressed in school uniform.

They were on a school trip and visiting a museum.

James somehow knew that this was the British Museum, and that the school trip was to visit the Eirby Hoard.

Of which the star was the Mighty Sword of Eir.

James knew that he was one of those teenage boys.

And he realised that he was about to meet the Sword again for the first time since he was a child.

"Come on, Sleepy Head!"

His mother's voice roused James from his deep sleep.

The vision vanished in a flash.

"We need to get ready to go home!"

James almost cried.

He needed to find out what happened next.

But it had all gone.

Sometimes parents were pests!

James started to pack up his toys. He picked up Timmy Rex and looked at him.

Now he came to think about it, the plastic did seem to be very old…

James went down to breakfast.

James's mother's suitcases were already in the car.

Just as he was about to bite into his toast, Great Aunty Marion's phone rang.

It was Great Aunty Pauline.

She asked to speak to James.

Great Aunty Marian handed the receiver to him.

Great Aunty Pauline asked James if he had had any dreams last night.

He said that he had.

Great Aunty Pauline realised that he couldn't talk about them in front of his mother. So, she asked if she could call him when he got home, and to not forget what he had dreamt.

When they next talked, she would write it all down and keep it safe.

As she had said yesterday, once he and the Sword were separated, he shouldn't have any more dreams. Not until they were reunited.

It was important that she and James kept a record for when he next met the Sword.

Although James couldn't go into details then, he did feel able to say that he would probably visit the British Museum when he was older.

The rest would have to wait until he could talk when he got home.

Chapter 1.19
Back Home

Mother and James got back home in good time. Even after a long stop at a motorway service station where they had enjoyed shepherd's pie with peas, they were still back by three o'clock.

James's mother reminded him that Great Aunty Marion would be pleased that they were back in plenty of time for tea. James smiled.

That phrase had become very important to James. It reminded him of all the strange things that he had experienced since last year.

They unpacked.

James's mother shouted for the cat, who sauntered in as if they had never been away.

He was glad they were back but there was no way he would ever admit it.

She made a big fuss of the cat and fed him.

Then she made beans on toast for their meal. James had quite got into the habit of calling it "tea!"

Great Aunty Pauline kept her word.

She rang James that evening. She timed the call so that James's mother was watching her favourite tv programme. That way she and James could talk on the phone in the kitchen without being overheard.

James shared his dream. He included every detail that he could remember. Even the warm glow of the amber stone.

When he had finished, Great Aunty Pauline told him that he had done very well. It was a shame that he couldn't have stayed asleep for even a few minutes longer. But at least they knew when he would next meet the Sword.

Great Aunty Pauline and James talked for ages.

His mother's tv programme ended, and she came into the kitchen. She was just in time to have a few words with Great Aunty Pauline before she hung up.

Now it was time for bed.

As he brushed his teeth, James realised that time was likely to do that strange thing again. That it would pass slowly until he could be reunited with the Sword. He wouldn't have to wait a whole year though.

It would be ten whole years. That was ages away!

Nevertheless, James felt a small glow of pride.

He was now the Keeper of the Mighty Sword of Eir.

He really was at the start of a long adventure.

But before it really got going, he promised to himself that he would work hard at school. That way, when it was time, he would be ready to be the Sword's Keeper.

How it would all work wasn't clear right now.

But he knew that it would all fall into place as he grew up.

He hoped Great Aunty Pauline was right about the Sword not messing with his life until he saw it again.

But he had a funny feeling that she was wrong.

Part Two
The Boy

Prologue

The British Museum had hit the news. Big time.

Not since the Tutankhamun exhibition in the 1970s had anything been so popular or generated as much interest.

The Eirby Hoard, now finally on display, was at the centre of the queues twisting their way round Bloomsbury. Everyone wanted to view this fantastic array of artefacts from the Dark Ages.

Not only was it an amazing collection, but it had also been discovered in the sleepy former mill town of Eirby in the north of England. It rivalled any collection in the world both in quality and quantity of its treasure.

People still couldn't quite believe that such a wondrous hoard had come from such a place.

Experts from across the globe had spent several years examining and analysing the find. They had formed and discounted more theories than there seemed to be pieces in the collection. But finally, they could all agree on one thing. It was time to show the public what all the fuss had been about.

The Eirby Hoard was the most magnificent collection of Viking treasure. Its content and preservation were both sources of surprise and delight for the experts.

Amazingly, the find could also be directly linked to an ancient historical document—the Codex Eiricus.

The Codex, written in Viking runes was now in pieces. The vellum on which it was set out had suffered greatly through time.

Nevertheless, experts had been able to match this mixture of artefacts with a dusty ancient historical document.

Context and content together for the very first time!

When he was interviewed for a BBC documentary, one expert was even heard to remark that where the fragments and artefacts mapped onto each other, it was like looking at an illustrated jigsaw puzzle.

The focus of public interest wasn't about what the Hoard might tell them about days of yore though.

The public wanted to see the treasure.

People wanted to view the worked silver, the hammered gold, the bejewelled brooches.

They wanted to be dazzled by the treasure's beauty and mystique.

And, of course, everyone wanted to view the Mighty Sword of Eir.

Apparently, it was discovered by a Professor of Physics and his great nephew.

How it came to be where it was discovered though was not known.

It should have been buried in the ground. But it was found inside a tree.

How it came to be there was one of the mysteries surrounding this stunning piece of workmanship.

The Sword was the centrepiece of the exhibition. It lay on a sheepskin pelt which was an exact replica of the tattered remains in which the Sword had laid undiscovered for hundreds of years.

It's almost legendary amber stone, still intact in the Sword's silver hilt, glowed majestically.

The darkened swirls on its blade hinted of mysteries that were yet to be uncovered.

The Mighty Sword of Eir was magnificent.

And so very mysterious.

Chapter 2.1
Past Times

The day had finally arrived.

After ten long years of waiting, James was getting ready to go on his school trip to see the Eirby Hoard.

The trip had been organised by his school as a reward for all the hard work he and his classmates had put in over the past two years.

The "A level" exams had finally come to an end. In a few days, so would the boys' time as school children.

James dressed slowly and with care. Although he had to wear his school uniform, he made sure that he was wearing the St Christopher medal given to him by Great Aunty Pauline underneath his shirt. It seemed right.

James recalled that she told him that the medallion had been given to her by an old friend—a Professor Manu from the University of Baghdad—when she and Great Uncle Gordon had married. It was very precious to her, but she was now passing it to James because she knew that he would be travelling a lot when he was older. The medal would keep him safe.

Today, James and his class were travelling to London with their teacher to view the famous Viking treasure.

To his classmates, this was a school trip to see a famous set of old things.

For James, though, it marked the fulfilment of a vision that he had had when he was a mere eight years old.

There was an air of excitement and anticipation as the boys clustered on the station platform.

The train arrived and the schoolteacher and her helpers shepherded the boys into their reserved carriage. The boys might well be eighteen now, but until they officially finished school, the teachers were still responsible for them. It would be very unfortunate if anything happened to any one of them during these last few days before their final end-of-term.

The boys found somewhere to sit as the train pulled out of the station. The teacher walked up and down the central aisle to make sure that they behaved themselves.

Although his friends didn't know it, James had a particular interest in this visit.

This would not be the first time that he had seen the Sword.

Their paths had last crossed over ten years ago.

In fact, it was he and his best friend Gordon who had first found the Sword.

Gordon had tripped over it as they played pirates.

James had been staying with his Great Aunt in Eirby.

He had met Gordon at the local playground.

They didn't tell anyone about the Sword when they first found it. They thought they would get into trouble if they did. So, they hid it in a tree, where it stayed, safe and sound, until the following year.

When James next returned to Eirby.

For his Great Uncle's 70th birthday.

From that day on, James's life had never been the same.

Everything that he had thought he knew had been turned upside down by that visit.

By finding the Sword.

The discovery of the Sword had caused quite a stir at the time. But James's mother had been quite insistent that her son was not named in the news reports.

All that was published was the name of his Great Uncle Gordon. The physicist.

For James, the discovery of the fabulous weapon was more than simply finding something.

The Sword was steeped in mystery and magic.

James had found out that it had the power to bend time.

It had already worked its magic on him by the time the Sword was retrieved from the tree.

He discovered that his best friend Gordon who he had played out with during the summer holidays when he was seven years old was none other than his Great Uncle Gordon. James discovered this fact at his Great Uncle's birthday party the following year. When James was eight years old. As his family celebrated his Great Uncle Gordon's 70th birthday.

And then there were the dreams.

Vivid, powerful dreams.

Some which looked back, and some, though fewer, which looked forward.

Luckily for James, his Great Uncle's wife was a specialist in Viking history and archaeology. She had guided him since.

She had told him that he had been chosen as the Sword's next Keeper.

He had been chosen by the Mighty Sword of Eir.

Based on her expert knowledge, James's Great Aunt reassured him that the Sword would not harm him.

But it wanted to work with him.

To right wrongs. And make things better.

It would bide its time.

The Sword would wait until he was ready.

But James needed to prepare.

This was an awesome responsibility and he needed to make sure that he could meet the challenge.

He could not fail the Mighty Sword of Eir.

Since that day ten years ago, James had worked hard and was now getting ready to go to University in the autumn.

"Hey, James," shouted his best friend, "You're thoughtful! This is meant to be a fun trip!"

James snapped out of his reverie and smiled.

"Soz, Mate! Was miles away!" he replied.

"We're almost at King's Cross!"

James had been gazing out of the window throughout the whole journey.

But he hadn't seen a thing.

The teacher counted the boys off the train and marched them down to the tube station. Then she issued instructions.

"Remember, Boys, we get off at Holborn tube station! If any of you get lost for some reason …"

She paused and took out her mobile phone and waved it at them.

"I know you all have my number on your phones. Call me IMMEDIATELY!"

The boys wove their way down the escalators.

Some stood on the right-hand side and waited to arrive at the bottom.

Others ran down the left-hand side and waited at the bottom.

When the teacher was satisfied that everyone was present and correct, they made their way on to the underground platform, and within a minute or so, onto the tube.

Amazingly, they all arrived at the British Museum together.

The teacher told them to wait while she found out more about where they should be to gain their entry to the exhibition.

"Do not wander off for any reason!" she commanded as she left the two hapless helpers in charge.

The boys stomped their feet and blew into their hands.

Chapter 2.2
Welcome to the British Museum

It had been an early start and even now the day had yet to warm up.

But James could feel the glow of the Sword again, seeping into his bones. Between his chilled toes.

It knew he was here.

Suddenly, James felt very, very nervous.

The Mighty Sword of Eir might be able to bend time, but he couldn't. He had to wait for things to happen.

He didn't know what might happen next. To be fair, he didn't really want to know right now.

Just as the boys' feet had started to freeze in their boots, the teacher returned.

She was accompanied by a man with straggly ginger hair and wearing a white coat.

"Listen up, Lads," she said, "This is Dr Magnus Ivar. He is one of the lead researchers who is working on the Eirby Hoard. He has kindly volunteered to be our host…"

His friend nudged him again.

"Wake up, Dozy!" he whispered, "Miss is still talking. We don't want her to get cross for any reason!"

James looked up briefly. He realised, with a start, that he recognised this man standing at the front of them.

If only he could remember from where.

Things felt like they were starting to move. First, the warm glow, and now someone who looked familiar arriving.

Yes, he thought, this was likely to be an adventure and a half, for him at least.

Now he wished he could see a little further into the future…

The teacher droned on in the background.

"We are very lucky to have Dr Ivar as our guide today. He was one of the first researchers to work on the Mighty Sword of Eir, all those years ago, when it was first discovered.

Since then, he has enjoyed a long and prestigious career as one of our foremost Viking experts. If you take notice of what he tells you, you just might learn something!"

Dr Ivar looked across the sea of uniformed faces. They all looked pretty much the same. Dark trousers, school blazers…

And then he saw James.

Then James realised that he knew Dr Ivar. From many years ago. From when he, James, was only eight years old.

Dr Ivar must have worked with James's Great Aunt back when James found the Sword. In fact, James had some vague recollection of Dr Ivar taking charge of the Sword after he and his Great Uncle had brought it to the party all those years ago.

James thought that Great Aunty Pauline must have worked closely with Dr Ivar since then, and that he must know her very well.

Great Aunty Pauline was a famous scholar who had spent so many years trying to piece together the Eirby finds with the historical record.

She had also been James's mentor and guide over the past ten years.

James realised that Great Aunty Pauline must have confided in Dr Ivar.

After all, although she was a very active 80-year old, she was now retired, and based up north. She wouldn't have been able to get to the British Museum for today's trip, even if she wanted to!

James realised that even though it had been so long since their paths had crossed, Dr Ivar knew who he was and probably something about how important today was.

Dr Ivar addressed the class.

"I am looking forward to showing you the Eirby Hoard. It is incredibly precious for so many reasons. It is treasure and extremely valuable. But it is also helping us to understand more about the Viking culture. And let's not forget how the Sword linked to the ancient Codex Eiricus!

All in all, this Hoard has helped us join up so many separate pockets of knowledge.

It is rather like finding the answers to clues in a crossword…"

The boys laughed obediently as they knew they were supposed to.

"And, then," Dr Ivar concluded, "There is the mysterious legend of the Sword…"

A shiver ran across James's back.

Dr Ivar's voice took on a muted, almost reverent, tone.

"The Mighty Sword of Eir! The Sword, which it is rumoured, has the power to rip the curtain that separates the past from the present. But only for the Him whom the Sword choses!"

All the boys, except James, laughed again, but this time more nervously.

This was getting to be a little theatrical for them, but they were loving it!

Except for James, who was again lost in thought.

James's friend nudged him again.

"Lighten up," he demanded, "We are going to go behind the scenes of this exhibition! We are going to have the chance to see the Sword without all that pesky glass or security in the way!"

James looked at his friend and asked, "Why are we being allowed to have this access when no one else can get close?"

James looked over to the long queues of visitors who were already gathering.

"I heard a whisper that one of the first researchers on the team knows someone in our class. But I don't know who that is… I wonder if it's one of us?" his friend replied, "But I think it's because of that fact that they arranged for us to have this privileged viewing."

Before James had a chance to reply, the teacher began to move the boys along. It wouldn't do for them to be seen to have special treatment in this chilly weather. The public waiting patiently outside in the freezing cold would be upset to see the boys in the warmth of the Museum.

When the group finally stopped by the bottom of a wide marbled staircase, James found himself at the front.

He wasn't at all sure how that had happened. He was trying to hang back.

He didn't want to be at the front. If anything, now he was here, he really wanted to be as far away as possible.

After a brief pause while the teacher made sure no one had wandered off or got lost yet, they resumed the slow pace of a guided tour.

They wandered through the Ancient Greek exhibits without as much of a glance.

The Mummy Room was slightly more interesting though. It had preserved dead bodies wrapped in old bandages for a start off.

But the Mummy Room was only a minor distraction.

The boys wanted to see the Hoard.

Dr Ivar led the way. He talked loudly, dishing out facts all the while.

He told the boys about the archaeological dig which had discovered the Hoard.

He spoke about how there had been two digs.

The first had been unsuccessful. It had found nothing.

But the second dig, which started over ten years ago, had uncovered the Hoard as it was displayed today.

Dr Ivar mentioned that the Sword was not found with all the other pieces of the Hoard though.

It had been discovered in an old tree trunk by a physicist and his great nephew.

As he said this, James could have sworn that Dr Ivar winked at him.

James hoped that she had sworn Dr Ivar to secrecy.

After all, how the Sword came to be resting in a tree was a huge public puzzle in its own right. The media had come up with all manner of theories. Not a single one of them was even close!

James thought that only he, his Great Uncle, and his wife, Great Aunty Pauline, knew the truth of what had happened. How the Sword came to be resting in an old tree trunk!

Had Great Aunty Pauline told Dr Ivar? Did Dr Ivar also know about James's link to the Sword?

If so, then James was not alone today, on this most special but scary day of his life.

He found that thought strangely comforting.

Chapter 2.3
The Eirby Hoard

The grand tour of the British Museum continued.

Now the boys were led away from the public areas and down long fluorescent light-lit corridors. At certain points there were doors with windows.

When James peered through one, he saw people in white coats bending over tables, or staring at large statues.

"We are now walking through our conservation laboratories," announced Dr Ivar, "These rooms are where the Eirby Hoard was cleaned up properly and authenticated!"

"But wasn't the Hoard investigated by a university up north first?" asked one of the class. The class swot to be precise. Who always wanted brownie points from the teacher.

Who, by the way, was nodding approvingly!

"Indeed, it was," came the reply, "But they could only undertake a preliminary analysis there. The university, well-equipped though it was, did not have access to the same facilities that we do here."

Then another question, this time from James.

He couldn't help himself. He had to know.

"But weren't you one of the staff that used to work up there?"

Dr Ivar looked at him.

Then smiled.

In a friendly, helpful way.

"Indeed, I was," he agreed, "I was lucky enough to get a placement here when the Hoard was transferred. I was there at the start of this adventure, and I am here now!"

James thought that Dr Ivar might be talking in code to him. Or rather, he hoped he was.

It would be good to have a friend close by right now.

Especially as James could feel the forcefield of the Sword getting stronger.

Just at that moment, Dr Ivar opened one of the corridor doors.

Into the tearoom!

What a time to break for lunch!

That said, once they were inside and looking at the buffet lunch that the Museum had put on for them, the boys realised that it had been quite a while since they had left home.

And being boys, they were now VERY hungry.

They fell on the sandwiches and sausage rolls like a swarm of locusts.

James managed to help himself to a few bites and then stood to one side.

As he was tucking into his second cheese and tomato sandwich, he realised that Dr Ivar was by his side.

"Hello, Young Man," said Dr Ivar, "Your aunt has told me all about you. And the Sword!"

James felt like a huge weight had dropped off his back.

He wasn't alone today. He had an ally.

And it got better.

Apparently, Dr Ivar wasn't just a Viking expert. He was a modern-day Viking. Well almost. He could trace his family tree back to the Vikings. Not the really old ones. But back far enough!

In fact, even his name had Viking origins.

"My first name is Magnus which means Big and Mighty!"

James thought this might be more than co-incidence, given that the Sword's full title included the word "Mighty!"

But it got even better.

Apparently, the doctor's surname—Ivar—meant Archer in Viking!

If James had put all this information together properly, perhaps Dr Ivar was more than just someone who knew James's real story.

Perhaps he was also a guide for James on this auspicious day.

Maybe even a protector?

Or would that be too much to hope for?

Just as he was about to ask Dr Ivar this question, his teacher came across to them.

Speaking to Dr Ivar, she said, "I really think we should be getting on. We have a train booked for six o'clock, and we need to cross London as well as finish this tour."

Dr Ivar smiled, put down his plate and agreed.

"Then onwards, my Good Lady!" he said, as she and the helpers started to move the boys back towards the door.

The boys trudged along the corridor. To tell the truth, they were starting to get a little bored by all this walking now. It had been ages since the Mummy Room, and they hadn't spotted a single thing of interest since then. Unless you counted the lunch, of course.

Just when they thought that the visit had been a complete waste of time, Dr Ivar threw open a door.

"This is the private entrance to the Eirby Hoard display! The exhibition closes between midday and two thirty to allow the curators to tidy up and make sure the public space is clean for afternoon visitors.

While it's all clear, I can show you the Hoard without all that glass to distract."

The boys were stunned into silence.

This was something that they could never have hoped for.

They had expected to have to wait in line along with everyone else. And they had expected to view the fabled collection from the public space.

To be here, less than a metre away from the Hoard, with nothing between them except air, was beyond their wildest dreams.

Except for James.

Since leaving the tearoom, he had felt the power of the Sword increasing.

Throbbing. Demanding. In time and tune with his heartbeat.

He knew that something would happen when he was close enough to the Sword.

But he didn't know what.

Couldn't imagine what.

"Be careful as you move around," urged the teacher.

Not that the boys needed any such warning.

They were awestruck by the beauty of the Hoard. Amazed by how much of it there was, and how even the smallest pin had delicate detailed filigree decoration.

All the while, the Mighty Sword of Eir stood proud at the centre of the Hoard.

Its amber eye seemed to follow James around the room.

All the while, he could feel its power drawing him closer.

Dr Ivar moved forward.

"I have one more special treat for you today," he said as he moved to the centre of the display.

James noticed that he was now wearing white cotton gloves.

Surely he wasn't going to…?

But he did.

Dr Ivar carefully lifted the Sword from its mounting.

Then he came towards James.

"How would you like to be the first boy to hold this precious artefact?"

James jaw almost hit the floor.

Whatever else he had been expecting from today, it wasn't this.

His teacher handed him a pair of white gloves. He put them on in stunned silence.

The boys around him moved away in awe.

James took the Sword from Dr Ivar.

As he did so, he felt a jolt of electricity like he had never felt before.

The room went black.

And then, nothing.

When he came to, it was still dark. Not a single chink of light.

"Hello?" he called out nervously. Then realised that he was still holding the Sword.

A voice came out of the darkness.

It was Dr Ivar.

"I'm here!" came the reply.

A small relief.

At least James was not alone.

But where were his classmates?

As the darkness cleared, he asked another question.

Where on earth was the British Museum?

And more to the point—where on earth was he?

Chapter 2.4

The Adventure Begins

James sat up and rubbed his eyes.

What had just happened?

Where was he?

Where was everyone else? His teacher? His best friend?

Dr Ivar sat down next to James.

But he wasn't wearing his white coat anymore.

He was wearing a very strange mix of clothes. All seemed to be made from coarse woollen cloth. There were no zips or buttons. Just pins and what seemed to be string holding the outfit together.

The white gloves had disappeared.

James looked at himself.

He wasn't wearing his school uniform either. He was dressed just as strangely as Dr Ivar. He must have left his school uniform in the 21st century.

He hoped this new outfit wouldn't itch!

James's comfortable trainers had also gone. In their place were leather sandals with thongs which wove up his legs.

The Sword was in its lambskin scabbard, attached by a sturdy leather belt across his chest.

James felt his neck. He still had his St Christopher's medal around his neck.

Something very strange indeed had just happened.

The Sword had begun to assert its power.

Wherever he and Dr Ivar were, they were not in the British Museum anymore.

Why were they here?

What did the Sword want of him?

And how was James going to achieve it?

Dr Ivar saw James's confusion.

"I think I know what has happened. You and I have moved back in time, but I don't know precisely to when.

I believe that I have been transported with you because we both had hold of the Sword when the shift happened.

Your friends and teachers are still where they were. I don't know whether time will stand still for them or not.

All I know is that we are no longer with them.

The Sword has awakened. It wants you, its Keeper, to undertake a mission. It will be dangerous. You will be at great risk.

The Sword will protect you as much as it can. As will I.

But we must fulfil the Sword's wish if we are ever to return."

James saw that Dr Ivar was now kneeling in front of him.

This was becoming seriously strange.

James wondered if the electrical jolt had upset Dr Ivar.

Dr Ivar went on, "My liege Lord. Keeper of the Sword. It is my destiny and duty to help the Sword protect you as you undertake your mission. I have waited long for this moment. I am here to help!"

That was all well and good.

But where were they? And equally important—when was it?

Dr Ivar continued.

"If my research is correct, we are still in London. We are still at the British Museum.

Only it hasn't been built yet. Neither will it be built for another nine hundred years.

We have been brought here because the Sword has detected dark forces.

A critical moment in English history is coming.

If all goes as it should the future will be as you know it. But if it doesn't……"

James gulped. Crikey!

"The future will change!"

The amber stone began to glow.

The gentle halo of light enveloped James.

In the soft yellow light, James could catch a glimpse of his home. But it only looked like his home. Instead of his mother happily tapping away on the computer, she was scrubbing the floor. Down on her hands and knees. Her face was etched with pain and lines. A man—James couldn't see his face—was seated in his mother's favourite chair. He was picking his nails and telling her to get a move on. There was still the doorstep to clean and the dinner to make.

James could feel his mother's unhappiness. And he could feel that this was a normal day for her—not just an isolated incident.

He knew that the Sword was showing him that life would be very different if he couldn't help. And not in a good way.

James knew that he had to work with the Sword. No matter how dangerous it may be. He wanted the future to be as he knew it. Not how it could become.

"What do we need to do? Where do we start?" he asked.

"To begin with. Please stop calling me Dr Ivar!" suggested Dr Ivar.

"Call me Magnus."

Magnus then shared his theory of what was happening with James.

Clearly, they had moved back through time.

Magnus looked at what they were wearing, and what they could see around them.

To be fair, there wasn't a lot to see. The landscape appeared to comprise open countryside which had a distinctive ridge and furrow pattern to it. In the distance, smoke curling skywards suggested that there may be a settlement.

"We need more information so that we can work out what we need to do!" stated Magnus, "I suggest we walk towards that smoke and hope that it is coming from some sort of village."

James looked at him. How was he going to walk that far wearing these sandals? His trainers were far more practical. However, James thought, there was a slight problem with that as his trainers were nowhere to be seen!

Magnus continued.

"If I am correct—and all the evidence—or rather lack of it—suggests that I am—I believe we have arrived in the Dark Ages. You can see that this countryside is used to grow crops. You can see the wheat and barley growing in neat stripes."

James nodded.

"The pattern of ploughing is typical of how they used to farm in the Dark Ages."

James was now very glad that he had studied the Dark Ages as part of his History "A" level. It seemed that it might come in handy!

"But that doesn't tell me a lot," replied James, "The Dark Ages covers a lot of centuries, and it would be really helpful if we knew what year we are in!"

Magnus agreed.

"That's one very good reason why we need to get to that village! We can ask. But we will need to make sure to ask in a roundabout way. We don't want to be thought of as wizards or magicians!"

Neither he nor James knew what people in the Dark Ages did to wizards and magicians, and they didn't want to find out!

Magnus and James started to walk towards the smoke.

They followed a track between the furrows which looked as if it went straight there.

As they walked, James turned to Magnus and said, "Most people in the Dark Ages stayed in their villages. They couldn't travel far because they had to walk everywhere. Horses were only for the super-rich. We will stand out as strangers no matter what we do!"

Magnus thought about this for a few moments and then came up with a suggestion.

"We know that the Keeper of the Sword mentioned in the Codex..."

"And my dream when I was eight..." interjected James, "... was a storyteller. Perhaps that is what you should be. I will be your manservant."

James liked the idea.

The Storyteller and Magnus the Manservant. It had a positive ring about it.

If they could entertain the villagers, the villagers might feed them and even let them sleep there for the night.

Now all they needed to do was think of stories to tell which would be exciting but not so mysterious that they would get into trouble!

After further thought and a few more steps, James had a brain wave.

"Why don't we tell them stories like Little Red Riding Hood, the Three Little Pigs, Goldilocks? They all have characters that are familiar to people in the Dark Ages. For example, I think there are still wolves roaming wild in the forests at this time. But the villagers won't have heard the tales before!"

Magnus agreed that this was an excellent idea and that it would hopefully guarantee them a bed!

They arrived at a cluster of wattle and daub buildings.

In between the houses—well—hovels might have been a better description—the space was filled with farm animals and people going about their daily work.

A large wooden loom stood outside one home. A man was laboriously pushing a shuttle filled with coarse thread back and forth.

Further along, the blacksmith was busy working over a blistering hot fire.

Pigs, cattle, sheep, and dogs seemed to be everywhere.

To add to the confusion, the way ahead was lined with baskets of produce and women shouting.

Children darted in and out between the baskets, around the cattle. They teased the dogs and shouted at each other.

It was a scene of disorganised chaos.

"I think we may have arrived on Market Day!" observed Magnus, "Or possibly some sort of celebration."

As they walked on, the whole place fell silent, and it felt like every single person was watching James and Magnus.

The blacksmith left his fire and stood in the middle of the street.

"Who are you?" he demanded as he waved the red-hot piece of iron he had been working on.

Thank goodness James and Magnus had prepared their story.

First of all, James carefully took out the Sword in a determined but non-threatening way.

He shouted so all could hear.

"Behold, the Mighty Sword of Eir…"

There was a collective gasp of admiration. It was indeed a fine weapon.

Then, as the villagers came closer, he introduced himself as the Storyteller and Magnus as "Magnus the Manservant".

The Sword's amber gem glowed approvingly.

"We have travelled far," continued James, "and need rest. But we wish to prove ourselves to you so that you can see that we are worthy of your kindness."

One of women ran into a house and brought out a three-legged stool. She placed it in front of James and gestured him to sit. Magnus sat cross-legged on the ground next to him.

The blacksmith was more interested in the Sword. He could see that it was of high quality and made with true skill. He wanted to know more.

The blacksmith said, "Tell us, Storyteller. Tell us about the Sword. If we like your story, you can tell us more. And then, we may feed you and give you a bed for the night."

James gave a shortened version of the Sword's history, but he did not mention the Sword's powers. Apart from anything else, he still didn't know where he and Magnus were, what year it was, or how superstitious his audience might be.

So, he stuck to the facts.

How the Sword had been made in ancient times, with love and care.

How it had been stolen and used in hate.

And then buried until he, James, had found it and become Keeper of the Sword.

His audience listened with rapt expressions on their faces.

Then, the blacksmith spoke again.

"I know that this Sword is old. Very old. I can tell that from the writing on its side.

I know that the Sword is of the highest quality and worthy of a nobleman. And I can see that your hands are soft and clean.

It is clear to me that the Sword was made with love. Its jewel is warm. It is not cold as many precious stones are.

I can see you tell the truth that you have travelled far. Your clothes are dusty, and your faces streaked with dirt.

So far, I believe that you have told us the truth.

Now we need to hear one of your tales before we decide to feed you."

Magnus spoke.

"Before the Storyteller begins, may we beg a cup of water or thin ale. It has been many hours since our journey began, and we are right thirsty."

One of the children ran away and returned with a terracotta jug and two beakers. Then the child poured a brown liquid from the jug into the beakers and handed them to James and Magnus.

James took a long refreshing gulp of the ale.

Then he began his tale.

Just as his mother had read to him when he was little, James started with "Once upon a time…"

Chapter 2.5
Lord of the Manor

James's tale drew to a close.

His audience had been spellbound.

Even the cows had shut up and seemed to be listening.

Who would have thought that the story of the Three Little Pigs would have proved to be so engrossing?

As James finished with "The Big Bad Wolf ran away, and the Three Little Pigs lived happily ever after", Magnus suddenly stood up and bowed in the direction of a man who was riding a horse.

The villagers also saw the man, and they, too, bowed respectfully.

The blacksmith stepped forward again.

This time, he addressed the rider.

"My Lord. These strangers entered our abode a little while ago. They have travelled far and carry a most magnificent Sword."

He pointed to James who was still seated on the three-legged stool.

"This man is James the Storyteller. He has just shared a most wondrous tale of how three little pigs outsmarted a wily wolf. It was truly amazing!"

There were murmurs and nods of agreement from the crowd.

The blacksmith then pointed to Magnus and introduced him.

"This is James the Storyteller's servant. He is called Magnus the Manservant!"

The Lord of the Manor thanked the blacksmith for this information and then turned to James.

"Show me your Sword!" demanded the rider.

James stood up and unfurled the weapon again.

The rider gasped.

"This Sword is indeed a fine object. I can see that your hands are smooth. You have not been toiling as a peasant. You must be of noble birth!

You will not eat or sleep with the rabble tonight. You will come to the Manor and entertain us with your tales. We will feed you and give you a bed for the night."

James looked at Magnus.

This was a turn up for the books, he thought. What do we do now?

In turn, Magnus looked at the blacksmith, who said, "You are indeed honoured to be asked to stay with his Lordship. He will care for your needs far better than we humble folk ever could.

We thank you for your story, and hope that you will pass by another time to share more!"

That settled that then!

The Manor House it was!

The rider dismounted and held his horse's bridle.

"Come," he said, "Allow me to introduce myself. I am Alfread, Lord of Holborne Manor. I see you have already met my vassals."

A-ha! They were in what would one day become modern day Holborn.

Alfread continued, "It is but a short distance to my abode, where I invite you to join our feast. We are celebrating the feast of St Swithun."

Magnus looked up. Here was another useful piece of information.

If his memory was correct, that meant that today was July 15th.

Alfread, Lord of the Manor kept on talking.

"This is an auspicious day. Had it had rained, then there would have been 40 days and 40 nights of rain. But, as you see, today is fair. That means that we will have dry weather for 40 days and 40 nights instead. Our harvest this year will be plentiful. We will not starve over winter! It is a miracle of St Swithun. I am sure that a couple of your tales will help us celebrate our good fortune."

As they walked onwards, the Lord talked more about St Swithun.

Apparently, he was an English saint, who had been Bishop of Winchester. As well as his meteorological talent, he had worked many other miracles since his death.

This told James and Magnus that the people here believed in miracles rather than science. James made a mental note definitely not to mention modern day life! It might be tricky to explain aeroplanes, rockets, and mobile phones in terms his Lordship could understand.

Clearly magic and mystery were very much a part of these people's lives, and James needed to make sure that he and Magnus stayed on the right side of them.

Did they burn wizards and magicians in these days, he wondered?

It wasn't mentioned in his "A" level syllabus if they did.

The Lord was still talking.

The topic had now moved to the city of Winchester.

His Lordship believed that it had a magnificent cathedral.

Indeed, it must be grand for it was where King Harold Godwinson had been crowned just this January!

Magnus smiled.

With that snippet of information, he had worked out the year.

It was 1066.

An auspicious year indeed.

Magnus turned to James and said quietly "The chronicles show that Harold was crowned at Winchester Cathedral by the Bishop of York on January 6th, 1066!"

Alfread, Lord of the Manor, paused.

He spoke directly to Magnus.

"From what you say, I believe that you know the Chronicles which are the preserve of priests and monks. You are learned and I think that you can read and write. But you are not in holy orders. Why is this?"

James was very glad that they had had a chance to think of an answer to this question before they had reached the village.

Magnus replied, "I was destined for holy orders. But then I was given the task of protecting my liege lord. Now, that is my mission."

Alfread seemed happy enough with this explanation.

They reached the threshold of a drawbridge to what appeared to be a small castle. It was built of stone rather than wattle and daub. It was a clear indication to James and Magnus that they were in the company of someone who was not poor.

"We are here!" Alfread announced.

Two grubby boys ran across the drawbridge and towards the Lord. He handed them the horse's bridle.

"Take my horse to his stable. Groom him and feed him. He has served me well this day," he said.

Then he turned to James and Magnus.

"Come with me."

Once over the drawbridge, Alfread was greeted by another servant carrying a bowl of hot water and a clean linen cloth.

Alfread looked at the servant and demanded that he get two more bowls for James and Magnus.

Then he began to wash his hands and face.

When their water arrived, James and Magnus did likewise.

It felt so good to freshen up.

After drying their hands on the linen clothes, the little group walked into the Great Hall.

The feast had already begun.

It was a confusion of colour, smoke from the open fire, and sweaty people.

Alfread, Lord of Holborne stood at the entrance and clapped his hands.

Silence fell.

He spoke.

"Behold, my friends. I bring two guests. They are from afar but are of noble birth."

He grabbed James's hands.

"See, this man's hands are soft and clean. He has never worked the fields."

Then he asked James to show the Sword.

James lifted it high.

There were gasps of admiration from around the room.

Alfread then turned to Magnus. He raised up Magnus's hands too.

"This man is a servant. Yet his hands show no signs of hard labour. He is a servant of learning, who can read and write. We welcome both these men to our feast tonight!"

Chapter 2.6
The Feast

It took a little while for James's eyes to adjust after being outside. But as they did, he began to see that he was now standing in a large space. He thought back to his studies and realised that it must be the Great Hall which formed the centre of the Manor House.

James remembered from his studies that when it was not being used for feasting, the Great Hall was where the Lord of the Manor would sit and listen to his villagers' complaints. He would act as a judge. If he thought someone had done wrong, he could punish them!

James's history books were right about the Great Hall.

The room was huge. There were magnificent tapestries hanging on the walls, and prickly rushes underfoot.

Alfread led the way towards a long table at the head of the Great Hall. It was raised up on a platform so that everyone else in the Hall could see the guests seated around it.

At least they would have if it wasn't piled up so high with food!

Clearly, James and Magnus had arrived in time for dinner!

Alfread told the servants to make space for James and Magnus Unfortunately, that included having to move two guests who were already seated, and who were not happy at having to move. They were directly in front of the roast boar which smelt delicious!

Thankfully, it was a very long table and so they didn't have to move too far along.

Alfread took his place in the centre and gestured for James to sit next to him.

James realised at once that he was the honoured guest at this feast.

Magnus was allowed to sit next to James. A rare privilege for a manservant.

Alfread hit the table with his fist.

The room fell silent again.

"Today, we celebrate the fine and glorious weather sent to us by St Swithun. Not a drop of rain has fallen since dawn. Our harvests will thrive, and we will not go hungry this winter!"

The room erupted into cheering.

Alfread hit the table again.

"Tonight, we feast. Tonight, we will sing and dance. And, as an extra-special treat, we will listen to the wonderous tales our Storyteller has brought with him."

Alfread sat down and all the guests applauded and banged the table in approval.

James had been looking forward to the food. But now he had butterflies in his stomach.

However, as the panic was starting to rise, James felt a comforting warm glow.

The Sword's amber stone was gently glowing against his chest. He felt its warmth giving him confidence.

Magnus looked on and smiled. He understood.

There were many courses. Potage, fish, fowl, and of course, the pig.

As the servants cleared away the last of the dirty platters, James realised that it was almost time for him to begin a Story.

But which one?

The servants replaced the meat dishes with sweet pastries.

The feast was almost at an end.

The servants filled up everyone's goblets and beakers.

Alfread stood up again.

The guests fell silent.

"It is time!" he announced.

"We need a story to amuse us as we digest this fine food and savour the sweet things in front of us. Come, Storyteller—stand here—"

Alfread pointed to the edge of the platform.

There was just enough room for James to stand without falling onto the other diners below.

"Amuse us!"

James decided to tell the story of Goldilocks and the Three Bears.

As with the villagers, he began with "Once upon a time…"

The room remained quiet. All were intent on hearing the tale of bears and porridge.

They had never heard the like before.

Bears living in a cottage? Amazing!

Bears wanting porridge for breakfast and leaving it to cool while they went out for a walk? Beyond belief.

But James was very convincing.

He had each and every guest hanging on his every word.

Magnus looked on with pride. His liege Lord was doing a fine job.

Eventually, James reached the end of the tale. He had made everyone jump when he told of how the Bears came home to find a pretty blond girl in their baby bear's bed. And how they chased her home!

By now, the minstrels were gathering and were ready to play their tunes. Alfread beckoned to James to return to his seat.

"That was indeed a fine tale!" Alfread said as James sat down, "I hope you will share with us the story that you told to the villagers before we finish tonight. I am intrigued by pigs that live in houses by themselves rather than in mud!"

James readily agreed, although he was now feeling extremely tired.

Magnus noticed that James 's eyelids were starting to droop.

"Perhaps the Storyteller could tell his tale when your minstrels have completed this merry tune?" he suggested, "My Master is becoming tired and needs sleep. Would you consider it rude if we were shown to our beds when he has finished?"

Alfread readily agreed.

And so, the Lord of the Manor's audience was regaled with the tale of the Three Little Pigs.

It turned out to be a perfect story to end the evening with. All in the Hall were enthralled.

Each and every guest joined in to huff, and puff, and blow the house down. Until it got to the house built of stone. At that point, the guests waited to find out what would happen next.

James told how the wily wolf huffed and puffed long and hard. But the stone was too strong. Too solid to be blown away. The wolf fell to the ground breathless and exhausted.

How the Three Little Pigs grabbed sticks and chased the wily wolf away. The wolf was so ashamed of being outsmarted by them that he never showed his face there again.

Of course, James had to end it all off by telling his audience that "The Three Little Pigs lived happily ever after!"

The room erupted with applause. Yet again, the guests had never heard the like before.

Usually Storytellers told of battles won or lost long ago. Of blood and sadness.

They didn't tell tales about bears and porridge or wolves and pigs…

This was such a refreshing change!

Alfread beckoned to his servants as the minstrels began to play again.

James was completely exhausted now. It was all he could do to keep his eyes open.

"Take my guests to my dressing room and make them a space to lie on. They need sleep!"

James and Magnus were led away by the servants. As they left the Great Hall, it was clear that the feast would continue for quite a while yet. But it didn't really matter how noisy or loud it all was because James was just about asleep even before he lay down on the straw and lavender mattress.

Chapter 2.7
A Night of Mixed Dreams

As James lay sleeping, the Sword began to weave its magic around him.

James saw a time before now. A long time before now. He knew, because the Sword told him, that he was watching the past.

James looked upon a man whose face was filled with hate and violence as he strode away from a distant village. He didn't need to see any more.

James knew, because the Sword told him, that this man had destroyed the village. He had killed everyone there—men, women, and children.

James felt that the Sword had not wished this to happen. But because the man was not the Sword's Keeper—merely the man who had the Sword—it could not halt his actions.

James's eyes were full of tears as he watched the man leave the village, his bag full of stolen goods.

The village burned behind him.

As the man marched on, James saw that he, too, was set upon by robbers. They beat him and stole his ill-gotten gains. Then, they pushed the man into a ditch where he lay bleeding and in pain.

The Sword was showing him that the man who did bad things had bad things done to him.

James felt a shift. It was almost as if he was being dragged along a fast-flowing river.

It was all he could do to stay afloat.

Eventually, he felt himself reach a bank and he pulled himself out.

He was greeted by another vision.

This time it was of Alfread on his horse and wearing armour. He was talking to his troops who were assembled all around him.

Alfread was clearly ready to do battle.

"We fight to the death if we must. We must protect England from this foreign invasion!"

His crowd of men murmured assent.

James felt a jolt as his vision changed again.

Now he was looking down on the aftermath of a battle.

It wasn't a pleasant scene.

As he scanned around the dreadful landscape, he let out a cry. There, below him, with some of his now weary and bloodied attendants surrounding him, was Alfread.

He was clearly dead.

Then, in a blink of an eye, the scene shifted again.

James saw his mother asleep. But she wasn't in her bed, or even her room.

Her face still bore the lines of pain he had seen in his earlier vision.

It was night, and she appeared to be sleeping in the small box room at the back of the house.

At least James thought it was the box room. It wasn't how he remembered or expected it to be.

Instead, there was just a narrow bed with thin blankets. The pretty floral curtains that James remembered his mother making were no longer hanging at the window, and the window was cracked.

James had finally seen enough and woke up with another loud cry!

It was so loud that it woke Magnus who was sleeping next to him.

"What's wrong?" Magnus whispered quietly. He had only just got to sleep himself because of all the noise from the revellers in the Great Hall.

He knew that they had now retired and wouldn't appreciate being woken up at all!

James and Magnus had to be quiet.

"Magnus, I have just had the most strange and horrible dreams…"

Magnus asked if James could remember them.

Of course, he could.

Magnus asked if James would share them. That way, Magnus might be able to help him understand them. He reminded James that helping James to understand was all part of his mission.

In a quiet, urgent voice, James recounted what he had seen.

Magnus listened intently.

It was clear that the Sword was sending messages to James. It was vital to understand them properly if they were ever to get back to where they had come from.

James concluded his tales of woe by telling of how his mother was no longer sleeping in her own room. How she looked so old and worn.

Magnus thought about what he had heard.

Then, he said to James, "I think the Sword is telling you several things at once. It's important that we don't get them muddled up or we won't be able to help or fulfil our mission. It must be urgent because the Sword has sent you so many very different visions on the same night."

James was very glad that Magnus had been able to travel back with him.

His knowledge and insight were going to be so helpful if James was to succeed.

In particular, Magnus's ability to help understand these mysterious visions was going to be vital!

Magnus set out what he thought the visions might mean.

The first dream told of the past.

How the Sword had been used in hate, against everything that the Sword stood for.

Magnus thought that the Sword wanted to remind James that it had been made with love and to protect. Not to hurt and maim. And certainly not to be used as James's first dream had shown.

"I think the Sword was telling you that if you use it to do evil, then evil will happen to you!" concluded Magnus.

James thought that could make sense.

"But what about the next part—about Alfread?" he asked.

Magnus felt less sure about what James had seen. However, he knew what year it was and what the history books had said.

Magnus told James that it was now July 16th 1066.

James knew, from his "A" levels studies that 1066 had been a pivotal year in English history.

He remembered how Harold Godwinson had been crowned at Winchester Cathedral in January of that year.

How Harold's brother, Tostig, had been Earl of Northumbria. But there had been massive arguments which led to Tostig going into exile the previous year.

And he didn't like it that Harold was now king of England.

Neither did Harald, King of Norway. He was also a relative of King Harold Godwinson, and he thought he should be king of England instead.

Between the two of them, Tostig and Harald raised a massive army. They and their men sailed to Hull. They needed over 300 boats to fit everyone in.

Then they marched to place a near York.

They had expected a battle with the English, but just not yet.

But Harold had other ideas. He took them by surprise.

The battle would take place on September 25th. Harold's army would include Alfread and his men.

A mere ten weeks away from where James and Magnus now were.

The history books report that the English were massively outnumbered there. But they fought valiantly.

They weren't expected to win, even though the Viking army was taken by surprise.

After a long hard battle, the English prevailed.

Many Englishmen were killed on that day at Stamford Bridge. But there were many, many, more Vikings lost.

Indeed, of the 300 boats filled with warriors which landed, only 30 were needed to take the fleeing tatters of the losing army away!

Could Alfread be one of the English dead?

James shivered.

It was possible.

Magnus agreed.

It was clear that the Sword felt it to be essential that Alfread should not die!

Magnus hadn't finished though.

"Our task may not be complete even if we do keep Alfread alive at the Battle of Stamford Bridge. Don't forget there is another, and probably more important, battle this year that we need to protect him from!"

The Battle of Hastings.

It would take place only three weeks after the Stamford Bridge triumph.

On October 14th 1066.

Which everyone knows is where King Harold Godwinson was killed, and the battle lost to William of Normandy.

But something was still puzzling James.

After all, the would-be invaders were Vikings. The same culture as the man who made the Sword. Why would the Sword want them to protect Alfread, and Anglo-Saxon?

Magnus answered the bigger question first.

He reminded James that the Sword had been forged with love. It wanted peace and harmony. Not war and hate running the land.

It may have been made by a Viking, but it knew that the Vikings could be cruel, especially in war and its aftermath.

It recognised the quality of mercy, and of kindness.

Such virtues transcended where you were born.

James sort of understood, even though it all sounded a bit hippy-dippy to him.

"So why does the Sword want us to protect Alfread? How will his death change the fabric of history as we know it?" asked James.

"I'm not sure," replied Magnus, "but it is likely to be linked to the vision you had of your mother. You say that she looked tired and worn. And she wasn't sleeping in her room. Maybe something doesn't happen in the future which means that instead of how we think it is, life is very different.

I think I know what we have to do for now though. We have to make sure that Alfread stays alive.

And I hope that the Sword will tell you more as we try to do that!"

James nodded.

"Shall we try and get a little more sleep?" suggested Magnus, "It's almost dawn but I think we need our rest if we are going to succeed."

James agreed. He was feeling very sleepy again.

He snuggled back down into the lavender-scented rushes and fell soundly into a dreamless sleep.

Chapter 2.8
The Manor in the Morning

The following morning, James and Magnus were woken up by the noises of the servants cleaning up the Great Hall after the previous night's frivolities.

It was fair to say that the guests hadn't been as tidy as they could have been. The Great Hall was more than a little messy. There was a lot to do. Right from clearing away the ashes from last night's fire to changing the rushes on the stone floor.

Then there was the washing up! Even though the guests had only used one platter each throughout the meal, the table was still piled high with dirty dishes.

James sat up and scratched his hair. He wondered if there would be somewhere for him to have a wash and maybe even a comb to tame his locks. He had already decided that he was going to try and grow a beard for now so that he didn't need to find a razor!

He stood up and shook the last of the dried lavender heads from his cloak.

That hadn't been the most restful of nights.

As he did so, Magnus jumped up, bright-eyed and full of energy.

How dare he be so awake and alert after the broken sleep they had had?

Magnus called to one of the servants hurrying by.

Where might they find water to wash, he wanted to know. Also, was there an old comb that they might borrow?

The servant went to search and came back quickly carrying a wide-toothed comb made from some sort of animal bone.

"I hope this will serve your master's needs!" the servant said as he handed over the stained object.

"There is water in the well next to the kitchen!" he added as he went back to sweeping and brushing the floor.

It was going to be a cold wash then!

James and Magnus found their way to the well. Much to their relief, it had a bucket tied to it.

"At least we can rinse ourselves and comb our hair!" Magnus observed.

James didn't really fancy the look of the comb but there wasn't much choice if he wanted to get the tangles out of his hair!

After cleaning themselves up as best they could, James realised that he was quite hungry.

It was breakfast time after all.

But Magnus had bad news for him.

Apparently, in this era, people didn't eat breakfast.

They only ate two meals a day. One at midday and the other in the evening.

And it was a long time until noon!

Magnus had an idea.

"Let's see if we can beg anything from the kitchen. There must be lots of leftovers from last night!"

They followed the servants as they ran back towards what must surely be the kitchen.

It was so very different to anything James had ever seen before.

At the far end was a huge stone arrangement on which an enormous iron pot was sitting. James could hear the roar of the fire underneath it and saw steam rising.

A large table was placed down the middle of the room and it was covered in a rapidly growing pile of washing up and leftover food.

"That must be the potage pan!" observed Magnus as he looked at the iron pot, "There was always a large cauldron of potage boiling away in these places!"

James wasn't that keen on another bowl of potage. He had had terrible indigestion from last night's serving.

Perhaps he could find some bread.

One of the kitchen lads noticed James and Magnus. He wanted to know what they were looking for.

He explained that he had been present near the door from the Great Hall to the kitchens last night. He had listened intently to James's tales. He thought that the stories were wonderful. So different to what he had expected from a Storyteller.

As a result, he knew who these two strangers standing by the kitchen door were.

More importantly, he wanted to help them!

Did they want something to eat?

Could he get them some bread? Perhaps some cheese?

Perfect.

Then the kitchen boy asked if James and Magnus wanted something to drink.

James wanted to know what might be on offer.

It turned out that the lad could only offer ale, or a drink made from wine and honey. He did not advise drinking the water. People got sick from drinking cold water!

James didn't fancy drinking the wine or ale. Apart from anything else, it was still only first thing in the morning, and he couldn't face that sort of drink!

How James wished he could be at home tucking into toast with orange juice and a large mug of tea!

But there was no chance of that, and he was very thirsty.

Magnus had an idea.

"Do you have a kitchen garden?" he asked the boy.

"Aye, Sir!" came the reply, "It's across the yard."

Magnus looked in the direction of the lad's finger and saw a cultivated section of land.

As he started to walk over there, he asked the lad if he could put a pot of water on the kitchen fire to boil.

The lad did as he was asked. Meanwhile Magnus found a patch of mint growing wild in the garden.

He picked a handful of tender leaves and returned to where James was standing.

The lad returned.

"The water is right hot now, Sir," he told Magnus.

Magnus asked the boy if he could find a couple of beakers.

When they arrived, Magnus divided some of the mint leaves between the two beakers.

He went over to the pot of boiling water.

"Have you a ladle that I might borrow?" he asked.

A large spoon was thrust into his hands.

James watched as Magnus filled the beakers with the boiling water.

A delicious smell of fresh mint permeated the kitchen.

"Drink this!" said Magnus, "It's fresh mint tea. The boiled water is safe now. The heat has destroyed whatever was in the water and made people sick. The mint imparts a refreshing taste."

James did as he was bid.

The taste was just as Magnus had said.

Gently warming and refreshing at the same time.

"Is there more?" he asked as he handed the beaker back to Magnus.

"Indeed, my Lord. We have a pot full of boiling water and I can pick as much mint as we need. It grows plentifully and the Manor will not run out of it."

With that, he prepared another beaker full of the mint tea.

The young kitchen lad handed them both a platter of bread and cheese.

Not quite the breakfast James was used to but a welcome alternative.

When Magnus and James had finished eating, James wondered what they were going to do next.

"We are going to prepare for battle!" stated Magnus.

It made sense. If there was going to be a major fight happening in ten weeks' time, James and Magnus needed to be as ready as they could be. Neither of them had been involved in a medieval battle before. It was likely that they would need to be in the thick of it is they were to fulfil the Sword's mission.

Magnus led the way to the stable yard where a group of young men were practising Sword fights with each other. The young men didn't use real Swords of course. They thrust and parried using wooden lookalikes. They were watched all the while by a tall man who was clearly in charge of it all.

James suddenly felt nervous again. The only time he had even played with a pretend Sword was with his best friend Gordon just before they found the Mighty Sword of Eir. That was when he was seven years old.

He was eighteen now.

But he did have a Sword that was the envy of everyone in the Manor.

What if he couldn't show any skill now?

James felt the Sword's amber stone glowing again. He was reassured. He knew that he could trust the Sword.

It would all work out.

Magnus asked the man in charge if James might join the Swordplay. The man readily agreed. He wanted to see what sort of stuff this strange storyteller was made of. It was still possible that the storyteller could be an imposter.

He might be able to tell a good tale. But could he fight like a nobleman?

James took off the scabbard and handed it, together with the Sword, to Magnus.

In return, he was handed a coarse wooden Sword.

One of the young squires came over to him and asked if James would spar with him.

This was it.

It was time for James to prove himself.

James took a deep breath and thought about the Sword.

Then faced his opponent.

Chapter 2.9
Preparation Begins

James waited for his sparring partner to make the first move. He sensed that this was what the Sword wanted.

He remembered that the Sword had been forged with love. Its purpose was to protect rather than kill.

James trusted the Sword to help him now. He could feel it watching his every move.

He beat off each thrust and parry that his opponent made. Several times, James could have finished him off with a pretend killer blow. But every time that was possible James held back.

Magnus and the knight-trainer who was teaching the squires how to fight watched on.

"Your master is adept at Sword fighting!" said the knight.

Magnus nodded.

"But I see that he does not have the urge to kill or maim. He seeks only to protect and repel. That is good. Although we need knights to fight and win in battle, we also need knights who are prepared to protect our leader and keep him safe. It is vital for the winning side to have a leader who is alive at its fore."

Magnus agreed.

He remembered James's dreams from the night before. He knew that the Sword which he was holding so carefully wanted this role for James.

As the play fight progressed, everyone in the courtyard gradually stopped what they were doing and turned to watch.

Eventually, James's sparring partner threw down his Sword and shouted, "I surrender. I am exhausted! You have blocked every lunge that I have made. You had several chances to overcome and yet you did not. You have true

Swordsmanship tempered with mercy and patience. I bow to my worthy opponent!"

Those watching applauded.

It had been a skilful and entertaining match with an unexpected end.

As the clapping subsided, Magnus realised that the Lord of the Manor had joined them.

"I see that my Good Knight has been exhausted by your Master," observed Alfread.

As the knight-trainer moved away to order the squires to pick up their wooden Swords and clear up the yard, Magnus quietly returned the Mighty Sword to James.

Alfread continued quietly, "I hear rumours that England may soon be at war," he said as James headed back, "We need to be ready for when we are called!"

Both Magnus and James looked at Alfread.

There was more.

"My friends last evening told of a rumour that we will soon be attacked. Come, let us walk, so I can say more without others listening in."

Alfread led Magnus and James out of the courtyard and over the drawbridge.

"My purpose is two-fold," he said to them once they were well away from the others.

"I have marvelled at your stories. Today I have also seen how you can fight. You possess qualities that I find useful."

Magnus and James looked at each other. What was Alfread going to offer?

"In return for a bed and food, I would be obliged if you would stay and join my knights. All that I ask in return is that you entertain us with more of your tales, and should the need arise, protect me as I lead my men into battle!"

James felt the Sword's glow of approval. It seemed that this was the outcome it wanted.

Magnus wanted to know more about the rumours.

They told of a big falling out between King Harold Godwinson and his brother, Tostig, Earl of Northumbria. It had been so bad that Tostig had had to run away. Now, it appeared that he was working with one King Harald of Norway who thought that he should be king of England.

Messages were starting to circulate that Harald and Tostig were building an army. When it was ready, it would set sail and then there would be war with England.

If Harald of Norway won, and became king, things would change. And not for the better.

It was vital that all knights, lords, and freemen were ready to fight alongside their King Harold Godwinson to protect and preserve England.

Alfread was already increasing the training for his men.

He turned to Magnus and said, "I believe your name—Magnus Ivar—means Mighty Archer in Viking. I believe that once upon a day you used a bow and arrow.

It is time for you to hone those skills. I would like you to train with my other archers.

I need every man fit and ready for the time is drawing nearer when we will be called.

I know your hands are soft now, but by the time we are battle ready, you will be able to handle a bow and arrow as well as any man here."

So, James and Magnus agreed to join forces with Alfread.

James could feel that the Sword approved.

The next weeks passed in a blur of training and storytelling.

James and Magnus spent every day practising the skills needed to meet the Sword's needs.

Initially, Magnus had been sent to train with the archers. But it soon became clear that, despite the promise of his name, he would never master the art of the long bow. He didn't even have enough strength to stretch the bow, never mind load it with an arrow!

After much thought, Alfread and James decided to test Magnus's skills as a Swordsman. It turned out that he was surprisingly good!

Both James and Magnus next had to demonstrate their ability to ride a horse while brandishing a Sword. If they couldn't do that, then they would be no use to any army.

Luckily for them both, they had had riding lessons as children!

After that, it was practice, practice, practice.

Alfread had the view, which he freely shared, that you must be as prepared as possible for war.

It was important to ensure that the men were ready but fully rested so that they had as much energy as possible for the coming demands.

And he wanted to be sure that there was enough food and water otherwise the men would not be at their best when the time came.

The coming conflict was going to be hard.

James and Magnus had been allocated the important task of protecting Alfread as he rode out into the middle of the battle to encourage and fight with his men.

There would be no room for error on either James' or Magnus's part.

As well as training to be a knight, James was also required to continue his storytelling every evening after dinner.

James was starting to worry that he might run out of stories soon and that he would need to make up some new ones.

That way was dangerous as he might accidently include references to things that the Lord and his household knew nothing about. Then he would be condemned as a wizard. And he still hadn't discovered what the punishment for being a wizard was!

It was evening again.

The Lord and his household had completed their evening meal and were settling back in their chairs for another story.

James was starting to worry. He felt that he had just about run out of new material.

Then, inspiration!

He remembered the tale of the Gruffalo.

His mother had read it to him so many times when he was little that he could recite the story off by heart.

The story was simple but very effective.

How the men laughed at the tiny mouse taking on a sly fox and outsmarting him.

They loved how the snake and the owl were fooled.

They particularly loved the description of the imaginary Gruffalo— especially the purple pimple on his nose!

At last it was time for James and Magnus to leave the Great Hall and get some sleep.

As they shook out their cloaks to lay on the lavender and straw, James said to Magnus, "I ache all over! I know I have to learn to ride and fight on horseback. But it's not easy, is it?"

Magnus had to agree.

But they knew they had to keep working hard to ensure that they could do their job when the time came.

Both Magnus and James knew that time was near.

The full moon shone almost bright as day. The guards on watch over the drawbridge spotted the King's Messenger from afar. He was clearly in a rush. His poor horse was galloping as fast as it could manage, and yet he urged more from the beast, such was his hurry.

The guards waited at the drawbridge. They had orders from Alfread to allow no one to pass until they had been identified, and permission given from Alfread himself.

Magnus heard the clip clop of the horse as the rider was escorted over the drawbridge and into the main courtyard.

He nudged James awake.

"Listen—I think the King's Messenger has arrived," he said.

James rubbed his eyes and struggled to rouse himself.

As he did so, he felt the glow from the Sword's amber eye.

This was it.

The beginning of their vital mission.

Both Magnus and James realised that not only did Alfread's life depend on them, but the future fabric of time.

They shook their cloaks free of the straw and lavender, and adjusted the clothes that they were sleeping in.

Then they rushed to the Great Hall.

They were just in time to hear the King's Messenger deliver the news that they had all been waiting for but hoped would never arrive.

It was time to prepare for battle.

Time was now of the essence.

Alfread called forward his knights and instructed them to wake their men immediately. They were battle ready, but they still needed to make sure they prepared for their journey to it.

The Manor House erupted into a hive of activity. Men, pages, and servant boys ran hither and thither. Fetching, carrying, checking, packing.

Even with all the effort that night though, it was still another full day before Alfread considered his army of men were fully ready for the coming conflict.

Chapter 2.10
Onwards to Stamford Bridge

It was a long hard march from the Manor of Holborne to the wild mists of the Yorkshire coast.

Most of the men making their way there under Alfread's banner hadn't even left the village before, never mind travelled so far beyond it.

James felt very relieved that he and Magnus had been allocated horses. Walking would have been just too difficult for them.

Alfread tried to make sure that his men travelled only as far as they were able without becoming overtired each day. They were carrying heavy armour, bows and arrows. Behind them rumbled the clumsy but reliable carts pulled by ox. They were packed as high as they could be with supplies to make sure that the men were well looked after as they marched purposefully onwards.

It was slow but steady progress.

Even so, the journey north took a full four weeks. Fortunately, Alfread and his men were welcomed at every village they passed through. No one wanted war. And no one wanted to live through another period of confusion. Memories were long and folk still remembered how it was when the rich fought for the throne of England.

Everyone hoped that the coming conflict would sort things out one way or another. They really didn't care who won just so long as they were left well alone to get on with their lives.

Alfread and his men gladly accepted their hospitality. His men were allowed to bed down on proper straw mattresses when these were available. Alfread let the men partake of the food and drink offered to them.

But he made sure that they didn't abuse the hospitality offered.

Alfread looked to all possible outcomes. He knew that if Harold Godwinson lost this battle, he and his men would have to retreat rapidly. If Alfread and his men respected folk on the way to battle, there was a better chance of them helping if it were needed on the way back.

James thought that Alfread was very wise to prepare for any situation.

Even if James thought he knew what was going to happen, he couldn't be sure. The Sword's ability to twist time had put paid to that belief!

For now, though, the most important thing was that James and Magnus did their job and protected Alfread!

The small army walked and rode at a steady pace.

Before they had set off, the King's Messenger had told Alfread that Harald of Norway had been seen amassing a large fleet of boats.

Over three hundred boats by all accounts! Over eight thousand warriors!

When all was ready, those boats would set sail. Indeed—some may have already done so!

As Alfread and his men marched north, more information started to come through.

First, it was that the Vikings had indeed left Norway and were heading towards England.

Magnus told James that the sea journey would take at least three days or even longer if the weather was poor. The boats were only powered by sails after all.

Alfread's army stopped and made camp on the afternoon of 24th September.

As the men began to set out their cloaks to rest on, a messenger arrived at the makeshift camp.

Apparently, King Harold Godwinson and his men had arrived at Tadcaster—not far from where they now were.

The king was preparing for battle.

Things had not been going well for the English. The enemy had landed and was beginning to raid and plunder. Harald and Tostig had burnt down Scarborough, after which they had raided other towns in the area, spreading pain and misery wherever they went.

Their plundering continued apace, and the latest information was that they had defeated the earls of Northumbria and Mercia's armies a mere two miles outside the city of York. As a result, the citizens of York were due to surrender the following day.

At this point, the messenger paused to gulp down a welcome beaker of thin ale.

It had been a long ride to reach Alfread, and he still had more to tell.

The next news was far more interesting to Alfread, James and Magnus.

Apparently, King Harold Godwinson's scouts had managed to find out more about the Viking plans.

It seemed that Harald and Tostig planned to march into York on the following day to accept the formal surrender.

The scouts understood that they would only take some of their army as they weren't expecting any more trouble. More importantly, the men they would take with them would only be wearing light armour.

The King's Messenger told Alfread that he had left his most trusted man there, hidden in a safe place so he would wait and watch.

He would return to Harold's camp at dawn to tell the king whether anything had changed.

If it had not, King Harold Godwinson would attack them as they made their way to the formal surrender!

By taking Harald and Tostig by surprise, the English could defeat the Viking invasion and banish the enemy for ever even though they were heavily outnumbered.

Alfread thought about what he had heard for a little while, and then decided.

"Saddle up, my men," he ordered, "Pack the wagons and pick up your weapons. We have another three miles to go! We need to reach King Harold's army before dark. Then we can join with his forces to defeat the foreigners!"

Although his men were tired and weary, they were still hungry for a fight.

A loud cheer went up, and before you knew it, Alfread's army was back on the road!

Three miles was a long way to trudge when they were fully laden and after a full day's march behind them, but now Alfread's men had a purpose.

They were going to rendezvous with King Harold's army.

Every step was a step closer to joining forces.

Alfread sent James and Magnus to ride ahead to forewarn Harold's troops that they were coming. He didn't want his men to be slaughtered because they were mistaken for the enemy.

James and Magnus rode hard and fast. They covered the ground in double quick time until they were standing on a small hill just above Harold's camp.

They could see Harold's men in the distance. A number of small tents had been erected in a cluster around a larger one.

Elsewhere, fires had been lit. Men sat around, laughing quietly, and joking. It was clear that they were relaxed and resting in advance of the attack they knew would happen on the morrow.

James heard the approaching horse first. He drew his Mighty Sword from its scabbard. He was ready for trouble if trouble it was.

"Halt! Who are you, and why are you here?" asked a very authoritative voice.

James turned his horse around to face the voice. He held the Mighty Sword of Eir above his head. Its amber stone glowed welcomingly. He said, "We are scouts for Alfread, Lord of Holborne Manor. Lord Alfread and his men have travelled far to join forces with King Harold Godwinson. They are marching towards your camp as we speak. My Lord seeks King Harold's permission to help rout the invaders!"

The rider took note of what James said, and saw the magnificent Sword. He decided that he should take these two stray horsemen into the camp where they could be interrogated further.

If what they said was true, King Harold would welcome the additional forces. But if they had lied…

He led James and Magnus into the camp, between the fires and towards the large tent.

He told them to dismount. They did.

"Come," he ordered as their horses were led away.

They followed the rider into the large tent. There, seated at the end of it, on a rather beautifully carved wooden chair sat someone who could only be King Harold Godwinson.

James and Magnus immediately knelt.

The rider also knelt before the king. He said, "I found these two men on the hill above our camp. They claim to be scouts for Lord Alfread of Holborne. They claim that he is marching towards our camp as we speak. Lord Alfread comes in friendship to offer himself and his men to support our cause!"

Then he stood and backed away.

King Harold smiled.

"Rise, young men. I believe your story. My scouts have been tracking your movements for several days now. Indeed, one of my best men contacted Lord Alfread earlier to tell him of our position. I am delighted to welcome your Lord and his army. We are expecting a vicious battle on the morrow. I think we will need Lord Holborne's men if we are to defeat Harald of Norway!"

James and Magnus smiled at each other.

That was a relief!

"Welcome to you, and we will welcome Lord Holborne!"

James addressed King Harold.

"Your Majesty," he said, "Lord Holborne will arrive here soon. We had just made camp when your messenger arrived. Lord Holborne roused his men as soon as he realised how close we were to you. He will arrive here within the hour, I am sure."

King Harold Godwinson clapped his hands.

Two servants appeared, one either side of his chair.

"Bring food and wine!" he ordered, "And hot water and towels. Lord Holborne will be in need of food and rest. Likewise, tell the men to make Lord Holborne's soldiers welcome. Tonight, we prepare for battle. We must be sure that we are all fully fed and rested!"

As Harold finished giving orders, a distant rumble of horses, carts and men could be heard.

Just as James had said, Alfread and his troops had arrived.

Now all was ready for the morrow.

James and Magnus's work was about to begin.

Chapter 2.11
Let the Battle Commence

It was an uneasy James who snuggled into his cloak that night.

He was all too aware that the next 24 hours were not going to be pleasant.

He also knew that he had an important role to play. He and Magnus had to keep Alfread safe. He could not allow the vision he had had back at the Manor to become reality.

James did not know why, but it was vital that Alfread did not die on the morrow!

James wondered if the Sword would send him another vision on this eve of battle.

He didn't have to wonder for long.

James fell asleep almost as soon as his eyes closed. Then the dreams began.

Magnus watched his master as he slept. He could tell that James was dreaming. He saw that James's eyes were moving rapidly back and forth beneath their eye lids. A sure sign!

Magnus waited patiently until James shuddered awake.

James realised that Magnus was there and was comforted. His visions had not been good, and he needed Magnus's wise counsel to help understand them.

Magnus listened as James related what he had dreamt.

How he could even smell and taste the battle. The cries of the wounded were painful beyond belief.

But, as the smoke and confusion cleared, he was able to see Alfread, on his horse, with James and Magnus flanking him. King Harold Godwinson was standing proud on his horse as the victorious English drove the few remaining Vikings back down the hill and into the distance.

If James and Magnus worked with the Sword on the morrow, all would be well.

For Harold and Alfread and their men at least.

But pity the defeated and dead Vikings.

Talking with Magnus calmed James's nerves. When he fell back to sleep, there were no more dreams. The Sword had told them what it wished to achieve.

Now all they had to do was deliver it.

The men woke with the dawn. It was a chilly morning and the mist rose gracefully from the valley below.

King Harold had told the men to pack their things quietly so as not to alert the enemy. He thought they were camped far enough away, but it was wise not to take chances.

The trusted scout who had been spying on the Vikings returned quietly to camp. He reported to the king directly.

The Vikings were on the move. They had left many men—perhaps even 3000 of them—with their ships at their landing place. Harald and Tostig were taking only a proportion of their army to York. They clearly expected its citizens to surrender peacefully as they had not bothered to wear anything other than light armour. The rumours of how Scarborough had been plundered and raided had preceded them and the citizens of York did not wish to suffer the same fate.

Harald of Norway and Tostig gathered their men at a place called Stamford Bridge. They waited for the burghers of York to arrive. They were expecting to discuss how the city would be managed now that they were in charge.

But, as they waited, an awesome and fearsome sight came into view.

Harold Godwinson's forces approached relentlessly. They outnumbered the lightly armoured Viking army, and they were most definitely ready for a fight.

To the death if needed.

The Viking army watched in growing horror as the sea of men advanced ever closer.

The suddenly, a brief spark of hope for the Vikings.

As Harold's army came to the bridge, a lone brave Viking stood firm. He managed to delay the troops' advance.

Briefly.

Harald and Tostig did their best to use this precious time to group their men into shield-wall formation. This would allow the reserve men from the ships a chance to reach them and repel Harold's men.

Indeed, just as the battle seemed lost, Harald's men arrived. But they had run all the way to the battlefield and could do little to help.

Just as James's dream had predicted, it was a bloody, nasty battle.

The Vikings fought with what weapons they had with them. Some even fought with their bare hands.

James and Magnus never left Alfread's side throughout.

James wielded the Mighty Sword of Eir with skill and kept any Viking threats at bay.

Magnus protected the rear. While it was unlikely Alfread would be attacked from behind, it could not be discounted.

Alfread rode forward, encouraging his men. He was almost parallel with Harold's entourage.

A wall of force!

Harold's men fought valiantly onwards.

Alfread's men fought valiantly onwards.

They dispersed the enemy in every direction, until it was clear that there was no more enemy to disperse.

Chaos surrounded them. Tattered remains of clothes, Swords abandoned in the rush to escape, and most poignantly, the remains of those who had fallen during the conflict.

Alfread's men were moving back to Harold's camp to celebrate.

As he looked around at the carnage and pain on the battlefield, James felt sick to the pit of his stomach.

James watched as the dust settled. Shadowy men appeared, seemingly out of nowhere, to pick and pull at the dead bodies.

He shuddered in horror as he realised that these men were scavenging for anything of value or use.

Magnus noted James's revulsion and said quietly, "Remember, these men have nothing at all. And the dead have no use for their things now. Let us leave them be. Times are hard enough. We don't need to interfere."

Although James knew that Magnus was right, he still couldn't rid himself of his feelings of disgust.

Indeed, it was at that point that he realised that he so desperately wanted to go home.

Back to his home, and his mother, and boring old fish and chips for dinner.

He had had enough of watching his "A" level studies come to life.

What wouldn't he give for a quiet evening in with his mother and to watch her favourite soap opera with her.

James and Magnus turned their horses around and left the battlefield.
They both knew what was going to happen next though.
There would be no respite yet.

Chapter 2.12
Just When They Thought It Was All Over

James and Magnus dismounted when they reached the camp's perimeter.

They could hear the laughter and singing echoing around. King Harold Godwinson had won a splendid victory. All thought that the Viking threat to England was done for.

Never again would its shores be at risk from a Scandinavian invasion.

James and Magnus remained solemn.

They knew that there would be no more trouble from the north.

However, they were all too aware that another battle, which would change the course of English history, was imminent.

Because of that, they knew that their task to protect Alfread was not yet finished.

James and Magnus walked slowly towards the royal tents. They could hear Alfread and Harold regaling each other with anecdotes from the day's events.

All James wanted to do was sleep.

He had witnessed so many horrible things that day. He really wished he hadn't had to. In fact, James was starting to question why the Sword had forced him into this situation. He knew the facts about the Battle of Stamford Bridge from his studies. Perhaps there was some merit in seeing the carnage for himself—although James could not for the life of him imagine why.

He sat down outside the royal tent and prepared to lie down. Every bone in James's body ached. He hoped sleep would come quickly and that it would be dreamless.

There was still some small part of him that hoped that the past weeks had all been a way too vivid fantasy. That he would wake up at home in his own bed. The day would begin again. And none of this would have happened. At least not to him.

However, deep in his heart of hearts, James knew that was not the case.

Magnus saw that James was troubled.

"We must do the Sword's bidding," he said.

James wearily agreed.

"But I am not sure I can face another battle like today's!"

"We know what happens next," agreed Magnus, "At least we think we do…"

James sighed.

"I haven't forgotten my vision of Alfread lying on the ground. He was so still, so pale. His men, and us, we were all standing around him. There was a clear sense that we did not know what to do next.

I know we have prevented that situation from happening today. But we still have the Normans to think about!"

Magnus turned slightly. He could still hear the men's laughter and relief.

Suddenly, he, too, felt very tired indeed.

James fell asleep first, and it wasn't long before the Sword started to weave its magic around him again.

James felt his body being pulled forward. He could sense the stars and planets whizzing by him as the Sword transported him through time. Then, as soon as the rush had started, he came to sudden halt.

The dust settled.

Slowly, more images became clear.

He was back in his own time. James knew that he was still in the north, but not at Stamford Bridge. He was back where his family came from.

James was watching an auction market. He could see people—farmers, he supposed—standing around a large, enclosed arena. James supposed that they were waiting for sheep or cattle to be paraded round.

James watched as the auctioneer climbed the steps to his podium, then nod to his men to open the gates to allow the stock in. James saw that the men had huge prods at the ready. To control any wayward cows, perhaps?

The stock was allowed into the arena.

Oh, my goodness me! What a shock!

It wasn't cattle, or sheep, or even pigs that wearily trudged through the gates. It wasn't farm animals that had been brought to sale.

It was a crowd of people.

All had metal collars round their necks. His mother was one of them!

With growing horror, James realised that he was witnessing a slave market.

But before he could even shout out, the Sword whisked him away.

Again, James felt the whizzing of time, but he had no clue whether he was heading back or forward. He didn't care either. He was far more afraid for his mother.

What had he just seen?

Just as suddenly, James came to halt.

He was in a very different place.

He couldn't be too sure where or when it was. It was so different to what he knew, but he thought he might be in Parliament.

But the politicians looked very different. They all were wearing white wigs for a start. They looked more like a collection of lawyers waiting to go into court!

It must be a Parliament from the past, from many years ago.

James seemed to be suspended in the air above the debate that was going on. He could make out some of the words on the papers in front of what he assumed was the speaker of the House.

He realised that he was watching Parliament debate a very important bill.

The bill to abolish slavery!

He had been brought there just in time for the vote.

The speaker stood up to announce the result.

The bill had failed.

But why?

James remembered from his studies that in 1792, a chap called William Wilberforce had brought a bill to Parliament to abolish slavery.

After much debate, it had passed, and by a sizable margin.

Those who wanted to get rid of the evil trading of human beings to other humans had won by 230 votes to 85.

No way had it failed.

James was both horrified and confused.

What was the Sword doing?

He wanted this to stop.

He thrashed around wildly in his sleep, and shouted loudly, "NO!"

And immediately woke up.

Magnus was by his side.

"Tell me?" he asked. "Perhaps I can shed light on what you have seen?"

James looked at him in wide-eyed terror.

"I hope you can because if what I see really happens, our world is horrible!"

Then he began.

First, Magnus and James had discussed the Alfread vision days ago.

It seemed that this night's offering added little to what they already knew.

Magnus felt that not much had changed at all except that they had survived the Battle of Stamford Bridge.

But Alfread was clearly still at risk.

Magnus then interpreted what James had witnessed next.

He thought that because the slavery bill had failed on that day back in 1792, England still kept slaves.

The Sword wanted James to realise just how wrong it was by showing him that his mother was one.

James realised that the images he had seen in his earlier visions were of his mother as a slave.

Magnus felt that these images were key to all of these nightmare visions.

The Sword had shown James that slavery had not been abolished as he had thought.

The bill had failed because the man who was responsible for it wasn't in Parliament.

He wasn't in Parliament because he hadn't been born.

Then came Magnus's bombshell—William Wilberforce hadn't been born because Alfread had died before he could have any children.

Although Wilberforce was many generations in the future, he was a direct descendant of Alfread.

That was why James and Magnus had been brought to this time and place.

That was why they had met Alfread.

And that was why it was vital to make sure he came to no harm!

It was still dark as Magnus finished his interpretation.

The chill of the night was seeping into their bones.

But that wasn't why they found themselves shivering.

As they stared at each other, they heard the distant sound of a King's Messenger approaching the camp.

It would soon be time to begin the next stage of their mission.

Chapter 2.13
Bad News

The King's Messenger brought bad news.

Terrible news!

Just as King Harold Godwinson and his troops had started to recover from the trauma of the Battle of Stamford Bridge.

The King's Messenger brought urgent news of another threat to Harold's kingdom.

This time from France. From Normandy.

Another rival for his throne had raised an army and had set sail to make war with Harold.

The indications were that this army would land on the south coast, in the bay of Pefensea.

Harold must defeat this second invader if he was to stay king of England!

Never mind that it was late.

Never mind that his men were still exhausted from the day's exertions. There was no time to waste. Never mind that it was the middle of the night.

The men must be woken immediately.

They must start the long journey south immediately!

Harold gave his orders.

His men must be ready within the hour.

And it was vital that they travel as quickly as possible to confront the Normans.

James and Magnus gathered up their things and were ready mounted in good time.

As were Alfread and the rest of Harold's men.

James and Magnus took up their protective positions on either side of Alfread.

On Harold's command, his army moved off.

It was fortunate that it was a clear moonlit night. Hazards could be seen and avoided.

Which was true until the army had to make its way through a dense wood. The tall trees blocked out the moonlight. It became increasing difficult to see where the track was. Branches which grew at horse head height were only spotted as the knights came close to them. The ground was pitted with tree roots and fox holes.

Suddenly, Alfread's horse stumbled and fell. One of its front hooves had caught in a tree root.

Alfread shouted as he fell.

James and Magnus halted immediately and were relieved to see that the horse had managed to struggle to its feet. It did not appear to have injured itself at all.

Just a nasty tumble. That was all.

Or so they thought.

They waited for Alfread to jump up and get back on his steed.

But he didn't.

He lay there on the ground. Still as still could be.

Magnus jumped down from his horse and rushed over to where the prone Lord lay.

James did likewise.

It was an eerie tableau, the prone Lord, flanked either side by his loyal knights, lit only by the chilly moon light.

It was just as well that Magnus had been one of the British Museum's first aiders. He knew what he had to do next.

He spoke in a firm voice to Alfread.

"Can you hear me?"

No response.

He gently shook Alfread's shoulder and asked again in a loud voice, "My Lord, can you hear me?"

Still no response.

Magnus decided that he needed to use the final test for unconsciousness.

He dug his fingernail into Alfread's ear lobe.

Nothing.

Magnus took hold of Alfread's wrist. He felt for Alfread's pulse.

Then he knelt over Alfread's face and turned his cheek to it.

James looked around.

He saw Alfread's men had stopped marching and were starting to cluster behind. They were all straining to see what was happening to Alfread.

"Is he dead?" asked one of them.

Magnus looked up.

At that point, James suddenly recognised what he was seeing.

His vision.

Was Alfread dead? Had they failed in their mission?

In such a mundane way? Not in battle, but a simple fall from a horse!

Magnus turned to the man who had asked the question.

"No, he is not dead. But he is unconscious. We cannot leave him here alone to recover. He will be in grave danger from robbers, thieves, and other dark forces of the night. Neither can he continue to march with King Harold. And he will need someone with him when he does come round."

James thought quickly.

He turned to the knight who had asked if Alfread was dead. James realised that it was his sparring partner from training, Alfread's Good Knight.

"Take your horse!" James ordered, "Find King Harold's knights. Tell them what has happened. Explain that Alfread is not dead but is seriously injured and may yet still die. Seek the King's permission for Magnus and me to remain with him."

"What about us?" asked another of Alfread's men.

This time, Magnus spoke.

"Our Master's fall has already delayed us by at least an hour. King Harold is moving his men at a great pace. I fear that those of you who are on foot or with the carts may not be able to catch him up if you do not leave now."

He turned to the Good Knight.

"You have a horse," Magnus observed, "You can ride quickly and perhaps catch up with the King? Could you alert the King that Alfread's men have fallen behind as well? They will do their best to catch up, but will likely arrive late? Also, pray warn the king that Alfread will not be able to fight. He is sorely injured, and we must seek help."

The Good Knight sped off on great haste.

Magnus turned to the rest of the men.

"Now go, all of you! If you leave now, there is a chance that you might be able to catch up."

James had another thought.

As the other men were preparing to leave, he realised that Alfread would need to be carried to help somehow.

"Hey, you with the ox and cart there!" he shouted, "You must remain to help us!"

He pointed to drover, seated on a sturdy-looking cart attached to what appeared to be a healthy cow.

"We are still not too far away from York. We will use your cart to take Lord Alfread there. We are sure to find a Monastery there which has an Infirmary attached!"

Although it had to be said that it was less clear what a medieval Infirmary might achieve.

James remembered from his studies that such places were very basic.

But, if they could even just find Alfread a warm bed, there was a chance that his broken body might recover.

Some of the men left once they saw Alfread was seriously injured. But several men showed no sign of moving, let alone leaving. Their master was seriously injured. They were going nowhere until they knew what was going to happen to him. They stayed resolutely by their Lord's body.

James quickly shared his plan with them.

He asked that four of the men stay to help with Alfread, so that he could be taken to York. All the rest must now depart.

Magnus selected several men to accompany them and the cart back to York. The rest he sent on their way, with orders to try and re-join the King.

Although they didn't say so out loud, both James and Magnus felt it unlikely that Lord Alfread's men would catch up with the army. But they had to try.

All but the helpers left.

James moved the remaining men back.

"Give us some space!" he ordered.

The men shuffled back slightly.

James spread his cloak on the ground by Alfread's still body. He and Magnus gently lifted Alfread onto it. They took great care to not move his head any more than absolutely necessary. After all, it was entirely possible that Alfread may have shattered one of the bones in his back.

It took quite a while to do this because they had to be so careful.

Once Alfread was securely placed on the cloak, James asked the drover to clear a space in the cart.

Then James called on the men standing by to help lift Alfread by his cloak onto the cart.

While they were so engaged, James's sparring partner returned with news.

He had managed to speak with one of Harold's knights. After brief deliberation, permission had been granted for Lord Alfread's men to proceed as James had proposed.

King Harold's knight hoped that the Lord Alfread would soon recover and be able to join the King in time for the coming battle at the coast.

James privately thought that this would be highly unlikely, even if Alfread regained consciousness now.

He thought that the Battle of Hastings would be over and done long before Alfread would be fit to travel.

James and Magnus flanked either side of the cart. The Good Knight positioned himself at the head of the cart, while another placed himself at the rear.

Dawn was breaking as the cart and its escort passed through the walled gates of the city of York.

The townspeople were starting their day. The streets were already busy and full of people.

James jumped down from his horse. As he led the beast along, he stopped and sought directions to the nearest Monastery.

It wasn't hard to find. It was the largest stone building in the area, and right next to the magnificent Cathedral.

James looked at it all in awe as they drew closer. It was just mind-boggling that here he was, looking at a Cathedral which predated York Minster!

The cart pulled up by a thick wooden door.

James knocked long and hard.

After what felt to be a lifetime, he heard the sound of a small grille being opened.

Then a voice from within asked "Hello?"

James quickly explained what had happened, and that he and his small group were seeking sanctuary and aid for their Lord who had been thrown from his horse.

The voice told James to wait. Then the grille was slammed shut.

Now what? James's studies had told him that medieval monasteries were bound to offer sanctuary and help to all who sought it. Were his history books wrong?

They waited and waited. Just when James and Magnus were ready to give up, the grille slid open again.

"You are welcome, Travellers. I can see from your clothes and demeanour that you are part of the army which saved our beautiful city yesterday. Even if you were not, we would have still offered you sanctuary. You are indeed welcome, Sirs.

Come in, and I will direct you to the Infirmary. Our Monk Physician will advise on what will happen next."

The wooden doors swung open.

James, Magnus, and their precious cargo entered.

Chapter 2.14
The Infirmary

The unconscious Alfread, flanked by his loyal retainers, passed through the arched doorway. They found themselves in a courtyard, where they were met by several monks. There was an older monk, wearing the hessian cassock tied with a rope belt that James had expected, who was clearly in charge of the rest of them.

He quickly assessed the situation and began issuing orders.

He first moved quickly to the cart, climbed on board, and gently examined Alfread.

"He lives. Gather the patient up gently. Brother Luke will not be happy if we handle him roughly!"

He then turned to James and Magnus.

"Were you with this man when he was injured?"

James and Magnus nodded.

"Good. You will accompany him to the Infirmary where you can tell our physician about the accident!"

The older monk explained what would happen next.

"These young men will carry your Lord Alfread. They will try to be gentle, but they are novices who are still learning. Please let them know if you think they are too rough!"

One of the young monks ran off to one side of the courtyard and retrieved what appeared to be a flat board. As he returned to the cart, James could see that he was carrying a purpose-built stretcher. Made of solid wood and very heavy—but definitely a stretcher!

James, Magnus, and the other escorts watched as Alfread was carefully transferred from the dusty cart and placed on the stretcher.

"Now there's a turn up!" observed James quietly, "I wasn't aware they had those in the 11th century!"

The older monk turned again to the visitors.

"May I respectfully suggest that the rest of your party break bread with us? I invite you to join our table for the first meal of the day!"

James looked surprised at this—breakfast? It wasn't that long since dawn. What had happened to the two meals a day rule?

Magnus pointed out that the monks had probably been up since the small wee hours, praying in the Cathedral. For them, this would be the right time to have their first meal of the day.

However, there would be no morning meal for James and Magnus. They followed the novices as they carried Alfread to the Infirmary.

The rest of the group happily followed the older monk towards the refectory. They might not have been praying since before dawn, but they had been marching long before then. It was fair to say that they were more than ready for food!

Alfread was carried along the cloisters and through another courtyard, and past what seemed to be a kitchen garden. Eventually, his bearers reached another building.

All the while, Alfread neither stirred nor showed any signs of life.

One of the novices paused before a large wooden door. He turned to James and Magnus.

"You must wait here. We will take your master to a bed where our physician will examine him. Brother Luke will want to do this without you being there so that he can form his own views on what is wrong, and what treatment he can offer. When he has finished, he will come and take you to see your master. Once there, Brother Luke will tell you his thoughts and ask questions of you."

James and Magnus looked at each other in surprise. This wasn't how medieval doctors behaved. From what they had read, medicine in the 11th century was very basic. It wasn't even understood how important it was to keep a patient clean!

The young novice noted their expressions and continued.

"You are fortunate that you found us. Our Infirmary is very good. We cannot save every hurt soul who seeks our help. But we have saved many, many patients who would have likely died had they not been treated by Brother Luke."

The novice knocked on the Infirmary's doors and waited for them to open. He returned to the stretcher. As the door opened, he and his fellow bearers picked it up.

The stretcher disappeared inside.

James and Magnus sat down on the cloister wall. They weren't quite sure whether they were allowed to sit there but did so anyway.

Now that they had a chance to rest, James felt the Sword's warmth flowing into his veins.

The Sword was pleased with what had happened.

James hoped that it would continue to approve. He wasn't sure that he ever wanted to find out what might happen if he upset the relic.

After what felt like an age, the young novice who had spoken earlier returned.

"Come with me," he said, "I will take you to Brother Luke."

He turned, and James and Magnus followed him into the Infirmary. James and Magnus braced themselves.

James had always thought that hospitals of this time were really just another part of the monastery. That they would be smoky and dark, with people having to share beds. That the floors would be dirty and covered in rushes—maybe even some lavender if it were available. Anything to keep the smell of sickness at bay.

But what a surprise!

They passed through another archway and found themselves in a bright airy long hallway. Everywhere was clean and light flooded the room. The place even smelt clean! And only one person per bed.

Monks hovered close by the beds. Some were checking brows for signs of fever, while others were fully occupied by washing the patients.

It almost felt like a modern-day hospital.

As James and Magnus looked at each other in amazement, one of the monks turned away from his charge and began to walk towards them. He stood head and shoulders above every other monk in the Infirmary. As he drew closer, they could see that was clearly not from these parts. Could he have travelled from a faraway place like Persia? Both James and Magnus knew that a few such travellers came to Britain at this time.

"Greetings," said the monk in a rich baritone voice, "I am Brother Luke. Welcome to our Infirmary!"

James was still looking around and took a little while to react.

Brother Luke noticed that James was stuck dumb.

"Are you surprised by me?" he asked gently, "I know I am not from these parts, but I can assure you that I am a very good physician…"

James finally found his voice.

"No," he said, "I am delighted to view your Infirmary! It is not at all as I had expected!"

Brother Luke smiled.

"I came to my Lord late in life," he began, "Before I found His love, I travelled far and learned much. I have tried to use my knowledge in the service of my Lord to improve the care of my patients here."

Magnus joined in.

"We would love to hear more of your travels, Sir, and I hope you find us a willing and credulous audience. We, too, are not from here, and we know we have much to learn! But first, do you have anything to tell us of our master?"

Brother Luke guided them to Alfread's bedside, where a novice was mopping Alfread's brow.

Brother Luke waited as James and Magnus moved to either side of Alfread's bed.

Then he told them his thoughts on what had passed.

"I believe your master has had a fall from some height. He has fallen backwards and banged his head. There is a wound at the back of his head. It had bled a lot, but I believe that head wounds do that. The amount of blood you had seen does not necessarily mean that this wound is serious. But lack of awareness is seriously troubling.

Tell me now what you know."

James told of how they had been riding with Harold's army through a dense forest. How Alfread's horse had stumbled in a fox hole, and how Alfread had been thrown.

"So far my diagnosis and your story match well. Is there more?"

Magnus took up the tale.

"I have learnt some elementary medicine in my travels too," he began.

Brother Luke smiled encouragingly.

"As my master lay on the ground, I did not move him. Instead I knelt by him. I shouted at my master but got no response. I shook him gently. No response. And I dug my fingernail into his earlobe—see here," Magnus pointed to a red weald on Alfread's left ear, "Again, there was no response. Then I tried to find a heartbeat. I did this by feeling for a blood vessel in his wrist. My Lord Alfread's pulse was strong and regular. It was not too fast or too slow. Finally, I checked that he still breathed. I did this by placing my cheek next to his face to feel his breath on my face. I could.

But my master lay still. We realised that he needed more help than we could give, so James and I carefully placed him on the cart—taking care not to move his head any more than we needed to—and brought him here."

Brother Luke breathed out slowly.

"First of all, I must commend you on your thorough and proper examination. You tested for his vital signs and did your best to make sure he did not incur further damage before arriving here. You have done well.

Secondly, I must also observe that you are not from these parts. You possess knowledge that only a learned scholar would know and have applied it well. I hope that we will have time to talk more of your travels later.

Finally, though, I must give you my thoughts on your master.

It is clear that although your master is deeply unconscious, he is alive. That is good. But there is little we can do until he comes round. But please be aware, he may not do so..."

At this point, James felt the Sword pressing against his chest. It was reminding him not to lose hope yet.

Magnus asked, "So for now, all we can do is wait?"

Brother Luke nodded.

"I will ask my best novice to watch over him. He will find us if there is any change!

Now come. Let us move away from here and let Brother Mark do his job. From what you have told me, there has not been much time for you to eat. And you must. You will need to keep your strength up if you are going to help your master!"

Brother Luke led James and Magnus back through the warren of cloisters and into the refectory.

As they entered, they could see that their men had just about finished their meal and were wondering if there was any news.

James had to tell them that there had been no change to Alfread. He was still deeply unconscious, and no one knew—not even the physician—whether he would live.

The Good Knight spoke first.

"What shall we do?" he asked.

James and Magnus looked at each other. King Harold's army would now be more than half a fast day's travel away. There was no way these men would be able to catch up with them now.

James privately thought that those of Alfread's men who had decided to follow the King straight after the accident could not have caught up with the fast-moving army. These loyal retainers, who were now delayed by almost a day, would have no chance.

James spoke first.

As the Sword glowed in its scabbard, he said, "I believe that even if you journey now, it will be too late for you to help King Harold. I believe that you will better serve your master if you return home to your families. They are going to need you in coming days.

The harvest may be gathered in, but there is work to be done if your families are going to see this winter through."

Brother Luke looked on benignly.

"I believe your Storyteller has spoken wisely. Pray follow his advice and travel swiftly and safely home. Your families need you."

James and Magnus looked at each other in surprise.

How did Brother Luke know that James was known as the Storyteller? Alfread's men may have mentioned it as they ate their food, but they were in the refectory at that point, while James and Magnus were in the Infirmary.

But as they were about to ask Brother Luke how he came by this information, Alfread's novice came rushing into the refectory.

Alfread was waking up.

All thought of food was forgotten. Brother Luke, James, and Magnus followed the novice back to the Infirmary.

They clustered around the foot of Alfread's bed.

Alfread lay on the bed. His head was moving from side to side. But his eyes were vacant, staring out, looking at nothing.

Brother Luke stepped forward and bent over Alfread.

Alfread tried to twist away.

Brother Luke did not try to do more. Instead, he moved back to the foot of the bed.

There, he gave his opinion.

"I believe that your master is starting to emerge from the fog which enveloped him after his fall. What we see now is very good news.

However, there is still much progress that needs to be made. I fear that could take days, if not weeks."

James and Magnus wondered what this might mean.

"I propose you do the following," continued Brother Luke, "James, Magnus, I propose that you stay here to oversee your master's progress. It will be long and slow, but from what you have told me, I believe that you possess skills which will enhance my own. And by so doing, you will hasten your master's recovery. If you are content to do this, I will seek the Abbot's approval for this course of action."

James and Magnus nodded. What other choice did they have? It was what the Sword wanted.

And they wanted to find out how Brother Luke knew James as the Storyteller!

Chapter 2.15
Brother Luke

The Abbot gladly gave his consent to James and Magnus remaining while Alfread recovered.

It was, after all, the Christian thing to do!

James and Magnus were still at the foot of Alfread's bed when the novice returned with the news that they were welcome guests.

Brother Luke said "Come with me, I will show you where you may sleep. You will be housed in one of cells. It is not grand. But it is warm dry and clean!"

It sounded wonderful to James and Magnus. Over the past few weeks, they had travelled far on horseback. Beds had been few and far between. Even finding a dry patch of flat grass to lie on was a luxury!

As they set off towards their lodgings, Brother Luke instructed the novice monk to fetch food and drink. These men had still not eaten, and the day was drawing late.

When they reached their accommodation, Magnus was pleased to see that it was as Brother Luke had described. It was indeed warm, dry, and clean. More importantly, it had thick stone walls, which meant that they might have a chance to talk privately with the mysterious physician.

It also had two beds. They were rather like the one that Alfread lay on in the Infirmary. James was beside himself with joy. Here was a chance that he would wake up on the morrow without those annoying knots and aches in his muscles! Or any unwelcome biting insects!

The two beds were separated by a rough trestle table on which a candle in a holder rested.

The novice returned with a large platter of bread and cheese and a couple of apples to savour as well. It felt like ages since either James or Magnus had eaten anything. Particularly fruit of any kind!

The novice put the food down on the table, and then placed a steaming jug of something that smelt fresh and minty next to the platter. He then rummaged in his robes and produced three clay beakers. James decided not to think about where they had been hidden. Sometimes it was definitely better not to know!

Brother Luke invited James and Magnus to sit down on the bed to eat the feast. He would join them to talk but would leave soon. He felt they should rest. He would eat later with his fellow monks in the refectory.

It was at this point that both James and Magnus realised just how hungry they were. They tore into the bread, ripping the rough-hewn slices with their teeth, and biting into the juicy apples. Brother Luke quietly watched on.

Both James and Magnus were young men and they quickly sated their hunger. Now they were thirsty.

Brother Luke filled the three beakers with the steaming liquid.

"I think you already know what this is," he said as he passed the beakers across, "But I know it from my own country, which is many, many miles away!"

As they took long gulps of the refreshing liquid, James realised that it was fresh mint tea, just as they had enjoyed when they had first arrived at Alfread's manor all those weeks ago.

Indeed, there was a lot they needed to talk about.

First of all, though, James wanted to know how Brother Luke knew that he was the Storyteller.

Brother Luke gave a very simple—even prosaic—explanation. No mystery at all.

James hadn't realised how his talent had been talked about, or how far his tales had spread.

In part, it was because James had told such rattling good yarns.

In part, it had happened because of the Battle of Stamford Bridge, where Alfread's men had laughed and joked with King Harold Godwinson's army.

After the battle, some of the wounded soldiers had been brought to the Infirmary. As they lay in the beds, having their wounds dressed, the men had told the monks about an amazing young Storyteller, who could tell a great tale. And that he possessed an ancient and mysterious Sword.

And so, Brother Luke knew who they were, and he had been told of the Mighty Sword of Eir.

But that was all he knew. Or so he told them.

But Brother Luke had a secret. A really big secret.

In truth, he knew all about the mystery of the Sword. But the time was not yet right for him to share this knowledge with James.

He wondered if James would show him the Sword. He really wanted to know if it was as magnificent as the wounded had said.

James gently pulled the Sword from its scabbard and lay it on the bed next to him.

Its amber eye glowed warmly.

Brother Luke gasped.

The Sword was as wonderful as he had heard.

"Is it true that you are a skilled Swordsman, but will only use the Sword to protect? You will not kill?"

James nodded.

"That is indeed a good thing. After all, our commandments say quite clearly that you shall not kill!"

To be honest, James hadn't looked at things in that way before. All he knew was that the thought of killing another human being made him feel very sick indeed and said so.

Brother Luke smiled. He could sense that he had learnt as much as he could for now.

Now it was his turn to tell his story.

The two young gentlemen sitting on the bed next to an empty platter of food were more than ready to listen.

Brother Luke began his tale.

As he had previously said, he was not from these parts.

In fact, he was from many, many, many miles away.

"My father was a trader in a far-off city known as Baghdad. We were rich and lived a happy life there. It was there that I first discovered my thirst for knowledge and learning!"

"You were in Baghdad in the Golden Age of Islam?" asked Magnus in wide-eyed wonder. He had read much about this time in his lunch hours in the British Museum Reading Room.

Apparently, at this time, Baghdad was part of what was known as the Caliphate. It wasn't ruled by a king, or a Lord, but by a Caliph. Which as far as Magnus could understand was not too different.

The city had a reputation as a centre of learning and had the most amazing collection of manuscripts, scrolls and books. All bursting with knowledge.

Brother Luke looked surprised.

"You know about Baghdad? You know about Islam?"

Magnus nodded. He turned to James and explained further.

"In this time, Baghdad is a very important city. It is a vibrant and bustling city. It is at the centre of trade. But it is also of the Islamic faith, and there are tensions between it and the Christian world."

Brother Luke was amazed.

"Your knowledge of my city and the religion of my birth is impressive. It is indeed clear that you must have travelled far and wide to know these things."

Magnus merely nodded again.

"Please do continue," he asked Brother Luke.

So, he did.

Brother Luke decided at an early age that he wanted to become a physician.

He learnt much from his teachers and experiences in Baghdad. Persian medicine was very advanced.

But Brother Luke felt that there must be still more to find out. The world was a big place, after all.

This was how his travels began.

First Brother Luke—or Manu as he was known then—decided to travel to Egypt. He had heard much about the ancient art of mummification, and he wanted to know more.

As well as preserving bodies, he wanted to explore whether the processes might be applied to the living in any way.

It had been difficult to find anyone who remembered the ancient ways though. But eventually he managed to trace a small group of practitioners. They were part of a hidden sect, living in the waste lands behind the old temple ruins at Thebes. The old religion was no longer acceptable to either Islam or Christianity, and they feared for their lives if they were ever found.

But the sect did possess the knowledge he sought. Amazingly, the devotees were willing to teach him their secrets, but on condition that he would never share them outside.

After several months with the sect, Manu took his leave. He still had more to discover.

He continued his journey until he reached Constantinople. It took him many, many days.

Once there, he was able to continue his education. Constantinople was another experience for the young man. Like Baghdad, it was a thriving metropolis where many different cultures and people crossed. As such there was even more to absorb.

But still Manu was not satisfied.

He decided to walk to Jerusalem. He had heard about Christianity and wanted to know more about this rival religion.

It was in Jerusalem that he found his Lord.

It all happened so quietly, so simply.

Manu decided to follow the road to Calvary, so he could see where this Jesus had died. On the way, he was struck by the sheer number of pilgrims, in bare feet—some sick, some with terrible injuries—all seeking the place where their Lord had died.

He reached the place—Golgotha it was called, or Place of the Skulls,—when he was suddenly blinded by a sharp ray of sunlight.

As his eyes recovered from the shock, he realised that the sunlight had been a sign from God.

Manu was baptised in the River Jordan, just as his Lord was. It was an incredibly special and moving ceremony.

He became a Christian.

But the baptism did not wash away his thirst for knowledge. Brother Luke, as he was now named, decided to stop his search for knowledge for its own sake, but to use what he already knew to help the sick and poor.

That wouldn't mean that he would stop learning. No one ever stops learning. But he would be able to apply his knowledge to help ease pain and suffering.

He did not know where he might begin his mission, and so he began to walk to Europe.

He met a trader on his journey who told him of the pain and suffering in the Island of England.

Brother Luke realised that God was speaking through that man that day.

He had no choice. God wanted him to go to England, and it was his bounden duty to obey.

And so, he came to York.

As Brother Luke came to the end of his amazing story, one of his novices came rushing in.

Alfread was trying to get out of bed.
The group rushed back to the ward.

Chapter 2.16
Recovery

The novice had reported correctly.

Alfread was trying very hard to get up but was being held down by two monks.

It was clear that he still did not realise that he had been injured, and even where he was.

As one of the novices held onto Alfread's arms, Alfread shouted "Ready my horse, ready my men. We have a battle to fight and fight to win…"

It was very clear that Alfread was still very confused.

"Methinks his brain is still addled from the fall," observed Brother Luke, "I fear it is going to be a long wait until he fully recovers!"

Privately and based on what he had just witnessed, James wondered whether Alfread ever would.

And if he didn't, would that mean that James had failed the Sword? And his mother?

Brother Luke noticed the worried expression.

"Try not to worry," he said, "I have seen men more addled than this recover completely. But it will take time. We still do not know what he can and cannot remember. We can't let him leave until he has fully recovered all his faculties. It would not be right."

James and Magnus were very relieved to hear Brother Luke's words.

There were so many reasons why they wanted Alfread fully recovered.

And many more why they did not want that to happen just yet.

Indeed, James quietly hoped that it would take two, perhaps even three weeks before Alfread healed. That way, the Battle of Hastings would be well and truly over before Alfread could even think about travelling.

In fact, it took a full four weeks before Alfread understood where he was, and another two before his memory fully returned.

During that time, James and Magnus busied themselves in the Infirmary. They both wanted to learn as much as they could from Brother Luke.

And Brother Luke loved willing pupils.

They learnt how to make soap using potash and tallow. It was a complex and tedious process, but the end result was used to ensure that the ward was washed clean at least twice daily. Brother Luke insisted!

James and Magnus watched as Brother Luke distilled alcohol from honey wine and used it to wash his medical instruments. It had to be said the process required a flame to heat the wine. As the resulting alcohol was highly flammable it was all quite dangerous. Magnus had whispered to James that watching Brother Luke was very similar to watching his old Chemistry teacher, just before he had set the laboratory on fire. Magnus and James made sure that they watched from a very safe distance!

Then there was the herb garden. It was brimming full of lush plants. Each one had its own use. Chamomile to help sleep, foxglove to aid heart disorders, and many more obscure but valuable plants for aiding the sick.

There was so much to learn that James almost forgot why they were there!

Thankfully, day by day, Alfread grew stronger. As he continued to improve, both James and Magnus knew that they needed to think about what should happen next.

After several weeks, Alfread was sufficiently recovered that he was allowed to take short walks.

It became quite a routine. James and Magnus would take it in turns to accompany the healing Lord around the Monastery grounds. There was much to see when the weather was fine.

On this day, it was James's turn to help Alfread stroll quietly through the courtyards.

As they ambled gently back towards the Infirmary, James heard a voice calling Alfread's name.

The couple turned to find the Good Knight standing there.

James was very surprised. The last time he had seen his sparring partner was as he followed the monks to the refectory when they had all arrived.

But that was several weeks ago.

Even then, Alfread's men were starting to look bedraggled and dirty. The Battle of Stamford Bridge had not been a clean encounter.

The man standing there now was in far worse condition than anyone of Alfread's men after the Battle.

James wondered if he brought news. And if he did, whether it would be welcome.

He felt the Sword start to glow against his chest. This was going to be important.

"How can we help you, Good Knight?" he asked.

"I have come to tell my news to the Lord Alfread. I also need to report back to the people of Holborne as to his state of health. I have much news to share."

"Then come," said James, "Let us return to the Infirmary. We will meet with Magnus and Brother Luke there. It will be safe to discuss whatever we need to."

Alfread said nothing. But it was clear that he had understood what the knight had said.

They rushed back to the Infirmary. Brother Luke and Magnus met them as they entered.

"Come, let us go to your lodgings," suggested Brother Luke.

It was a bit of a tight squeeze for all of them to fit in the tiny monk's cell. But they managed. They even made sure that Alfread had some space around him so that he would not feel too crowded.

Brother Luke smiled at the Good Knight.

"You are among friends here," he began, "And these walls are solid. No one will be able to overhear what you tell us!"

The Good Knight looked relieved. It seemed that he had bad news to impart. The worst.

Alfread's men had not managed to catch up with the King's army. But they did meet some of its soldiers as they fled the battlefield.

They told of a nasty, dirty, conflict. It made the Battle of Stamford Bridge seem like a child's game.

These Normans were not nice people at all.

The knight grew more and more agitated as he talked.

It was clear that there was worse news to come.

The King's army had reached Senlac Ridge in good time, but at a cost. The men were exhausted.

But there was no time to recover.

They had to march straight into battle.

The men fought valiantly, but the Normans were too strong.

Their archers were too accurate.

"When King Harold was killed…"

"Wait, and say again," begged Brother Luke.

The knight repeated the dreadful news that King Harold had been shot by an arrow.

This was indeed startling news.

If Harold had been killed what did that mean?

It meant that the country had a new king.

William the Conqueror!

Alfread's confused expression spoke for all of them.

What would happen now?

Magnus spoke first.

He spoke very carefully.

"James and I know of these Normans from our travels. You are indeed right that they are vicious thugs who want to exploit our land. But I fear that we will have to learn to live under them!"

James nodded in agreement. So far, Magnus hadn't departed from what the history books said.

Silence briefly fell as Brother Luke and Alfread absorbed the news.

Then, much to everyone else's surprise, Alfread spoke.

"You bring distressing tidings, my friend. But you also enable us to think about what we need to do next. I fear for my Manor and for my villagers. We must keep them safe as best we can."

No one disagreed with that. But the big question was "how"?

James could feel the Sword urging him to talk. To share his thoughts.

He held up his hand.

"Speak, James," encouraged Brother Luke.

James began by repeating what had just been said about how important it was to make sure the villagers were kept safe. His concern was that because Alfread had been aligned with Harold, the Normans might decide that the village should be punished.

And that must be avoided at all costs.

If it hadn't already, the Manor would soon be seized and given to one of William's knights as a reward. Alfread could not return.

For now, the Manor's Lord was absent, believed injured and recovering here, in York.

James looked thoughtful. He was just thinking out loud, you understand.

But what if the village believed that Alfread had not recovered? That he had died after being left at the Infirmary?

It would be clear to the Normans that Alfread's men had not fought at the Battle of Hastings. They tried to catch up with King Harold's army, but they were too slow. And now, they had all returned home, alive and well.

Perhaps the Normans would see that the villagers were not that loyal to Harold after all.

The Sword had told James in no uncertain terms that Alfread must be allowed to live. And to marry. And have children.

James coughed. He had to say something that would make Alfread understand why he must live. He wasn't too sure what to say. He quietly grasped the Sword's hilt and took a deep breath.

"My Lord, you know we are not from these parts. You know that we have seen and learnt many things in our travels. What I say next I say in the light of that knowledge."

The room was completely silent. All waited to hear what James said next.

"Until now, you have led a quiet, happy life. You love and are loved by your knights and your vassals. But things have changed seriously over the past weeks. Life is no longer the settled existence that you are used to. If you try to return to it, you will surely die. We cannot allow that to happen. It must not happen," James was becoming increasing agitated as he thought of his mother being a slave.

He spoke again, "Life is like throwing a pebble into a pond…"

Magnus looked at James. Had he lost the plot?

But no.

James continued, "The pebble drops into the water, and immediately sinks. But the ripples caused by the pebble spread out and disturb the whole pond.

I believe that you are like that pebble. What you do next may not seem very exciting now. But it will have a major impact on England's future in years to come. You must survive, find love, marry, and have children. And they, too, in time, will do likewise. In many years to come, it will be one of your descendants who will have a pivotal role in English history!"

Alfread looked like he had been hit across the face with a fish. The Good Knight looked extremely worried.

What James was saying was perilously close to magic. It was as if he was foretelling the future. And in a House of God at that!

Brother Luke did not appear at all perturbed by what James had just said. It was almost as if he had expected it.

He spoke next.

"There are many things in life that we do not understand and must take on trust. We do not know if the sun will rise at the start of the day, but we trust that it will. I believe that James is like that. We must take what he says on trust. If he says that Alfread must live for the good of our future, then we must do all we can to ensure that he does."

Magnus was amazed at how understanding Brother Luke was.

James had uttered words that could be considered heresy or witchcraft.

"You are truly a remarkable man, Brother Luke," he stated.

And so, thanks to Brother Luke's acceptance, Alfread and the Good Knight relaxed.

If it was important that Alfread should live, now it was time to think about how they might help Alfread escape.

He could never return to the Manor of Holborne. But Holborne was not the world. As Brother Luke had said, the world is a very big place.

Neither could Alfread remain here in York. Too many people knew that he was here.

The safest thing to do would be to spirit Alfread well away.

It would mean exile from his home and all that he knew, but he would live.

He would not die as a traitor.

But where could he disappear to?

For now, the most important thing would be to get Alfread far away from York and find him a safe place while he worked out what to do next.

James had an idea.

Did Brother Luke know of any religious houses where Alfread might seek refuge?

Alfread thought about this possibility briefly, then slowly nodded his head in agreement.

He didn't like the idea of never returning home but knew that it was the only way to protect him and the future. It had to happen.

It was Brother Luke's turn to look pensive.

"I believe that there is a group of friars heading towards Whitby. It's a small town on the coast, and not too far from here. But it is sufficiently small that it should not attract attention.

I think the friars are exploring whether they should set up a new mission there. Alfread could perhaps help?"

"But I wouldn't have to take Holy Orders, would I?" asked Alfread.

Going into exile was one thing, but he wasn't ready to become a monk.

Brother Luke smiled.

"Indeed no. The friars need help from lay people such as yourself, and that is what you can do. Offer help. You can read, you can write. You have watched me in the garden with herbs and observed me in the Infirmary. You could help teach the friars to read, you could share your herbal skills, or aid the sick and needy perhaps?"

The Good Knight held up his hand. He had a question.

"I realise that I have no ties to Holborne, other than my liege Lord, who is here and healing well."

He paused to smile at Alfread, "But I need to be clear. Will I ever be able to return to the Manor?"

Magnus spoke up.

"In time, most certainly. But I would strongly propose that you wait until the new regime has settled down and they are less likely to regard knights such as yourself as a threat. As you say, your first loyalty and duty is to Alfread. As we are all too aware, although he is much recovered, Alfread still has a little way to go before he is back to his robust self. You would be both helping Alfread and fulfilling your duty if you could stay with him until he is settled in his new life."

Magnus now wanted to think about details.

"We know what we need to do. Now we need to consider timing. If you, Good Knight, are here with this news, I fear that, even if they are not already here, it is only a matter of time before others arrive with the same information. They could be less friendly. They may even want to take Alfread prisoner for William to try as a traitor."

Brother Luke agreed. They had to move quickly.

"There is no time for delay. We must act swiftly. We need to smuggle Alfread out of the Infirmary tonight."

Chapter 2.17
Escape to the Country

Brother Luke quickly shared his plan.

For it to work, several things would have to happen. And quickly.

Brother's Luke's first task would be to write a note of introduction for Alfread and the Good Knight to take with them when they left.

That was the easy part.

The next part was for Alfread to leave the Infirmary and the Monastery. The safest time to do this would be under cover of darkness when the rest of the monks were at prayer and the city slept.

Alfread would have to leave on foot and hide until The Good Knight, and their horses, could rendezvous with him.

However, it was equally important that Alfread was not missed by the monks. And he could not be in two places at the same time.

Brother Luke's idea was risky, but it could work. It had to work.

Alfread would have to die.

Not really—but the good monks of the Monastery and the Infirmary must believe that he was dead.

Alfread would need to literally trust Brother Luke with his life.

Brother Luke would use his knowledge and skills to prepare a draft of medicine. It would have two effects.

The first dose of the tisane would make Alfread agitated and appear quite mad.

Then, he would fall into a deep sleep.

At this point Brother Luke and one of his novices would examine him and announce him to be dead.

The Infirmary preferred to bury its departed souls as quickly as possible after they had died, and so Alfread's "funeral" would take place on the following day.

Alfread would be placed in a coffin. The coffin—with Alfread inside—would be placed on trestles in the chapel's aisle. Brother Luke, accompanied by Magnus, James, and the Good Knight, would keep vigil through the night.

They would follow the coffin as it was carried from the Infirmary and into the chapel.

Magnus and James would carry Brother Luke's old cassock, hidden about their persons. The Good Knight would have sacks from the pharmacy secreted about him.

Alfread looked a little worried at this thought. He wasn't keen on being at his own funeral and did not relish lying in a coffin one little bit.

He particularly did not like enclosed spaces, whether he was asleep or not.

Brother Luke reassured him.

It was the Monastery's tradition that coffins were kept open until the deceased was buried. That way, those who kept vigil could watch for any signs of life. After all, even monks were known to make mistakes sometimes.

Once the coffin was on the trestles, the novice monks would leave and return to their prayers in the Cathedral. Only the friends and relations of the deceased would remain. In this case, that would be James, Magnus, and the Good Knight. And, of course, Brother Luke. The novices would not think this strange as they knew how hard Brother Luke has tried to save Alfread's life!

Rather than watch, though, Brother Luke would use the vigil to administer the antidote to Alfread and wake him up.

Once he was awake, they would have to work swiftly.

Alfread would dress in Brother Luke's old robes. They would be slightly too long, so he would have to take care not to trip.

Once the coffin was empty, James and Magnus would take some of the stones from the pile by the building works at the rear of the chapel.

They would wrap these in the sacking and place them in the coffin.

Brother Luke would use more of his knowledge to create a bad smell which would flood the chapel. The smell would give them the excuse to put the lid on the coffin as everyone would think it came from Alfread's body.

While they undertook these actions, Brother Luke suggested that Alfread leave the chapel and walk out of the Monastery through the gardens at the rear.

He had spent the past few weeks walking the Monastery grounds. He knew how to get out.

And there was nothing unusual about a lone monk walking the streets of York at night.

Alfread's "funeral" would be held on the morrow. He would be buried in the chapel graveyard.

As he was Lord of Holborn Manor, it would be a grand affair, with the Abbot presiding.

After that, James, Magnus, and the Good Knight would leave. They would take their horses, including Alfread's, and leave the Monastery and York.

"You three will need to ride for quite a distance away from York before meeting with Alfread," stated Brother Luke.

"Where shall we meet?" asked the Good Knight.

"I suggest that you make your way back to Stamford Bridge. It is not too far from here. I recall that Alfread's men were able to walk from there to here within a couple of hours. I believe that Alfread is fit enough to walk the return journey!"

James took up the train of thought.

"We three will leave the city together. But once we are away from prying eyes, I suggest that the Good Knight heads off to meet Alfread. We will return to Holborn with the sad news of Alfread's passing. We will also say that you, Good Knight, are undertaking a pilgrimage to Lindisfarne for his soul. It's a long way from York and will explain your absence.

However, in reality, you will head towards Stamford Bridge with Alfread's horse in tow.

Because you ride, even though you will depart York later than Alfread, you should both be at the battlefield at about the same time.

From there, you and Alfread can travel to Whitby and start your new life!"

It all sounded possible.

Now all they had to do was carry out the plan!

Brother Luke stood up and bustled out. He had robes to find and potions to concoct.

The others decided to have a gentle stroll around the Monastery grounds, just as they would do most days.

Only this time, they took the opportunity to make sure Alfread knew where he had to go once night fell. It also felt like the four men were saying goodbye to each other.

Which in a sense, James supposed, they were.

Even if everything went as they hoped, it was unlikely that he and Magnus would ever see Alfread again.

After ambling around the grounds for what felt to be hours, they all returned to James and Magnus's room.

Time did that strange thing again of passing both slowly and yet quickly.

It seemed to take for ever before Brother Luke returned with the robes and potion.

Alfread looked nervously at the beaker of liquid in Brother Luke's hands.

After reassuring him, Brother Luke told Alfread what was going to happen once he had taken the potion.

"The potion will begin to take effect about ten minutes after you drink it. I suggest that you head over to the latrines now before imbibing, and then we will walk down to the Infirmary. Good Knight, you will come with us. You will have to bring the news back to James and Magnus!

James, Magnus, you remain here until the Good Knight returns. Then simply follow your instincts and allow yourselves to be caught up in the drama!"

Alfread needed no ordering to head over to the latrines. He was terribly nervous!

However, he couldn't stay in there for ever. He finished what he had to do, and then purposely (and rather bravely) rearranged his clothes and headed back to Brother Luke.

Then, before he could change his mind, grabbed the beaker, and swallowed its contents in one go.

He handed the empty beaker to Brother Luke, looked across to James and Magnus.

"Thank you from the bottom of my heart for what you have done for me. I will always remain in your debt. I am sore sad to have to leave you."

Magnus coughed to cover up a sob, and James wiped his eyes. They must have had some grit in them.

The Sword throbbed reassuringly against James's chest, reminding him that this was the right thing to do.

Brother Luke led Alfread and the Good Knight back down to the Infirmary.

"Now we wait," observed Magnus.

"I doubt it will be for very long," replied James.

Even as he spoke, they heard the Good Knight clattering up to their room as if there was a fierce fire behind him.

"Come," the Knight shouted, as he burst into their room, "You must come at once. Alfread is having some sort of seizure, the like I have never seen before. Brother Luke is seriously concerned. We know not what to expect!"

Magnus and James didn't need telling twice. Either the Knight was a very good actor, or something had gone wrong.

They ran as quickly as they could to the Infirmary and towards a circle of monks.

They pushed through and saw Alfread writhing on the floor.

He had been violently sick, and his eyes were rolling back in their sockets.

Brother Luke was kneeling over Alfread. He appeared calm, but everyone present could feel the tension emanating from him.

"There will be time enough to ask what has passed when this has been sorted!" he said quietly to James and Magnus, "But we must try to get him to a bed."

Suddenly, Alfread became still.

Too still.

"Quickly," ordered Brother Luke, "Get him to the nearest empty bed so that I can examine him. Brother Mark, come with me. I will need your eyes and ears!"

It was clear that Brother Mark was delighted to be asked. He had spent many years as the physician's pupil. Now would be his chance to show everyone what he had learnt.

Once Alfread was laid on the bed, Brother Luke ordered the huddle of observers, including James and Magnus, back so that he and Brother Mark could see what they were doing.

Brother Luke followed the same process as Magnus had when Alfread had fallen from his horse. The response was exactly the same. But this time, when Brother Luke felt for a pulse, he couldn't find one. He asked Brother Mark to do likewise. He could not find one either.

Then, Brother Luke put the side of his face next to Alfread's nose and mouth.

"I do not believe he breathes. Brother Mark—what do you observe?"

Brother Mark produced a small mirror from his robes. He put it close to Alfread's nose and mouth.

"We will see a mist on the mirror if he breathes," he announced.

The mirror remained stubbornly clear.

Brother Luke turned to the Good Knight, and to James and Magnus.

"You have seen the tests that we have carried out. I think you will agree that we have been thorough."

They nodded. James was concerned that perhaps the potion had been too strong for Alfread. Perhaps it had indeed killed him.

Brother Luke behaved as James had seen him do when other such sudden demises had taken place in the Infirmary.

"If we are all in agreement, I must perform the Last Rites on this poor dead man. Then, Brother Mark, will you lay him out in one of our coffins? I will go and inform the Abbot!"

With that, the huddle of observers dispersed. Brother Luke conducted the solemn sacrament, after which he carefully put his stole away. Then he went to see the Abbot.

Brother Mark, meanwhile, instructed two of the other novices to bring him a coffin.

It all seemed to be so normal and routine.

Magnus whispered to James, "In these times, death was almost as common as birth. While it was still painful, it was far more matter of fact than we have become."

That didn't mean to say that either of them had to like it!

They moved to where Brother Luke had his table and stool so that they did not have to watch as Brother Mark could do what he needed to do to Alfread. But the Good Knight stood his ground, guarding his master.

By the time Brother Mark had finished, Brother Luke had returned. He was accompanied by the Abbot.

James and Magnus bowed low.

"We are humbled and honoured by your presence, My Lord," muttered Magnus.

James thought that he always seemed to know the right thing to say!

"Indeed, indeed," replied the Abbot who seemed very distracted.

James nudged Brother Luke and asked, "What's wrong?"

Brother Luke replied, "There are reports of a King's Messenger heading towards York. He has a mission to seek out those not loyal to William."

The Abbot looked up from viewing Alfread's body.

He announced to all standing there, "I had to view for myself. Alfread of Holborne is indeed dead. To one more cynical than I, I would say that this man's death is timely. We must bury him as soon as it is light tomorrow."

The Abbot them moved to Brother Luke and said, "We will bury him at dawn. The King's Messenger should not arrive before then. Once Alfread is disposed of, we should not have any problems entertaining the new regime."

Janes and Magnus looked at each other. Things were getting very serious and they would need to move quickly.

If Brother Luke could revive Alfread, that was.

And given the manner of his demise, they were not too sure that was possible.

Brother Luke gave the order for Alfread's body to be moved to the chapel. He also ordered two other novices to dig a grave in the cemetery next to the chapel.

The novices gathered up the coffin on their shoulders and reverently carried it into the chapel. Two trestles had been made ready for it to be gently lowered onto.

Brother Luke lit two candles, placed one at Alfread's head, and one at his feet.

The vigil had begun.

All but Brother Luke, the Good Knight, James, and Magnus remained.

It seemed to take for ever for night to fall.

But eventually, Brother Luke deemed it safe to move to the next stage of their plan.

He silently moved to the coffin, took out a small glass bottle and uncorked it. He opened Alfread's still mouth and poured the contents in.

Almost immediately, the coffin started to shake and Alfread coughed loudly.

"Shush!" ordered Brother Luke quietly, "We cannot afford to draw any attention to ourselves. Not with a King's Messenger on his way. We have to be even more swift than we had planned!"

He helped Alfread out of his casket.

James and Magnus quickly filled up the space as planned. Then they screwed on the wooden lid.

Meanwhile, Brother Luke helped Alfread into his old cassock.

Just as they had finished, they heard a movement at the chapel door.

"Quick," ordered Brother Luke, "Alfread, hide behind that stone pillar. If you are spotted, fold your hands so you look like you are at prayer."

Alfread scurried across to the pillar. James had to confess that it was almost impossible to spot him hiding there. The candlelight was so dim.

Brother Mark came through the chapel door. He was carrying two additional candles.

"I thought that you may need these," he said, "It's a long time till dawn!"

James breathed a silent sigh of relief, and he was fairly sure that the Sword did too!

After accepting the candles and thanking Brother Mark for his thoughtfulness, Brother Luke escorted him to the chapel door and closed it after he had left.

They all then waited for the longest period they had ever experienced. But they had to allow enough time for Brother Mark to return to the Infirmary before they did anything else.

Once it was safe to do so, Brother Luke opened the chapel door again, and beckoned to Alfread.

It was time.

"God's speed, my man!" he said as he hugged Alfread, "I believe you to be a good and kindly soul, It is vital that you go now and start your new life. Take a care. We will pray for you!"

James stepped forward. He too gave Alfread a hug.

Then he said, "Go and be safe, my Lord. It is vital that you escape and lead a long and happy life. You are a very important cog in the wheel of history…"

Alfread looked puzzled. This was a very strange farewell.

James quickly continued. He had to share his knowledge with Alfread now. This was the only chance.

"You, My Lord, will sire many children with the wife you have yet to meet. They, too, will go on to have many offspring. One of your future descendants has a vital role in destroying the evil trade of slavery in this fine country. But he will only do that if you survive and your life unfolds as it should…"

Alfread heard but he did not understand. And there was no time to ask more. He had to go.

He would ponder these words when he was safe and far away from William's men.

The Good Knight knelt before Alfread, and said, "I will be at Stamford Bridge as soon as I can. I will hoot like an owl when I arrive. As it will be light by then, you will know it is me and not the bird!"

With that, Alfread seemed to melt into the night.

"Come," said Brother Luke, "We still have things to do!"

They resumed their places around the now-sealed coffin.

"I have brought linen squares for you all. This smell will not be pleasant!"

He handed the squares to each of them. And then, making sure he had one held against his own nose, opened another bottle, and poured an oily substance underneath the coffin.

"If it is spotted, the monks will think that it has dripped from the coffin. Along with the vile smell..."

James started to sense the malodorous aroma weaving its way through the linen. It was disgusting. A sort of mixture of stink bomb and chemistry laboratory.

"They will not wait to bury the coffin. We will have this funeral completed as the sun rises."

Fortunately for all, things started to happen much sooner than they had expected.

The novice monks retuned to the chapel after completing their morning prayers in the Cathedral. Dawn was still an hour away.

But all were worried about the arrival of the King's Messenger.

The novices were not expecting the stench as they opened the chapel door. It was highly unusual. But then, Alfread's sudden demise had been peculiar. Perhaps this oozing of body fluids was linked to that.

No matter, they didn't want to waste any time finding out.

The smell clearly came from the coffin—which they had to carry—so they wanted to get things over with as quickly as they could!

The novices were amazed that the vigil was still taking place, given the evil smell!

Alfread clearly had inspired much loyalty and dedication.

The Abbot wasn't too far behind. He turned a funny shade of green.

He decided that he would make his announcement from just outside the chapel door, where the air was distinctly more pleasant.

"It is time for us to say our farewells to the dear departed Lord Alfread!"

With that, and trying to hold their breath, the novice monks picked up the coffin and carried it out to the graveyard. Brother Luke and the others followed.

As the Abbot recited prayers and readings, Alfread's coffin was gently lowered into the ground.

Brother Luke, the Good Knight, James, and Magnus each threw a small handful of soil onto it.

When they were finished, the Abbot invited them back to his rooms for a small meal. It wasn't just about being hospitable though. What the Abbot really wanted to know was when were they planning to leave. There was no reason for them to stay now that Alfread had passed. And given the imminent arrival of the King's Messenger, he felt it might be prudent for them to leave sooner rather than later.

James spoke first.

"Father Abbot, we are grateful beyond words for your kindness and patience. You granted us sanctuary in our hour of need. You permitted us to stay and help as Alfread recovered.

Sadly, although things seemed to be progressing well, it was not to be.

We are sad that our brother Alfread has gone ahead of us to meet his Lord but are truly thankful for your succour in this difficult time."

Magnus followed on.

"We are all too aware that we live in troubled times, and we have no wish at all to bring misfortune and pain on your house. We will leave you as soon as we can be got ready!"

This was just what the Abbot wanted to hear.

So much so that he already had ordered their horses to be made ready!

They said their farewells.

James took Brother Luke to one side.

"I must thank you from the bottom of my heart for everything, particularly your trust and understanding!"

Then, he carefully removed his St Christopher's medal—the only item he had with him other than the Sword from his time—and gave it to Brother Luke.

"Take this as a token of my esteem and gratitude. It is not much, but it means the world to me. It was a gift from my Great Aunt Pauline, a wise and clever woman! I believe that you would like her very much!"

Brother Luke was amazed.

But he also had a parting gift for James.

"I made this cross as I travelled from Jerusalem. Each night, before I lay down to sleep, I carved a little more. I was told that the wood came from the one true cross. I don't think it did. But this crucifix holds very special memories and is full of Christian symbology. It is very precious to me. I hope you will treasure it and think of me as you do."

James was deeply touched.

But time was against them.

James, Magnus, and the Good Knight left the Monastery with only minutes to spare.

Chapter 2.18
Return to Holborne

It felt to be a very long and lonely journey back to the Manor of Holborne.

James and Magnus could only hope that their plan to ensure that Alfread lived had worked. Certainly, the Sword gave every indication that it had. It lay warm and cosy in its sheepskin fleece, strapped tightly across James's chest.

The weather matched James and Magnus's mood. It was cold, damp, and drizzly.

"I suppose this is what an anti-climax feels like," observed James as they trotted alongside a beautiful little stream without noticing.

"I think so," replied Magnus, "But we still need to get home. For us to do that successfully, we need to return to where our adventures started. I can't see any alternative!"

Neither Magnus nor James knew what might greet them when they got to the village. Neither did they have any idea of how they might return to their own time.

All they could do was to return to Holborne and hope something would happen to them there which would get them back to all that was familiar again.

It felt to be a much-chastened country that they passed through. In part, no doubt, that was due to autumn turning to winter. But the mood of the country felt to have changed. In each and every town or village they passed through all was quiet. Almost as if they were holding their collective breaths. Waiting to find out what the new King would be like.

Would there be peace and stability? Would there be tyranny and over-taxation? For now, it was too soon to know. But the people wanted to, needed to know. Until they did, this uneasy calm would hang over them.

Eventually after several weeks of uninspiring riding, James and Magnus spotted the weaving curls of smoke that was Holborne on the horizon.

Now it was their turn to feel nervous.

They had no way of knowing what would greet them.

If they were fortunate, the village would remember their happy times, and the tales told and enjoyed. They would remember Alfread with love and mourn his passing.

Or, the Norman Knight could be in charge, and they would be taken prisoner and tried as traitors.

They rather hoped not. From what James remembered from his history books, traitors were considered the lowest of the low.

If they were found guilty, they would be hanged, drawn, and quartered. Even he didn't think the Sword would be able to magic them back to the 21st century if that happened.

They paused momentarily on the low ridge above the village. After a few moments, Magnus said, "Come on. We have to do it. The sooner we start, the sooner we will leave this uncertainty surrounding our fate."

They spurred their horses onwards and arrived at the village boundary.

It was a very quiet scene that awaited them. So very different to their entrance on St Swithun's Day, not that long ago.

The doors were closed, and windows shuttered. No children ran in the road, and no animals meandered across the thoroughfare. Only the lonely barking of a chained-up dog greeted their arrival.

James and Magnus rode on to the blacksmith's forge.

They dismounted and knocked politely on the door.

A blast of deliciously warm air greeted them as they entered inside.

The blacksmith was still doing what he did best. He was hammering out another horseshoe, which glowed red from being in the fire. Every time he hit it sparks flew in the air.

"Good Morrow, Master Blacksmith," said James.

The blacksmith looked up. He clearly had heard neither the polite knock nor them entering.

He put down his hammer and put his hands on his hips.

"'Tis the Storyteller and his Manservant, back again!" he stammered in amazement, "We thought that we would never see you in these parts again!"

He bade them sit on two stools by the roaring fire.

"How go things in Holborne, Master Blacksmith?" asked James.

The blacksmith sighed.

"Much has happened since you rode to Stamford Bridge," he began, "But before I tell you of what has passed, pray tell, do you have any news about our Lord Alfread?"

James and Magnus looked at each other and slowly shook their heads.

"I fear that we bring bad news," said Magnus.

The blacksmith staggered slightly and sat down.

"Please do tell. The village must know. Our fate depends on it!"

Magnus was sorrowful. He knew that this news would not be welcomed.

"You may have heard that our Lord Alfread fell from his horse after the Battle of Stamford Bridge. He was sorely injured. My master and I, together with some of your fellows from the village, took him to an Infirmary in York. I presume the men have now returned back here?"

The blacksmith nodded slowly.

James took up the tale.

"For the next few weeks, our Lord Alfread made good and solid progress. We all thought that he would recover and be able to return here. But, several days ago, I am sad to report that our Lord Alfread had a major relapse. He had some sort of seizure. He foamed at the mouth, writhed in agony and then was still. I am afraid that he passed that day."

Both James and Magnus looked bereft. James had made it sound as if Alfread had died. But he didn't actually say it.

All that James had said was true.

It was just that he had chosen his words very carefully!

Magnus continued the story again.

"Lord Alfread's Good Knight was with him when he passed. But so sorrowful and shocked was he that he decided that he must make a pilgrimage to pray for your lord's soul. We understand that he is going to the Island of Lindisfarne in the far north where he will pray and say masses.

He gave us the task of returning here to tell you all of what has happened."

The blacksmith wiped his brow and looked sad.

"I am sore sad to hear that my Lord has passed," he began, "but I think that it is perhaps for the best. The new King has given us a new Lord who now lives in the Manor. We haven't seen much of him, but we understand that we must be careful. He has a mission to root out any supporters of King Harold Godwinson."

James and Magnus looked at each other. It was as they had feared.

They would need to tread very carefully.

But before they had a chance to tread anything, two burly soldiers burst into the blacksmith's forge.

They roughly grabbed James and Magnus.

The larger of the two thuggish men announced loudly, "We are arresting you on behalf of the Lord of Holborne Manor. We have tracked you for the past week and believe that you are aligned with the traitorous Lord Alfread. You will come with us!"

Magnus and James looked at each other.

They didn't have a choice!

The blacksmith went back to bashing the half-finished horseshoe with his hammer. He was keeping well out of things.

James and Magnus understood. It was safer this way.

They could not see anyone at all watching their passage to the Manor, flanked by the two thugs. But they could feel that they were being observed from behind every shuttered window of the village.

James hoped that the blacksmith—or someone else from the village—would be able care for their horses. The horses had served them well. They were valuable creatures. And James doubted that he or Magnus were likely to see them ever again.

The group walked onwards, along the path James and Magnus had trod with Alfread in happier times.

Eventually, they reached the Manor House, and crossed the moat into the house itself.

They felt, rather than saw, the Manor's drawbridge closing behind them.

Whatever was happening to them did not appear to be good.

James grasped the hilt of the Sword, hoping for some sort of sign that he should not worry. But the Sword remained resolutely still.

James and Magnus were pushed, rather than led, into the Great Hall. It was so very different from their first visit, when the feast of St Swithun was taking place.

Now it was a sombre, chilly, space only dimly lit by flares set into the solid stone walls. At the far end, seated on a simply carved but oversized chair, sat someone who could only be the new Lord of the Manor.

The thugs forced James and Magnus to kneel.

The new Lord looked disgusted by what was in front of him. Then he turned to the two thugs.

"You have done well this day," he said, "You have captured the two traitors who we know were with Alfread in York. Take them to the dungeons where you can find out more about what really happened in the Infirmary."

The two thuggish soldiers grinned a broken-toothed smile.

James and Magnus looked at each other.

This was not good at all.

Why wasn't the Sword doing something to help them? They had done its bidding after all. And at great cost to themselves.

Now, it looked as if they were going to be tortured regardless.

As they were being manhandled towards the dungeons, someone else clattered into the Great Hall. He was clearly in a great rush.

"My Lord, I am sorry to be so late," the person said as he bowed, "Bad weather in Yorkshire delayed my journey. But I have returned as quickly as I could. I have news about Alfread. And it is good."

The thugs stopped their pushing. They wanted to hear what this person had to say.

James and Magnus realised that this was the King's Messenger who they had just managed to avoid when they left York.

"I arrived in York and made haste to the Infirmary, where Alfread was reported to be hiding," he began, "but I arrived too late!"

"Continue," ordered the new Lord, "I arrived just after Alfread had been buried. I asked the Abbot to dig up the coffin as it had just been laid in the grave. I wanted to be sure that he was indeed dead! I wanted to spit on his cold dead face!"

The new Lord of the Manor nodded his approval.

James and Magnus were now seriously worried. What had happened next? Had their plan been uncovered?

"The Abbot agreed that we could exhume the coffin. I ordered the novices to start digging. They were unhappy to do so, but I gave them no choice."

"Go on," came the order.

"As the novices dug, a foul stench began to permeate through the soil and around us. The novices reported that they had experienced the same smell as they lay Alfread's rotting corpse to rest. The smell was so disgusting in its intensity, I decided that I had seen enough. The smell could not have come from any living thing, and I was sore afraid that I would not be able to hold my guts down if we exposed more!"

196

James felt a sudden throb from the Sword.

Brother Luke's super stink had lasted long enough to make the King's Messenger feel ill. The plan had worked so far.

Now all he and Magnus could hope for was that they would not be tortured.

The new Lord absorbed this new information.

"You bring excellent news," he decided, "And you have travelled quickly in terrible weather to make sure I heard it as soon as possible. Go to the kitchens and eat. You have done well!"

With that, the King's Messenger was dismissed.

"Now, where was I?" he muttered.

One of the thugs coughed.

"Ah yes," he remembered.

"Take these traitors to the dungeons where they can enjoy our hospitality tonight. But do not harm them…"

The two thugs looked disappointed.

"I have another job for you once they are locked up. And do this job quickly. I need you back here as soon as you can. I require you to build a bonfire!"

James and Magnus looked at each other again.

"Tomorrow we will burn these two traitors at the stake in full view of the village. It will be a timely lesson for them. They will see what happens to those who are traitors!"

The thugs seemed happy with that proposal and began to push and shove James and Magnus down a stone stairway to the smelliest, most filthy cell that they could have imagined.

One thug held James while the other unlocked a set of manacles which were fixed to the wall. Then James had them fitted around his wrists and ankles. They repeated the exercise with Magnus.

Once the thugs were satisfied that neither prisoner could escape, they slammed shut the cell door and locked it.

James and Magnus really were in trouble now, and there didn't seem to be any escape!

"At least we still have the Sword," said James.

"But it seems to have abandoned us in our hour of need!"

"Hold the faith," replied Magnus, "I am sure things will work out!"

James nodded, but privately wished that he could share Magnus's confidence.

Yet again, time did that strange things of passing both incredibly slowly and in the blink of an eye.

The thugs were back before James and Magnus knew it.

They unlocked the manacles on each of them, and then tied James and Magnus's hands behind their backs again.

James and Magnus were pushed and shoved back up the spiral stone stairway and into the manor courtyard.

A terrifying scene greeted them.

By the drawbridge, the villagers had been gathered together, flanked by more of the new Lord's soldiers. Directly ahead was an enormous bonfire with a stake at the centre of it.

Dawn was just breaking. It was an angry sky. It felt like a storm was brewing. Not that James or Magnus cared. They were far more concerned with what was unfolding in front of them.

It was definitely the stuff of nightmares, only it was real!

James and Magnus were forced onto the bonfire and tied to the stake.

There was still no reaction from the Sword. It merely nestled against James's chest, as if it, too was awaiting a fiery fate.

One of the thugs began to pour a black gooey liquid around their feet.

Magnus turned to James and said, "That's pitch! It will help us burn better!"

Thanks for that. Trust Magnus to be a scholar right to the end! James did not need to know that fact!

All the while, the Sword was silent.

The sky grew darker and more threatening.

At the command of the Lord of the Manor, the other thug loosened a flare from the wall.

He brought it to the Lord.

As he put the flame to the bonfire, the Lord announced to the crowd, "Take note, all of you! I am a fair man. But I will not tolerate traitors. This is their due punishment!"

The flames started to ignite the wood.

James took his chance to address the crowd while he still could.

"Go in peace," he shouted, "Stay calm and be loyal to your new Lord. It is the only way."

The flames were starting to rise higher.

As they did so, the wind started to blow hard, and there was a distant rumble of thunder.

James felt the heat starting to burn through the soles of his sandals.

He prayed that this would be quick.

The storm hit.

A flash of lightning……

Chapter 2.19

Back in Time

"Wake up, James."

James wondered what was going on.

He nervously opened an eye.

The last thing he remembered was the heat of the fire eating through his sandals and the smell of thick black smoke.

He coughed.

The air seemed surprising clean. No hint of charcoal at all.

Where was he? He certainly wasn't in the middle of a bonfire, that much was for sure.

He gingerly opened the other eye.

All he could see as his eyes came into focus was a bright light.

"Where am I?" he groggily asked.

But there was no answer.

James could sense that there was a lot of excitement around him though, What on earth was going on?

After what felt to be an absolute age, his eyes saw a most welcome vision.

Perhaps he had been burnt alive and was now in heaven? Or somewhere like it at least?

"Welcome back," said the vision, "You and your partner in crime had us all worried for a while!"

Now James was really confused.

He felt, rather than saw, someone bend over him and fit some sort of contraption round his arm and put another block of something on his finger.

The band round his arm tightened then loosened.

James realised that he wasn't dead. He was having his blood pressure taken. And that sort of thing most definitely didn't happen in the 11th century.

The bright light was a fluorescent light, and the heavenly vision was an Intensive Care Nurse!

Someone else entered the room. She was wearing a white coat. She noted down the readings, and then looked at him.

"What do you remember?" she asked.

Although he was still quite groggy, James thought it best just to tell her about what he recalled of what had happened before he ended up in 1066.

"I remember Magnus, I mean Dr Ivar, handing me the Might Sword of Eir to hold. It was a special honour. I am not sure why he chose me. But I can't tell you what happened after that!"

The doctor wrote it all down, muttering, "Good, good."

Then she looked up again.

"You've been unconscious for a couple of days," she said, "But seem to be recovering well now. Rather like your colleague, Dr Ivar!"

James needed to know more.

"Where am I? And how did I get here?"

"You're in the Intensive Care Unit at St Thomas's hospital. It's the one closest to the British Museum. We think that there was a power surge just as Dr Ivar handed you the Sword. The electricity formed a circuit using you, the Sword and Dr Ivar as conductors. Between the three of you, you managed to black out most of Holborn! You and Dr Ivar were knocked unconscious. It was similar to you being hit by a thunderbolt or flash of lightning. You were both lucky not to have been killed."

"So, what happened then?"

The doctor consulted her notes then continued.

"Electricity must always find a way to earth. In this case, we believe that the power surge flowed first through Dr Ivar, then the Sword, and lastly through you and into the ground via your foot. You will see that you have a very nasty burn there!"

James peered down at his foot. It was covered by a blanket so all he could see was a lump at the bottom of the bed. It was quite painful when he tried to move it.

What about Dr Ivar?

The doctor was able to reassure James that he, too, was recovering well. He had just regained consciousness too. The doctor thought it was strange that they both came round at the same time, but then, strange things happen, don't they?

The doctor was delighted with their progress and hoped that they would both be able to go home in a couple of days if they continued to do so well.

At this point, the doctor went to the door, saying, "I think there are a couple of people who want to see you now!"

James struggled to sit up. When he looked round, his mother was by the side of his bed, and surprisingly, so was his Great Aunty Pauline.

James had thought, nay, hoped, that his mother would be there. But Great Aunty Pauline? The last he had heard, she was still at the university up north, translating the writing on the Mighty Sword of Eir. It was a long trip to get to London, especially at her age. She was no spring chicken!

"You have had us all quite worried," said his mother as she tried not to cry.

Great Aunty Pauline was more pragmatic. She suspected there was more to this accident that might be thought.

"I am here because I think you might have things to tell us…"

That one sentence told James everything he needed to know as to why she was here.

She knew that the Sword had been up to something and she wanted to know all the details.

Well, that could come later.

For now, James was so glad he was back where he should be. And even better, he was unsinged, apart from his foot, of course.

James's mother couldn't stop herself. She hugged her son so tightly that the doctor had to remind her that James had only just come round.

James had to confess that he didn't care. Being hugged by his mother after all he had been through was the best medicine he could have hoped for.

While she was hugging him. James tried to feel round her neck.

Was there a metal collar round it?

Or had they succeeded?

Relief—his mother was exactly as she should be! Not a hint of metal!

She reassured James that Dr Ivar was recovering well in the next room.

But was there any news about the Sword?

James would hate to think that it had been damaged by all that had happened.

Great Aunty Pauline answered that question almost as it was forming in his mind. He recalled that she was very good at that!

"You will be pleased to know that the Mighty Sword of Eir is completely undamaged by the power surge. When you collapsed on the floor the Sword landed on your chest!"

James was amazed but not surprised to hear this. After all, he had been wandering around the 11th century with the Sword strapped across his chest! Probably in the same position as it had fallen two days ago.

The doctor didn't want James to get overtired. But she could see that he was full of energy. It was clear that he would benefit from having a few more moments with his relatives without her hovering in the background.

The doctor decided to use her discretion. She told James that it was time for her to check on her other patients. She told James that she would be back to see him before she finished her shift. Then she left.

All too soon, a bell rang somewhere in the distance.

A nurse bustled in.

"I'm afraid it's time for you to leave now!" she said to James's mother and to Great Aunty Pauline, "There is every chance James will be sufficiently better that we can move him to the main ward this evening. Then, tomorrow, you will be able to visit him for as long as you want and when you want! Call us when you get home to find out what's happening!"

James 's mother gave James another kiss, moved to the door, and waved her goodbyes.

Great Aunty Pauline merely said, "I look forward to learning more!"

Then she left too.

Chapter 2.20
Epilogue

James, Magnus and Great Aunty Pauline were sitting in the British Museum's seminar room.

It had taken some time to organise a place where they could meet and talk in privacy. None of them felt that what they needed to talk about should be overheard.

Apart from anything else, and despite all the historical detail, there was no doubt that James and Magnus's story sounded wacky, even to academics.

And both Great Aunty Pauline and Magnus were all too aware that academic credibility could be destroyed in a moment but take years to build up again. Their reputations as serious scholars could be compromised!

Great Aunty Pauline had listened to James and Magnus tell of what had happened to them after the power surge.

The details were amazing to hear.

Great Aunty Pauline's ears really pricked up though when James started to talk about how their clothes had been changed to match the era. James was still upset that he had not been able to keep hold of his trainers, even though he fully understood that they would not have fitted into the 11th century at all.

James also mentioned that he had been deeply embarrassed when the hospital had returned the clothes that he had been wearing before the power surge. They had had to be cut off him and were now essentially rags. It had been just as well he had been wearing his school uniform as he wouldn't be needing it now, he had finished school for good.

However, and much more interestingly, when his mother had gone through the ruined uniform before she threw it out, she had discovered a beautifully carved wooden crucifix.

Naturally, she had asked James where it had come from as she didn't recognise it.

But James did.

It was the cross carved by Brother Luke during his travels around Europe.

At this point, James handed the crucifix over to Great Aunty Pauline.

It was a truly wonderful object. It was in the medieval style. But it looked like it had only recently been carved—which was even more amazing!

Great Aunty Pauline looked a little worried.

"How on earth was that allowed to return with you?" she wondered, "From what I understand of the Sword, you are not allowed to bring anything between times. The runes are quite clear on this. It is how the Sword is able to bend time. Things have to be kept in balance. I hope you haven't accidentally caused an imbalance—that could undo the good you have done!"

Magnus suddenly remembered a detail that they had both forgotten about.

"Didn't you give your St Christopher's medal to Brother Luke?"

James nodded.

"Then we should be fine. The exchange of your medal for the cross means that we have balanced things out!"

Great Aunty Pauline kept quiet. She thought they were right but made a mental note to keep her fingers crossed!

Brother Luke, the cross, and how James had acquired it prompted Great Aunty Pauline to remember a dig that she had been involved in. It had taken place in York over fifty years ago, long before her collaboration with Magnus, and many years before James was born!

York had been in the throes of an economic boom. The dig had been part of what was known then as "rescue archaeology".

That meant, she explained to James, that the land that the archaeologists were going to dig up would be developed once the dig had finished. Whatever was in there buried in the ground would be destroyed. It was vital to find out as much as possible before that happened. It was the only chance.

At the time, Great Aunty Pauline's team had hoped that it would provide evidence about the impact of the Vikings just after the Romans left.

"But that was well before 1066!" exclaimed James.

"Yes, it was. But as you know, we have to dig through many layers to reach the one we want to examine," Great Aunty Pauline replied.

James nodded.

"We were on the site of an ancient Monastery, which had been destroyed during Tudor times. We had to dig down though nearly a thousand years of archaeology.

The top layers were fairly boring and didn't really tell us very much that we didn't know already. We uncovered a lot of broken tiles and crockery from the 19th century, but nothing of real interest.

However, as we dug deeper, we uncovered a mystery which remains unsolved to this day."

Magnus and James sat quietly as Great Aunty Pauline told her tale.

She might be in her eighties, but Great Aunty Pauline was still as bright as a button and had an amazing memory for details.

And there were records to back up what she was saying—so they could check if they wanted to!

She paused to clean her glasses and then continued with her story.

"As they dug deeper, my team realised that they were uncovering an ancient cemetery. The archaeologists decided to take a little more care as it became clear that it was a monastic resting place from about the 10th—11th century. Although it wasn't our first choice of research, we knew that it was important for two reasons…"

James and Magnus were all ears.

Great Aunty Pauline continued

"The first reason it was important is that we didn't know very much about burial traditions and practices of that time. This excavation was an excellent chance to find out more.

Secondly, and perhaps most importantly, this would be our only chance to explore what that the layer contained.

As well as needing to dig through it to reach our fifth century layer, the whole site was going to developed into a shopping centre shortly afterwards."

Great Aunty Pauline paused again, then added as an aside, "At least those were the original plans. But as you know, sometimes things can and do change quickly. After we had completed the dig, it was decided that there was far too much information still there for it to be destroyed and so it all became part of the Jorvik enterprise!"

Great Aunty Pauline was referring to a major museum and continuing archaeological dig which was now a major tourist attraction in the city. Indeed, it had been so successful in raising money to support the research that other major digs had followed its example. James remembered that it had been the model on which the Eirby Hoard museum and dig had been based.

Great Aunty Pauline told of how the team had carefully excavated all the graves that they found. They didn't expect to find skeletons in all of them. After all, the graves were a thousand years old. Their contents had been in the ground for a long time and bone doesn't survive that well. Which was all well and good, until they came to dig out one grave in particular.

The archaeologists hadn't expected to find any bones. But they certainly hadn't been prepared to uncover a line of large stones, which at some point appeared to have been wrapped in some form of material!

James and Magnus looked at each other.

Great Aunty Pauline smiled.

"I know it's not proof of what you say happened. But it is rather strange, don't you think, that the dig found a grave left has you have just described to me?"

Indeed!

It was time to make a move.

The British Museum had long since closed.

Only they, a few intrepid researchers, and curators, and of course, the trusty security guards were left in the building.

"I don't suppose we could have one quick look at the Sword before I go home?" asked Great Aunty Pauline.

Magnus smiled at his former boss and agreed.

"It would be very impolite if we left without saying a quick hello!" he agreed.

James felt a small qualm, bearing in mind what had happened the last time he had viewed the Sword.

However—it had to be said that while it had put them into some pretty hairy situations—it had also managed to extract James and Magnus from them as well!

But James was not going to handle that Sword in any way, shape, or form just in case.

Not until he was ready. And the way he felt at that moment, that wouldn't be for a long, long, time. He still thought that the Sword could have found another way to transport them back home. Being burnt at the stake was just a bit excessive!

Magnus led the way from the seminar room, through the winding corridors and to the service door to the Eirby Hoard display.

He punched the security code into a keypad by the door.

It opened and he walked in, followed by Great Aunty Pauline and James.

The Sword seemed to be bathed in its own light as Magnus switched on the lights.

Great Aunty Pauline stood directly in front of it and breathed deeply.

It had been a while since she had seen the Sword, but it had lost none of its mystery and charm.

James stood quietly to one side. He could feel the Sword's pleasure at seeing its friends. He could also sense that all was calm.

Great Aunty Pauline gave the Sword one of her looks and said "You really led these two a merry dance, didn't you? But it all seems to have worked out. And it has meant that I have been able to see you again after all these years. You are still so much more impressive than your photos!"

Was Great Aunty Pauline flirting with the Sword?

James could swear that the Sword's amber stone winked at her!

With that, Great Aunty Pauline turned back to Magnus and James.

"Come on, boys," she said, suddenly all briskness and efficiency, "I have a train to catch!"

"And if I miss it, I won't be back in time for tea!"

Part Three
The Man

Chapter 3.1
The Oxford Exhibition

It was the Exhibition the world had been waiting for.

The British Museum had worked hard with its counterparts in the UK and across Europe to bring together the first pan-European interactive Exhibition of "Life as a Viking—warts and all". It had worked closely with the University of Oxford. Its world-famous experts in the both the Archaeology and History of Art departments, had been pivotal to the overall structure and staging of the Exhibition at various key establishments across Europe.

The narrative built on the Jorvik concept where everyday life was depicted alongside recovered artefacts. It was a multi-layered concept, layering class and social strata within the Nordic culture through time and space. After all, the Vikings had been a major influence across Europe for over 600 years.

Now, it was possible through interactive software to be a fly-on-the-wall in rich and poor households alike. Visitors could track the development and spread of Viking technology and trade in seemingly real time, complete with smells and sounds.

It was now possible to virtually visit the Exhibition in real time and space as well as use the technology to further enhance the experience at the Exhibition proper.

The virtual reality techies had excelled themselves. The reviews said it all.

"The next best thing to travelling through time"—The Sunday Times, UK

"The one historical show you must not miss"—The New York Times, USA

"Like living the dream"—the Sydney Morning Herald, Australia.

The list of stellar reviews seemed both endless and five-star.

After travelling, almost fairground- or circus-like across the globe, visiting venues in London, New York, Paris, Munich, Canberra to name but a few stops, it had reached its final stage.

It returned to where it had started—the University of Oxford's Ashmolean Museum.

Like all good things, it had to come to an end. The individual museums and collections wanted their exhibits back, after the extended period of a four-year loan.

The permanent staff who had organised and managed local temporary help at each stop-over were looking forward to a nice long rest. Four years is a long time to be on the road!

Included in that cohort was Dr Ivar of the British Museum.

As a young man, he had been the fast-tracked protégé of the famous Emeritus Professor Holden. Even now, as she reached the second half of her eighties, she was still publishing erudite and learned analyses of the Eirby Hoard, and its mysterious links to the now famous Codex Eiricus.

Dr Ivar had been there from the start of this mammoth project and was now a celebrated expert in his own right.

After his long and dedicated research and conservation of the Eirby Hoard, the British Museum Board of Directors could think of no one better equipped to guard their precious contribution to this global collaboration.

So it was that Dr Ivar and the Eirby Hoard had circumnavigated the globe to display its complex content.

Dr Ivar's primary task was to ensure the safe keeping of the Hoard's most prized object.

The Mighty Sword of Eir.

This beautiful and well-preserved weapon was the centre piece of the global exhibition and all but worshipped wherever it went. It even had its own fan club in America.

As well as the amazing runic messages etched into the Sword's blade, the Sword possessed a silver hilt into which a perfectly formed amber stone was set.

The Sword was at least 1300 years old. It was part of the Eirby Hoard but had not been discovered with it.

Its discovery was still a bit of a puzzle. According to the records, it had been found in a tree trunk by an eight-year-old boy and his Great Uncle. The tree was close to the archaeological dig where everything else had been uncovered. But it wasn't actually part of it.

By pure co-incidence, so the story went, the young boy had had the good fortune to give the Sword directly to Emeritus Professor Holden who had immediately recognised what it was.

Since that fateful day, all those years ago, much had happened. Emeritus Professor Holden and her team had established strong collaborative links with the British Museum as a result.

Of course, there was another not-so-public story. Emeritus Professor Holden was the young boy's Great Aunt. It was her great-nephew, James, who had found the Sword with his Great Uncle. They had been playing truant from the Great Uncle's 70th birthday party and gone exploring.

Dr Ivar was the first person to see the Sword once it had been found. He had been on the Eirby dig and had come immediately to the party to collect the Sword from Great Aunty Pauline so that it was kept safe.

Since that fateful day, Great Aunty Pauline had become much more than a distant relative. She was most definitely James's mentor and adviser.

Dr Ivar and James's paths had crossed again during the Holborn Power Surge. James had been on an end-of-school trip to the British Museum. Dr Ivar was showing the class around when the power surge hit. Both he and James had been injured and had had to go to hospital.

There was also a lot more that had happened to the two of them. But that was most certainly not in the public domain.

Suffice to say, James and Dr Ivar had formed a solid friendship as a result. Emeritus Professor Holden—or Great Aunty Pauline—had encouraged this. She was getting on, much as she didn't want to admit it, and knew that James would need someone else as well as her to advise him as he grew up. She was sure that Dr Ivar's wise counsel would be welcomed.

Dr Ivar had been so important in helping James in the aftermath of the Holborn Power Surge.

Now, he and James were very much on first name terms!

After things had settled after the power surge, James and Dr Ivar had gone their separate ways.

Dr Ivar returned to his work on the Eirby Hoard, before being picked to take it round the world.

After his experiences at the British Museum, James went to the University of Oxford. What he really wanted to study was a degree in science-based archaeology. But Oxford didn't offer that.

Instead, he thought about studying archaeology. After all, he had studied history at "A" level. But it was an extra subject that he had taken because he enjoyed it. His other subjects had been chemistry, physics, and maths.

James briefly considered studying for a degree in physics. But he had struggled a bit with maths at "A" level, and he thought that degree-level mathematical requirements might be a little too demanding.

After much thought, he opted to study Chemistry. It would provide him with the foundation knowledge to better understand science-based archaeology.

He had had to undertake a placement during his study. Usually students would opt to work in pharmaceuticals or other universities. But James decided to try and fulfil his dream of working in science-based archaeology. He'd got a placement in one of the facilities at the University and enjoyed every moment, even the most tedious ones! He learnt an awful lot.

Now, as the Viking Exhibition returned to Oxford, James had just completed his final year and gone home to await his results, and hopefully, graduation.

It was at this point that Dr Ivar called him.

He didn't need to tell James who it was. After all they had been through, he would know Magnus's voice anywhere!

Dr Ivar didn't even bother with a "Hello!"

"I'd like to offer you a temporary job! I need a reliable and knowledgeable person to help me with packing and shipping the Viking artefacts back to their homes," were his opening words.

James was immediately interested. He hadn't had a chance to visit the Exhibition at all because he'd been so busy with his studies. He had had to revise and revise and revise. With only sleep in between. Now Magnus was offering him an opportunity to see it, and from a professional rather than public view.

James was most definitely interested in taking up Dr Ivar's offer of a job. Even if it was just packing away the exhibits prior to shipment back to their original museums, he would get to see them in much closer detail than the public had.

It would also mean the possibility of a reunion with another old friend.

The Mighty Sword of Eir.

If it had plans, it would need him.

Chapter 3.2
Reunion

Four years had passed since James had last seen either Dr Ivar—or Magnus as he had come to know him—and the Sword.

The three of them had had a scary adventure when all of them had last been together.

There was a very good reason for this.

The Sword held magical powers. It could, in the right circumstances, bend the fabric of time and space. Many years ago, when James had found the Sword, he realised that the Sword had chosen him to be its Keeper.

The Sword could not exercise its powers without its Keeper. And for reasons only known to the Sword itself, it had selected James to take on this responsibility.

From before James had found the Sword, he had experienced its mysterious gift.

The first time he had been exposed to the Sword's abilities was when he was a mere seven years old. He had made friends with a local lad who lived in the same town as his Great Aunty Marion. James had been staying with her during the school holidays and had gone to the park because he was bored.

It was there that he made friends with Gordon who was a whole year older than him and was heaps of fun. They vowed to meet up the following year, which they did. Only while James was now eight, his friend Gordon turned out to be his Great Uncle and 70 years old!

Oh yes, even then, the Sword had wielded its powers.

His Great Uncle's wife, who was also Emeritus Professor Holden, was a world-renowned expert on the Viking culture. She had winkled the mystery from her husband after he and James had given her the Sword they had found. She had realised that something strange was afoot which could not be explained away by academic theories or science. It was good, old fashioned magic. And so, she became James's mentor, and helped him adapt to accommodate his newly acquired responsibilities. No mean task!

Four years ago, Magnus had taken on some of that task.

Between Magnus and Great Aunty Pauline, they had played a vital role in helping James understand the vivid dreams he sometimes experienced when the Sword required action to be taken.

Most recently, Magnus had been there with during the Holborn power surge, when they were transported back to the 11th century.

So not surprisingly, James felt his trepidation growing as he travelled back to Oxford to take up his temporary job. He felt under his tee shirt for the delicately carved wooden crucifix that he always wore. He was reassured by the feel of wood under his hand. James remembered how Brother Luke had given him this precious carving just before James and Magnus had left the priory in York, back in 1066. It had become his good luck charm, and James did not feel safe without it.

He touched it as he boarded the train for Oxford. He stroked it as the fields rushed by. James wondered what had happened to Brother Luke. Did he still remember the Storyteller and his Manservant? Did Brother Luke still have the St Christopher's medal that James had given him? All these questions, but no answers.

To be honest, James wasn't sure that he really needed to know.

Enough of looking back, James decided that he must look resolutely forwards.

It would be lovely to meet up with Magnus and catch up properly.

But what did the Sword want?

While the Sword had been travelling across the world, James had been free of any visions. But the closer James now came to Oxford, the more conscious he became of the Sword's influence.

He could feel it pulling at him.

By the time James stepped on to the station platform at Oxford railway station, he was sure that there was something afoot.

The Sword had plans and it needed him to make them happen.

James didn't have long to feel nervous though. As he reached the ticket barrier, Magnus was waiting on the other side.

"Long time, no see!" he greeted, "Come on, I have so much to tell you, and even something to celebrate!"

James remembered that Magnus used to live in London. Clearly though, he wasn't any more. He had been away for four years though, so he had probably sold his flat in Paddington.

James wondered if Magnus was renting a place here in Oxford until the Exhibition was completed, or whether he had even bought somewhere.

Underlying all these thoughts, James had a sense of coming home. Seeing Magnus standing there in the flesh reassured him that he had made the right decision.

Magnus had arranged for James to stay with him while he helped with the dismantling of the Exhibition.

They picked up a Thai meal for their dinner and headed back to Magnus's cosy terrace house in Jericho.

While they were waiting for the meal to be prepared, Magnus shared his news.

He had just accepted a post with the Archaeology Department here in Oxford. He would start his new job just as soon as all the Exhibits had been safely returned to their owners.

Travelling the world had shown Magnus that there was more to life than just the Eirby Hoard. He had discovered a need to be settled in a place where he could concentrate on a wider field of research. Although he would be based in the Archaeology Department, he would straddle the boundary between that and the History of Art. It was the perfect job for him. He could maintain his interests in both areas but explore a wider range of topics.

He would still be involved in the work around the Eirby Hoard, but in a more dispersed way. He would be able to link that highly focused knowledge more directly with research taking place in other countries across the globe. Thanks to this Exhibition tour, he had already made many strong links across the field.

Definitely something to celebrate.

Once back at Magnus's home, James and Magnus sat down to enjoy their Thai meal. The Pad Thai noodles were absolutely delicious. Sticky, garlicky and most definitely moreish.

As they tucked in, Magnus regaled James with many tales and anecdotes about his travels with the Exhibition. Most of them seemed to focus on either setting up or dismantling the thing. James listened intently. Although the stories made him laugh, he didn't want to make the same mistakes when he began his new job tomorrow.

Eventually, it was time for bed. They had an early start the following day.

James would be starting his job and renewing his friendship with the Sword.

He wondered what the morning would bring.

He didn't have to wait long. After brushing his teeth and enjoying a gloriously hot shower, he just about fell into his bed in Magnus's spare room. He had enough time before falling fast asleep to note that Magnus had done his best to tidy the room. However, despite those efforts, it was still very much a spare room with piles of academic journals and books scattered on the chair and bedside table.

If James had hoped for a dreamless peaceful night, he was out of luck.

The Sword was clearly keen for them to meet as soon as possible. The dreams started immediately. And they were not pleasant.

A familiar feeling of being dragged through the stars and space enveloped the young man. Then he juddered to a halt.

As the mists around him cleared, he witnessed a terrifying sight. He watched in horror as men, women and even small children were tied to stakes on bonfires. There seemed to be so many of them. As he watched, he saw the bonfires covered in pitch, and lit.

It was all too familiar to the lad. Only the last time he had seen anything like this, it was he and Magnus who were tied to the stake.

James remembered from his "A" level history from several years ago about the religious turmoil which had engulfed England during the 16th century. Following Henry VIII's break from the Catholic Church, things had been very difficult.

For a while you had to be a protestant, or you would die by burning. Right the way from Henry's reign and throughout that of his young son, Edward.

But, when Henry's daughter, Mary, ascended the throne, you had to be catholic again. Or you would die by burning.

Then when she died and his other daughter, Elizabeth, took over, it was back to being a protestant otherwise you would be burnt.

Was the Sword showing him a snapshot of those times? If so, when exactly was it? Which year and which religion? Were the folk about to be barbecued catholic or protestant, or simply in the wrong place at the wrong time?

And more to the point—what was this to do with him? What did the Sword want from him?

James woke up in a cold sweat.

He checked his watch. It was still only two o'clock in the morning. A long time to go before breakfast at seven!

He decided to quietly head back downstairs and make himself a cup of cocoa. Perhaps that would soothe him back to sleep so that he was fully refreshed when he met with his old sparring partner later that day.

As James opened the door to the kitchen, he was surprised to see Magnus sitting at the table nursing a steaming mug of cocoa, and another similar cup was waiting for him.

"I heard you thrashing about as you slept," explained Magnus, "I thought you might appreciate some cocoa and a chat. I suspect our old friend has been working his tricks again and that you have had another of your visions."

James nodded.

Magnus asked, "Do you remember how I knelt in front of you when we were in Holborne in 1066?"

James nodded again.

He remembered that Magnus had told him that he, James, was Magnus's liege Lord. That it was Magnus's job to serve and protect him.

Magnus told James that this was still true. They may now be in the 21st century, but the Sword had given Magnus this role, and he couldn't escape it even if he wanted to.

Just as they had, back in 1066, James and Magnus talked about James's vision. It was far more comforting to do it over a cup of hot cocoa than lying on a straw mattress though, it had to said.

The clock ticked slowly towards three o'clock. James shared his vision. Magnus could barely suppress a shudder. He, too, had bad memories of how they had been returned to the 21st century. Their last memory of 1066 was being tied to a stake themselves and set alight.

However, Magnus could not make any sense of James's vision. There was both too much detail and not enough information.

Maybe James would dream some more when he returned to bed?

Or they could find out more when James and Sword met up again in the morning?

James finished his cocoa and decided to try again to get some sleep. This time he slept like a log.

Chapter 3.3
Packing Up

Despite his interrupted night, James felt well rested as he set out with Magnus to the Exhibition.

He was looking forward to his first day at work. Although he wouldn't be paid a lot, he would get something for his labours. That he would be working with things that he loved was very much a bonus.

James did have a few qualms about what the Sword might be planning. But for now, as he and Magnus walked through the main entrance, he had managed to push them to the back of his mind.

Magnus introduced James to the professor-in-charge of the Exhibition.

"I have heard very promising things about you from Magnus," said the professor, "Magnus tells me that that you want to get into the field of science-based archaeology!"

James nodded. He hoped Magnus hadn't been too flattering about his abilities. He didn't want to let anyone down!

The professor began to show James around the various stands and areas where the exhibits had been housed. These spaces were now mainly filled with large wooden crates which were overflowing with straw. The precious artefacts were laid out on trestle tables next to the crates. Alongside the artefacts were piles of bubble wrap, sheets of polythene, non-acidic tissue paper, and sticky tape. And, strange to James's eyes, a small camera.

The professor took out a pair of white cotton gloves from his trouser pocket and put them on. Then he picked up a beautiful gold Viking brooch from the nearest table.

"This artefact was loaned to us by the Hedeby Museum in Germany. We have to pack it carefully and make sure it is put in the right crate for shipping back there. Everything that we do to this marvellous piece of history has to be carefully documented as we pack it up and send it on. That includes taking photographs at every stage. We cannot afford to allow anything to be damaged or even worse, lost. I think I speak for every archaeologist and historian when I say that we want to organise more of these sorts of Exhibitions in the future. For that we must be 100% sure that we get everything right. There can be no mistakes!"

James gulped.

Wrapping presents suddenly seemed so simple by comparison.

The professor walked James through the main exhibits at a rattling pace. It was clear that he thought that James only required the bare minimum of training before he was going to be allowed to touch the precious displays.

Finally, they reached a trestle table at the far end of the Hall. Magnus was already there and was wielding an enormous pair of scissors as he cut through bubble wrap.

The professor looked at Magnus and then at James.

"I believe that you have some familiarity with our star," he said.

James nodded again. He felt that he was getting very good at nodding. It seemed to be all he had done since he walked through the door!

"Magnus will guide you through wrapping the Mighty Sword of Eir. It is to be shipped back to the British Museum later today!"

James looked across to where Magnus was standing. Securely attached to a wall behind him was the Mighty Sword of Eir, glinting in all its glory.

James's qualms returned. He was suddenly incredibly nervous. He remembered all too vividly what had happened when he had last touched the Sword. Looking back, it would be a great story for a book or film.

However, he wasn't sure that he was ready to undergo a repeat performance. He still had a nasty scar on his foot from his adventures in 1066!

There wasn't time to protest, not that it would have made any difference.

Magnus went over to the display and gently, almost reverently, picked up a screwdriver and loosened the supports holding the precious artefact in place. He carefully took the Sword from its supports. He turned to James as he held it up.

"Behold, the Mighty Sword of Eir," he announced, "At last, we reunite!"

James looked on with a mixture of fear and familiarity.

The professor had a benign expression. He thought these researchers had a great sense of humour. As long as the artefacts were handled carefully and with respect, he could enjoy a joke or two.

James could feel the Sword's amusement as its amber eye watched the tableau.

"Go on, take it!" ordered the professor as he handed James a pair of cotton gloves, "But be careful not to drop it!"

Now James was feeling really nervous. Those words were perfectly designed to enhance the nervous tremors rippling up and down his back.

He gingerly took over holding the Sword from Magnus.

No flashes! No power surges. Nothing!

James was relieved and then realised that the Sword was laughing at him. It was almost as if the Sword was giving him a big soppy hug!

It was welcoming him back.

It was pleased that he was here.

What a relief. Things would stay calm for a little while yet at least. Until James had become used to being with his old friend again, he hoped.

As James looked at the Sword, the professor-in-charge wandered off to oversee how packing up was progressing elsewhere in the Hall.

Magnus looked at James and said, "I wish you could have seen your face just now! You were as white as a sheet!"

"So, would you have been if this was the first time you had seen the Sword since it nearly had us burnt!"

Magnus's smile faded. That had been a horrible experience.

"Here, put the Sword on the tissue paper. I will then wrap it in the polythene, before finally padding it with the bubble wrap, and then I will secure it with sticky tape."

James held the Sword close to his chest—just as he had done when they were brought back to now. He felt its warmth permeating through his body.

They were reunited. It felt strangely right.

With more than a little reluctance, James carefully lay the Sword down in the centre of the bubble wrap. He watched as Magnus folded the plastic padding around the weapon, and then secured the wrapping with sticky tape. He hoped that the Sword would not feel suffocated.

"Pull that crate over here," demanded Magnus, "We need to place the Sword at its centre then make sure it's well covered with straw. You know how bumpy the roads are nowadays with all those potholes. We can't afford for the Sword to be hurt."

Magnus laid the Sword in the crate. James did as he was bid and began padding the space around it with straw.

Just as he had finished packing one side of the Sword into the crate, James was distracted from his job by a sudden commotion.

He and Magnus looked across to the door that James had only recently come through.

They saw two masked men, armed with guns, heading in their direction.

Everyone else had either fled or was hidden under the trestle tables.

This was not good at all.

The two masked men stopped in front of Magnus and James.

"Hand over the Sword!" demanded the first man.

James and Magnus were terrified. Never mind how you think you would behave when threatened with violence—it is very different when it actually happens!

"Come on, hurry up," demanded the other masked man as he waved his gun at James.

Magnus bent down and reached into the crate. He picked up the bubble-wrapped Sword.

He passed it to James. James almost handed it over.

But just as he was about to let go, his instinct—and some influence from the Sword perhaps—made him pause.

He yelled "NO!" in a very loud voice, and began to run towards the fire exit, the Sword still clutched to his chest.

A shocked Magnus followed closely behind.

As did the two masked men.

James pushed open the fire exit and began to clatter down the iron steps. Magnus followed.

So did the men.

As James almost jumped down the steps, he somehow managed to secure the end of the Sword in his jeans' waist band. That way he only needed one hand to hold the Sword. He could run faster and hold the stair rails at the same time. It might only save seconds, but every one of those counted at the moment.

Just as James reached the bottom of the steps, one of the masked men, who was at the back of the chase, slipped and fell forward.

He tumbled onto the other man. The guns fired. There was a flash of light and a deafening bang. The men tumbled down and landed on top of James and Magnus.

Then all was still.

James came round. He was face down on the pavement. As he slowly tried to move, he realised that the Sword's tip was still in his waistband, but that he had somehow managed to clutch the rest of the precious object to his chest. He felt rather than saw that Magnus had landed on top of him.

Magnus was coughing as all the wind had been knocked out of him.

"Are you hurt?" he asked James as they both sat up.

"I don't think so," came the reply, "But I think the Sword has saved us! Look around!"

The two masked men were nowhere to be seen.

Then, as they looked further, Magnus and James realised that neither was the Ashmolean Museum either.

Magnus and James looked at each other and thought more or less the same thing at the same time.

"Oh no! Not again!"

James stood up shakily.

"Is the Sword safe?" asked Magnus.

"It is," James replied, "It was tucked into my waistband as we fell. I suppose I was lucky not to be stabbed by it!"

However, James was sure he must have a Sword-shaped bruise on his chest!

"Take off the wrapping so we can check!" ordered Magnus.

James felt for the Sword and removed it from his clothing.

To his astonishment, it was no longer encased in bubble wrap. Instead, it was wrapped round with linen.

This was definitely a "Not again!" moment.

James carefully unwrapped the Sword. Magnus looked up to see and then said, "Have you seen what you are wearing?"

James looked down.

He was no longer wearing his old jeans, comfortable fleece, and well-loved trainers.

He had some sort of black tights on his legs and black breeches layered over them. Instead of his lovely warm fleece, he was wearing some kind of black jerkin. And over all of this, he had a black heavy gown.

A veritable man in black!

James looked across at Magnus and saw that he was similarly attired.

Except that he was now sporting a rather jaunty almost beret-style hat as well.

James heaved a small sigh of relief that he hadn't been given such a thing to wear until he looked down at the pavement. There, on the ground just next to him was another of those silly things.

He supposed that he had better put it on. It was essential that he fit into whatever time they had arrived in. If wearing a hat was part of it, then he had to do it.

James and Magnus looked at each other.

James felt the amber glow from the Sword.

It had done it again.

The three of them were now truly reunited, and the Sword had a mission for James to complete.

Now all they had to do was work out where they were, what year it was, and what that mission might be.

The only clues so far were their new clothes and James's dream from the previous night.

Judging by their clothes, James and Magnus realised that they had not been transported to the 11th century. Indeed, once Magnus had stopped smiling at James's outfit, he noted that he thought that James had a look of some Elizabethan courtier. He wasn't an expert in fashion, but his best guess was that they had probably been brought to Oxford in the late 1500's or even early 1600's.

James and Magnus looked at each other with a mix of disbelief and resignation.

Then they set off along the path that they hoped would take them into the centre of Oxford.

Chapter 3.4
An Unexpected Meeting

Magnus had only been living in Oxford for a short while. For most of that time, he had busy with the Exhibition. As a result, he only had a vague idea of where he was trying to go. It wasn't helped by the fact that he and James were no longer in the familiar territory of the 21st century.

"But you may recognise more than me," he said to James, "After all, you are at a University which was founded in the 13th century."

James thought that this was highly unlikely. His time at Oxford had been spent either studying for his degree or in the Junior Common Room at his college, which was regarded by some others at the University as a "Johnny-come-lately".

Magnus felt that he and James had one factor in their favour.

Although Oxford had been built on and over through many centuries, the town design was based on its original medieval street plan. Or so he had read somewhere. Medieval Oxford wasn't his specialism.

However, if he was right about the street plan, he and James should try to find the cathedral. After all, remembering the history of that period, religion played an extremely important part of people's lives, regardless of whether they were protestant or catholic. So, there must be a cathedral. And people they could ask.

As they walked on, James looked around.

It was very different to either where they belonged, or where they had been on their last adventure.

The buildings that they walked past actually looked like houses now. They had the characteristic wooden framework that James had associated with the house in Stratford-on-Avon where Shakespeare was born in about 1564. The houses didn't look new though, so he suspected that they were now in a time after that.

At least the city's appearance agreed with Magnus's thought that they had been brought by the Sword to a point somewhere around the turn of the 1600's.

But there were still no clues about why.

James could feel the Sword gently emitting an aura of peace.

It was clear that the Sword was very pleased with what it had achieved so far. It was sure that James and Magnus would work out the whys and wherefores. It didn't intend to leave it all up to their intuition and chance. It would throw in some clues and guidance along the way.

But the Sword had its limitations. It had to be its Keeper who would right the wrongs it detected.

The streets were busy, but they were not filled with animals or rubbish.

"This is very different to last time," James observed, "The place is so clean!"

Now it was Magnus's turn to nod in agreement.

"I wonder why the place is so clean?" mused Magnus, "Even in the 16th century towns were not exactly pristine?"

Suddenly James stopped and pointed.

"Look over there!" he demanded, "Although it's nothing like I know it, I am pretty sure that is Christ Church!"

Magnus looked in the direction of James's outstretched arm. In front of it was what looked to be the ruins of an old priory with a rather magnificent church at its heart.

"There seems to be a lot happening," observed Magnus.

The area seemed to be either a demolition site or a building site. It was impossible to tell. There were piles of rough-hewn stone everywhere, interspersed with wooden beams. Men were chipping at stones, while others were carrying smaller burdens back and forth. Tools and dust lay everywhere. It was a real hive of activity.

James and Magnus could see ladders placed at certain points around the site loosely tied to rudimentary scaffolding. Workers who James assumed to be masons scurried back and forth along the narrow platforms. There was a lot of banging and chipping, but what those intrepid masons were doing was anyone's guess. They could have been putting stones in place or removing them. James and Magnus were too far away to see. However, not one of them looked in the least bit safe. If a sudden gust of wind had blown, Magnus was sure that there would have been some serious injuries.

The air was filled with orders being issued, and instructions being given. In short, it was a scene of not-very-organised chaos.

"I wonder if they are rebuilding or destroying?" pondered James.

They both knew that Henry VIII had closed all the catholic religious houses. Some were converted to vast estates for his favourite nobles. Others were just allowed to rot. But in each and every case, anything that was of value and could be carried away had been seized by Henry's men and given to the king.

Magnus thought a little.

"Perhaps they are converting the church into a protestant place of worship for the city? I haven't seen any other churches around here that might be of cathedral status?"

James agreed and added, "From what I can recall of Christ Church's history, the church was part of the old priory. But, when Henry broke with Rome, the church was given to the university and the city. It had cathedral status. Even in the 21st century, Oxford still uses Christ Church as its cathedral."

Magnus and James drew closer to the building site. It was obvious that there was no health and safety in these times. Men scrabbled around in the rubble and dust without any safety clothing at all. Not a protective hat in sight.

The two men gingerly picked their way through the strewn tools and rubble, hoping to find out more.

Suddenly, out of nowhere, a person rushed into them, shouting "Look out".

James and Magnus fell to the ground. The person who had pushed them landed right on top of them.

As James started to ask what was going on, a huge lump of masonry crashed down within feet of them.

Had they not been shoved out of the way by this stranger, James and Magnus would have been killed before they had had a chance to do anything!

They stood up.

"Sir, we must thank you," began James, as he brushed himself down.

"Without your timely intervention, we would have been crushed to death," added Magnus.

They picked up their hats, which had been knocked off in the commotion and dusted them off.

"Tis my honour to be of service!" came the reply.

Magnus and James recognised the voice. It was deep and rich. A perfect baritone.

But what on earth was it doing here, now?

For that voice belonged to none other than their old friend from the 11th century, Brother Luke!

Both James and Magnus were stunned.

Of all the things that the Sword might have organised for them, they would never have thought of this.

James stepped forward and looked closely into his rescuer's face.

"Brother Luke, is it really you?"

"James, my Storyteller," came the shocked reply, "Indeed it is. But what in heaven and earth are you doing here?"

"We're as surprised as you are!" said Magnus, "After leaving you at York we managed to return to our own time and hoped that you would be safe. And now, here you are!"

It was clear that the three men had much to discuss.

None of them could ignore the fact that magic was afoot.

It was also clear that they needed privacy so they could talk freely.

As ever, the Sword had brought James and Magnus to an era where anything that could not be explained was considered to be evil and witchcraft.

It wasn't only hapless worshippers who suffered death by burning.

Brother Luke spoke again.

"Come, let us walk, and I will tell you more.

First, I must tell you that I am now a Student of Christ Church college. It is very new and is being built up from the ruins of St Frideswide's priory.

I will relate how I come to be here when we get to my rooms. But now, since we are here, I will tell you a little more about where we are."

James and Magnus were far more interested in what year it was. But no matter.

Brother Luke continued, "Christ Church has had a long and chequered history.

It was first established way back in 1122. Then, in 1564, the infamous Cardinal Wolsey decided to use it, together with those of other adjacent religious houses, to found a new college to be called Cardinal College. But these were turbulent times. And it did not stay as Cardinal College for long. Henry VIII decided to take it over and renamed it Christ Church.

The work you see around you today is to demolish part of the priory church. It will be replaced by a quadrangle for our new College!

It is a good use for the place. If it is not to be used for the glory of God, it is best that it be used for the glory of knowledge. 'Tis a far more suitable use than merely being available for the locals to steal away the stones for their own ends."

James and Magnus looked at each other. Brother Luke had mentioned a date—1564. And he had said that it was in the past. So, they must be somewhere after that!

Not much to go on, but a good start.

And it still didn't shed any light on how a monk from a monastery hospital in York back in 1066 came to be here in Oxford sometime after 1564.

The Sword agreed. Deep in James's jerkin, it glowed with pleasure. Its Keeper and Manservant were doing well. It enjoyed puzzling and teasing them.

As they strode on in companiable silence, James, Magnus, and Brother Luke remembered how they had done a similar circuit of the Monastery gardens so many times when they had last been together in York.

"It's just like old times," observed James as they walked away from the dangerous site.

"Indeed," agreed Brother Luke, "But let us continue in silence for now. We can talk freely and without interruption when we reach my rooms. I can also organise food and drink," and turning to James, he smiled, "I remember that you have a bottomless pit for a stomach!"

James grinned.

Even though they still had no clue about where they might exactly be in time and space, it felt so right and reassuring to have Brother Luke's calming influence beside them again.

Chapter 3.5
Catch Up and Reflection

Brother Luke led the way along what had, until comparatively recently, been the church of the Augustine canons.

Now, Brother Luke explained, it was planned that this construction site would become new buildings where the Students of Christ Church could live in comfort as they pursued their academic dreams.

Admittedly, now, it was all a bit of a mess, but he had seen the plans and they were very ambitious.

After what felt to be a trek across a moonscape, they arrived at Brother Luke's rooms.

It was dark inside, and it took a few moments for James and Magnus's eyes to adjust. When they did, James and Magnus saw an academic environment surrounding them. There was a long bookshelf filled with leather-bound books, and there were even more books covering every available space, except for a narrow bed and a couple of chairs.

James remembering his bed the previous evening, looked pointedly at Magnus, and said, "It seems that untidy academics exist in every era!"

Magnus sheepishly grinned back. He knew he wasn't the tidiest of people at the best of times.

Brother Luke told them to sit down. Then he went outside and pulled at a small rope.

A bell jangled somewhere in the distance.

A short man came almost at once.

"What do you need, Master Luke?" he asked.

"Bring me a flagon of hot water and some fresh mint for myself and my guests. Also, some bread and cheese would be most welcome. My guests have travelled far and are very hungry."

The short man tugged his forelock and asked, "Will you be requiring food and rooms for your guests tonight as well?"

"That would be most welcome," Brother Luke agreed.

The short man walked briskly away and returned almost immediately with the food and drink. He also informed Brother Luke that a room for the two gentlemen had been secured for them at the Bear Inn.

"Good, that is very good," replied Brother Luke as he gave the man a few coins.

He turned to Magnus and James and explained that the Bear Inn was a local hostelry not too far from where they were now.

Magnus cleared a space on the crowded desk. Brother Luke carefully placed the tray of victuals in it.

As they ate and drank, Brother Luke began his story.

His tale started where they had last met. In York in 1066.

How Brother Luke now came to be in Oxford was a complicated tale, and one that he didn't really understand himself.

Especially now as it was early August 1605.

A-ha thought James and Magnus together. We have a date!

Before Brother Luke could begin, he needed to tell them about what was happening now.

Firstly, he was no longer known as Brother Luke.

As a Student of Christ Church, he was now known as Master Luke.

He would explain how that change had occurred later. But there were things that James and Magnus needed to know before they went to their lodgings, so that they would not slip up with their stories.

The Sword throbbed persistently against James's chest. It felt like he had a second heart.

It was the Sword's way of telling James to let Master Luke continue with his tale NOW!

Before Master Luke said more about his journey to Oxford, he had to share just one more thing.

The King was due to visit the city in a mere week's time. Most excitingly, he and his queen were to be accommodated in Christ Church.

Master Luke did not know if this might be the reason why James and Magnus were here, but it was something to think about.

It was important to know this in case James and Magnus spoke with anyone at the inn that night.

James felt the Sword go silent.

Clearly, the Sword did not consider the royal visit to be the reason it had brought them here. But James felt sure that there would be some sort of link to it.

Now, though, Master Luke was ready to share more of his story.

"Within minutes of you leaving us at the Infirmary, the King's Messenger arrived. He bade us exhume Alfread. The novices did not want to. They felt it would desecrate Alfread's grave and risk his immortal soul. But the Abbot gave his permission, and so they began to dig. Very slowly, and very reluctantly.

They did not have to dig very far before my stink began to filter out. The poor novices could not continue to dig as they were violently sick—right at the graveside. As the stench reached the Abbot and the King's Messenger, they decided that they had seen—or rather smelt—enough. Only a putrefying corpse could produce such an evil aroma!"

James and Magnus smiled at each other. They remembered how Brother Luke sprinkled noxious liquid around the coffin. They would never forget that smell. Even though they had linen cloths to muffle the stench as they buried the coffin, it had seeped though.

Master Luke continued.

"The King's Messenger left immediately. I think he was trying to escape the smell!" he chuckled.

Several weeks passed peacefully after that. Then Brother Luke had a dream.

It told him to see for himself what had become of his charges.

It took a little while longer for him to depart the Infirmary. He had to convince the Abbot that Brother Mark was ready to step into shoes, for example.

But, just as the first snows fell, Brother Luke strode out of the Infirmary for the last time.

First, he walked towards Whitby in pursuit of any knowledge of Alfread. He was fortunate. As he rounded the coast, he heard reports of a band of monks who were trying to establish an abbey at Whitby. They had been blessed by having two clerks with them who were able to liaise with the noblemen in the area. Already great progress had been made. It was hoped that land would soon be available for the venture.

Armed with this knowledge, Brother Luke changed course. Alfread was safe. That was all he needed to know.

He walked on to the manor of Holborne.

There, he was greeted with a terrible tale.

The villagers told him of how their Lord Alfread was dead, and the two messengers who brought the news had been burnt as traitors by the Norman lord.

"However," continued Brother Luke, "The villagers talked of witchcraft or a miracle. They couldn't quite decide which. For it seemed that as the bonfire was lit, a huge fork of lightning hit the stake. The whole pyre burnt immediately to white ash.

When the soldiers came to clear things up there was only ash. No bones, no Sword, no nothing.

The villagers were afraid. The lightning had clearly been an omen of some sort.

As for the new Lord—he was frightened too. So much so that he decided that he would have to rule these people kindly from now on!"

James was delighted to hear this outcome.

"That flash of lightning was how we were returned to our own time," he said, "It happened in the nick of time. I still have a nasty scar on my foot from where the bonfire was starting to burn me!"

The next stage in Master Luke's story told of how he came to be in Oxford in 1605, rather than the 11th century.

"I believe it was your St Christopher medal which brought me here," he said to James.

Magnus remembered how Great Aunty Pauline had been concerned that it had been left behind.

Master Luke continued, "After Holborne, I decided to walk to Oxford. I know not why. It took many days. I celebrated Christmas with the monks in Abingdon. Then I set off again towards Oxford. It was a beautiful bright crisp morning as I walked. The snow was frozen solid on the road and you could see the outlines of the cobwebs in the frost. Again, I cannot explain it, but I decided to look at my St Christopher's medal. Maybe for inspiration? Guidance perhaps? As I held it in my hand, it caught the rays of the sun. For a few seconds I was blinded. When I regained my sight, I was no longer dressed as a monk. I was dressed as I am now. And I was no longer in 1067! Regardless, I decided to continue my journey to Oxford. When I arrived, I was fortunate to meet with sympathetic scholars who were interested in my learning and knowledge."

Both James and Magnus remembered how Luke had travelled the world before reaching York in the 11th century. He was a true scholar. He had not only learnt much of different cultures, but he was also well versed in ancient and current religions. Not to mention his medical skills!

"The scholars got me a position here at Christ Church and started to refer to me as Master Luke. So, here I am," Master Luke concluded.

Now it was James and Magnus's turn to share their story.

Of course, James had to produce the Sword so that they could all admire its beauty once again.

Then, he took out the wooden crucifix. Master Luke looked at it with tears in his eyes.

"Oh, what sweet memories..."

It was growing dark as they finished sharing their stories.

"Come, let me walk you to the Bear Inn. We will enjoy a late supper there and then you can rest," Master Luke decided.

A good night's sleep sounded perfect to James and Magnus.

They would meet again with Master Luke on the morrow.

Chapter 3.6
The Bear Inn

A rowdy warm fug greeted the travellers as they walked through the door of the Bear Inn.

It appeared that Master Luke was well-known here. As he strode ahead of James and Magnus, it seemed that everyone there either wanted to shake his hand or slap his back. Master Luke was clearly a very popular fellow.

Master Luke led James and Magnus to a small table. It had been occupied a few moments before but had been emptied and even wiped down by the proprietor especially for them.

"Greetings, Master Luke," he said as he clanked past them, his hands full of dirty tankards.

"And a fine evening to you too, Master Harrison," replied Master Luke, "How is that bear of yours? I hope he is not too bored now that he has retired from amusing your patrons with his dancing!"

So that was how the inn had got its name!

It seemed that Master Luke had first met the innkeeper's bear several months ago. Although the bear had been here for far longer. The poor creature was now retired as it had developed a nasty ulcer on its feet. Luke had offered to treat the bear. Using his 11th century knowledge, and basic hygiene, Master Luke had been able to relieve the ailment so much that the bear could walk again.

"But," explained Master Luke to James and Magnus, "I encouraged our good host to allow the bear to enjoy his last days in quiet retirement. I don't hold with treating animals cruelly, particularly not for entertainment. While I could not undo the pain that poor creature must have endured through his life so far, I could at least ensure that his last few years would be pain free and calm. The bear now lives in a holding pen which I designed for him. It has plenty of room to move around, and warm shelter as needed. I also advised Master Harrison as to the bear's diet. And now, Mr Bear is very content in his life."

James and Magnus agreed wholeheartedly with Master Luke. They both held very strong views about how animals should be allowed to live where they belonged and not used for pleasure or amusement.

The innkeeper returned to the table with three tankards filled with something that had a head of froth.

"These are from those gentlemen over there," he said as he plonked the drinks on the table and pointed into the crowd, "They want to thank Master Luke here for his help. Without his magic liquor, they would not have been able to stay alert to complete their studies!"

James and Magnus looked quizzically at Master Luke.

"What do they mean?" asked James.

"I discovered these beans whilst on a visit to London," explained Master Luke and dug out some reddish coloured nut-like objects from within his breeches, "You roast them in a flame. Then when cool, they are ground into a coarse powder. I then boil the powder in water. The resulting liquor, which is both brown and very tasty, has the property of keeping folk awake and alert!"

Magnus looked at the object and said, "It sounds very much to me like they are coffee beans. They were just starting to become known in England at this time. Coffee Houses, however, are still to come, but you won't be able to move for them in another 50 years!"

"I can see that you have been using your medical and herbal skills to help, just as you did in York," observed James as he sipped his frothy drink.

The Sword, still secure in his jerkin glowed in agreement.

Master Luke continued, "As I had no means to live on in this time, I had to rely on my skills and knowledge. I must admit to feeling an ungodly amount of pride in the fact that they have served me well! Indeed, my understanding of medicines got me a bed here when I first arrived. I managed to soothe our host's bad cough with a tincture of my own making. Then shortly afterwards, my knowledge secured my scholarship!"

The innkeeper returned.

"Will you be wanting to eat this night?" he asked.

"Indeed," replied Master Luke, "What have you to offer?"

The innkeeper puffed up his chest. He was very proud of the inn's catering.

"For you, Master Luke and your guests, I am pleased to offer you the finest mutton, served with a goodly helping of carrots, and for today only, some of those new-fangled vegetables called potatoes!"

It sounded delicious and three portions were ordered immediately.

Just before he went to chivvy the serving wench to bring food, the innkeeper turned to James and Magnus.

"Do you plan on staying long? Only that with the visit of the king, we have a huge demand for rooms. As you are friends with Master Luke, I can offer you beds regardless, but it would aid me greatly to know now!"

Master Luke looked at the innkeeper and replied, "I believe that my guests will have need of your hospitality for at least a couple of months. Of course, they want to witness the king's visit. The university has many things planned and I know that my guests wish to witness them, and after that, we plan to do some research together."

James and Magnus nodded in agreement even though they hadn't got a clue what was likely to happen!

They rather thought that Master Luke didn't have a clue either. But as the Sword throbbed warmly in James's jerkin, he knew that it was the right decision.

And they trusted Master Luke. That was enough, truth to tell.

Master Luke continued chatting to the innkeeper, "I will sort out the little matter of money with you separately, when my guests have retired!"

James and Magnus would have argued that they should be paying for their bed and board, but they were all too aware that they had brought nothing with them except the Sword. And that was most definitely not to be used for payment.

The exchange was interrupted by the arrival of three very crowded platters of steaming hot food. If it tasted half as good as it smelt, they were in for a real treat!

"Master Victualler, you excel yourself!" exclaimed Magnus.

James was too busy sniffing and hunting out the eating irons. He wasn't sure what to expect.

The question was answered by the serving wench who had returned with a tray of bread. Then she put spoons on the table. The innkeeper dug under his apron and pulled out three knives.

"Just for you," he said as he placed them in front of the hungry threesome.

As the innkeeper bustled away, Master Luke said, "We are honoured guests. Our host does not make knives available to everyone. We must make sure that we return them directly to our host when we have finished!"

James and Magnus would have replied but they were too busy tucking into their food before it went cold!

Although there seemed to be a veritable mountain of food on the platters, not to mention a pile of crusty bread to mop up any last dregs of gravy, it all seemed to disappear in the blink of an eye. Master Luke had been right about James's bottomless pit of a stomach. But he had forgotten that Magnus also possessed one as well!

But the warmth and whatever had been in those tankards were starting to affect both James and Magnus.

They suddenly felt extremely tired and could barely keep their eyes open.

Master Luke noticed.

He called over to the innkeeper.

"Good Sir," he asked, "I would be much obliged if you could show my friends to their room. It is clear that your excellent food and drink has relaxed them both to the point where they can barely stay awake!"

The innkeeper looked on in wry amusement. He had lost count of how many guests he had helped to their slumber over the years.

But he was very aware that although these two young men were replete, they hadn't overdone things. He felt that Master Luke had chosen his friends wisely, even if they were now tired out. He wondered how far they travelled that day.

Little did he know!

Master Luke returned the knives, and then he nudged James and Magnus.

"Come, it is time to retire! Our host will guide you to your beds. I will return here on the morrow and we can sort out what happens next then."

With that, James and Magnus sleepily followed their host, through the noisy crowd of drinkers, up a rickety staircase, and finally into a small clean room with two beds and a bowl of water for washing which stood steaming on a small table.

"Here we are, Sirs" said the innkeeper, "I hope you will find this sufficient for your needs. When you awake in the morning, there will be something for you to eat!"

James sleepily opened one eye.

Breakfast on the morrow! When they woke up! 1605 was definitely an improvement on 1066!

For now, all James wanted as a good night's sleep.

He managed to get ready for bed although it was the quickest catlick of a wash! He placed the Sword by his side, climbed between the rough but spotless sheets, and fell instantly into a deep slumber.

The Sword realised that its Keeper was exhausted. It glowed benignly as James enjoyed a peaceful night's sleep.

There was time enough to guide him and Magnus on their mission. Things would keep for now.

Chapter 3.7
August in Oxford

James and Magnus woke to the sound of birdsong interspersed with various banging and sawing noises from the Christ Church building works.

It took a moment for James to remember where he was. Then he remembered that he had somehow ended up in Oxford in 1605, just before a king's visit.

James thought that he might take a quick look around the inn before anyone stirred.

He quickly dressed, making sure that the Sword was securely fastened in his jerkin, then crept to the bedroom door. He opened it quietly so as not to disturb Magnus who was still fast asleep. As the door creaked open, he was greeted with a smell that he had not expected.

Fresh coffee!

This was an unexpected surprise!

People were already up and about. They had made coffee! But what if it had all been drunk by the time he got downstairs? Or even worse, before Magnus got to it?

He had to wake Magnus.

He roughly shook Magnus awake. Once the initial shock of being disturbed had worn off, Magnus registered what James was telling him.

There was a smell of fresh coffee. Really! He wasn't imagining it.

However, they had better hurry in case the source ran out before they got to it!

The promise of freshly brewed coffee did the trick.

Magnus was dressed and halfway down the stairs before you could say "I will take mine black!"

As they came to the bar area, James and Magnus were surprised to see that Master Luke was already seated by the fireplace. By his side, on a small trestle table, was a large pot of something which was steaming hot alongside three beakers.

"Good morning," he said, "I trust you slept well?"

James and Magnus could not deny it. They had slept like logs all night.

"Following on from our discussions last night, I thought I should test your theory about my beans," continued Master Luke, "What do you think? Is this liquid what you know as coffee?"

He poured a beaker each for them.

James sniffed his. It smelt like a little drop of heaven.

He nodded enthusiastically. Real coffee!

What wouldn't he give for some orange juice to go with it?

But never mind. A truly unexpected pleasure.

The innkeeper arrived, wiping his hands on his apron. James wondered if he had managed to go to bed at all last night.

"What can I get you young Sirs for breakfast?" he asked in a jolly voice, "I have fresh bread, out of the oven at first light, with cheese or cold mutton?"

James decided that he could face bread with the mutton. Magnus was more circumspect, opting for the cheese option. Master Luke claimed that he had already eaten.

The coffee was just right. Not too strong, but definitely not weak or insipid.

The three gentlemen made plans as James and Magnus munched.

It was decided that James and Magnus should familiarise themselves with Oxford. It could be important when the king came to visit.

However, Master Luke would have to leave James and Magnus to their own devices after midday.

An important meeting, chaired by the Vice-Chancellor, had been called to discuss the king's visit.

It wasn't an order, but there was an expectation that Master Luke, together with other Students of Christ Church, should attend.

As soon as they had finished their breakfasts, Master Luke suggested that they explore the route likely to be taken by the king.

None of them had any idea why they had all been brought here by the Sword. However, it made sense to be familiar with the parts that were going to be used by royalty in the coming days. Just in case.

Master Luke called the innkeeper over to ask if he could make up packed lunches for them.

Then suitably armed with a bag of bread and cheese and a skin of ale, the threesome ventured out into the bright summer morning.

Master Luke suggested that they walk along the route that the king would take in a few days' time. James and Magnus could find the best vantage points to watch the proceedings that way.

Master Luke had heard that the king would stay at his palace in Woodstock in the run up to the visit. His entourage would therefore likely enter at the North Gate to the city.

They decided to head in that direction.

James wondered what Broad Street looked like in this time.

James asked Master Luke very politely if he thought there would be sufficient time. Particularly given that Master Luke had to be back for his important meeting by noon, and such a detour could add too many minutes to their exploration. But Master Luke felt that they could afford to indulge James and so they set off.

As they walked along Broad Street, James recalled that the thoroughfare had once been known as Horsemonger Street. It was a wide street because horse markets were held there.

Master Luke suddenly stopped in front of where the street met the city wall. He pointed to a small, blackened area just by the junction and said, "This is where Archbishop Cranmer was burnt at the stake back in 1556 on the orders of Queen Mary!"

It was indeed a horrible episode in England's history. Archbishop Cranmer had been instrumental in Henry VIII's wish to break from the Catholic Church. He had worked with the king to put together laws that all had to swear loyalty to the king first, then God. If you didn't swear loyalty to the king, you would be burnt at the stake. It was all part and parcel of becoming a protestant country.

Then Henry died. Cranmer continued his work to sever links with Rome throughout Edward's short reign.

On Henry's death, his daughter, Mary, became queen. She was a fervent catholic and worked hard to restore England to being catholic again. She made new laws to ensure that everyone became catholic again. If you didn't, you would be burnt at the stake.

Archbishop Cranmer decided that he really believed that he was a true catholic. All that stuff about swearing loyalty to the king first and burning Catholics at the stake was a huge error.

But the judges weren't convinced by his sudden conversion, and condemned Cranmer to die by burning.

Right there. In 1556.

Strangely, as the flames licked about his feet, Cranmer had another change of heart. He recanted his recanting. Then died.

To the protestants, he was a martyr. To the Catholics, he was a heretic of the worst order. An opportunistic heretic!

James and Magnus looked at each other. They really were not impressed at all by this era.

As they did so, they heard a commotion behind them. Then an urchin, clutching a small bag, ran in front of them.

Someone behind them shouted, "Stop, thief!"

James felt the Sword throb inside his jerkin. He was being called to action.

He ran after the urchin, threw himself at the boy's legs, and wrestled the bag from his hands. As James's fingers closed on the bag, the youngster managed to break free and disappeared down the back alleys.

No matter. James had saved the bag, whatever it was, and it could be returned to its owners. He could tell that the Sword was pleased.

He walked back towards Magnus and Master Luke. Master Luke was talking to someone who was clearly a gentleman, as Magnus patted the delicate hands of someone who was obviously his wife.

James handed the small bag to the lady who was so overcome with gratitude she began to sob.

The gentleman turned to James and said, "We can't thank you enough. This bag is quite precious to my wife. She calls it her good luck charm. She would have been devasted to lose it!"

Being attacked like this had taken its toll though, and the lady suddenly went as white a sheet and looked like she was about to faint.

Master Luke took charge.

"Your wife has had a nasty shock. Let us retire to the White Horse, just over there," he said as he pointed in the direction of what seemed to be a traditional house of the period, "I am sure that the innkeeper will prepare some tea while your wife regains her composure! It will also allow us to introduce ourselves, perhaps?"

Master Luke then led the way to the hostelry and ushered them all inside.

The landlord rushed over immediately. He wasn't used to seeing guests at this time of day. When he heard what had happened, he went to make tea immediately.

"Good Sirs, we must thank you again," said the gentleman, "and allow me to introduce ourselves. I am Sir Francis Tresham, and this is my good lady wife, Anne. We are here to witness the visit of the king next week. It was such a pleasant morning, though, that we decided to venture out and view the spot where the heretic Cranmer was burnt in 1556!"

Master Luke introduced himself, and then his two friends.

They all agreed that it was indeed fortunate that they had all been here in Broad Street at the same time.

James could feel the Sword pulsating. It disagreed that they had met by pure chance. It was no accident. This was a meeting that had to happen.

Lady Tresham recovered quickly once the tea had been drunk, and it was agreed that she and her husband would return to their lodgings in her husband's old college.

"And we must carry on," said Master Luke.

However, time had gone by, and Master Luke had to leave James and Magnus to work out the likely royal route by themselves.

He would meet them back at his rooms later.

James and Magnus discussed what had just happened as they made their way over to North Gate.

"That was all very odd," said Magnus.

James agreed. Then told Magnus about the Sword's reaction to it all.

"I know I have heard the name Tresham somewhere before," he added, "But I can't for the life of me remember where!"

However, given the Sword's reaction, James and Magnus were sure that their paths would cross with the Treshams again before long.

However, it was now time to concentrate on the king's route through Oxford.

"I believe that the mayor, together with the civic dignitaries and the University's senior academics, will meet the king and queen here at North Gate. I suspect the plan is then for them all to process on towards Christ Church to the royal couple's lodgings!" said Magnus, based on what Master Luke had said.

"Let's make sure that we know the way they will take. Even though the Sword is quiet now, it may send me a dream to help us work out what we are supposed to do tonight?" hoped James.

"I am sure that Master Luke will have more information to share later," agreed Magnus, "If we understand the possible routes now, it will save us time, I am sure!"

And so, James and Magnus spent the rest of the day trekking between places that they thought the king might visit. They memorised short cuts between them and explored alternate routes. They paused only once, and that was to eat their simple lunch.

It was a very tired pair of young gentlemen who knocked on the door to Master Luke's rooms later that day.

And it was a very excited Master Luke who opened his door to them!

After ringing the bell and ordering refreshments for the three of them, Master Luke bade James and Magnus to be seated.

James and Magnus were very glad to do as they were asked. They hadn't noticed as they trudged along the streets of Oxford, but now they realised that their feet were quite sore.

"Tell me how you got on," asked Master Luke, "and then I will share my exciting news!"

Master Luke was rightly impressed with James and Magnus's efforts. They had indeed walked miles! Most importantly, they both felt sure that they had been able to commit all their explorations to memory too. Should they need to rush from North Gate to St Mary's Church, for example, they were confident that they could do so quickly. Magnus even thought that they knew which shortcuts to take to avoid the crowds which would most probably line the main thoroughfares.

Now it was Master Luke's turn.

Apparently, the Vice-Chancellor had shared the University's plans to entertain the king while he was here.

There were going to be three days of events.

Master Luke wasn't too bothered about what was happening on the first two days—even if one of them was likely to be an outdoor production based on a play by that famous playwright, William Shakespeare. Indeed, the Vice-Chancellor had even hinted that the great man himself might be in the audience! Who wanted to watch a play about witches?

No, Master Luke had to prepare for something far more important which was scheduled for a couple of days later!

Master Luke explained that the University was rather fond of organising what it called "disputations". From how he described them, James thought that they sounded to be what he would recognise as debates. Certainly, if that were true, Oxford had kept that tradition going! However, unlike their modern-day equivalents, these disputations had to be delivered in Latin!

The Vice-Chancellor had told the meeting that the king was renowned for his intelligence and knowledge. With that in mind, the Vice-Chancellor had decided that the University was to deliver no less than five of these disputations over two days. They were designed to show off the University's specialisms. Of course, the king would have a front seat at them all, in St Mary's church.

James thought that this all sounded a bit dry, and he was at a loss to understand why Master Luke was so excited.

Then Master Luke told Magnus and James that the Vice-Chancellor had invited him, Master Luke, a humble Student of Christ Church, to give the disputation on Physic!

James looked a bit blank—he hadn't got a clue what "Physic" was, although he could appreciate that Master Luke had been given a great honour to deliver one in front of the king.

"It's an old name for medicine," explained Magnus.

Now it made more sense.

Master Luke had more to tell though.

The topic he had to talk about was the new world weed that was proving incredibly popular. His disputation would be entitled "Whether the often taking of Tobacco be wholesome for such as are in health!"

Gosh—what an opportunity. Would Master Luke be prepared to listen to what his 21st century guests might have to say on the subject? Or even include some of it in his disputation? If he did, then his disputation would be well ahead of its time.

Chapter 3.8
The King's Visit

The next couple of days were spent in deep discussions and a flurry of translation. Master Luke wanted to hear every last detail about what James and Magnus knew about tobacco. He wasn't sure how he would use the information, but it was all helpful.

Of course, once he had decided what he wanted to say, he then had to translate it into Latin—which had to be word perfect. There was no leeway for errors in front of the king. Of course, Master Luke's fellow Students would also be listening carefully. After all, they had not been selected for this great honour, and one or two of them would be all too keen to draw his attention to any errors later. Probably in front of the king and Vice-Chancellor!

While Master Luke wrote, James and Magnus wandered the city.

They joined the crowds of city folk who lined the thoroughfare as the king and his entourage arrived at North Gate. It was a spectacle to observe. The mayor was in his official robes as were the other dignitaries and senior academics. It was all very colourful and formal.

The first of the four plays that Master Luke had mentioned was performed just outside North Gate. Magnus and James were so glad that it hadn't rained. While Magnus enjoyed the acting, James was more interested in the audience. He wanted to see if Mr Shakespeare was observing the proceedings.

The procession of dignitaries and kingly retinue then made its way to Christ Church where the king and queen were to stay for the duration of the visit. The crowds followed which made for slow progress and a tiring experience.

By the time James and Magnus reached their lodgings at the Bear, they were exhausted. They decided to have an early dinner and then get some sleep. They wanted to be at their best for Master Luke's disputation the following day.

Even though the king was in town and the inn was full, Master Harrison's catering was of its usual high standard.

James and Magnus enjoyed a supper of poached fish, which was served with a dollop of parsley sauce. James thought this was quite unusual for the time— but that didn't stop it tasting delicious.

Then there was just enough time for a wash before falling into bed.

Only the night was not to be a restful one for James.

The Sword had decided that there was work to be done. It wove its magic around James and whisked him into another world.

As the mists cleared, James saw that he was in modern-day Oxford. But it didn't feel like modern-day Oxford. Or look like it either.

He was standing in front of Christ Church. The cathedral looked very different to how he remembered it. It was brightly coloured. Every niche and statue had its own rainbow of brightness.

James looked around. There were students and scholars all around him. But instead of the short gown over jeans standard University dress of the 21st century, they all seemed to be wearing clothes that wouldn't have been out of place where he currently was. More to the point, they were all men.

Before James had a chance to do anything, say anything, the Sword lifted him up again.

This time he was on Broad Street. Again, it looked strange.

He recognised the spot where Archbishop Cranmer had been executed all those years ago. It didn't look like it should. In fact, it looked like it had only recently been used! It was blackened and there were still one or two glowing embers.

With a shudder, James realised that in this world, the punishments for being on the wrong side were still as brutal as they had been in the 16th and 17th centuries.

What was the Sword showing him? And why?

But the Sword hadn't finished its work.

James found himself inside the cathedral proper. As he watched, he recognised some of what was going on. It was a church service. But it wasn't one that belonged to the Church of England. This was High Mass, complete with incense and bells. And it was in Latin.

Very strange. But then, James did recall that some protestant churches did sometimes use the Latin forms of worship.

What was the Sword trying to tell him?

The service came to an end. James noticed that the main worshippers seemed to be dressed in red flowing cassocks. They made their way to the priest and spoke with him.

As James listened in, his horror grew.

For these red-robed worshippers had travelled from Rome. They were here on business. The Lord's business. They had paused their investigation to take Mass. Then they would return to their duty.

They were here to root out any dissenters from the One True Church.

Those dissenters would be allowed to recant their heresy. Then, to properly save their souls, they would be burnt. For only through the purification of fire could those poor misguided creatures be brought willingly to God.

James was horrified. He recognised these men in red. But he thought that they had long since disappeared into the mists of history.

They were members of the infamous Spanish Inquisition which was set up hundreds of years before. Its original purpose was to bring non-Catholics to God. But over time and space, it had become more and more cruel in its pursuit and punishment of them.

James woke up with a jump.

Magnus was immediately alert.

"Tell me what you saw!" he demanded.

James was white as a sheet as he recounted what he had just witnessed.

Magnus sat there in silence until James had completed his tale.

It was a lot to take in.

And it was difficult to untangle. Magnus was worried. If he got it wrong, he and James might end up doing more harm than good.

He tried to think about where they were. It was clear that the Sword had brought them to Oxford in 1605 for a reason. But what was it? Were James and Magnus here to stop James's vision becoming real? And if so, how?

So many questions.

Magnus recalled that the years since Henry VIII had died had been some of the most brutal in English history. The country had swung between catholic and protestant faiths, depending on who was on the throne at the time.

"People—rich and poor alike—took their religion far more seriously than we do in the 21st century," explained Magnus, "People in these times really did fear for their immortal souls! If you got it wrong, you were damned for all eternity!

Of course, the religious leaders of the time wanted everyone to go to heaven using their version of Christianity. It was their job to get you into the right belief so you could!"

The challenge was making sure that you were in the right camp!

Magnus moved on.

"The monarchy was very much intertwined with religion at the time. It wasn't that the catholic faith itself was cruel and harsh. Rather, it was the monarch, as God's representative, and his Parliament who decided the best way to punish those who flouted the faith.

From what you say, it seems that modern-day Oxford—if not the whole of England—is still very much part of this close relationship.

If I am right, then we have been brought here to try and make sure that history continues to unfold as we know it, and not how you saw it in your vision."

James felt a warm glow from inside his jerkin.

The Sword agreed.

Now all they had to do was to work out exactly what it was that they had to do and then how to do it!

For now, James and Magnus could do no more.

James fell back to sleep. There were no more visions.

They were again greeted with the welcome smell of coffee for breakfast.

As Master Luke poured out two beakers of the steaming hot liquid, Magnus told him about James's vision.

Master Luke did his best to concentrate, but his thoughts were elsewhere. Magnus could see that Master Luke was far more focussed on his disputation, which was to take place later.

"You will come and listen, won't you?" he kept asking them both.

Neither James nor Magnus had seen Master Luke nervous before. That was what made them realise just how important this event was going to be.

"Of course, we are going to be there!" assured Magnus, "Where else would we be?"

Master Luke took his leave—he still had some minor adjustments to make to his speech.

Magnus and James decided to spend their time until the disputation, strolling around where they knew the Ashmolean Museum would be in future years. If they got back to the 21st century, it would be something to talk about!

They were enjoying the calm so much that they lost track of time. It wasn't until they heard the church bells chiming that they realised that they were running late.

They got to St Mary's Church just in time. But to their horror, they could see that it was absolutely packed. They walked up and down the aisle trying to spot a space, but there didn't seem to be any.

Then, as they matched up towards the altar one more time, James heard a voice say, "Master James, Master Magnus! We thought it was you! Our rescuers from earlier this week!"

James and Magnus bowed. It was Sir Francis Tresham and his good lady wife who were already settled most comfortably in a pew. Ready and waiting.

"You are here to listen to the disputation?"

They nodded in agreement.

"But it seems that we are too late!" said James.

"Indeed, not!" exclaimed Sir Francis, "After all you did for us, the very least we can do now is to squeeze up so you can fit into our pew!"

Sir Francis turned to someone sitting on his other side and said, "Squeeze up, Catesby—make room for these two gentlemen!"

It was a tight squeeze indeed, but James and Magnus just about managed to fit in between Sir Francis and his friend. There was just enough time for everyone to introduce each other.

Sir Francis explained to his friend how James and Magnus, together with the chap who was about to speak, had saved his wife's lucky charm.

"Allow me to introduce myself," said Sir Francis's friend, "I am Robert Catesby. I am an old boy of Oxford too. Although I did not graduate. It is an honour to be here and watch these disputations!"

James was about to reply, but a sneeze erupted in his nose. He had to quickly rummage inside his jerkin for his linen square to blow it. As he did so, Brother Luke's hand-carved cross, which he had been keeping safe, clattered to the ground.

Catesby picked it up as James sorted himself out.

"This is a fine crucifix," he said as he handed it back to James.

James grabbed it slightly more quickly than he had intended. It was so very precious to him.

"Indeed," he replied as he put the cross back where it belonged, "It was carved by a very dear friend of mine, a monk, who is very learned and who I regard as my personal mentor."

James didn't notice, but Magnus saw that Robert Catesby was suddenly very quiet. Almost as if he were thinking deeply.

Catesby took a deep breath, and then turned back to James and Magnus.

"You must come to dinner when you are next in London. I am sure that my friends and I will have much of interest to talk about with you."

This invitation clearly came as a bit of a surprise to Sir Francis. In fact, Magnus would have said that he looked shocked. But there was no time.

Master Luke was climbing the steps to the pulpit to deliver his opening lines.

It is fair to say that neither James nor Magnus understood a single word of Master Luke's presentation. But it was clear that just about everyone else in the audience did—including the king.

Then as Master Luke concluded, the whole church erupted into a storm of applause.

Sir Francis and Robert Catesby talked over James and Magnus to say "Absolutely masterful! Sheer brilliance!"

James whispered to Magnus, "I think they liked it!"

Chapter 3.9

New Friends

It was a jubilant Master Luke who sat at the table in the Bear Inn, regaling all who would listen to his telling of the day's events. He was very happy and more than a little relieved.

It had been a huge undertaking to put together such an erudite piece of work in the timescale demanded by the Vice-Chancellor. It was even more of an undertaking to translate it all into word perfect Latin. But Master Luke had done a splendid job. Even the king had stood up to acknowledge the power of Master Luke's arguments.

It was clear to James and Magnus that Master Luke was very happy indeed. It was going to take quite some time for him to calm down and return to more mundane activities. Both Magnus and James were heartily proud of their friend. They did not begrudge him his moment of glory. They suspected that once things had reverted to normal, Master Luke would be in as dangerous position as they were as they tried to work out the Sword's latest riddle. Let him enjoy his moment while he could.

Master Harrison was equally pleased with his friend's performance and provided Master Luke, Magnus and James with a dinner fit for the king himself.

As they ate, James told Master Luke about how they had renewed their acquaintance with Sir Francis, and they had met Robert Catesby. James mentioned that he had dropped the crucifix on the church floor but added hastily that it was undamaged. Then, he relayed Catesby's strange reaction to it.

Master Luke's mood changed abruptly. James thought that this was because Master Luke thought him careless. But no, it was for a different reason.

Master Luke explained that the crucifix which he had carved on his travels had great symbolism for some who were of the catholic faith. It was quite dangerous to expose it in public for that reason. If people saw that James was carrying a catholic artefact, they would suspect he was catholic himself.

From what Master Luke had learnt about this time, being catholic was very dangerous.

James wondered if Robert Catesby's reaction was because of this.

Meanwhile, Magnus was still trying to remember where he had heard that name before. He could feel in his bones that it was significant.

It was on that mysterious note that the friends decided that they should retire to their respective beds in preparation for the morrow. All was quiet now. James felt that the Sword was sleeping.

It had been another long day, and without much to show for it, truth to tell. Although James and Magnus had sought clues at every stage, they were still no wiser as to what the Sword was seeking from them.

James slept peacefully until almost dawn. Just as the first chinks of light were starting to fight their way through the coarse curtains, the Sword sent another vision.

Unlike the previous night, this one seemed factual. It merely showed that James took delivery of an envelope. It was from their new friend, Sir Francis. James could tell this from the seal on the back. It contained a formal invitation from Sir Francis to James, Magnus, and their scholarly friend to join him and his friends for two weeks' time in London. James could feel that the Sword wanted them to accept this invitation.

The key to why they were all here in this time might be revealed at the meal! Certainly, the Sword made it feel like it would be.

And so, it was, a fortnight later, that the three men found themselves outside a small property in central London.

It didn't seem to be in the most salubrious part of town, although it was close to the river. It was very different to the Westminster of the 21st century. Magnus had to remind James that they were still in 1605. And, as Magnus also noted, the house was well situated. It was almost next door to the old House of Lords.

These Houses of Parliament weren't due to be burnt down for another 200 or so years. They were still part of the medieval Palace of Westminster. They would be destroyed later in history and rebuilt in the 19th century and take the form that James knew from his sauce bottle after that. But for now, the entrance to the House of Lords—or Royal Approach—was in the south east corner of the Old Palace Yard and was the main way in!

Master Luke reminded Magnus that there was work to be done. There would be plenty of time to discuss their impressions of London when they returned to their overnight lodgings at the Duck and Drake. He also noted that it had been kind of Sir Francis to suggest the hostelry for them. It was very convenient, and if dinner did not finish until late, they would not have far to walk in the dark.

James marched up to the door and knocked loudly. It slowly creaked open, and they were ushered inside by a manservant. There, waiting in the hallway were their hosts, Sir Francis and Robert Catesby, together with another gentleman.

"Welcome," said Sir Francis, "I must admit that I am but a guest here myself. However, there are several people I would like you to meet. First, I must introduce our host for the evening, Thomas Percy!"

As James, Magnus and Master Luke all shook hands with their newly introduced host, Sir Francis continued, "Thomas was appointed Gentleman Pensioner in June. It is a great honour as it means that he is a member of the king's bodyguard. A very important job, I am sure you will agree! It is one that needs a base in London too. Hence this magnificent property!"

James, Magnus, and Master Luke nodded. James privately thought that it looked slightly dowdy and down at heel. But he was a guest in this house. It would have been impolite to say anything. Anyway, he thought, it could just be a trick of the candlelight.

The Sword gently throbbed away inside James's jerkin.

"Come, let us eat!" continued Sir Francis as he ushered them into an ornate room with a table set for 12, "Our servants have prepared a fine meal for us. We are 12—just like at our Lord's last supper!"

James and Magnus looked at each other. That was a bit strange. They thought that they had been invited to a posh dinner, but that comment made them feel like they had been invited to some sort of religious gathering instead.

Then it got even more strange.

"Before we break bread, we must make prayer around the table. James."

Sir Francis looked directly at him, "Would you lead the prayers?"

James was taken aback. He might be able to manage "grace", but a full proper prayer? There was no way he was equipped to do any such thing. He did the only thing he could think of.

He passed.

"I am not worthy to undertake such an honour. Perhaps you will permit me to defer to my learned friend and Student of Christ Church. I believe he is better placed than I to do justice to this great honour!"

"Master Luke," asked Sir Francis, "Would you?"

It seemed that Master Luke had not forgotten his life as a monk in York.

He folded his hands together and intoned something which neither James nor Magnus could understand. But it seemed that everyone else did. And that they approved wholeheartedly.

James and Magnus were mystified. What had Master Luke just done?

Master Luke whispered quietly to Magnus, "You must trust me for now. I think I know what is going on, but I need a little more information before I am sure."

James was still confused. However, the Sword's steady throb calmed him. He knew that he must trust the Sword. All would become clear soon.

It was a simple meal but made enjoyable by the company and candlelight.

The three guests ate and listened. Much of the discussion around the table was about the king and his visit to Oxford. There was much made of Master Luke's treatise that tobacco could cause cancers. While there was some debate about how something that tasted so good was bound to be good for you, there was another view that anything that tasted good like that must be bad for you!

Then, the topic broadened. Now, the diners talked about how religion was still an issue despite the promises made by King James. He had apparently promised that Catholics would be treated better but had reneged. Now, it was even more difficult to follow the true faith!

James and Magnus felt that they were completely out of their depth. These subjects were not your usual 21st century dinner table topics for discussion!

But all the while, James felt that the Sword was asking him to watch and listen. This was very important.

Suddenly, the conversation turned to James. He realised that Sir Francis was asking him to show his crucifix.

He had no choice. Mouthing a "sorry" to Master Luke, he carefully retrieved it from his jerkin, and lay it on the tablecloth. The other diners clustered around the small cross, but not one of them touched it.

"It is just as you described," said Thomas Percy to Robert Catesby.

"The detail and symbolism are truly magnificent," said Sir Francis.

"How did you come by such a wonderful object?" asked other guest.

James told them that it had been given to him by a very dear friend who had been in holy orders many years ago.

James was allowed to put the crucifix away, and the meal recommenced.

Now the chatter was far more general, and it was obvious that the guests would soon be making their excuses to leave.

Before long, James, Magnus and Master Luke had said their thank-you's and goodbyes and started on their way back to their lodging.

It was a calm night, with a full harvest moon in the sky.

Suddenly, out of what seemed nowhere, Magnus was knocked to the ground.

"Hand over the cross!" demanded a masked voice.

Magnus could do no such thing. It wasn't his cross to hand over. And more to the point, he didn't have it.

The person who did have the cross also had the Mighty Sword of Eir. He had drawn it as soon as he saw Magnus fall. Instead of looking at a crumpled figure on the ground, the masked voice found himself looking down the twinkling blade of what looked to be a very sharp Sword.

He decided very quickly that he did not want the cross after all, turned round and ran away as fast as he could.

"Are you alright?" asked James as Magnus got up.

"Indeed, but I wonder what that is all about?"

Master Luke looked at them both and said, "I believe I have some idea of what is going on. But I do not want to talk until I am sure it is safe. I do not trust where we are staying. We must return to Oxford now. It is too dangerous for us to remain here any longer than we have to!"

The men were very glad that they had left nothing at their lodgings. It meant that there was no need for them to return to the Duck and Drake.

So, they didn't. They set off back to Oxford instead.

Chapter 3.10
Back to Oxford

It was a footsore and exhausted trio that trooped into the Bear Inn at noon two days later. They had walked all day and all night so that they could get back as quickly as possible.

How James had longed for a 21st century train!

The innkeeper was surprised to see them back so soon. He had understood that they were going to be in London for a few days yet. But no matter.

Master Harrison could see that the travellers were tired. He also saw that they were in need of good wash and clean clothes. He called for the serving wench and ordered her to heat up water—a lot of water. These gentlemen were going to have a good soak. It might be in what was formerly a beer barrel, but it would do the job. He sorted out sets of clean clothes and then rustled up bread and cheese for the hungry trio.

Master Luke quietly thanked Master Harrison as James and Magnus tucked into the food. He explained that they had been set upon by thugs as they had left the dinner. As a result, they had decided that London was not for them and had made their way back immediately!

Master Harrison shook his head sorrowfully. London was indeed a den of thieves and iniquity!

Once James and Magnus were replete and clean, Master Luke left. He would meet with them at his rooms on the morrow. They should rest for now, but not discuss any of what had passed—not even with each other—until they were safe with him again.

Even though it was still only early afternoon, James and Magnus needed rest. They wearily made their way back to their room, lay down and fell fast asleep.

James began to dream immediately.

The room melted away and he was suspended in the air. James saw a lone man, dressed in rags lying on a dirty straw mattress. He was surrounded by rough-hewn stone walls. A thick wooden door with iron fittings was in the middle of one wall. James felt rather than knew that the man was in prison, awaiting trial. He heard blood-curdling screams from outside the door. Whatever was happening beyond it was not good, and it felt likely that it would be the man's turn next. But for what?

As James felt the man's terror building, the Sword whisked him away.

He was back at the house in Westminster. But James wasn't a guest. It seemed that he was suspended above the table so he could watch and listen.

There were a number of men around the table. James recognised Tresham, Catesby and Percy. However, there were other faces there who had not been at the dinner.

This was clearly a meeting of some sort. And judging by the furtive glances that each and every person at the table kept making in the direction of the door, it was a secret gathering!

James strained to listen in.

He could hear the odd word here and there, but for some reason, he couldn't make out whole sentences. Never mind—the words he heard were enough to chill his blood.

Catesby leaned into the faces around the table. James heard one word.

"Gunpowder!"

And then, "Kill the king"

He realised that he was witnessing the planning for the infamous Gunpowder Plot.

As he reached this conclusion, the Sword whisked him away yet again.

Now he was in Westminster Abbey.

There was a huge ceremony taking place. Every seat was filled, and the abbey was bedecked with flags and tapestries.

The doors opened. A procession of men, who were obviously very important, walked on ahead. They were followed by a little girl, who could not have been more than 10 years old. She was dressed in flowing heavy robes and looked completely terrified. She was the centre of attention and was not enjoying it at all.

James looked towards the altar.

In front of it was a beautifully carved chair with a large stone underneath. Beside the chair were priests and bishops, and at their head, someone dressed in red robes. Clearly it was the Archbishop of Canterbury.

James realised that he was watching the coronation of the king's little sister.

Which meant that the Gunpowder Plot had succeeded.

James woke with a start. He was cold but covered in sweat.

He thought that he now knew what he and Magnus were here for. But he felt that he must check his thoughts with Magnus to make sure.

After splashing his face in the now-cold water in the wash bowl he went over to where Magnus was snoozing peacefully.

"Magnus," he said as he shook him awake, "I need to talk…"

Magnus immediately woke up, without even rubbing his eyes.

"The Sword has sent you another dream!" he stated.

James nodded.

"And I think I know why we are here because of it!"

Magnus's face grew more and more solemn.

Then he spoke before James could share his terrors.

"Stop right there. Remember what Master Luke said? How he was nervous about who might be listening in? Say no more until we are with Master Luke. I do not think that we can do much tonight anyway."

Now it was James's turn to feel frightened. He'd forgotten that!

What if all that he had just said to Magnus had been overheard?

As if he had read James's mind, Magnus went over to the bedroom door. He opened it quietly and poked his head outside.

"I think we are okay," he said as he returned and got back into bed, "There is no one outside!"

But James was not convinced.

"What about the rooms either side of us?" he worried.

Magnus reassured James that they were both empty. He had noticed that the serving wench had been busy cleaning them as they had retired earlier.

"The doors were open, and I could see right in!" he said, "It looked as if the maid was dealing with the mess from the king's visit. From what I saw, our fellow guests were not as tidy as we are. I got the impression that she would not finish the job until tomorrow."

James wasn't totally convinced, but he was still incredibly tired after their long trek from London. And to be fair, all he had done was wake Magnus and tell him that he had had another dream.

No, the safest thing to do now would be to try and catch up on his rest and be properly alert on the morrow. Then they could discuss their thoughts in safety with Master Luke.

James wasn't at all sure that he would get back to sleep. But the Sword had one last piece of magic to weave, and that was to ensure that James would now sleep well!

Both Magnus and James woke with the dawn. They still felt weary after their trek, but they wanted to get to Master Luke's rooms as soon as they could.

Master Luke had only just risen. Nevertheless, he welcomed them inside, and rang to order breakfast. He apologised to his manservant for the sudden addition of two guests but hoped that they could be accommodated regardless.

The manservant tugged his forelock and assured Master Luke that it would not be a problem at all. It would be a pleasure.

Suitably fortified by strong mint tea and fresh bread, Magnus began.

"Master Luke, you have warned us to be careful about what we speak and to whom. Are you sure it is safe for us to talk freely here?"

Master Luke assured Magnus and James that it was. He was glad that they had come—he had much to share about what he had uncovered.

Master Luke suspected that why they had come would be closely linked to what he had discovered. If Master Luke were right, it would explain why the Sword had brought them all together, and what they had now got to try and do!

They sipped their mint tea in companionable silence, enjoying a brief moment of calm.

Then, Master Luke put his cup down and asked James if he would care to begin.

James related his dream in detail, feeling its full horror again.

Magnus looked more and more worried. Master Luke merely nodded his head in an almost absent-minded way.

When James had finished, Master Luke spoke quietly.

"It is as I had feared. Your dream closely mirrors what I have heard whispered about the university. That there is a plot brewing to assassinate the king and put his sister on the throne. The king has incurred the hatred of the catholic nobles by reneging on his promised reforms. The king had promised to allow Catholics more freedom to practise their faith. But then decided not to. As a result, the catholic nobles have lost confidence and patience with him. They want to replace him with his younger sister. They believe that they will be able to manipulate her into allowing England to return to what they see as the true faith."

The vision you experienced when you first arrived showed what life will be like in your time if that happens. The society that you know and value—particularly elements such as freedom of speech and the like—will simply not exist.

Master Luke's words provided a logical explanation of what James and Magnus had been through so far.

Now they understood what was going on.

But Master Luke had another comment which made their blood run cold.

"I believe that we have been brought together to halt the conspiracy. But we need to work out how. The Sword has brought us to the right time and has introduced you to people who are directly involved in the plot. But I fear this next part is going to be up to us!"

Chapter 3.11
Plots, Plans and Schemes

Master Luke had more worrying information.

It seemed that James and Magnus had come to the attention of the government. In fact, the dreaded name of Robert Cecil, who was James I's much feared head of State Security, had been mentioned!

Magnus and James's knowledge of Stuart history wasn't great. However, they did remember that Robert Cecil was a minister that James I had inherited from Queen Elizabeth. He had spies everywhere and was constantly looking out for threats and plots to get rid of the king. It was not good to be noticed by Robert Cecil.

Master Luke shared their concerns. It seemed that he, too, had been mentioned. Being involved in the disputations had been a mixed honour, it would seem.

"What can we do?" asked James, "From what I remember, all the Gunpowder Plotters were already known to Cecil. All he was waiting for was proof of a plot before he could strike. It must appear to Cecil that we are aligned with them."

"Indeed," replied Master Luke, "However, I have a plan which might prove to him that we are not. If it works, then we will be exonerated, and the schemers caught before they can do any damage!"

James and Magnus wanted to know more. However, before they did, Magnus had one last question.

"Wasn't torture used to find things out? If we are shown to be innocent, will we be responsible for condemning the plotters to unspeakable pain?"

Master Luke nodded in agreement.

"That is very much a risk, I am afraid. But we have to look at the bigger picture. Your vision from a few days ago showed us what will happen if the Gunpowder Plot succeeds. The religious turmoil and hatred that everyone—rich and poor alike—experienced throughout the reign of the Tudors will continue. Because there is no need for the Catholic Church to adapt over time, its doctrine will remain rigid.

Everyone will have to think the same or risk the wrath of the church. There will be no learning or advances in knowledge. Remember what the church did to Galileo? He was tried by the Inquisition, found "vehemently suspect of heresy", and forced to recant. He spent the rest of his life under house arrest.

The Spanish Inquisition that did that to him will still exist, to torture and maim those who dare to think for themselves."

Both James and Magnus were white with horror.

When all of this sort of thing was in the past, it was easy to forget that real people were involved. But now, being part of that history, living it, and experiencing it, it was all so very different.

However, when they thought about what their future might be like if they did nothing, it was almost unbearable.

Magnus and James drew closer to Master Luke. Master Luke dropped his voice to a whisper. They thought they were safe and couldn't be overheard, but it was only sensible to not take any chances. Whichever side might hear, they were all at risk!

Master Luke's plan was simple but dangerous. Basically, what the three of them had to do was to become spies themselves.

They would do their utmost to have Tresham, Catesby and their friends believe that they were on their side.

James interrupted at this point.

He was worried that for them to be convincing they would need to know all the nuances of 17th century catholic faith. He barely knew any Christmas Carols. Wouldn't that be a problem?

Master Luke paused and then reassured James.

"We are all in this situation together. Although I have adapted well to this current age, pray do not forget that I was, until comparatively recently, a monk in the 11th century church. I am more than familiar with the subtleties that will be required. But I accept that your lack of knowledge is a risk. We must stick together at all times until we have resolved this issue."

Master Luke also noted that James still had the crucifix. Even if he couldn't come up with an appropriate form of words, mere sight of the cross would grant him credibility. He remembered the reaction around the dinner table when James had produced it!

Further, Master Luke believed that it had been one of servants from that dinner who had attacked them as they left. He was presumably acting on orders from his master who wanted the precious artefact for himself.

"So, for now, we watch and wait for something to happen?" asked Magnus.

"Yes," replied Master Luke, "But if the rumours have even a grain of truth, we won't have long to wait!"

"Then what?" asked James.

"I must ask two things of you now," said Master Luke, "Firstly, that you trust me completely and do as I ask, and secondly, try not to be surprised by anything that I do ask of you."

With that, he picked up his academic gown and suggested they take a stroll around the college. He had a feeling that they would not have to wait very long at all.

It was very pleasant walking around the college grounds where building work had been completed. Master Luke explained what was happening, and what was expected from the works.

Just as they rounded a corner, they were accosted by a boy who shoved a piece of paper into Master Luke's hands before running off.

James wondered if it had been the same boy who had tried to steal Lady Tresham's bag. But he hadn't really seen whoever it had been in any detail.

Master Luke unwrapped the scrap of paper, read it and then, much to James's amazement, ate it.

After swallowing it down, Master Luke turned to James and said, "We can't afford to have anything which links us to anyone!"

This had suddenly become too real. James felt another of those shivers down his spine as he realised that he wasn't part of a rattling good yarn. He was up to his neck in subterfuge and spying. Hanging would be the best he could hope for if he were caught!

Master Luke walked on, oblivious to James's fears.

"Come," he ordered, "We have been invited to a rendezvous!"

He led them briskly to the White Horse, where they had taken Lady Tresham only a few weeks earlier.

This time, it was clear that they were expected.

They were shown to an upstairs room, where a rather sinister-looking gentleman waited. Although he was seated, it was clear that he was small of stature, and had something wrong with his back.

"We need no introductions," he growled, "You read my message, and I hope you have destroyed it."

Master Luke nodded. James and Magnus tried to make themselves as small as possible and hide behind Master Luke.

"What do you know?" the sinister-looking man demanded.

"Nothing beyond what I have already told you," replied Master Luke, "We wait for contact to be made."

The sinister-looking man nodded.

"You must expect to be contacted very soon indeed if my sources are correct."

James suddenly felt a little braver.

"If it please you, good Sir, how will we let you know when we are contacted?"

"I rely on your good Master Luke. I trust that he will have a means of telling me," replied the sinister-looking man, "For if he does not, it will not bode well for any of you. My men are everywhere."

With that, the meeting was over.

Once James, Magnus and Master Luke were outside, James looked at Magnus and said, "I did not enjoy that one little bit! Even the Sword seemed to be scared into silence! What a nasty little man!"

Mater Luke quietly spoke.

"Have a care, James. That man was none other than Robert Cecil, Secretary of State to the king. And Spymaster. If he promises something, he will deliver. The terrible thing is that what he usually delivers is painful!"

Magnus looked thoughtful.

"Our mission must be incredibly important if he is here meeting directly with us. After all, it is a long way from London to Oxford."

"Indeed," Master Luke replied, "We cannot, we must not, fail!"

They decided to walk to the banks for the river, where Master Luke thought it would be safer to talk freely.

"Now what?" asked James as they passed by a weeping willow, its branches gently dipping into the Thames.

Master Luke gave the same answer as he had earlier.

"We wait. I believe that we will be contacted shortly by Sir Francis or another of his colleagues. I have let it be known that you, James, are a graduate of natural science, and in particular, have a deep understanding of potions and powders. I think that our conspirators will have some questions that you can help with!"

They made their way back to the Bear Inn. It was now well past noon, and hours since they had eaten. They hoped that Master Harrison might have more bread and cold mutton that they could feast on while they waited.

As they entered the inn, Master Harrison asked Master Luke if he would visit his bear. It had been sleeping a lot recently, and Master Harrison was concerned that the bear might be ill. He was uncommonly fond of the creature who had shown itself to be gentle and kind.

Master Luke agreed immediately and asked if James and Magnus could join him. He knew they would be interested in meeting the creature after which the inn was named.

Master Luke knew where the bear lived and so he led the way.

"I will have some food for you when you return," shouted the innkeeper as they left through the back.

When they got outside, James, Magnus and Master Luke were given no chance to see the bear at all.

Instead, they were greeted by Sir Francis.

"Good Sirs," he said, "Please come with me. We need your help urgently. We must travel to London immediately. There is no time to be lost. I have horses ready."

Sir Francis pointed to four horses, already saddled and ready for the journey.

They knew they must go, but James was cross—he had been looking forward to something to eat!

Then he thought of Robert Cecil and what he could do to them all and decided that food could wait.

Chapter 3.12
Problems with Powder

Just as Master Luke had predicted, things were happening quickly.

The horses were fleet of foot, and the four men were back outside the house in Westminster just as the stars were starting to shine.

They were met by a couple of servants who helped them dismount.

Sir Francis led the way into the house.

Once inside, he turned to the three men and said, "I am sorry for the subterfuge, but we are on a dangerous mission. It is not something I wish to be involved in, but I fear there is no other course of action. Come!"

He took the lead again, and ushered Magnus, James, and Master Luke into the room where they had only recently been dinner guests:

There, already seated at the table, were Thomas Percy and Robert Catesby.

"We believe that you practice the one true faith. We also understand that you have knowledge and understanding that will help us to restore that faith to its proper place," said Robert Catesby as they entered.

James and Magnus did not know what to say. They looked to Master Luke for guidance.

As ever, Master Luke was calm. He thanked the gentlemen and asked them how he and his friends might be of help. But first, Master Luke wondered, should they perhaps commence this gathering with a short prayer? He would be happy to lead.

With that, Master Luke folded his arms and intoned something in Latin. All James and Magnus recognised was the "Amen" at the end, but they could see that it had had the desired effect on those around the table.

They were ready to trust them.

Robert Catesby began.

"We have lost our trust in the king," he began, "We do not believe that he will ever introduce the reforms needed to enable the Holy Roman Church be a full part of our society. If we are to restore those rights, we need to get rid of the king. It is as simple as that."

James and Magnus looked at each other and gulped. This was treason. High treason. The sort of treason that would get you hung, drawn, and quartered.

Or put it another way—something that they most definitely did not want to be involved in at all.

But James, Magnus and Master Luke were already involved. They knew too much already. If they tried to leave now, they would be killed.

On the other hand, Robert Cecil and his spies were watching and waiting. Wanting information that only they could find out. And if James, Magnus, and Master Luke failed them, they would likely suffer a similar fate.

They really were between a rock and a hard place!

Robert Catesby didn't notice. He continued, "We planned to kill the king when he opened Parliament. That was supposed to have taken place earlier this year. We had everything ready. We even invested in the gunpowder. Then, because of the plague, it was decided to put off the opening.

We had heard rumours that gunpowder is unstable and does not like the damp. So, we thought it wise to test our consignment ahead of the new date. It was difficult to find someone with the right knowledge to be able to undertake this important task. When we did, he discovered that it had gone rotten. It was fit for nothing. Afterwards, our tester disappeared. He wanted no further involvement. I haven't asked about what happened."

James swallowed. He did not like what that implied.

Robert Catesby didn't notice and carried on, "Then, we learnt that the opening ceremony would take place on October 3rd..."

"But that's tomorrow," thought James.

"We bought another 36 barrels of gunpowder, ready for the occasion. But, just today, we have learnt that the opening has been postponed again—this time to November!

Master Luke tells us that you have skills in alchemy, even though you are a true follower of the Church. Will you test our batch so we can be sure that it is still good?"

How could James refuse? There was no other option. Now he wished he had studied archaeology at university after all!

Robert Catesby moved over towards the door.

"Come, we must leave immediately. The gunpowder is stored in my house across the river. We need to take the wherry to reach it. Then you can conduct your tests and advise on what else we need to do to ensure its effectiveness when it is needed. We cannot afford for a second lot of our precious weapon to go bad."

With that, Catesby ushered Master Luke, James, and Magnus from the house in Westminster, down twisting side alleys, and along the river, until they reached a rickety dock.

A short pier butted into the water, and a rather unsteady wooden boat with a grubby disreputable man standing at its prow, sat at its end.

James had some concerns that the boat might not be able carry all of them, but somehow it managed to get them safely across.

"Welcome to Lambeth," announced Catesby as they disembarked, "Come, my house is close by!"

After walking briskly for a short distance, Catesby stopped then knocked at a door. It was clearly a coded knock, and the door was opened by someone who was also involved. Here was another member of the conspiracy that they had not met before. He had the most amazing moustache. While James, Master Luke and Magnus had never seen this person before, Robert Catesby clearly recognised him.

There was no time for formal introductions while they all stood at the door. It was important that they were admitted into the house as quickly as possible.

The man with the moustache asked Catesby, "Were you followed?"

"No, we took especial care that we were not. Come, Guy, let us show my guests to the cellar."

Catesby then bade everyone enter.

James and Magnus looked at each other. They realised that they were in the presence of the most infamous of the Gunpowder Plotters—Guy Fawkes. James recalled that it was he who had eventually been discovered with the stash of barrels in the House of Lords cellars!

This man had become so famous after this time that the English still celebrated the 5th November by burning effigies of Guy Fawkes on top of bonfires! Not to mention magnificent firework displays.

Strangely, not one of the others seemed to get mentioned outside of the history books...... And none of them had their effigies burnt on bonfires.

James briefly wondered why that was so. But not for long. There was no time for reflection. Time was pressing on. James had vital work to do!

Catesby and Fawkes took them to where the gunpowder was stored.

As James followed Catesby and Fawkes, his scientific curiosity overcame his caution. James became a scientist for a few moments. From somewhere deep in his memory cells, he realised he knew what to do.

He noted that the barrels were being kept in the obvious place—in the cellar.

James also saw that despite its proximity to the river, the cellar was dry and even had a couple of vents to allow the air to circulate.

He nodded his approval. So far, so good.

"I need to open some of the barrels, and I need to see their contents in the light!"

Even as James said this, he realised what a high-risk operation he was undertaking.

The barrels were full of explosives, and the only source of light was a lantern with a naked flame.

He decided that he must make sure all were aware of the dangerous task he was about to undertake.

"We must take care to ensure that not a spark hits the powder as I examine it. For, if as you hope, the powder is good, then we will all be blown into the next world!"

Guy Fawkes volunteered to hold the light. He held the lantern high about James's head as James carefully opened the first barrel.

Master Luke, Magnus and Robert Catesby decided to stand as close to the cellar door as they could.

Once the lid was removed, James sniffed the powder. He couldn't smell anything was amiss. He invited Guy Fawkes to do likewise. But carefully for he was still holding the lantern.

Then James addressed the others who were trying hard not to look like they were ready to scramble upstairs away from the explosives.

"The powder smells good. There is no aroma of alcohol or acetone, or similar solvents. Had I smelt anything like that, I would be suspicious of the quality. For my next test, I need a sheet of white paper."

Master Luke reached into his jerkin and handed one over. Magnus had no idea where it had come from. Perhaps he never went anywhere without a ream or two of white paper about his person.

Again though, time was of the essence. This was serious stuff.

James explained what he was going to do next.

"I will make a funnel and tip some of the powder through it. If any of the powder shows up as a rust colour, or adheres to the surface of the paper, there is a strong risk that the barrel's contents have gone bad. If that happens, I will need to undertake far more risky tests."

After allowing some of the gunpowder to run through the funnel, James opened up the paper and held it up for all to see. Not a trace of rust-coloured powder to be seen.

"I believe that this barrel contains good gunpowder," James announced, "Which is excellent news. Now we need to make sure the rest of your cache is the same.

I can do checks on all your barrels. However, I would prefer to undertake a series of random checks on your stocks.

I would suggest that you pick perhaps three more barrels from different parts of your consignment. I will test them.

If you are content to accept my advice, I propose that I only open more if we find one of those barrels to be bad.

I have solid reasons for proposing this way forward.

Firstly, I have noted the conditions in which you have stored your unstable cargo. I see that your cellar is dry and well ventilated. That tells me that your stock should not have turned rotten, for it is the moisture in the air which does the damage.

Secondly, the more barrels we examine, the greater the risk of a spark finding its way to one of them. As you know, it will take only one spark to blow us all to smithereens!

Finally, from your demeanour, I also sense that time is of the essence. It would take me until the morrow to complete testing all of your barrels."

Robert Catesby was impressed with James's reasoning. He decided that James's approach was wise. Guy Fawkes agreed. After all, it would be he who would be taking care of the precious powder once it left Catesby's house.

It was important to remember that the gunpowder had been difficult to source, and very expensive. It hadn't exactly been bought through legal means.

Neither Catesby nor Fawkes wanted to take more time than was absolutely necessary to make sure the barrels were good. Fawkes wanted to move the barrels as soon as possible. The longer they remained in Lambeth, the greater the risk of their discovery there.

Neither did they did want to take any more risks than absolutely necessary. As James had already pointed out, a stray spark here in this cellar plus explosives was not a good mix. They couldn't afford any accidents here in Lambeth. The barrels were destined to blow up a very different House! And if all went to plan, the king as well.

However, Catesby and Fawkes did need the assurances that James could give. They could not afford to go to all this trouble if the powder was not going to do its job. Catesby and Fawkes didn't want to have to try and find a third lot of gunpowder, particularly at this short notice. Truth to tell, they rather doubted that it would even be possible.

Master Luke handed James more sheets of paper as Catesby and Fawkes decided which barrels should be tested. They picked one from the middle of the pile and two from opposite ends of the cellar.

James repeated his sniff and pour tests on each and declared them all to be in perfect working order.

The House of Lords would not stand a chance. And neither would the king!

The group finally left the cellar and the house as dawn was breaking.

James was mightily impressed that he had met the infamous Guy Fawkes. How he wished he could tell his mother. But she would never have believed him. Of course, he would be able to share his experiences of testing gunpowder with Guy Fawkes with Great Aunty Pauline. However, he strongly suspected that she would only have an academic appreciation of his encounter. She wouldn't be enthusiastic about how this character had inspired magnificent firework displays around the country ever since 1605! Even though he was now in his twenties, James was still impressed by the celebrity of this man. James wanted to brag that he had met and worked with the man who almost blew up the Houses of Parliament.

However, for now, he knew he had to be practical.

"We must return to Oxford," said Magnus as they approached the Lambeth pier, "I hope the tide will still be with us. We should not be absent from our base for any longer than is possible."

Catesby agreed.

"The king has spies everywhere. If you had not had the crucifix, and Master Luke demonstrated his deep faith, I would have even suspected you three. You must head back before you are missed. I have horses waiting for you in Westminster. You must leave immediately you get to them!"

James groaned. He hadn't eaten since the previous midday and he was starving.

It was almost as if Master Luke had read James's mind.

"When we are back at my rooms, I will make sure we have a feast fit for a king—or some sort of royal personage!" he added hastily, "Your hunger will spur us onwards to make the best possible time!"

Chapter 3.13
Analysis and Action

Leaving the horses at the Bear Inn, James and Magnus followed Master Luke back to his rooms. James was already planning what he would eat.

Master Luke rang the bell for the manservant, who appeared as if by magic. It was as if he had read their minds as he was already carrying a tray of food and drink.

"I understand you have had a busy night," the manservant remarked as he placed the tray on Master Luke's desk, "I hope these few morsels will settle any hunger pangs that you may have. I understand it is long ride to London and back!"

With that, he turned and left the room before anyone could say anything or ask him anything else.

"That was strange!" observed Magnus.

"Indeed," pondered Master Luke.

James was too busy munching to care. He hadn't eaten anything for the past twenty-four hours and he was very, very hungry.

The Sword stayed still. There was no reaction to what had just passed.

James, Magnus, and Master Luke ate in silence. They would discuss what had just happened when they had finished.

They completed their meal, and then without needing to say a word, James, Magnus, and Master Luke stood up and headed to the door.

"Let us partake of the good weather," suggested Master Luke as he held the door open for the others to pass through.

"An excellent idea," chimed James and Magnus together.

They walked away from the college for a good ten minutes before James stopped and said, "Your manservant knew that we went to London."

Magnus agreed, "And he knew that we had not had time to eat while we were away!"

Master Luke scratched his chin. He was deep in thought.

He looked up and spoke carefully.

"First of all, I must offer my deepest, most sincere apologies. I thought my rooms were safe. It is now all too apparent that they are anything but. But I also have a second conundrum to resolve."

James and Magnus waited.

"I need to know which side my manservant has been spying for. And for how long."

Magnus spoke first.

"How are you going to do that?"

James felt a twitch in his jerkin, and it wasn't the pickled onions that he recently enjoyed. It was the Sword, reminding him of its presence.

He looked at Master Luke and said, "You plan to ask him questions while I am there. The Sword's reaction to his answers will tell us whether your manservant is one of Cecil's men or if he is part of the conspiracy!"

"If you agree, that is indeed my intention."

James nodded his head in agreement.

Magnus chipped in.

"Your manservant must not realise that we have spotted his error until we have him securely in your rooms. Either it was deliberate—in which case he is testing us for whichever side he supports—or it was foolishness. Either way, we must ensure that we are subtle."

Now all they had to do was think up some questions to ask which would answer their queries without the manservant realising.

After more walking and thinking, James suggested that they ask the manservant directly.

"After all," he reasoned, "if your manservant is innocent, but foolish, he will simply tell us a straightforward tale. If he is spying, I am sure that his response will be far more complex."

The Sword glowed hot inside his jerkin. It agreed.

And so that was decided.

They continued their walk a little longer, returning to Master Luke's rooms as dusk was falling.

"May I suggest some refreshment before you return to the Bear?" suggested Master Luke.

James and Magnus agreed.

Master Luke rang for his manservant who appeared almost immediately.

"Good Sir," began Master Luke as the manservant entered, "I would like to request more refreshments for my friends."

The manservant tugged his forelock and was almost out of the door before Master Luke continued, "I wonder, too, if you could help us clarify a mystery."

The manservant looked frightened.

"Come in for a few moments," invited Master Luke, "I think that you may be able to help us."

The manservant moved away from the door carefully. Magnus went and stood in front of it. The only way that the manservant could leave was if he decided to move.

James could feel the Sword's interest growing.

"You mentioned earlier that you knew we had been to London and had not had time to eat. It was a sudden and surprise decision on our part, and so we wondered how you came by this information?"

The manservant's reaction surprised them all.

He fell down in front of Master Luke and began to cry.

"Good Sir, please forgive me. I had no choice. I have been forced to report your comings and goings to Lord Sainsbury's men for some time now. When you did not return yesterday evening, I was forced by his men in black to find out what I could. I went to Bear to see if you were there. I asked Master Harrison. He trusts me and he told me of your mission."

The Sword throbbed. The manservant spoke truly.

James nodded to Master Luke.

"It seems you speak the truth. Do you know any more?"

The manservant shook his head slowly.

The Sword disagreed. It sent a short sharp bolt of pain through James's chest.

Master Luke saw James wince and understood.

"I do not believe you! You must be totally honest with me. Otherwise I will not be able to help you should it become necessary!"

The manservant flinched as if he had been hit.

"I fear what will happen to me if I say more!"

"Your fate will likely be the same; it will only be the instruments of your fate that will be different. It is best for you if you tell us now."

The manservant thought for a brief moment and then poured out his story.

It seemed that Master Luke had been watched ever since he had arrived at Christ Church. No one and nowhere was safe from Cecil's informants.

When James and Magnus had arrived, the manservant had been asked to keep a particularly close eye on them all.

Everything that he had seen and heard since had been reported back to Cecil.

The Sword glowed gently. It knew that the manservant had told them all that he could. He knew no more. He was but a small cog in a very large machine.

Master Luke looked at the manservant.

"I understand your situation entirely. We live in difficult and testing times. Please believe me when I say that we are honourable folk who bear you no ill will. We will not force you to do anything that your conscience would be uncomfortable with. But we do need your help if only to let us know when you have been approached by Cecil's lackeys. Are you willing to do that?"

The manservant looked totally bemused. He had expected to be kicked or punched for his duplicity. Instead he was being treated with mercy and kindness.

He couldn't speak. He was so full of gratitude he merely nodded his head.

The Sword continued to glow. Master Luke had done exactly the right thing.

It was time for James and Magnus to return to their lodgings. They agreed to meet with Master Luke on the morrow—this time at the Bear Inn. They would discuss their next moves at that point.

Chapter 3.14
The Plot Thickens

After a hearty breakfast, James and Magnus made their way to Master Luke's rooms.

It was a chilly, frosty morning. Both James and Magnus were very glad of their thick academic gowns as they picked their way across rime-covered ground.

They were almost at Master Luke's rooms when they saw someone coming towards them. It wasn't Master Luke, as they had anticipated. It was his manservant.

"Good Sirs," he gasped as he reached James and Magnus, "Master Luke has sent me. As proof, he asked me to pass this to you."

The manservant handed over the St Christopher's medal that James had given to Master Luke all those centuries ago. Because of this, James and Magnus knew that the manservant was telling the truth.

"Did Master Luke give any indication as to where he was going?" asked Magnus.

"No, Sir," came the reply, "But he said that you would understand!"

With that, the manservant turned and walked briskly back in the direction of Christ Church without a backward glance.

"I think we know what that means," muttered James as he turned the medal over between his fingers, "Things are starting to happen."

Magnus agreed.

They decided to return to the Bear. There was nothing to see at Christ Church now. All they could hope for was that Master Luke would seek them out when he had completed his business.

As it turned out, they didn't have to wait for very long. Master Luke strode into the Bear just after they had got there. They hadn't even taken off their academic gowns!

"Come," said Master Luke without any preamble, "Let us enjoy this beautiful morning. I believe that the hoar frost has turned the trees by the river quite white. We should go and see it before it melts."

Magnus and James needed no cajoling. They merely nodded and went back outside.

The little group walked in silence until they reached the river. Then Magnus could keep quiet no longer.

"What has happened? Can you tell us?"

Master Luke paused and looked at them both. Now they were far away from walls that might have ears, or prying eyes, he could tell them what had just passed.

It seemed that Master Luke had been summoned to another audience with Robert Cecil.

Cecil wanted to know exactly what had transpired during the impromptu visit to London. He particularly wanted to know the details of the plan to assassinate the king. Where and how were of notable interest.

Of course, Master Luke had told Cecil everything. He had no other choice.

"Now," concluded Master Luke, "We have to wait for further instructions. I believe that Cecil has a scheme to thwart things."

"Is there no way that we can warn the plotters? I know that they are planning to undertake action which we must not allow to happen. But they are not evil people doing it for their own ends," asked Magnus.

James agreed.

But the Sword remained steadfastly silent. James wondered if it didn't know what to feel.

After all, what they did next would likely mean that their new-found friends would be arrested and, if found guilty, suffer the most horrendous of punishments.

Master Luke noted James and Magnus's qualms.

"We know that we have been brought to this time and place to ensure that history continues as we know it.

James, you have had visions of what life would be like if we do nothing.

I share your concerns about our friends. But if we do nothing, we will condemn many, many, more people to suffer.

Such a decision is not easy. And, in an odd way, we are mirroring our friends in that we must have faith and trust in what we are doing. That what we do is for the right reasons and for the greater good.

From what you know from your time, it is essential that history unfolds as intended.

From my time, I know that there were great divides between rich and poor, between men and women, and that is before we even get to religion or cultures.

We do have one major advantage on our side, which gives me confidence that we are doing the right thing for all. That is the Sword. For why else would we be here?

We must be brave now and do as we are bid."

James could tell that the Sword approved and agreed totally with Master Luke. It was almost red hot.

The die was cast.

James, Magnus, and Master Luke began walking back towards Christ Church.

As they drew close, they were intercepted by the manservant, who looked to be all of a fluster.

"Good Sirs," he gasped, "You are all requested to be at the White Horse immediately. Please do hurry. I fear that it will not bode well for you if you dawdle!"

This sounded very serious. So serious, in fact that James's blood felt a sliver of ice pass through it. The Sword, still safe within his jerkin, was silent.

Even Master Luke appeared to have lost a little of his usual calm.

They made double quick time to Broad Street and knocked on the door of the Inn. It was opened straight away by the innkeeper who ushered them straight upstairs.

He, too, seemed to be on edge.

James, Magnus, and Master Luke were shown into the room where they had met with Robert Cecil previously.

He was still there, seated at the head of a long table and flanked by two bodyguards.

Before they had a chance to bow before the Secretary of State, he growled, "Parliament is due to open in but a few days' time. I need you to make sure this plot unravels before then.

My plan is simple but needs you to implement it."

James looked terrified. What was going to happen?

He felt the Sword move. It had woken up. Perhaps this was now the time they had all been waiting for?

Robert Cecil passed a sealed note to Master Luke.

"I have thought of how to foil this evil plan, and I believe it is not only straightforward but that it will not harm you. You have been good loyal citizens."

James and Magnus looked at each other as Master Luke took charge of the sealed note.

"This note is addressed to one of the catholic nobles who is due to be at the opening of Parliament. The person in question is one William Parker, who is the Fourth Baron Monteagle. In a rather delightful twist of fate," Robert Cecil paused for effect, "He is also the brother-in-law of your good friend, Sir Francis Tresham!"

The more Cecil spoke, the more ingenious his idea became.

It seemed that Cecil's spies had discovered that Monteagle was going to have a dinner party at his London property in the borough of Hoxton. It would be a few days before the opening of Parliament.

That, in itself, was unusual as he hadn't visited the place in years. James wondered if the baron had been coerced somehow into organising it by Cecil's spies.

One thing was for sure, Cecil wasn't sharing that detail with them. They would never know!

Robert Cecil continued.

"One of you will need to make sure that Monteagle takes delivery of this note. I will have ears and eyes at that dinner, so I will know what happens after that. But the critical task is to ensure safe delivery to the right person. You must not fail!"

Judging by the heat that James felt deep within his jerkin, the Sword whole-heartedly agreed.

"Do we need to know what is written or an address?" asked Master Luke.

Robert Cecil replied, "You have no need to know the letter's contents. My spies will give you the address, but it is up to you how you chose to deliver the note.

The dinner will take place on October 26th. You must ensure that the note reaches William Parker, 4th Baron Monteagle at that meal."

Master Luke had one more question.

"Do you have any advice for us as to how we deliver this note?"

Robert Cecil replied, "You need to be vague when you knock on the door. You should imply that that the note was given to you by someone whose description matches one of those who we know to be involved. I would suggest, given the family bonds, that your friend Tresham would be the obvious person!"

At this moment James took his courage in both hands and asked a question. He felt honour-bound to do so. After all, Tresham had done him no harm and had indeed been kind to him.

"Good Sir," he asked, "I realise that I am asking much. However, I wonder, if Sir Francis is to be our letter writer, even by implication, is there any scope for mercy to be shown to him if he is to be arrested and tried?"

Robert Cecil smiled. It wasn't an evil smile either.

"You are a brave man, Master James, and I hear your plea. I cannot promise anything now. However, if you succeed, I will do my best to ensure that he is shown mercy."

With that, James, Magnus and Master Luke were dismissed.

Chapter 3.15
The Letter

Master Luke put the note safely away in his jerkin, taking care not to break the seal. He would examine it later.

He wanted to be sure that the note would convince the baron of its authenticity. If this William Parker did not believe that the letter came from someone who might reasonably be his brother-in-law, then the whole venture would fail. If that happened, there was every chance that the Gunpowder Plot would succeed.

James and Magnus were already discussing how they might affect their return to London. They had to be there to deliver the letter. Although who would do the delivering was also still not clear.

Although Cecil's plan was simple in outline, there were so many small details that they needed to consider. If they got even one small detail wrong, the letter might not get through. And it had to!

James, Magnus, and Master Luke needed to talk things through in depth. But where?

They could not use Master Luke's rooms now. They knew the Bear was out of bounds too. Master Harrison had shown himself to be a catholic sympathiser, so it was too risky.

Eventually they settled on another long walk by the river.

But before then, Master Luke wanted to examine the seal—and if possible— the note's contents to make sure that they were convincing. He would need to be in his rooms to do that. He was taking a huge risk by so doing, and so decided to not involve James and Magnus. He told them he would rest now and think things through. They could all meet later, after James and Magnus had eaten.

James's stomach thought this to be an excellent idea.

James and Magnus retired to the Bear for some well-earned food.

Master Luke did not have time to eat. He had important work to do.

Once he was safely back, he made sure that the door was securely closed, and the windows shuttered. Then, he lit his lamp so that he could examine the letter's seal more closely. He still had the seal from the invitation they had had to dinner all those weeks ago. He wanted to compare them. He hoped that they would not be markedly different. If they were, then he would have to think of what he needed to do.

He also wanted to ensure that the contents of the letter accurately mimicked Sir Francis's style of writing. Otherwise, the contents would not be believed, and Cecil's plan would fail.

Master Luke searched the top of his desk for the old seal. It took a little while, but he eventually located it under a pile of untidy papers. He set it alongside that on Cecil's note.

To his horror, they were nothing like each other.

Master Luke had some serious work to do.

He dug out his palette knife from the untidy heap of items by his desk. Then, he gently warmed the seal from underneath to try and loosen the seal. As he did so, he reflected that sealing wax was well-named. The seal on this note was very firm indeed. If he wasn't careful, he would shatter the fragile disc and by so doing, reveal that the notes contents had been opened.

It took a lot of time and patience, but after what felt to be far too long, Master Luke felt the seal finally loosen. He gently prised it loose so that he could try to adapt it. It had to at least resemble the Tresham official seal, even if it were not an exact replica.

Now that the seal had been removed, Master Luke decided that he should look at the note's contents. Much to his relief, he thought they might well have been written by Sir Francis as a caring brother-in-law. The words were not totally explicit, but their meaning was clear. That something was going to happen when the opening ceremony took place, and it was perhaps better if Baron Monteagle absented himself.

Master Luke felt that a lot of work had been put into drafting the note. It would be enough to warn, but not enough to give too much away. Very clever.

These Cecil spies were very good!

However, they had let themselves down with the poor workmanship of the seal.

As he worked, Master Luke wondered just how devious Cecil's spies were. Was the seal an example of poor workmanship or could it be a test of how trustworthy he and his friends were? After all, he thought, if the letter was deemed to be a forgery by Tresham and his allies, it would be James, Magnus and himself who would be seen as traitors to the Plot. If that happened, they would likely suffer the same fate as the first tester of the gunpowder.

Even if the contents were accepted, the seal could still point to them as traitors regardless. That would ensure their demise and another loose end being tied up. Very clever!

This thought spurred Master Luke on to do the best that he possibly could ensure that the seal was the exact double of the one on their invitation. His next test was to replace it carefully back onto the note in such a way that it did seem to have been tampered with. It all looked absolutely perfect when he had completed his task. Sir Francis himself would not have been able to tell the difference.

But it had taken a lot of time. As he rubbed his aching eyes, Master Luke realised that it was already dark. He carefully put the letter down on his desk.

As he pulled on his academic gown and made his way to the door, James and Magnus rushed in. They were wondering what had delayed him.

Master Luke told them that he had been doing some work and pointed to the note. He dared not say anything.

James and Magnus understood. However, now it was dark, there was little more that they could do.

It would be far too dangerous to walk by the river now. They might trip and fall in. Or perhaps be followed there and pushed in. Either way, once the heavy black gowns became waterlogged, they would be dragged under by the flowing water and drown.

They decided that they should eat. They returned to the Bear Inn to explore what tasty morsels might be on offer.

James and Magnus decided to have an early quiet night, and left Master Luke as soon as they had finished their meal.

Much as James wanted to sleep, the Sword had other ideas.

The now-familiar sound of rushing wind filled James's ears, and he knew that the Sword was taking him on another journey. One that would hopefully help them in their task.

First, James dreamt that he was with Master Luke. He did not know where. James was handing the St Christopher medal back to him.

Even in his trance-like state, James thought that this vision was a little mundane. However, the Sword clearly felt that it was very important, and so James made a mental note to return the medal to Master Luke as soon as he could.

Of course, there was more to come.

The Sword whisked James off to the end of Broad Street, guiding him down several back alleys until he was standing outside a dirty run-down building. James felt that the Sword wished him to enter. He wasn't at all sure what to expect as he nervously opened the door.

Once inside, it was a very different picture. Here was a clean, warm stables, with several horses munching hay.

James realised that the Sword was showing him where they could hire their transport for their trip to London.

Before he could do anything else, the Sword whisked him away again.

This time, he found himself riding one of the beasts. He recognised parts of the route he was being taken down. But then, suddenly, just as they reached the river, the horse turned along a street that he had never seen before.

Over the clatter of the hooves, James could hear the words "Onwards, onwards, to Hoxton," being repeated over, and over, again.

The Sword was obviously in a practical frame of mind for it was now showing James the way to where they would find Baron Monteagle!

Then, the vision stopped as suddenly as it had begun. As before, James woke up immediately. However, unlike the other times when he had dreamt, he felt energised and positive. James understood what he was being told. He also realised how useful the information was. It would save them a lot of time when they started their mission.

James decided not to wake Magnus. To be honest, he didn't see the point. He hadn't been traumatised by what he had seen. He didn't need Magnus to explain why he was being shown it. No, he would share his dream with Magnus and Master Luke on the morrow when it was safe to do so. After which, perhaps, they could check out whether the stables were where his dream suggested.

Chapter 3.16
Delivering the Letter

The following morning, as they went down to breakfast, Magnus asked James if he had experienced any dreams during the previous night. James nodded, but put his finger to his lips.

Magnus understood. James was being careful.

They ate rapidly and left the Bear as quickly as possible. They had much to discuss with Master Luke now it was light.

Given that the Monteagle dinner was but a couple of days away, James and Magnus knew that they hadn't much time to work out how they were going to deliver the letter.

Master Luke was feeling the same urgency. So much so that he had already left his rooms to walk to the Bear Inn when he bumped into James and Magnus outside Christ Church.

"Come, let us take a walk alongside the riverbank!" suggested Magnus.

As soon as they were sure they were safe and could not be overheard, the discussions began.

Firstly, Master Luke apologised for his tardiness of the previous evening. He explained that he had been examining the seal on the letter. He was fearful that Cecil might try to double cross them. It would not matter whether they were caught as long as the letter was delivered. For once the letter was read, actions would follow. But if the seal was an obvious forgery, James and Magnus would be the suspects! The plotters would have no qualms about getting rid of them. And it would tidy up a loose end for Cecil.

James wasn't too keen on being thought of as a loose end, but he did see Master Luke's point!

"How did you make sure the seal was good?" asked Magnus.

Master Luke told him that he had carefully kept the seal from the Tresham invitation. At the time, he hadn't really thought about it. Perhaps it was going to be a souvenir of an interesting evening? But as things turned out, it was a good job that he had.

When looked at in detail, Master Luke discovered that the seal was a reasonable forgery. It would pass light scrutiny, but it would not fool someone who was familiar with Sir Francis.

Master Luke had then spent this time working on the letter's seal. He now believed it to be totally indistinguishable from the real thing. But it had taken a lot of care and attention to detail. It could not be rushed. Hence, he had been late for their meeting yesterday.

At least Master Luke had confidence that the letter would now be accepted as genuine.

But time was now of the essence. They had lost a precious 12 hours of planning, and they still had so much to do.

Magnus said, "We know we have to deliver the letter to the Baron at some point during his dinner in Hoxton on October 26th. Which is only a couple of days from now."

Master Luke agreed, "And we need to organise horses to take us there—we do not have enough time to walk even if we wanted to!"

Magnus then added, "We don't have a clue where this house is in Hoxton— or even where Hoxton is! So much to organise and so little time!"

They both were close to despair. They had the perfect note, but no way of delivering it.

James quietly entered the conversation.

"The Sword sent me a dream last night," he said as he took out the St Christopher medal, "The first thing that the Sword wanted me to do was to return this medal to you, Master Luke. I have no idea why, but I am doing as the Sword wishes."

Master Luke took the medal and put it away in his jerkin, and bade James continue.

"I feel that the Sword was in a practical mood," he said, "For it showed me where we might find good horses for our journey. The Sword even showed me the route that we should travel. If we can find the stables, then we should be able to find Baron Monteagle's house in Hoxton too!"

Master Luke and Magnus brightened up immediately.

James had one more comment though.

"We must decide how we deliver the letter once we are in Hoxton."

Master Luke agreed.

"We need to be both obvious as we deliver it, but anonymous so that we cannot be found afterwards."

Quite a challenge.

Magnus was the first to suggest what they might do.

"I am the tallest of us all. I am also quite noticeable because of my red hair. Perhaps I should be the one who hands the letter over?"

Although neither James nor Master Luke liked the thought of Magnus putting himself in such a position, the suggestion made perfect sense.

"However," added Master Luke, "If we can think of a better idea as we travel to London, then we will use that thought instead!"

Now it was time to test whether the Sword had been accurate.

The group walked back into Oxford and over to Broad Street.

James led them through tiny alleys until he reached the door from his dream.

"Come," he said as he opened the door, "We will find our transport here!"

It was all exactly as he had seen in his dream. There was one small difference. There was a small fat man wearing a leather apron on the other side of the door.

He wiped his hands on a cloth, looked at James, Magnus, and Master Luke, and said, "How may I be of service to you good men?"

James turned to Master Luke and Magnus.

"This man is the ostler. He is responsible for these fine steeds!"

James turned to the man and asked, "We need three strong, fast, steeds to take us on with an important journey. We need them now. Can you help?"

It was almost as if the ostler had been expecting them.

The small fat man nodded and pointed to three mares who were happily grazing in beds of hay.

"These are my most reliable horses. For the right price, I can guarantee you a rapid journey wherever you may be going. They are fleet of foot and tireless!"

Master Luke moved forward and began to discuss prices as James and Magnus went across to pat the beasts. The horses looked up briefly from their munching and accepted the attention as their right.

As James and Magnus continued to admire the beasts, they realised that Master Luke and the ostler had moved. They were now gathering up saddles, bridles and getting the horses ready.

They led the horses into the alleyway.

As they turned to begin their journey, James asked Master Luke, "Are you sure that we have everything that we need?"

Master Luke leant forward on his horse, urging it to move, replying, "Indeed, yes. Come, time is short. Let us begin."

With that, the three men began their journey to Hoxton.

After leaving the city and covering many miles, they came to the outskirts of London.

Master Luke halted his horse. Magnus and James did likewise.

"It is time for you to take over," Master Luke said to James, "The Sword showed you the way. Now you must show us!"

James urged his mare forwards. He knew exactly where he had to go. As well as remembering the way from the previous night, the Sword was glowing warm beneath his jerkin. He would feel it change temperature if he even thought about deviating from the route!

Eventually, they reached the house that James had seen in his dream.

"We are here!" he announced.

"Good, good," said Master Luke, "Now we must find a place to rest up until dark. We should also seek out a vantage point for James and me to wait while Magnus delivers the note. It will need to be near so that we can leave quickly once you have completed your task. But it must not be too obvious, or we will be spotted."

They all dismounted and led their horses quietly through the streets. To a casual observer it appeared that they were allowing their steeds a few moments of rest before continuing onwards.

It was James who found the ideal place to wait.

"Over here," he whispered urgently, "I think we may be safe here."

Magnus and Master Luke turned to look. James was right. In front of him stood an archway between two halves of the street. It had been designed to allow carts, carriages, and the like to go round the back of the houses. They could wait there as darkness fell and Magnus delivered the letter. If all went well, they wouldn't need to wait very long.

There was just enough time to try and find a pie shop to help quell James's rumbling tummy. When they had set off from Oxford and Master Luke said that he had everything that they needed. He had lied. He did not have any food with him. James felt that seeking out something to eat now would be a good use of their time as they waited for night.

Time did that strange thing of passing both slowly and quickly. It felt to take for ever before darkness came, and yet, suddenly, there was no light to see by except from the house windows and the stars in the sky above.

Moving the horses under the arch, Master Luke handed the letter to Magnus.

"Remember to knock loudly on the door. Then hand this to whoever answers it. If you are asked who it is from, merely reply that it is from a friend. Then leave. But do not walk straight back here. Go to the other end of the street. By the time you reach it, you will be submerged in darkness and you won't be followed. We will wait here for you to come round the back of the houses. As you do that, we will watch the front of the house and make sure nothing goes wrong."

James reached out and shook the hand of his friend.

"Good luck!" he said, "I still wish there were another way…"

Magnus walked purposefully towards Baron Monteagle's house. He knocked loudly on the door.

From their vantage point, James and Master Luke saw the outline of a manservant against the candlelight. They watched as Magnus handed the letter over, and then begin to walk away.

The door closed. A few moments later, it opened again, and a figure slid out and started to follow the retreating Magnus.

But it was no good. Magnus was swallowed up into the darkness before the figure had a chance to see where he was going. James and Master Luke saw the door opening again, the figure returning inside, and then the door closed.

James and Master Luke continued to watch. The windows had not been shuttered and so they could see vague outlines through them. But it was impossible to make out too much detail. James and Magnus could see someone stand up and appear to open the letter.

But James and Master Luke did not have time to see any more.

Magnus was back.

It was time to return to Oxford.

They had done their duty.

What happened next was out of their control.

It was a more relaxed journey back to Oxford. They had done as they had been told. None of the three of them had any idea about what would happen next. James reported that the Sword was stubbornly quiet.

They arrived back at the ostler's in the early hours.

James tried the door to the stables. It wasn't locked.

"We should get these beasts back to their beds," he said as he led his mare indoors.

Magnus and Master Luke followed.

As they were about to tie the beasts up, they were surrounded by several men, all dressed in black.

"Traitors, all of you!" shouted one voice.

"You will die now, and join the king," screamed another.

Had they had the chance to think about it, they would have realised that they had been betrayed. By whom and when was not something that they had time to discuss.

James ran back to the door, followed by Magnus.

As they ran, their horses, startled by the noise and violence, reared up. They knocked Magnus over on to James.

It went quiet.

Magnus was the first to stand up.

James wobbled to his feet too.

As they turned round, they heard a voice they recognised.

It was the professor-in-charge of the Exhibition.

"Are you two hurt?" he was asking as he rushed to their sides.

"And where is the Sword? Is it safe? We caught the thugs with the guns thanks to the bravery of one of our colleagues who happened to be passing by. But they didn't have the Sword?"

James realised that he was back in his 21st century jeans and fleece, and the Sword was still encased in bubble wrap, partially tucked in his waist band.

He was still very shaken but managed to pull the Sword out and hand it over to the professor-in-charge.

After doing a quick check to make sure that the Sword was undamaged, the professor-in-charge took James and Magnus back into the Exhibition Hall.

As they entered, the whole room—and it was an enormous room—erupted into spontaneous applause. James and Magnus had risked their lives for the Sword.

And joy of joys, it was safe!

"You boys have exceeded all expectations. But I think you both need to go home and rest. I have some good news for you, but it can wait until tomorrow. I think we have all had enough excitement for one day!"

Chapter 3.17
Aftermath

James and Magnus walked back to Jericho. They were both shocked to find themselves back in the 21st century. They were also worried about Master Luke.

Now that the Sword was back in its packing case, James had no direct way of knowing whether Master Luke had been captured, or even worse, murdered by their attackers back in the 17th century.

The only positive thing that they could agree on right now was that whatever they had done in delivering the letter seemed to have worked as Robert Cecil had intended. Or, if it hadn't, something else had happened to ensure that life was as they knew it, and not some alternative reality.

Both James and Magnus decided that they would indulge in a takeaway for dinner and then have a decent long shower. It felt like ages since they had been able to enjoy a good wash. The 17th century was marginally better than the 11th century, but it still left a lot to be desired regarding hygiene and plumbing!

They both wanted to sit in front of a good soap opera, or even a talk show, and watch the world unfold.

But before that, they decided to interrogate the computer. They wanted to find out what had happened to the Gunpowder Plot. Had things unfolded as they had hoped? And more to the point, had James and Magnus been identified or were they just a cog in the wheels of history?

Magnus fired up his desktop machine as soon as they walked through the front door. He typed in "Gunpowder Plot". The computer whirled and the first thing that appeared was a list of related subjects. At the top, the first item began, "The Gunpowder Plot was a failed attempt to blow up England's King James I (1566-1625) and the Parliament on November 5, 1605. The plot was organised by Robert Catesby (c. 1572-1605) in an effort to end the persecution of Roman Catholics by the English government."

Magnus and James read on.

It was all there. Everything about the king's visit to Oxford, how the plot was postponed and finally unravelled because of an anonymous letter to William Parker, the 4th Baron Monteagle, at his house in Hoxton......

Goodness me. They had done it! They had foiled the Gunpowder Plot!

If only they knew what had happened to Master Luke. They really hoped that he was safe somewhere.

James also felt a slight twinge of regret that they hadn't had an opportunity to spend a little more time with Guy Fawkes while in 1605. After all, Fawkes was the name everyone associated with the Gunpowder Plot.

James felt that he had enough knowledge to write a book on Tresham, Percy and Catesby. It would include information about them that only he and Magnus knew.

But other than that rather tense meeting in the Lambeth cellar, Fawkes had not really been part of this adventure.

James and Magnus felt that they needed to know what had happened after they left 1605. In particular, James really wanted to know if Cecil had been able to keep his word, or whether his friend, Sir Francis, had suffered a traitor's death.

First of all, they looked up what had happened to Guy Fawkes. It seemed that he was the first to be captured. He was caught red-handed with the gunpowder under the Houses of Parliament. Taking all the evidence into account, there was no way he could not be found guilty of treason. He was sentenced to be hung, drawn, and quartered.

But it seemed that Guy Fawkes was a very brave man. As he was led to the scaffold to suffer the first part of his terrible punishment, he broke free from his guards, leapt from the platform, and broke his neck. He died instantly.

Catesby and Percy ran away to try to find refuge. After all, there were many catholic sympathisers across the country. If they could seek aid from them until they could escape to France, they might have a chance.

But Cecil's men were in pursuit. They had to keep moving.

Catesby and Percy, along with two others, sought overnight refuge at a place called Holbeche House. It had been a horrid night to have to travel but they had no choice. As they rested by the fire, they discovered that their stash of gunpowder, which they needed for their muskets, was soaked through.

As James had told Catesby on that night in October 1605, wet gunpowder is useless. So, they decided to dry it in front of the open fire.

James could not believe it.

Catesby clearly did not understand what could—and did—happen.

A spark flew from the fire. While the gunpowder did not explode, it caused a fierce inferno. Catesby was badly injured as a result. Percy managed to avoid getting hurt, but the other conspirators were killed.

But it got worse. Just as Catesby and Percy assessed the damage, Cecil's men arrived. They opened fire on the two men.

Apparently, it was the same musket ball which killed both of them.

James and Magnus looked at each other. They knew these people. While James and Magnus could not support their cause, they felt that Catesby and Percy did not deserve that.

And so, it was time to find out what had happened to Sir Francis. James particularly wanted to discover whether Cecil was a man of his word. Did he show mercy to Sir Francis?

He couldn't bear to look to the computer. He asked Magnus to do it instead.

It seemed that Sir Francis was arrested a week after the plot fell apart.

He was taken to the Tower of London to await trial, where he died in December 1605 of natural causes.

"I think I am glad that Sir Francis didn't suffer like the others," remarked James when Magnus told him, "He was a kind man, and his wife was lovely. But given that he hadn't even come to trial, I don't think we will ever know whether Robert Cecil would have been merciful!"

Magnus nodded.

"Sometimes, it is better simply not to know!" he agreed.

They didn't need to find out anything else. James and Magnus had discovered the fate of the men they had met in 1605. It was now time to rest and recover from their activities.

They sat down to eat their meal. They had thought that perhaps the activities of 1605 as recorded on the computer might have spoiled their appetite. But, as they opened the cartons of food, they realise just how hungry they were.

Having demolished every last morsel of the takeaway, and caught up with the day's news, they put the dishes in the sink to soak.

The promised long showers and good night's sleep in comfortable beds beckoned.

The following day, they returned to work. There was still a lot of packing from the Exhibition which needed to be completed.

However, when they walked into the Exhibition Hall, all was quiet.

Where was everyone?

The professor-in-charge appeared, seemingly out of nowhere.

"Good, good," he said as he rushed to their sides, "I am so glad that you are here. And here early!"

It turned out that while they were in the 17th century, Magnus and James had become used to rising as soon as it was light. They hadn't quite adjusted to the 21st century!

As a result, they had arrived at the Ashmolean Museum well in advance of everyone else.

No matter. The professor-in-charge wanted to catch them by themselves.

"I have some brilliant news. It came through just as those thugs attacked you. I would have told you yesterday, but as we know, events rather got in the way! You both seemed very shaken by what happened, and I am not at all surprised. You don't expect to be threatened with firearms when you're clearing up an Exhibition!"

But now the professor-in-charge was determined that they should hear his news.

First of all, the professor-in-charge told James and Magnus that the two thugs were now in police custody and were, as the police so delightfully put it, "spilling their guts".

The professor-in-charge thought this a rather indelicate way of saying that the thugs were confessing to everything, but no matter.

It seemed that some rich multi-billionaire wanted the Sword for his private collection. When he discovered that it was not for sale, he hired the thugs to steal it instead. It was only a matter of time now before the multi-billionaire was arrested!

Secondly, the professor-in-charge had some exciting news about the Sword itself.

The British Museum board of directors had had a series of meetings after Magnus had announced his move to Oxford.

After much careful thought, the board had decided—unanimously—that for scholarship purposes, the Sword should remain with the Ashmolean Museum on long term loan. Should Dr Ivar decide to move elsewhere, the board would review that decision. However, for the medium term at least, the Sword was to remain in Oxford. The secretary to the board had telephoned the news through as James and Magnus were heading down the fire escape.

This was indeed good news for Dr Ivar. He had dedicated his life's research to the Sword! This decision would mean that he could work with the Sword without having to travel to London all the time.

"Now, after that, I think we deserve a cup of coffee!" said the professor-in-charge.

He led them out of the building and into a local coffee shop. He invited them to sit down while he ordered.

James looked at Magnus and asked, "This doesn't feel normal. Have you any idea what is going on?"

Magnus answered, "Not a clue, But I don't think it's bad. At least I hope not."

The professor-in-charge came back to the table with the three flat whites and sat down.

"Now I have more news to share as well."

He looked directly at James.

"Do you remember that you applied to study for a D Phil here in our Centre for Environmental Sciences?"

James nodded. It was his ambition. He wanted desperately to become a researcher like Magnus, and perhaps even, if he were bright enough, a professor like his Great Aunty Pauline. Studying for a D Phil here in Oxford would be a giant step towards this long-term goal.

However, funding was tight, and only the very best students would be able to undertake such a project. He didn't believe that he could match the requirements.

The professor-in-charge thought otherwise.

He had received James's degree results (a first—no surprise there), and the references from his tutors. The professor-in-charge had also taken note of how James had opted for a placement in archaeological sciences rather than industry during his year out.

There were, of course, many other applicants for the small number of places. But James's application had stood out.

Taking all these facts into consideration, the grant committee had made its decision a couple of days ago.

The professor-in-charge was delighted to inform James that there was a scholarship with his name on it if he wanted it!

James was over the moon. This was fulfilment of the first stage of his career. He had done it. He had a place in Oxford to study for a D Phil. If he succeeded in that, he would become a doctor, just like Magnus.

James wanted to kiss the professor-in-charge but thought that he better not.

Instead, he smiled, and said, "Thank you ever so much. I can't tell you how happy I am. Are you sure? Absolutely sure? Can I call my mother to tell her?"

Of course, James could tell his mother.

Chapter 3.18
Epilogue

It had been a busy few months.

James had helped to sort out the dismantling of the Exhibition—with the exception of the Sword—of course. It had been taken to one of the University's archives for safe keeping while the University decided how best it should deal with this precious artefact.

Somehow, he and Magnus had managed to find time to go flat hunting too. James enjoyed staying with his friend. However, it was becoming a little tiresome to be constantly referred to in private has "Liege Lord". They were mates.

And the house in Jericho was small. It was clear that James was taking up space that Magnus really needed for his books and papers.

It was time for him to find his own space.

James found his ideal accommodation just before he began his D Phil studies. It ticked all the boxes. It was close to the laboratories where he would work. It had a bedroom, kitchen, and bathroom. It also had a small lounge area with a sofa bed which he could happily sleep on should his mother visit.

Most importantly, he could afford to rent it on his grant.

James discovered that studying for a D Phil was very different to what was expected of him as an undergraduate. For a start off, he was expected to follow up his own ideas and design methodological approaches to investigate them. He would meet with his supervisor often to discuss progress, but he was treated more as an equal than a pupil.

Things had started to settle down as Trinity Term began. James loved this new phase of his life. It had been fun as an undergraduate. But being a postgraduate was infinitely better. He particularly loved the looks of respect and awe he got from the first-year students.

James was walking into the University to begin another day's research when his mobile rang. It was his mother, and she had a request.

James's Great Aunty Pauline, also known as Emeritus Professor Holden, was soon to celebrate her birthday. She would be 85 years old. She was a sprightly as ever, though, and keeping well.

James's mother told him that she had asked his Great Aunt what she would like to do to celebrate this auspicious anniversary.

Emeritus Professor Holden knew exactly what she wanted to do. Great Aunty Pauline didn't want a party. Neither did she want to holiday.

It seemed that Great Aunty Pauline had just heard from one of her dearest friends.

He was to be awarded an honorary degree from the University of Oxford.

What Great Aunty Pauline wanted to do for her 85th birthday was to be in the congregation to see him receive his degree. She also wanted to stay at a posh hotel while she was in Oxford, enjoy a decent meal, and possibly an afternoon tea or two. If there was time to have a browse round Blackwell's bookstore as well, so much the better.

James's mother could sort out hotels once she had dates and an assurance that she had tickets for the ceremony. She'd checked on the web, and it seemed that places were quite limited. James told her that the ceremony would be held in the University's wonderful but rather small Sheldonian theatre. It had been designed by Sir Christopher Wren back in the 17th century, when the University was much smaller. Its atmosphere was grand, but it could only hold around eight hundred people at a time. Given the demand for tickets, James wasn't at all surprised that they had to be limited.

James's mother sounded disappointed, so he immediately agreed to look into it for her. He might be able to get a ticket for Great Aunty Pauline and his mother, as her helper, but that might be all.

James's mother cheered up immediately. It wasn't ideal. It would have been nice to have James with them as well, particularly given how close James was to his Great Aunt. However, she knew James would do his best.

At coffee time, James met up with Magnus. Usually they would discuss the challenges and frustrations they were experiencing as they followed their research. But today, James wanted to sort out tickets. Magnus agreed to apply for a ticket alongside James. They would have the right number for Great Aunty

Pauline and James's mother. James could ask if there were more tickets, but Magnus thought it unlikely.

But they needed to apply immediately. Apparently, there was a deadline for applications. It was the following day. Magnus and James cut short their coffee break and rushed back to their respective computers. After wrestling with the forms for 20 minutes or so, each had a reply from the University's administration to say that their applications had been received and would be processed. James and Magnus would hear back within a few days whether they had been successful.

It was a tense wait. James knew how much Great Aunty Pauline would be looking forward to seeing her old friend being given such a great honour by the University. After all, there were only seven or eight such awards made each year!

Just as James was losing hope, there was a ping on his email. He had been successful. He had been awarded a ticket.

James immediately called Magnus, who confirmed that he had been successful too.

Now all they had to do was to tell James's mother, and she would do the rest. They could relax until the ninth week of Trinity Term—or mid-June as mere mortals know it—when the ceremony would take place.

Mid-June arrived. James and Magnus collected his mother and Great Aunty Pauline from the station in a top of the range luxury taxi. James had briefly considered a stretch limo, but realised that Great Aunty Pauline might not see the joke!

They rolled up to the Randolph Hotel. It looked very buttery in colour as the June sun shone on it.

A man in a uniform and wearing a tall hat opened the taxi door and ushered the ladies towards the grand entrance. Another lackey opened the boot and carried the luggage inside.

James and Magnus waited until the ladies had registered, been shown to their rooms and then come back down.

"Are your rooms ok?" asked James, "We can try and change them if not?"

All was satisfactory. There was now just enough time for that browse round Blackwell's before getting ready for dinner.

The boys should go back to work. James's relatives would meet them back in the lobby for dinner later.

James had to admit it. The food at the Randolph was delicious. His only complaint was the portion size. His mother told him off saying that by the end of the meal he would be overfull if portions were any larger.

James replied that he would have enjoyed taking up that challenge!

In between courses, they worked out what was going to happen the following day.

James and Magnus would meet the ladies at the Randolph for lunch and then take them over to the Sheldonian Theatre and make sure they were seated and looked after.

At the end of the event, James's mother would ring James so that they could all return to the Randolph where an afternoon tea of scones, jam and clotted cream had been arranged.

It all went remarkably smoothly. James and Magnus got the ladies to the ceremony with just the right amount of time to spare. Magnus knew one of the stewards there and so the ladies were ushered to almost front row seats. They would certainly have a good view!

The ceremony ended when it was supposed to, and the group were back at the Randolph at just the right time.

James was sure he could smell freshly baked scones as he walked through the door.

A waiter took them to a table by the window looking out onto the street. He must have been instructed by James's mother because he indicated that Great Aunty Pauline should have the seat which looked out onto the busy Oxford street.

Then a multi-tiered cake holder arrived. Each layer was packed with tiny, delectable morsels, scarcely more than a bite in size. Fortunately for James, the number of treats far outweighed their size. As a snack between lunch and dinner tonight, he was sure it was all just fine!

Great Aunty Pauline looked delighted. This was exactly what she wanted for her birthday. There was just one more thing to make it complete.

She had invited her good friend to join them. She hoped that they wouldn't mind, but it had been such a long time since she had seen him.

It was her birthday treat—how could anyone object?

Just as they unfolded their napkins, Great Aunty Pauline jumped up and waved to someone in the distance.

"He's managed to get away from the garden party already! Oh, this is such good news. Now I can introduce you to my friend!"

Great Aunty Pauline was very excited. She almost knocked over the teapot in her rush to greet this stranger.

"This is my learned friend, Emeritus Professor Husam, from the University of Baghdad!" Great Aunty Pauline announced as she dragged a tall man towards the table, "He has been researching Viking trade routes in the Golden Age of Islam. It took a while for the visas to come through, but here he is!"

James and Magnus looked at Emeritus Professor Husam, and then at each other.

He might well be Emeritus Professor Husam now, but to their deep joy, they saw that this person was their Master Luke, or Brother Luke, or now Professor Husam! His hair was snow white and he looked much older than when they had last seen him. But he was safe. Alive and here!

They didn't care what he was called.

Both James and Magnus jumped up and went over to him.

Much to James's mother's surprise, they both gave Emeritus Professor Husam the biggest bearhug she had ever seen!

Great Aunty Pauline merely smiled enigmatically!

What a way to celebrate a perfect birthday!

Luke sat down next to Great Aunty Pauline, who said, "It's time for tea. Let's tuck in! I know James will be ready for this!"

The boys needed no further invitation. The scones disappeared in the twinkle of Great Aunty Pauline's eyes.

It wasn't too long after that the teapot emptied and all that was left was the cake stand and a few crumbs.

Great Aunty Pauline smiled.

"I enjoyed that. I love the blend of clotted cream with strawberry jam on warm scones. However, it's been a long day, and I am starting to feel a little tired. I think I should enjoy a short nap before we gather again for dinner."

Then she turned to James's mother and suggested that she do likewise— "That way we can stay up late this evening with the boys!"

James's mother knew when she was being told to do something. She nodded her agreement and followed Great Aunty Pauline out of the hotel lounge.

"Now we are alone," began Magnus, "Can you at least tell us a little of your travels?"

Given that time was limited, Luke could only give them a short outline of his adventures.

Luke recalled the time when he had last seen James and Magnus. It was all a mess of confusion.

However, Luke recalled the bemusement of the catholic thugs as they searched in vain for bodies after the horses were tied up.

It was a mystery where James and Magnus had disappeared to after being trampled under the horses' hooves. Master Luke was less fortunate. He had not been able to disappear. He had been captured by Catesby's men.

They dragged him back to the Bear Inn, where they put him in the cage with the bear. They didn't realise that the bear regarded Master Luke as a friend. They were very surprised when the creature merely sat down next to him.

So, they dragged him out of the cage to kill him themselves.

Just as they were about to do so, Cecil's spies rampaged through the inn and rescued him.

It was a mixed blessing, however, as he was then imprisoned in the Tower as a traitor, awaiting trial.

He could hear the screams of others being tortured as he awaited his interrogation.

Just as James had seen in his vision.

Before they came for him, Luke decided that he wanted one last look at freedom. He went to the barred window and stood on tiptoe and gazed out.

Luke did not have his crucifix, but he did have the St Christopher. He turned it over and over between his fingers as he worried.

As before, the sun's rays must have caught it, for he was again temporarily blinded.

When he regained his sight, he was no longer in that terrible place. He wasn't even in England or the 17th century.

He had been transported back to familiar territory—his Middle Eastern travels in the 11th century.

As he looked around at his surroundings, Luke felt something stir within him that he hadn't felt for a long time. An excitement that he had almost forgotten. His thirst for knowledge.

He realised that he now had the opportunity to discover much more about the Golden Age of Islam.

From there to here, there had been a few more leaps and bounds. It hadn't all been straightforward.

Luke told Magnus and James that he had much more to share, but it would be impossible to tell it all now.

However, Luke wasn't intending to go anywhere else soon. He told the boys that he had just been offered a visiting chair at the University. That meant he was going to be around for the next year or so at least. That should allow plenty of time for swapping notes.

Perhaps they should start that journey tomorrow?

With the Sword close by, who knows where their discussions would lead them.

Postscript

It had been a truly fulfilling day, thought James after he had made his way back home. In every sense. He had managed to ensure that he had a full stomach and spent an enjoyable time at the Randolph with his family and friends.

Most amazingly, he had been reunited with his comrade-in-arms, Luke. He'd almost lost hope of ever seeing the man again. Yet here he was.

He would meet up with Magnus and Luke again tomorrow. He would find out more about what had happened to Master Luke following Magnus's and his abrupt departure from 1605.

He also wondered what would happen now that they were all reunited again. He could sense that the Sword had plans. He could feel it starting to stir in its display case, its amber stone glowing into the dark museum.

He had so much to look forward to.

As he drifted off to sleep, James felt the gentle tugging of the Sword more strongly.

He could feel that it, too, was happy that the three friends were back together. They were a powerful team, after all.

The Sword had one last act on this night.

It wanted to share a vision with James to help him plan, to look to the future, or into the past? James couldn't tell which. All James could sense was that the Sword was becoming restless. It was preparing to bend the fabric of time and space again.

James slept on but it was a hot and steamy night. He woke and thought that he had perhaps not opened the bedroom window before he had got to bed. He sleepily made his way across the bedroom to open it.

Much to his amazement, the window wasn't there anymore. Neither was the bedroom wall.

James was looking down on a Viking village. He recognised it from when he was a child. From his very first vision at eight years old.

He saw a weary man, carrying the Mighty Sword of Eir, as he joined the villagers around the bonfire. As the man settled himself on the stool in front of the burning logs, he took off his helmet and looked up at James. And James saw.

Underneath the blue swirls was a face that James knew.

James recognised the man who was about to tell stories and tales to the villagers, and who was the Storyteller and Keeper of the Sword.

James realised that he knew who that Storyteller really was.

It was Luke.

It was he who would give the Sword to the village for safekeeping. Until the Sword found its new Keeper. Until it found James.

James watched as the Storyteller left the village. Just like he did in his vision all those years ago. But in this dream, the Storyteller turned and waved to James.

As if to say that they would meet again, and again, and again…